MW01706625

Put Your Name on It

ANGIE DANIELS

—THE DECADENT DELIGHT SERIES—

Caramel Kisses Publishing

THE DECADENT DELIGHT SERIES

A Delight Before Christmas

Say My Name

Naughty Before Christmas

Put Your Name on It

ANGIE DANIELS

—THE DECADENT DELIGHT SERIES—

Caramel Kisses Publishing

ISBN-13: 978-1-941342-14-5

For questions and comments about the book please contact angie@angiedaniels.com.

Caramel Kisses Publishing

Caramel Kisses Ink
PO Box 2313
Chesterfield, VA 23832
www.caramelkissespublishing.com

This book is dedicated to all the fans
of the series who asked for more.
You know who you are.

ONE

Christina Holloway climbed out the passenger side of my new Range Rover with a frown curling her painted lips. "Why in the world would someone want to have a party in this old dirty warehouse?" she asked.

Leave it to my girl to turn up her nose.

"Christy, all I know is that this is where our client wants to celebrate her fiftieth birthday. She said something about retiring from this place several years ago," I added as an afterthought.

"But the kitchen is probably gross," Christina pouted, although she quickly fell into step beside me. "Are you sure we have the right address?" I could tell she was hoping I was wrong.

"No, it's the right place. Remember the instructions said the building would have a red tin roof. And that's a tin roof." I noticed the way her eyes rolled upward before her shoulders sagged in defeat. Chuckling softly, I walked over to the warehouse door and produced a key from my purse.

"Claudia, I'm not sure about this place." She was looking around like she expected the Boogey Man to appear at any moment.

As I turned the key in the lock, I looked over and said, "Trust me. I've known Pearson for years. He said looks are deceiving." With that said, I pushed open the door. The power was motion detected so as soon as I took a few steps forward, the lights came on and the long narrow corridor was lit. "This place has been out of business for years."

"I can see why." Christina shuddered. It took everything I had not to start laughing. She's so stuck-up that somehow I wonder how we have managed to be friends for so long.

"Come on Christy, you have to admit the building has character and charm, and it's in much better condition on the inside." I loved the old industrial look while she preferred everything traditional and timeless.

"I think we need to suggest something different." She stopped and swung around. "Which client did you say this was for again?"

"Mrs. Mays. She's a new client," I mumbled without even breaking my stride. "Come on. I want to get this over with. The sooner we inspect the kitchen, the sooner we can go check out that new restaurant. I'm starving." I knew mentioning food would do the trick. She loves French food.

Christina walked beside me, clicking her stylish lime green pumps against the polished concrete floor.

"At least the building is well-maintained."

She responded with a rude grunt.

I had to stifle a laugh. When we reached the end of the hall and turned left, I pointed ahead at a pair of double doors. "That must be the room. Pearson said it's big enough to hold a large party," I said loudly. As soon as we reached the doors, I played with the knob.

"Is it locked?"

I yanked on the door, and shouted, "No, I think it's stuck."

Christina frowned. "Why are you talking so loud?"

"Because I love the way my voice echoes off the walls!" I replied and started laughing.

She gave me this look like I was crazy and then started giggling. "You are retarded."

"Yeah, I know. I think the lock is just sticking."

"Here, let me try," she said.

I stepped aside and Christina turned the key, then pushed open the double doors. "There's nothing wrong with this lock."

Shrugging, I replied, "I guess it didn't work for me." With a sweep of my hand I gestured for Christina to go inside first. She took a few steps and stopped.

"How come the light didn't automatically come on?" she asked.

"Hold up, I think Pearson said they're over here." I rubbed my hand along the wall near the door then hit the switch. And as soon as the room flooded with light…

"SURPRISE!" was shouted across the room and then there was collective laughter.

Grinning, I looked over at Christina's stunned face.

"What the…"

The large room was packed with friends, family and even some of our most loyal customers who had all come out to celebrate Christina Holloway's big day.

"What's going on?" she mumbled, but there was a smile on her face she couldn't have hidden even if she wanted to.

"Just wait and see." I playfully wrapped my arms around Christina and gave her a loud kiss on the cheek.

"You know I don't like surprises," she mentioned.

"Since when?" I retorted and then released her just as a tall, gorgeous man walked toward her, moving with so much swag and cockiness he had every woman in the warehouse's attention. Dereon Sanders had this style about him that was hard to resist. Mahogany skin, bald head, beautiful golden eyes, and a pencil thin mustache darkening his top lip…, he was a work of art. He was also in love with my best friend.

Lucky heifer.

He stopped directly in front of Christina and took her hand. When he smiled, deep dimples became prominent on both sides of his dark-chocolate face.

"Baby, what's going on?" she asked, looking from him to me and then back to her boyfriend. "Why are all these people here?"

"Boo, I invited all our friends and family here today because I wanted them present for one of the most important moments of our lives."

Her eyes widened as he continued.

"Sweetheart, a few months ago you came strutting into my life." He paused for the crowd's laughter because everyone knew her well. "Since then my life hasn't been the same. But one thing I do know is I never want to know what life is like without you in it. Christina, you are the air I breathe," he continued in a low voice. "... my last thought before I go to sleep and the first thought that brightens each and every morning. Well tonight I wanted to say in front of all our friends and family, I love you Christina Holloway."

My eyes were growing misty while I watched her shake her head in disbelief and whisper, "I love you, too." Dereon leaned in and kissed her passionately and I watched our guests grinning and elbowing one another.

Pulling away, Dereon looked down at Christina. "I have a question for you."

She didn't push, just waited, her eyes glowing with curiosity. He brought a hand up and slowly stroked the side of her face and anyone who wasn't blind could see how much that man loved my best friend.

"Christina, I want nothing more than to spend the rest of my life with you. If you'll have me, I promise to spend the rest of my life trying to make you happy, or die trying."

"What?" She gasped then looked up, searching his face.

Stepping away from her, Dereon reached into the pocket of his jacket and took out a blue box. Trust me, Christina knew Tiffany's when she saw it and with a choked gasp, she started waving her hands with excitement. "Oh my God!"

He dropped down on one knee. And when he popped the box open she was screaming and crying all at once. I don't blame her. Dereon showed me the ring a few days ago and if a man bought me a diamond like that I would be screaming too. "Christina, marry me."

Her lips parted. "I... well..."

"Marry me," he repeated, gazing deep into her eyes.

"Yes... yes I'll marry you!" she answered breathlessly.

The crowd started applauding. He took her hand and slid the ring onto her finger while Christina scrubbed at her face, wiped away the tears before they ruined her make-up.

Dereon rose and captured Christina's mouth in a kiss that even had me gasping for air. The crowd cheered while the engaged couple hurried out the room for a private moment. I raised my hand in the air, signaling the deejay who started spinning tunes. Within seconds, their engagement party was in full force. I still wasn't sure how I managed to pull this event off without Christina finding out, but I had.

Damn, I'm good.

I grinned proudly as my eyes circled the room, admiring the space. There were several raised platform stages with professional dancers inside cages. The deejay, who we had flown in from New York, used to be a regular on 106 & Park back when Free and AJ were the hosts. My gaze swept over all the small intimate tables covered with white linen. Christina was too bougie for the ghetto nightclub theme so I kept it upscale. There were bartenders set up in all four corners of the room and a buffet table with everything from caramelized baby carrots to prime rib.

I spoke to several guests. A couple of clients stopped and wanted to discuss business but I shut them down and asked them to call my office in the morning. After weeks of planning, I needed an evening off to finally breathe and relax. I waltzed through the packed room in a black mini-dress that showcased my long legs and boosted my C-cups, and made it to the bar.

"I'll take a tequila and pineapple please." I took a seat on a barstool.

"Coming right up for the lovely lady."

While I waited, my eyes traveled over to the dance floor where guests were already grinding to the beat as the deejay served it up. I found myself swaying my hips and getting caught up in the vibe.

Videos were rolling and cameras were flashing. I had allowed limited access to the media, but there were enough in the house to give Christina the attention she demanded. I shook my head. She was truly a diva.

Christina and I owned *Cater to You,* the hottest catering company in St. Louis. I was a confectioner, which means I'm all about the sweets, while Christina's responsible for putting together a fabulous menu of dishes for our guests. Last month we catered a party for Ludacris and his new wife that was so off the chain, our office phones had been ringing off the hook ever since. Our success had caught the attention of several A-list celebrities and with the growing demand we were planning to expand our business.

As soon as my drink arrived, I sauntered over to a large table that had been reserved for a select few. Christina and Dereon were standing there talking to her younger sister, Portia. She was married to a pediatrician who made you take your shoes off and leave them on the front porch when you visited their home. I hadn't been back to the mini-mansion since.

"You did good."

I took a moment to calm my nerves before I swung around. Not that it did any good. The moment I turned and spotted the man standing in front of me, my body started vibrating with wanting.

Maximilian James was coochie-clenching gorgeous. At six-four he had smooth nutty brown skin and eyes that were dark and seductive. And then there was his short-cropped curly hair and a perfectly trimmed goatee that surrounded a pair of the softest, juiciest lips I had ever seen. He was Dereon's best friend.

"Thanks Max." I was amazed at how calm my voice remained. And it wasn't easy, considering the way he was staring down at me.

"How have you been?" He moved in closer so he wouldn't have to shout over the music. Damn, that man smelled so good I was tempted to lean in and sniff.

"I've been great. Business is good."

"I didn't ask about business... I asked about you."

Why did his voice always do crazy things to me? The last thing I wanted was to be attracted to him and yet I was. To be honest, Max was the cause of my sexual frustration.

"I'm doing great. Just bought a house."

He nodded. "Dereon said he came out and inspected it for

you."

I beamed. Last month I had stumbled upon a foreclosure that was everything I had dreamed of but didn't think I would have ever been able to afford on my own, but I had given up long ago on the dream of finding a husband and decided to pursue a future on my own. The house had been the first step. And I couldn't be happier. It symbolized I didn't need a man in order to get ahead in this world.

"Thanks. I finally moved in last week."

"You should have called me. I gotta truck and the boys and I would have been more than happy to have moved you in."

Goodness, just the thought of the five men construction crew running around with their shirts off at my house was more than I could have handled. It also would have meant being around Max. The further I stayed away from him, the better.

"Give me a call if you need some help hanging anything. I'm pretty good with my hands."

I just bet you are. Instantly I thought about those large hands rubbing me in some of my most intimate places. "I'll keep that in mind," I lied. There was no way in hell I was giving him a call.

"Would you like to dance?" he asked.

I looked over at the dance floor at all of the sweaty bodies clinging together, imitating sexual acts. *Yeah right.* "I think I'll pass. But thanks for asking."

"Okay, then come and sit with me."

Max was persistent. I'll give it to him. At one point I had almost considered dating him.

"When's your baby due?" I already knew the answer but I could see I needed to remind him why I wasn't interested in him.

"The baby is due in six weeks. But what's that got to do with us?"

Men like him just don't get it. "It's got everything to do with us. I don't have time for baby mama drama."

"There's no drama with me."

"That what you say but I met her, remember?" We had been standing outside a house he and the crew were renovating when Parker came screeching up in front of the house. She waddled around the car and made sure I saw she was having his baby. As loud and ghetto as she acted, I knew if I got involved with Max, it would be just a matter of time before she would be smashing out the windows of my Range Rover. Nope. Don't have time for that bullshit.

"Listen, like I told you before I don't know if that's my child or not but until I do, I need to stand by her. But we're not together."

Maybe, maybe not, but the second the baby was born and he found out it was his he might have a change of heart. And then where would I be? Standing on the outside watching the happy family. Fuck that.

"Nah, the only babies I want my man to have are mine. But you hold that thought and holla at me after you get the paternity test results."

I didn't waste another moment standing there talking to him. Max was just too damn fine and a woman could only resist so much when it came to him. I was attracted to him. There was no doubt about that and I spent countless nights imagining him fucking me. But I wasn't interested in the real deal because I knew for a fact once with Max would not be enough.

I walked over to the buffet to make sure there was still plenty of food. Since there was no way I could have prepared a spread this size without Christina knowing, I had catered the event with another company we often subcontracted. They provided the foods while my staff and I prepared most of the sweets using their kitchen.

I made a plate, then went over to the table and took a seat. Dereon and Christina were on the dance floor locked in each other's arms. I was happy for them. Really I was. Christina had been dying for a husband and now she was about to get her wish. The St. Louis police detective was more man than any of those bozos she used to date. You know the saying, opposites attract? She came from money with a socialite as a mother and a millionaire father who had just recently come back into her life. Dereon kept Christina grounded and that was what she needed.

I sat with a few friends. Chatted nonstop then excused myself to the restroom. I followed the arrows away from the loud music. I was turning the corner when I heard a familiar voice.

"Have that pussy ready for me."

What the hell? I froze in my tracks. My mouth hung open and I then realized he was on the phone.

"I'll be there just as soon as I can. Just unlock the door." There was another pause and I eased my ear closer to the door and held my breath, wishing I could hear the response on the other end of the phone. "What color panties you got on?" *Was he for real*? "Take them off. I want you butt naked and spread eagle when I get there." He chuckled and I just stood there, listening and shook my head. Who is that? I wondered and I wasn't leaving until I had a chance to see who it was.

"Claudia, we have a problem in the kitchen."

"What's the problem?" I didn't mean to snap at Montel, but I was trying to find out who was on the other side of the door.

The culinary arts major continued. "Ummm…one of the servers is drunk."

"What?" I barked. It's amazing how quick I forgot all about being nosy and followed him toward the kitchen in back. To pull off an event this size, I had reached out to Culinary Resources, a staffing service for temporary personnel in the food and hospitality industry. Every now and again they sent me a problem child. But once I rounded the corner and spotted a young Meagan Good lookalike talking loud and staggering around the room, I cussed under my breath. My mistake. That chick was someone I had hired, doing a friend a favor.

I marched right up to her. "Shalisa, have you been drinking?"

She gave me a look as if I was bothering her. "Just a little. Why you trippin'?"

No she didn't. "I'm tripping because you're here to work."

She rolled her big bubble eyes at me. "I am working. Damn, we've been working all day."

"And that's what you're getting paid to do."

"I…" she began and then she dashed over to the trashcan and started puking her guts.

"Freda, please get her home."

"I'm sorry," Shalisa said between moans.

"Gary, please take out that trash. Nina and Rachel, let's get that area sanitized."

After that little fiasco, I was the one who needed a drink. I made my way to the ladies room. My mystery caller was long gone. I was pissed because I really wanted to know who he was.

I went back to the party, had a few glasses and made my rounds, networking and doing what I do best. I was talking to a previous client when I spotted Max over near the buffet talking to one of Dereon's cousin. That hoochie was smiling and throwing her big boobs in his face. I tried to act like I could care less what he did, but I knew I was lying. The sight of them laughing and having a good time churned my stomach. It was messing up my head. I don't remember when I have ever met a man I had wanted so bad and yet knew it was better just to leave him alone.

I was laughing with Christina's favorite cousin, Tamara, when I caught them on the dance floor bumping and grinding. Max was running his hands all across that female's ass and she looked like she had just come on herself.

"Goodness Max is fine! If I wasn't already married I would be all over him," I heard Tamara hiss. "Christy said he's single. How come you're not all over *that?*"

I gave a rude snort and tried to act as calm as I could. "Because he's got enough women on his plate as it is and I don't believe in being second to nobody."

"I know that's right." She gave me a high five.

"How that baby girl doing?" I asked.

"Getting so big." She was beaming with pride, the way all

new mothers do. I was happy for her.

"Have you allowed Christy to keep Summer yet?"

"Hell no. She doesn't know the first thing about babies." We laughed before Tamara's husband came over and dragged her out onto the dance floor. When I stole another look at Max, that chick had her head resting against his chest, her eyes closed, and lips parted. Oh my. She was already caught up under his spell.

I know the feeling. I almost made the same mistake.

By the time the two of them got off the dance floor I was rolling my eyes. Then I caught Max coming my way.

"Hey beautiful."

I shook my head. "Bumping and grinding… that's how you got yourself in the predicament you're in now," I accused and pointed my finger at him.

He simply chuckled and yet that sound vibrated through my body.

"Dance with me, CC."

"I already told you— Whoa, wait a minute… CC? How did you know my name was Claudia Ciara Winters?" I asked suspiciously.

"I have my ways."

"Nobody calls me CC but my family."

"I want to be your family." His voice was a little rough, lacking in the usual flirtation, but it was still enough to make my body heat. Oh, he was smooth, I'll give him that. "Now stand up." He took my hand. "I like this song. Let's dance."

"Why?"

"Because I want to." He clasped my hand and yanked softly, but I drew back with my feet firmly grounded.

"What are you afraid of?" He held out his other hand. "I want to dance with you. To be honest, I'd use any excuse to hold you in my arms." With a wry smile he added, "Come on, CC. What do you say?"

Damn, he looked too yummy standing in front of me "Fine." I blew out a long breath then took his hand. "You'd better not step on my foot."

Max nudged me off the stool and laughed. "I'm too good

a dancer for that."

I let him lead me out onto the crowded dance floor. Of course the song had to be something slow. My body was snug against him, his arms tightly around my waist.

I moved from side to side with my arms dangling by my side.

"I don't bite."

"Who said you did?" I snapped.

"Then put your arms around my neck," he said swaying just slightly to the music.

Damn him. No way in the world was I going to let Max know I was afraid of him because I was—afraid of the way he made me feel when I was around him.

I did as he asked, and when my breasts rubbed against his solid chest and he brought his lips to nuzzle the side of my neck, I heard myself sigh. Why couldn't my body listen to my mind? It was screaming, "Danger Will Robinson!" and yet my nipples hardened and refused to listen. As the song continued even my mind was no longer listening because I was now thinking about what it would be like to take him home with me tonight. The erection I felt pulsing against my belly button guaranteed a night I would never forget.

"You are so sexy," Max whispered close to my ear. "Would it piss you off if I kissed you right now?"

He was testing me, and had no idea how close I was to tugging him by his collar toward me and covering his lips with mine. "Yes, it would."

But now his lips were close, dangerously close. I could hardly breathe. Being in his arms felt right. Natural. Like I had found what I had been waiting for all my life.

Where the hell had that thought come from?

Jerking back, I dropped my arms and planted my hands lightly at his waist. The little distance between us was just what I needed to get my head on right, even though I wanted to draw him close again. As soon as the song was over, I was storming across the dance floor, and away from him.

For the next hour, I steered clear of Max, which wasn't hard to do. I made sure the buffet table was presentable. Sent my staff back to the kitchen for more salad and then helped set up the dessert table. My specialty is confections—truffles, cakes, cookies. Carbohydrates and sugar was what I was good at which was why I would never be considered a skinny woman. My mother was Asian and yet I had definitely inherited the hips from my father's family. He was a proud black man from Georgia.

I spent the next hour, mingling with guests and sipping one too many martinis. I was more than tipsy when I spotted Max and that same chick disappear together. For the longest time I sat there trying to act like I didn't care until I couldn't take it any longer. Whatever reason I had for getting up out of that chair I was blaming it on the alcohol. I sprung from my seat and went in search of them. Halfway there I ended up detouring to the ladies room and puking my guts out.

"You okay?" someone called from the other stall.

"Yeah," I lied. I had drunk more than my usual limit of two, maybe four. I wasn't even sure. I cleaned myself up. Bummed a piece of gum from the woman standing at the sink and walked out when I suddenly remembered I was looking for Max. I headed down the hall. It was ridiculous, but yet I was pissed. And my mind and body were screaming… if anyone was going to screw Max tonight it was going to be me.

"You looking for me?"

I jerked around to find him standing in the doorway of what looked like possibly Pearson's office.

"Nope. Why would I be looking for you?"

"Liar." Max stared me down as if I was an opponent and he was being challenged.

"I don't have a reason to lie."

"Sure you don't." Max yanked my arm, dragged me into the room, then shut the door.

Click!

My heart started racing as I leaned back against the door trying to get as far away from him as I could.

"Are you going to let me go?"

"Not until I kiss you."

I parted my lips to protest, only it ended up being an open

invitation as he pressed his lips to mine and slipped his tongue inside. The kiss was possessive and dominating ripping the air from my lungs while sending heat pooling into my panties.

My traitorous body responded and my tongue was sliding against his, meeting each and every confident stroke. My arms came around him and then I was raking my nails down along his back. Goodness, did I have any shame? Evidently I did not because I was rocking my hips and grinding against him. It was the alcohol I kept telling myself. The tequila had weakened my ability to resist. Max's hands roamed all over my body, exploring my curves. He found my nipples, straining against the dress, eager to accommodate his big hands.

"You like that?" he said encouraging me.

I whimpered in response. The dampness between my thighs was evidence I couldn't ignore.

The kiss deepened and I felt the need to knock him onto the desk and straddle his lap. His hands lowered to my ass and pulled me closer and I felt his penis pulsing. Not that it was easy to miss with him grinding his entire length up and down along my pussy until I was whimpering in pleasure.

"You want me to fuck you, don't you?"

"No," I moaned.

A laugh rumbled in his chest. "You are such a liar, CC. I might have to show you what happens to pretty ladies that lie."

Show me, was right on the tip of my tongue, but I clamped my lips down hard and moaned instead.

"I want to lick you, suck you, and bury my dick so deep you'll scream my name."

Oh I liked the sound of that so much I didn't even try to resist a moan.

I felt his hand slide up under my dress. Oh my, I was hot and so willing. He got the dress past my thighs and I arched forward so his fingers could slide across the crotch of my panties. And on contact, I was crying out with pleasure.

"I knew your lips would be fat. Just the way I had

imagined them."

Well, it was good to know that at least he had been thinking about me, too. With his fingers sliding across my folds, I didn't even bother trying to hold back, I whimpered and moaned and rocked my hips. Why did things have to feel so right between us?

I didn't have much time to mull over that thought when I felt his hand shoving my panties to the right and eased inside. "Damn," he groaned. "CC, you're so wet."

I was just getting started.

Cum was already sliding down my thigh, then he was pushing into my pussy and my body clasped around his finger.

"That feel good?"

"Yes," I whimpered. "Oh yes." I kept on rocking my hips, drawing his fingers deeper. Max brought his thumb up and rubbed across my clit. "Max!" I screamed.

"That's it babe. I want you to come for me." He removed his finger and rolled it around my swollen nub, while his lips and tongue trailed along my cheek and neck. And then his fingers plunged inside again and again, over and over and I was so close to an orgasm. But even as intoxicated as I was, I refused to let him be in control.

I stepped back, his fingers sliding out from inside me, sending moisture sliding down my inner thigh. "Sit," I ordered. I was trying hard to be in control, but I was shaking with both fear and desire.

Grinning, he walked over and took a seat on an old wooden chair and folded his arms.

I turned around then reached behind me for the zipper to my dress and slowly lowered it, letting it fall down around my waist. I wanted him to see the curve of my round ass in a pair of sheer white lace panties. As soon as the dress hit the floor, I heard a sharp intake of breath sliding through his teeth.

I couldn't resist a grin. I wanted Max. I would probably regret it in the morning but tonight I wanted him. Tomorrow, I would do like Jamie Foxx said, and blame it on the alcohol. Slowly, I turned. I was standing in nothing but a lace white bra, matching panties and come fuck-me shoes. The way he was watching, heightened my arousal and confidence.

My heart was pounding in response. My clit throbbed with anticipation. I knew what and who I wanted. I also knew that despite how much I tried to deny it, the only person I could get it from was Max. Reaching up, I unclasped my bra tossing it to the floor and my breasts hung free. His eyes were glued to me as I lowered my panties over my hips and kicked them away.

"Damn," he hissed under his breath.

Max sat there legs spread, saying nothing and yet his eyes never left my body. But the evidence of his arousal spoke volumes.

Slowly, I walked toward him, the heels of my shoes, clicking across the floor. I was completely naked except for my shoes and the way he was looking at me made me feel confident and sexier than I've ever felt before.

I approached the chair and stood between his legs, my breasts dangling in front of him. "You like what you see?" I said barely above a whisper.

"I like everything standing in front of me. Now c'mere." Reaching out Max drew me closer to him, bringing my kitty within an inch from his mouth. I felt his breath feather the hairs surrounding my clit.

Leaning forward, Max brought his lips to my stomach where he dropped light kisses, sending quivers of need straight to my core.

His hands slid up to my breasts, molding me, caressing. "I love these," he growled and I closed my eyes. He touched my nipples, rubbing the sensitive tips. My head rolled forward to his shoulder and groaned as his fingers closed on my nipples and pinched just enough for my breath to catch. He continued to caress and tease while dropping light kisses across my stomach. I always knew his touch would be confident and skilled. I tried to pull away, to evade his tongue but he was strong and in all honesty, I really wasn't that interested in stopping him.

Max let his hand drift up along my ass. "You are

beautiful. You know that, don't you Claudia?"

He kissed my stomach again, tracing a line with the tip of his tongue from my belly button to just above the place that was wet and aching for him. He looked up at me, his eyes locked with mine as he dropped to his knees. "You know I have to taste you, right?"

I swallowed hard in response.

He pulled me close, bringing my apex into the line of his mouth. Max then leaned forward, sliding his tongue along my damp folds, sending a bolt of pleasure through me.

"Oh Max," I sighed.

He growled and held onto me with both hands, bringing me up against his mouth.

I tried to keep from collapsing by clinging to his broad shoulders while his tongue continued its demanding assault.

"Open your legs for me, babe."

As I slid my thighs apart, Max adjusted his hold on me and then placed one hand between my thighs, teasing my slick entrance with his fingers as he continued to tease me with his tongue. I let out a cry of shock before I could stop myself.

Pleasure built and twisted in my stomach as Max pushed fingers inside of me, matching the strokes of his tongue with the thrusts of his fingers. His tongue was buried between my labia and he was holding me firmly in place. It wasn't long before I was whimpering until I was certain I couldn't take it any longer. And then his fingers went deeper and I was met by a wave of pleasure that sent cries of ecstasy from between my lips. Max didn't cease until my hips had stopped rocking and my breathing began to slow. I looked down at him and my body heated at the sight of the wicked smile on Max's lips.

He rose and while I leaned back against the desk, he began removing his clothes. First undoing the buttons of his shirt, then unzipping his pants, followed by lowering his boxers to his knees.

His cock was thick and proud and thrusting in my direction.

My mouth felt like it hung to the floor. There was no way in hell I could accommodate all that. "Uh-uh, what do you think you're about to do?" I managed between breaths.

"You're not gonna leave me like this, are you?"

He moved his palm up and down the length of his erection. Unconsciously, I shook my head and watched in awe as he reached down for his wallet in his pants and removed a condom

"Put it on," he said then handed me the foil packet. He leaned in and captured my lips in a deep kiss while I ripped open the packet. Reaching down, I wrapped my fingers around his cock and rolled it on. Max groaned with desire, then moved back to the chair and took a seat.

"Straddle me Claudia." His voice was rough, strained. "I need to be inside you."

I was shaking with anticipation as I walked over to the chair. I wasn't sure how he was going to make it work but I wanted him too damn bad not to try.

Lifting my legs, I positioned myself over his erection and felt his hardness sliding against my slick folds. I rolled my hips against the swollen head, teasing both me and him, and then lowered very slowly over his length.

"That's it babe. Take all of it."

I sighed as he filled me. The feeling was amazing. He brought his hands to my waist guiding me and yet not rushing to be buried and I was grateful. I stretched, swallowing his hardened length inch my beautiful inch.

So this is what it feels like to be with Max.

All the nights I had spent thinking about this very thing and now that it was finally happening, my fantasies were weak in comparison. He felt huge and I moved slowly at first, allowing for my body to adjust but once it did, I was in heaven. I braced my hands on his shoulders and before long, I was riding him hard until my ass was slapping against his lap. His hands were firmly at my waist as he started pounding his hips forward. I was crying out his name because nothing or no one had ever felt that good. I moved against him, rocking my clit back and forth, bringing myself closer to the peak.

His hands were at my waist guiding me as the pounding began. I flexed my hips one last time and then I was riding him fast and within seconds I felt Max pulsing inside of me and then I exploded. Max howled and came seconds later and then we rode it out to the end.

When it was completely spent, I leaned forward, resting against his chest and listening to the strong rhythm of his heartbeat. I waited until his heart slowed, and his breathing became even again before I drew back and met his stare.

"You're gonna be mine," Max murmured against my lips.

I was completely at a loss for words.

TWO

Hours after the party ended, I finally made it out to my vehicle. As soon as I climbed inside, I reached under my dress and yanked off my panties. Oh my! They were soaking wet.

Dammit, I was nasty!

Oh God! What in the world had I been thinking? That's the problem. I wasn't thinking. It had been mind over body and my mind had me now feeling like a slut.

Stupid! I clearly had had too much to drink. That was my story and I was sticking to it.

Somehow I made it home and decided not to push my luck trying to maneuver my SUV into my overstuffed garage. That took skill and a clear head because my parking spot was only so big with boxes still waiting to be unpacked lining the walls. So instead I pulled into the driveway.

I climbed out and was so anxious to get inside my twenty-five-hundred-square foot house, I left my heels and those damn drenched panties in the front seat. I'd get them tomorrow. I staggered up the stairs and into the door. The lips of my kitty cat were slick and wet, a reminder that I had gotten dicked down tonight. Oh, I was sore and even though I would never admit to him, sex with Max was one of the best experiences of my life.

After our rendezvous in the office, I had spent the rest of the evening hiding out in the kitchen. It was easy to stay distracted. Plates needed to be cleared, dishes required washing, and everything packed away in the van. I helped the staff and by the time we locked up at midnight everything was just as we had found it. Luckily, Max was nowhere in sight when I finally pulled off the lot.

I climbed the stairs to my master suite, then padded down the hall. I tossed my purse on the bed and fell back beside it on the soft mattress, taking one deep breath followed by another and another, then my head began to spin. Oh, I had drunk way too much, which left me wild and horny. It took me a moment to realize my phone was ringing. I fumbled for my purse, hit Accept, and brought it to my ear.

"Yes?"

"You make it in?"

Oh shit! "Max?" I whispered then tried to sit up on the bed, but the pain at my temple sank my head back onto the comforter. "Why are you calling me?"

"I wanna make sure you made it home safe."

"I don't need you checking up on me," I barked into the phone.

There was a chuckle. "Why're you always trying to act like you don't like me?"

Why couldn't he leave me alone? "Because I don't."

"Yes you do. You like me."

"No I don't. I tolerate you," I protested.

"Really? Then what was that all about?"

"What are you talking about?"

"Oooh, Max..., baby, yes...YES!"

I squeezed my eyes shut. Oh God! I was never going to be able to look that man in the face again. Dumb, Dumb! You hear me! Sex with him, although satisfying, was the stupidest thing I have ever done. "I can't believe you even went there."

There was that throaty chuckle of his again vibrating through my middle. "Yo, I'm just keeping it real. It's time you do the same."

"Max, I was caught up in the moment."

"*The moment*?" He actually sounded offended. "So you're saying the dick wasn't good."

Hell no. I was squeezing my thighs together just thinking about how good he had felt, pounding inside of me with long deep strokes. "I'll admit the sex was great, but let's not make it more than just casual sex."

"There is nothing casual about us, Claudia. I know it and deep down you know it too."

"Max, you can think whatever you want," I told him, then ended the call.

First off, how the hell had he gotten my number because I definitely hadn't given it to him? I'll admit I had been tempted at one time, but that was before I found out about his suspect baby mama. Ever since then, he's been talking to the back of my head.

I rose from the bed and started yanking off my clothes. I was angry and yet I couldn't believe how humiliated I felt. I went against everything I believed in and had sex with the last person I would ever pick as my man. And it wasn't because he was a contractor. At one time I wouldn't have dated anyone who didn't have a college degree but over the years I realized that educated men could be idiots too—instead I focused on the person and what they had to bring to the table. All the years I spent working hard, sacrificing to get where I was today, there was no way I would date a man who wasn't at least my equal. And then I met Max while Christina was visiting Dereon at a house they were renovating. He was sexy, funny, and had my body surging with energy. When he asked me out, I really thought I had met my match until I discovered he had some unfinished business with another female.

My phone rang again and I padded over to the bed, and looked down at the screen. "Are you serious?" I tapped the screen and barked, "What do you want?"

"Why you hang up on me?"

I felt this urge to smile but I held it together and resisted. "I don't wanna talk to you."

Don't you know he had the nerve to say, "Yeah, so you say." *Oh no he didn't!* "Yo, listen..., meet me for dinner on Friday."

"What... why?" The last thing I wanted was to be sitting across the table from him.

"Because I have an idea for my man's wedding I wanna run by you."

"What is it?" I'm not going to lie. I was curious.

"Nah, I'll tell you when I see you."

Now he was going to have me wondering. "Just tell me now."

"Claudia, just meet me at Tommy's for dinner at five."

"I have an appointment at six." I didn't really have an appointment until eight but just because we'd had sex didn't mean I was about to allow him to start bossing me around.

"Then I'll meet you at four. Just make sure you're there."

"Yeah, I'll be there."

"And wear something sexy. Make sure you show those pretty legs of yours."

I almost found myself smiling before I heard him chuckling. I hit the button and ended the call. My body was tingling and I was starting to get excited over seeing him again. Dammit! How was I turned on by a man I could barely stand?

That's because you like him more than you're willing to admit.

Once I was under the spray of the water all I could do was think about how pathetic my personal life was. Professionally, I had it together.

I guess it all started when my lifelong friend and college sweetheart decided he'd rather practice medicine in Africa than spend the rest of his life married to me. I should have known then I was doomed for a life of relationship disappointments. Yet instead of recognizing the warning signs, I subjected myself to years of dating fiascos. It wasn't until after wasting six months of my life with a man I was convinced was the one, I was finally ready to accept that what I'd read in those romance novels was simply make-believe. Love at first sight and that instant attraction crap only happened in the movies.

But it was hard to remember any of that when Max was around. That man had a way of screwing up my head and wishing for something that I knew was never going to happen for me. At least not with him. And it was a damn shame because he was so fine, with the prettiest smile. And now that we'd had sex..., OMG! He had raised the bar.

As I lathered my body, I pushed that last thought aside.

There was no way in hell I was going to start yearning for something that was all wrong for me.

I loved my life. I was a beautiful woman, with honey-brown hair that I had recently cut in a short stylish style; beige skin, and champagne colored eyes. I was tall and wearing heels all the time, I was over six feet.

I rubbed the sponge across my breasts and my nipples puckered as thoughts of Max resurfaced. Even now I could hear Max's grunts as he pumped at a frantic rhythm, thrusting upward into my body. Just remembering how good he had felt caused my body to pulse with need.

Oh, I was in for a long night.

By morning, I was pissed off. Max... Max... Max. That's all I thought about all damn night. He haunted my thoughts. He haunted my dreams. All night long I replayed our encounter over and over in my head. Every kiss... every lick... every suck. The way his hands felt on my breasts. His mouth. His penis buried deep inside of me. It was maddening. By the time the sun was set to rise, I'd ended up pulling out my dildo and riding that long device trying to satisfy my craving for Max. It provided a little relief but nothing was like the feel of Max being inside of me. I woke up aroused and exhausted.

I gotta get him out of my head.

I had a date later with Tyler, a lawyer who worked at my mother's law firm. Normally I didn't want to have anything to do with the men my parents tried to hook me up with but he had the prettiest teeth and was actually cute. So during one of my parent's social events, I gave him my number. Since then we had talked on the phone several times and I have to admit, he seemed like a great guy, and unlike Max, he doesn't have any children.

With that thought in mind I decided to focus on the evening ahead. Tyler had invited me to his house. He was cooking for me, and I was determined to have a good time. "Please let him be the one," I mumbled under my breath. I wasn't sure if I was talking to God or trying to get my mind to consider the possibility. Tyler had made it pretty clear that I had wifely potential. And he definitely had almost everything I desired in a man. The rest was yet to be seen.

I walked into the office. Mia, our office assistant, was behind the desk chatting away on the phone. Customer service was something she was definitely good at. She was also smart, organized and dependable.

Without breaking stride, I gave her a beauty pageant wave, then headed down the hall toward my office. I loved what we'd accomplished. Back in the day, Christina and I started our business in my parent's basement. Now look at us. We have a storefront building right in the heart of downtown Clayton.

I pushed open my office door, flicked on the light then walked across my carpeted floor to my desk. I was already fired up and ready to get the week started. But first on the agenda was coffee.

Who ever invented a Keurig coffeemaker deserved a kiss. A big wet kiss. I put my purse in the bottom drawer then loaded a K-cup in the system and logged onto my MacBook. By the time Christina came waltzing into my office, in a chocolate dress and red pumps, I was on my second cup of coffee.

"Good morning sunshine," she sang.

"What are you so happy about?" I asked as if I didn't already know.

"My party. OMG! I was so surprised. I can't believe you pulled that off." She went on and on as she walked over and made herself a cup of coffee.

"I had a little help," I admitted. There was no way I would have been able to pull the party off if it hadn't been for Dereon. He had ways of occupying Christina's time and freeing up part of the day so I could sneak off and make that night happen.

"From my boo?" She had this saucy grin on her lips.

My brow rose. It was weird hearing Christina refer to a man as her boo, but then nothing about her was normal since Dereon stepped into our office and into Christina's life.

Instead, she had been on the ride of her life. As fine as he was, that was one ride she was definitely enjoying.

"You know you're gonna have to start planning my birthday three years in advance to top that party, right?"

Laughing, Christina came over and gave me a big hug. "What the hell would I do without you? You're truly the best."

"I know and don't you forget it." I was smiling and hugging her at the same time. She really was my best friend.

She finally released me and reached down for her cup. "What happened with you and Max?"

I did my best to play dumb. "What do you mean?"

She was all in my face. "I saw the two of you coming from the back of the warehouse at the same time. Then you rushed toward the kitchen before I had a chance to talk to you."

"How the hell you have time to be watching me at your party?"

"I know how to multitask and quit trying to change the subject. What were the two of you doing? And don't you dare say nothing."

I knew she would never believe that, but that didn't mean I had to tell her the truth either. "He spotted me coming out the ladies room and wanted to talk."

"Talk?"

"Yes, talk."

Christina wasn't buying it for a second. "You don't talk to a man that fine."

She wasn't lying about that. Men like Max—the only conversation going on was body language. I just wasn't ready yet to tell her how far I had gone. "Okay, fine. We kissed."

"Oh shit!" Her eyes were wide as she flopped down in a chair across from my desk.

"Yeah, I know it's hard to believe, especially after I made such a big deal over the whole baby mama thing."

"I knew it!" she screamed. "And then what happened?" She was asking for details I wasn't about to give.

"Nothing. We kissed, then my phone was vibrating in my purse so I went to check on the staff while I called Tyler." Damn, I was good.

"Tyler?" I noticed the way she sniffed the air at the mention of him. "What in the world did he want?" Don't you know Christina had the nerve to look pissed off? Like she had been watching a movie and someone stepped in front of the screen at the good part.

"He wanted to remind me we have a date this evening."

She rolled her eyes the way she does whenever she isn't getting her way. Did I mention Christina is spoiled? She is accustomed to the finer things in life and getting what she wants. At least that was the case before she met Dereon. After that, everything changed. Now she wanted to be all up in my business.

"I thought you liked Max?"

Her eyebrow inched up. "Max?"

Dammit. I waved a frustrated hand at her. "I mean Tyler. I thought you liked Tyler?" I slipped up and she knew it.

Christina's eyes were dancing with amusement at the mistake. "Tyler's a nice guy, but he looks boring." He brought lunch by the office last week.

"Boring?" I knew she was right, but that wasn't what I wanted to hear.

She brought the cup to her lips, took a sip and said, "Look..., one thing I discovered with Dereon is I need a man who challenges me. I never had that before."

"You never had a man that made less than six figures either," I added sarcastically.

With a rude snort, she added, "Yes, that too. Dereon made me step out of my comfort zone. Now I look back at all the men whom I used to date and think how selfish, boring and superficial they were."

"Sound a lot like you."

"Whatever girl. This conversation is about you, not me."

She was sipping her coffee, her eyes never leaving mine like she was expecting me to slip up or something, and confess how I really feel. She was my best friend, but I wasn't about to admit something to Christina I wasn't ready to admit to myself. It just was not going to happen.

I shrugged my shoulders. "Tyler isn't like that. He is

really pretty cool. He's also single with no kids."

She held up a hand to silence me. "I don't even think that's Max's baby."

"Why, because he says it isn't?"

"Yes, I believe him, and you should too."

"I don't have to believe anything. He's a nice guy. Really he is, but I don't see a future with a man with a kid. I mean come on… if you found out Dereon had a child with another woman would you still want to marry him?"

"Girl, you know I'm too selfish for that."

"Exactly, so what makes you think I want a package deal?"

"Because you're not like me. I'm the one who's stuck-up and spoiled. Jeanna still thinks I'm ruining my life, but for once, I don't care what anyone thinks about Dereon, but me."

"So, I will ask you again, if you found out that Dereon had a baby on the way by another woman, would you still marry him?" I sat there with my arms crossed at my chest, hoping she would agree with my decision.

Christina gave me a long thoughtful look and took another sip before saying, "It's impossible for me to answer that question now."

"Why?"

Leaning back on the chair, she sighed. "Because I'm already in love with Dee. Once you love someone, things that used to be important, no longer are."

That was not at all the answer I was expecting. "What's that supposed to mean?"

"You'll find out."

A client called, marking an end to the conversation. Christina went back to her office and I spent the rest of the morning working with Mia, finishing up the final catering details for a wedding that was scheduled for the following weekend.

"By the way, Mrs. Sheaves called this morning to add five more to the guests list."

I was cussing under my breath even though I knew it was so unprofessional. It was taking everything I had at that point not to personally call and cuss that woman out.

"The numbers have already been finalized. The food has been ordered," I reminded as if she didn't already know. One thing about Mia, she knew her job.

"I know and I told her it was too late to add names." I noticed my assistant had this look on her face that told me I wasn't at all going to like what I was about to hear. Trust me, I've been dealing with that stuck-up woman for over a year, she was truly a piece of work.

"What did the heffa have to say?"

Mia's eyes grew twice as large and round at my shrewd comment. I didn't make a habit of talking bad about our clients, because I knew what hand buttered our bread, but the congresswoman and her daughter Rana were definitely pieces of work.

"She said as much as she's paying for us to cater the wedding, I needed to find a way to make it happen."

Her words felt like a slap in the face. "Did she now?" I was boiling with anger as I reached down for her client file, scanned through the contract for the information I needed, then reached for the phone on my desk. *No she didn't think she could talk that way to us.* I didn't care how much money she was paying, there was no excuse for disrespect.

She answered by the second ring.

"Good morning Mrs. Sheaves… this is Claudia at *Cater to You.*"

"Hello Dear, how are you?"

I wasn't about to fall for all that formality gibberish. Christina and I had been dealing with bride-zilla and her mother's venom for over a year. At some point the bullshit had to stop. "My assistant has just informed me you wanted to add five more guests to the list?" I actually was surprised how syrupy sweet my voice sounded. I'd learned as a teenager to kill them with kindness.

"Yes, that's sounds about right. We have cousins from Germany who have decided to attend."

"Okay, no problem… I'm going to need you to put that request in writing."

"Excuse me?" Don't you know she had the audacity to sound insulted? I, on the other hand, had decided to keep it professional. Even though I had the strong urge to suddenly go ghetto on her ass.

"As it states in your contract, any changes made less than thirty days before the event are to be done in either a letter or email."

"I don't remember that."

"I'm looking at it right now in your contract. Turn to page four, paragraph three." I knew she didn't have the contract in her possession, but I wanted to make damn sure she knew I had it right in front of me.

"I would think you would make an exception."

Why, because you are spending a ridiculous amount of money for your daughter's wedding? That was a personal choice. "Mrs. Sheaves we have several other clients and we hold them to their contracts as well."

There was dead silence on the other end and it took everything I had not to laugh out loud.

"Like I said, just put your request in an email and we'll make sure we do everything we can to make them possible... for an additional charge, as stated in your contract."

"Let me think about it and I'll get back with you." There was a click and then the phone went dead.

"That chick hung up on me."

Mia was chuckling like someone was tickling her. "I wish I could have seen the look on her face when you told her she had to put the request in writing."

I couldn't resist a laugh of my own. "I bet she won't call again with any other requests."

Mia quickly sobered and then rested her elbow on my desk. "Claudia, I would like to apologize for Shalisa's behavior. I really thought she was trying to get herself together."

She had been doing everything she could to help her younger sister, who'd been battling alcohol addiction. *So much for her twelve-step program.*

"Luckily, I was able to contain the situation before she

had a chance to make a scene."

Mia shook her head with despair. "You were doing me a favor hiring her. I'm really sorry."

I gave her a sympathetic smile. "Don't worry about it. I had everything under control." I tapped my nails against the desk. "Alright, hand me the next file."

We reviewed two additional catering orders, then Mia returned to her desk to finalize the changes. Christina returned to my office after lunch and we spent most of the afternoon preparing a menu for a birthday surprise for a new break-out artist who was having a launch party in December at a mansion in Chesterfield. The Memphis-based label was hoping to make her the next Rihanna. It was going to be a black-tie affair and everything had to be perfect.

THREE

It was almost eight by the time I arrived in Ladue. I looked at the numbers on the mailbox and grinned as I gazed up at the house. Tyler's place was breathtaking. Why in the world was a single man living in something so huge? I don't know but I definitely planned to find out.

Slowly, I pulled onto the driveway. Not only did he have a three car garage but there was another off to the right with the door raised and inside was a boat. I couldn't believe my luck and was getting all excited. This was exactly the type of man I needed in my life.

I quickly popped a mint in my mouth, then decided to make it two before I climbed out my Range Rover. I figured Tyler was probably standing in front of one of those large picture windows looking out at me so I wanted to make a grand impression as I sauntered up to the door. I was rocking a pink designer dress and lime green and pink open-toe pumps.

As I walked toward the porch, I admired his two-story brick house and was clearly impressed. My first thought was I couldn't wait to tell Christina, but she was so stuck on me and Max getting together that she probably would only half listen.

I climbed the steps to a beautiful double wrought iron door and rang the bell. Tyler didn't keep me waiting.

"You made it." There was something about a crooked smile that I found sexy.

"I got turned around a few times. But I finally figured it out."

"You should have called me." He seemed so concerned I had been riding around in circles. He was really a nice guy. Compassion... check!

"Well, I'm glad you made it. Leave your shoes by the door

and come back to the kitchen."

My brow rose. I had worn my Zanotti pumps just for his viewing pleasure and now I had to take them off. That was almost like Samson having to leave his hair at the door. He lost a point with that request, but one glance down at his beautiful gray hardwood floors I could understand why he didn't want the heels of my shoes scratching the surface. There was even a box of blue booties, the kind physicians use in the operating room, on a shelf beside the door. My toes were too cute for that, so I opted to pad barefoot down the hall.

"Your house is gorgeous!" It was almost as nice as my parents. Crown molding, textured beige-painted walls, tray ceilings in the living and dining room and expensive traditional style furniture. Trust me, I know expensive when I see it. "What did you do, hire an interior designer?"

He nodded and appeared pleased I had noticed. "Last year I retained Clements Interior Design to come in and have free liberty. It cost me a pretty penny but was truly worth it."

I smiled and as he continued the tour I oohed and aahed. I preferred to put my own personal stamp on my place, but he was a man and I was sure he didn't know the first thing about decorating.

What impressed me the most was his kitchen. It was something out of a magazine with white cabinets, granite countertops and a huge island in the middle with a cooktop. The room was surrounded by windows and gave a clear view of the large deck out back.

"Something smells delicious." I took a seat at the island while he moved over to stir a pot.

"I hope you like pasta."

"I love it."

Tyler looked pleased. There was soft jazz playing from an iPod and a bottle of red wine chilling in a bowl of ice. He must have noticed me eyeing the bottle.

"Go ahead and help yourself to the wine."

I was reaching for the corkscrew and thinking, *I bet Max doesn't know anything about wine*. Damn, I don't even know why I'd allowed thoughts of him to invade my evening.

I quickly shifted my attention to Tyler. He was standing at the stove loading garlic bread in the oven. Did I mention how much I love a man who can cook?

He had the curliest dark hair and a dimple at his right cheek that made him almost look like a boy when he laughed, and then there was that goatee. It wasn't as nice as Max's but it did look good on him.

Dammit, quit thinking about Max!

"How was your day at work? Your mother tells me your business has really expanded over the last year."

I couldn't help but grin. I love a man who shows a genuine interest in what I do.

"I thank God every day for what Christina and I have accomplished. I always thought we'd be successful. I just never expected it to happen quite so fast."

His dark eyes twinkled. "Consider that a blessing."

"Oh I do! Every damn day." I poured wine into two glasses, then handed him one.

"Thank you." he said and then took a sip. "Your mother showed me a photograph of a sugar sculpture you made."

My eyes sparkled as I took a sip of my own. "I made that for a christening ceremony last month."

Tyler was leaning over the counter staring at me. He really was cute. "Blown glass… how in the world do you make sugar do that?"

I was blushing now. "It took years of practice."

"I bet. It is truly a special form of art. I am amazed at your talent."

"Thank you." I was staring at him over the rim, thinking about how great this man was when his lip missed the glass and red wine ran down his yellow Polo shirt.

"Shit!" he cried as he jumped back. He put the glass on the counter, then pulled his shirt off and moved toward the sink. I know he was probably taking it off in the hopes of impressing me but as soon as he lifted the material over his head and flexed, it took everything I had not to cringe.

Taco meat.

It traveled from his nipples down past the waist of his

pants. I started coughing like I had grazed my tongue across those kinky hairs and caught a few in my throat.

"You okay?" he asked and rushed around the counter and started whacking me hard on the back. The moment his chest touched my arm, I jumped off the stool.

"I'm fine. Really," I managed between breaths. My high expectations were shattered.

While he dabbed at the stain, I took the moment to pull myself together. Instead my mind traveled back to the first time I had met Max, standing outside the house he and the team was renovating, and he had his shirt off. Max had wide football shoulders and a sculpted chest that tapered down to a flat ripped stomach and narrow hips. Fine dark hair traveled across smooth brown skin. It was enough to make a woman salivate.

"You ready to eat?"

I blinked and noticed he was wearing a clean shirt. Damn, I must have really zoned out. "Sure. I'm starved."

I spent the entire meal trying to focus on all of the positive things about Tyler and yet I couldn't stop thinking about all that thick beady hair on his chest. If the relationship continued maybe I could convince him to have it waxed. That thought caused me to chuckle.

After the meal, I helped Tyler clean up the kitchen while he talked about a case he was working on. I found myself fantasizing about evenings like this with him coming home from work and discussing his day. I could get used to that.

We moved into the family room and lay across the couch together. It was nice. Really nice, and I actually felt my body becoming aroused.

"Where do you see yourself in five years?"

I took a deep breath. I was lying on my back and he was on his side staring down at me. Tyler really did have pretty eyes.

"Well, Christy and I hope to expand our business with offices on both the east and west coast. I also hope to be married."

"What about children?" I could tell the question was

important to him.

"When the time is right I hope to have a kid or two." Apparently that was the right answer because he was grinning like crazy. "What?" I asked.

"I think you'll be a great mommy."

It sounded so weird hearing him call me a mommy that I laughed, but apparently he didn't see anything funny.

"What's wrong?"

I shook my head. "Nothing, just the way you called me a mommy."

"Did I say something wrong?" I couldn't believe the way his lip dropped and he actually looked like a little kid. Oh my God! There was nothing worse to me than a weak, wimpy man.

"No not at all. It just sounded strange coming from you."

He gave me this long look like he was trying to figure me out. "How do you feel about spankings?"

I thought the question was odd but I answered it anyway. "My parents spanked me when I was growing up and I don't see anything wrong with it as long as it is done lovingly and with a clear explanation as to why."

Tyler then climbed off the couch and bent over in front of me. "I want you to spank me."

"What?" At first I thought he was fooling around.

"Please spank me."

My mouth fell. Before I could figure out what he was doing he lowered his pants and his boxers to his knees. I saw something that looked similar to a Vienna sausage sticking out from a patch of thick knotty hair. There were even a few pieces of lint from his cotton briefs hanging from the ends.

I sprung from the couch just as he bent over again with his hairy ass in my face. "Go ahead, and spank me."

I hesitated then decided to play along and swatted him across the butt. And he started moaning. "Oh God! That feels so good. Mommy, harder please."

"*Are you fucking kidding me*?" Hell no. there was no way I was going to be part of his sick fetish. I pushed him out the way and with his pants at his ankles he tried to catch himself but instead tumbled over onto the floor. "I'm not into that weird kinky shit!" Don't get me wrong. I loved a little role play but not this kind of sick shit.

"Wait a minute, Claudia!"

"Sorry Charlie, but you got the wrong chick, you sick fuck!"

I stormed through the house, grabbing my purse from the kitchen then hurried to the door to retrieve my shoes.

"Let me explain!" He had the nerve to follow me waddling down the hallway like a duck with his pants at his ankles and that little penis of his sticking out like little Pinocchio's nose. "You have to understand what my life was like. The only time my mother showed me any love was when she punished me."

"I don't give a shit. Lose my number!" I hurried out the door before he could reach me and peeled down the street. I practically side swiped another car and instead of apologizing, I stuck my middle finger out the window. I'd feel bad about it later, but right now I needed to get as far away from that man as possible. I couldn't believe I had thought he could possibly be the one. Sighing, I eased my foot on the gas. What in the world had happened to all the good men in the world?

At the stop sign, I reached inside my glove box and pulled out a bottle of hand sanitizer and poured a big glob in my palm. And to think I actually touched his ass.

Five minutes later, Christina was screaming in my ear. "Oh my God! I can't believe Attorney Tyler Weber is a straight freak."

"There's nothing freaky about a man who wants you to pretend you're his mother."

She was getting a big kick out of my misery as I headed toward the highway.

"Are you going to tell your mother?"

I groaned. "Hell no. Would you?"

This time I couldn't help but start laughing with her. "And it's such a shame! He was really a cutie."

"Yeah I thought so too before I saw all that taco meat on his chest."

As I drove, I told her about Tyler taking off his shirt. By the end of the conversation I was laughing so hard I was practically in tears.

"I don't understand why you won't just give Max a chance."

Leave it to Christina to bring Max up. I have been trying to do everything I could not to think about him. "You know why," I grumbled.

"But he doesn't even know if it's his baby." She sounded exasperated.

"Well then... Once he finds out for sure it's not, then he can holla at me."

She sighed heavily and I know she wanted to say more. I can't stand Christina some times.

I put my foot on the gas and increased my speed as I admitted, "He and I are meeting for dinner on Friday."

"Really? Why didn't you tell me?" Christina sounded pissed and excited.

"I didn't tell you because I know you would make more of it than it really is?" I muttered.

"So is this a date?"

"No. He wants to run an idea by me." I wasn't buying it but I was willing to play along.

"Did he give you any idea what he wanted?"

I gave a rude snort. "No, but I'm sure it's just an excuse to see me."

"Well, can you blame him? You don't make it easy for a brotha," she snapped.

I couldn't help but laugh. "You got a lot of nerve. Don't you dare forget how hard a time you gave poor Dereon." It's amazing how quickly we forget. "You thought he was a thug...and that he was broke... and you were determined to marry a rich man."

Christina was chuckling again. "I know and it all sounds so crazy now. To think I had almost missed out on the best thing to ever happen to me."

"Well you need to finish packing your stuff and move in with him so we can start focusing on your wedding."

"I know," she said and I could hear the frustration in her breath. "I hate moving."

Dereon had been renovating a house that Christina loved so much, he bought it and the couple was supposed to move in together. Dereon had already moved his things, but Christina had been dragging her feet. Her reasoning had been why buy the cow if the milk was free, but now that the couple was official engaged, it was time for her to stop straddling the fence and make it happen.

"I told Jeanna about the proposal. She wasn't as disappointed as I had expected. In fact, she insists on hiring her wedding coordinator. Now she's calling me nonstop all day and already driving me crazy."

Her mother drove everyone crazy. Jeanna was definitely a piece of work. A gold-digger at its finest. She had rubbed off so much on her daughter I was amazed when Christina finally saw the light and had given Dereon a chance.

So what's the problem with Max?

I brushed that thought aside. That was a different situation all together. I liked him, but I was selfish. Have been all my life and that meant I didn't want to share my man with someone else if I could help it.

I talked to Christina all the way home, then went inside and headed straight to my bedroom. *Well at least I got a good meal out of the deal.* Although, I was starting to wonder if maybe there had been taco meat in the pasta and shuddered at the thought.

After taking a long hot bath, I felt slightly depressed. I had really hoped Tyler could have been the one. With a sigh, I climbed out and wrapped myself in a large yellow towel.

I was headed back into my bedroom when my phone vibrated. Hurrying over, I reached for it then glanced down at the message on my screen.

I LOOK FORWARD TO SEEING YOU ON FRIDAY.

It had come from Max.

My body tingled and yet I refused to acknowledge I also looked forward to seeing him again.

FOUR

I stepped out of my Range Rover, then scanned the parking lot until I spotted a black Tahoe. I didn't need to see the personalized license plate MRSIX4 to know who that SUV belonged to.

Maximilian James.

Just knowing he'd already arrived caused a smile to curl my perfectly painted mauve-colored lips.

I slid the pink Coach purse over my shoulder then hurried toward the tall brick building. I was late and although I rarely showed up anywhere on time, this was one appointment I did not want to miss. As I moved across the parking lot, I was met by a rush of warm air. It was September and already proved to be a gorgeous day in St. Louis for this time of the year.

As I neared the restaurant, I spotted a short, round man walking toward his car, checking me out.

"Excuse me Miss—"

I raised a palm shutting down his weak rap before he even got it started. "Uh-uh … ain't interested." I replied then sighed because I was partially to blame. I should have known the outfit I was rocking was bound to turn some heads. After all, I had on a two-piece, beige, Christian Dior suit with a pencil skirt that hugged every luscious curve of my voluptuous frame. The outfit was complemented with five-inch pink stilettos that made my long legs seem endless. I had spent hours picking out the perfect outfit for today, determined to show Max what he could never have.

I felt my heart begin to race. As I sauntered to the door, I forced myself to take deep breaths. *Relax girl. You gotta stay in control,* I chanted. I moved inside and a young female hostess was standing behind a podium. The smile she tossed my direction was about as fake as those eyelashes she kept batting at me. "Welcome. Would you like to sit on the floor or out on the patio?"

"I'm actually meeting someone. Tall… dark… goatee."

Her brown eyes twinkled with recognition. Go figure. She pointed outside.

As I headed for the French doors leading out onto the patio, I spotted Max. A beautiful mocha-colored woman was sitting at his table with legs crossed, showing off long slender thighs in navy slacks. She was smiling at the man I'd thought I was having dinner with… Alone.

"So glad you decided to come," he said politely, then rose.

I ignored him. I was more interested in the pretty woman rising from the chair.

"Well, Max. I'll let you get to your dinner. It was nice to meet you," she said tossing her hair away from her face. Didn't she know that only worked in the movies?

She turned and I saw the way Max was watching her walk over to a table near the door where three other ladies were seated. As soon as she sat down they leaned in close, probably asking for a full report.

Max's gaze finally slid in my direction. I felt a jolt that I quickly shook off.

"Who's that? Another one of your baby mamas?"

He chuckled and I immediately regretted letting my irritation show. So what if we'd had sex? Max wasn't mine.

He took a sip of iced water. "I just met her and when I told her I was a contractor she wanted to know if I would be interested in giving her a bid on a kitchen remodel," he explained.

Yeah I just bet. "Uh-huh," I mumbled under my breath. I then moved in front of his chair so Max didn't miss how the skirt hugged my perfectly toned ass. Years of running backwards on a treadmill will do that for you.

"Have a seat."

I took the chair she had vacated, then leaned in over the table and reached for a menu. The smell of his cologne infiltrated my nose. Cartier. He had worn it at the party and ever since, I've smelled it in my dreams.

"I didn't think you were coming," he said and looked so sexy sitting there in blue jeans and a red polo shirt, it irritated me even more.

I rolled my eyes and spat, "That's what you get for thinking." I then made the mistake of meeting his gaze. Damn! It didn't make any sense for a man to be that fine. I swear to you Max had been dipped in milk chocolate. Sexy mothafucka. Short cropped curly hair, a perfect goatee, and a body. And did I mention the brotha had swag? Believe me when I tell you he was everything a woman would want in a man. Trust me … I had sex with him so I would know, but he was a suspect baby daddy. And unfortunately, men like him thought with their little head instead of the one bobbing around on their neck.

"I have a seven o'clock appointment. What is it that you want?" I demanded impatiently.

"You. I want you," he murmured, those dark eyes fixed on my face. "And I thought your appointment was at six?"

"I changed the time." Lord, the man was unnerving. "And that's not happening. What else you got?"

Max chuckled. I was really getting sick and tired of him laughing at me. "My heart. It's all yours if you'd give a brotha half a chance."

My own heart lurched traitorously. Quickly, I reached down for the menu and pretended to be looking over the choices. Why was Max making it so hard for me to resist his sexy ass? "I thought you wanted to talk about the wedding, not us?"

He stared at me across the table and I forced myself to look back down at the menu. His eyes were just too beautiful and if he had asked me to 'come here', I would have dove over the table and onto his lap. That's just how bad of an affect he had on me.

"Why don't we order first and then I'll share my news?"

I rolled my eyes and didn't even bother to hide my annoyance. "Are you really that desperate that you have to con a woman into having dinner with you?"

"I don't know, you tell me?" he said with this cocky grin on his face. My nipples puckered, my lips parted and I was certain my tongue darted out. There was no denying it. I couldn't think straight when I was around him. Damn, I was going to have to start carrying an extra pair of panties in my purse.

The waiter arrived and I was so grateful that I didn't have to answer him. I listened to the sound of his voice as he ordered shrimp Alfredo. I was so caught up in the deep tremor that I didn't hear the waiter asking for my order.

"Claudia, babe… you a'ight?"

I blinked and snapped, "Of course I am. I'll have the same as he's having with a diet soda."

He nodded and left. Max sat there, sitting low on the seat, staring at me with this ridiculous smirk on his face.

"What?"

"Nothing, I'm just admiring how beautiful you are."

The fact he found me beautiful caused my insides to tingle, which annoyed me even further.

I pointed a finger at him. "Listen Max, I don't want your compliments. And I would prefer if you would stop."

"Tell me why."

Because I'm attracted to you too, dammit! "Because I prefer not to go there with you."

"Go where?"

I waved an irritated hand in the air. "I'm not interested in having a relationship with you."

"Tell me why," Max asked with a slight frown.

I glared over at him. "You know why?"

His smile returned. "Then if that's the only reason, I have nothing to worry about."

His confidence freaking scared the hell out of me. How in the world was it even possible for a man to be that damn sure about himself all the time?

"Listen, I have a meeting in a few hours that I need to prepare for, can we move this dinner along."

Our waiter returned with our drinks and a basket of rolls. Max took a sip before finally getting to the reason why I was there.

"I have asked my friends to sing at Dereon and Christina's wedding."

"Sing?" I was sure he could see the confusion on my face. "Christina mentioned this morning that one of Dereon's cousins would sing at their wedding."

"Nina… yes I know her."

I didn't at all like the way that sounded. It wouldn't have surprised me to hear the two of them once dated.

"What if I told you I got someone even better to sing at their wedding?"

Okay, I could see this was going to be a chore getting to the heart of the question. Truth of the matter, I needed to get away from him fast. "Someone like who Max?" I didn't even bother to hide my annoyance. I was sure he was used to women hanging on his every word. Well, not me.

"Jagged Edge."

"What?" I gave him a hard look. "The male group?"

He looked over at me and didn't bother to answer until the waiter left our garden salads on the table.

"Max, I asked you a question?"

He finally nodded. "Yes, the male group."

I didn't believe him for a moment. "And how did you get them to agree to that?"

Something in the way I asked the question caused him to shake his head. "CC, I'm starting to think you're hard of hearing. The guys and I are friends."

"Yeah right," I snorted and stabbed a grape tomato with my fork. "And how much is this going to cost?"

Max lowered his head, said grace and I closed my eyes. By the time he was done I was already searching his gaze.

"It's not going to cost a thing. They're doing it for me as a favor."

I didn't know what to say.

"It's my wedding present to them. Dee told me how much Christina loved the group."

She wasn't the only one. She and I used to spend hours listening to the group. "She's mad about them." I went on to tell him how Claudia had won a contest on the radio to have dinner with Jagged Edge as part of a promotional tour for their album, *Highway to Heaven*. They had made Claudia feel so special, she refused to talk about anything else for weeks. Occasionally I wondered what had happened that they had stopped making music.

"That's mighty nice of you," I said.

"You'd know how nice a guy I really was if you'd quit playing and give me half a chance."

My body was screaming yes and all I could think about was Max making love to me, but my mind quickly took charge of the situation and yelled, "Hell no!"

Our food arrived and not a moment too soon. I needed every distraction possible to keep my head on around Max.

"What song are they going to sing? Let's Get Married... Promise?" I asked, changing the subject once the server had gone.

"Nope, they're gonna sing something new," he answered.

"They're going to launch a new album at her wedding?" A sista could only hope.

"No, but they're planning to release the song on their next CD."

"Really? Then I can't wait to hear it." I stirred the sauce and brought a forkful to my mouth. "Christina is going to be floored!"

"That's what I was thinking which is why I want to keep this a surprise."

I quickly chewed and replied, "Huh?"

"It's not a wedding gift if she finds out about it now," he reminded.

That took some of the fizzle out of my adrenaline. "Sure, you're right. It's just so exciting, but the surprise will be seeing her face." I could see Christina now. She was going to practically pee her pants when she spotted the group standing at the end of the aisle singing her a love song. "If she faints it's going to be your fault."

Max shifted on the chair with this shit-eating grin on his face. "Then I guess you better bring the smelling salts."

Within seconds I had a visual and was giggling myself. "Does Dee know?"

He brought the fork to his mouth before shaking his head. "Nope. That dude can't hold water."

"Yes, he can. We had no idea he was undercover."

His eyes were twinkling with laughter. "That's different. Now that he's in love, he tells Christina everything. He doesn't believe in keeping secrets," he drawled humorously.

I don't know why but I had this sudden urge to flirt. "And what about you?" I was leaning over my plate batting my eyes.

"Only when I have to, but when I'm with my woman I believe in being honest and upfront about everything in my life."

One thing I had to admit, Max had wasted no time explaining about Parker and the baby, but that was only because she had confronted him while I had been standing there.

"What about you? Got any deep dark secrets?"

There he was looking all cocky again. *Yes, I have a secret – I'm dying to have you inside of me again.* I chewed my pasta and gave him a hard stare as I replied, "Sure, I have plenty of secrets, but I reveal them on an as needed basis." I could just see the two of us lying in my bed, sharing our deepest thoughts. Me on my back, and Max lying beside me staring down into my eyes. Just thinking about it made me shiver.

"And how does a man get to be so lucky?" It was his turn to flirt. Damn him, sitting over there licking his lips, his eyes were hooded and dark.

"Membership has its privileges." Oh damn, I was flirting again. Like I've said, Max brings out the worse in me.

"So then tell me, how can I become a member?" He looked so serious for a split second I was at a total loss for words. It was at that moment I felt this warm feeling in my chest and knew if I stayed a moment longer I was going to be in trouble.

"Uh-Uh… I'm not even going there with you." I went back to eating my food, ignoring the deep rumbling of laughter coming from him.

"My bad. I promised to behave," he said with a lopsided grin. "Any other wedding plan I can help you with?"

"Why don't you ask Jeanna? It seems she will be the one making all the major decisions."

"How about I just ask you. No offense, but Christina's mother scares me."

I was faintly amused as I looked at the frown on his face. "Jeanna can be a little intimidating." I giggled and met the laughter in his eyes and felt a jolt at my gut. Goodness, it was time to put some distance between us. I glanced down at the slender gold watch on my arm. "I hate to eat and run but I have a meeting at The Hole to prepare for."

His face hardened. "The Hole? Do you know how dangerous that hood is?"

I shrugged although I was touched by his concern. "I've lived in St. Louis my entire life. I'll be okay."

"Claudia… north county ain't no joke. Ever since the riots, the area has gotten even worse."

I took one last bite of my food. "I'm a big girl Max, really I am."

He wasn't ready to let up. "Who are you meeting with?"

"DJ Mecca. They're showcasing some new rapper who's been cast for a recurring role on this new series on FOX." I thought explaining would lighten his mood, instead it seemed to anger Max even more.

"Shiloh. He hit the scene last year. That's him singing the hook on that new Chris Brown song."

I nodded. "Yep. That's him."

Max frowned as he washed down his Alfredo with a long swig of iced tea. "There was an article about the role he landed alongside Angela Bassett in *People* magazine last week."

"Well then… it sounds to me like I have nothing to worry about tonight."

"He's not the problem. But the neighborhood is."

I wiped my mouth with the linen napkin, then swung the purse over my shoulder as I slid out from behind the table. "I got my Mace."

Max rose and his presence was overpowering as always. "Let me walk you out."

I stared at him. "You don't have to, really." And to be honest I didn't want him to. "Stay and finish your dinner."

"I insist." He reached for his wallet and tossed money onto the table. I was already headed for the door, but with those strong long legs he caught up with me in no time.

I was so uncomfortable with his large body beside me that I was searching for something to say. "I appreciate you wanting to surprise Christina like that." I started walking fast across the parking lot.

"No problem. She's good people. And my boy is crazy about her." He was right. Those two were so in love at times it was almost sickening to watch them.

"I want with you what Dereon and Christina have."

My head whipped around. "What?" I was at my vehicle and I stopped walking and turned to face him. "Why are you always saying stuff like that?"

"Because it's true. I want you. And I know you want me to."

His lips crushed down on mine before I could cry out in protest. After that, I pretty much gave in to the sexual tension that had surrounded us since I had arrived at the restaurant. When Max's tongue slipped into my mouth, I figured I might as well enjoy it. Later I would convince myself I had at least put up a fight regardless of how quickly I had given it. Dammit, it was Max. Something about that sexy beast made it literally impossible to say no to him. The smartest thing was to keep my distance and after today... after I got finished with our kiss, I would make a notation in my day planner to stay away.

My hands rose to Max's broad shoulders. I guess he had expected me to shove him away because he moaned and then deepened the kiss even though I wasn't sure how that was even possible. The longer he kissed me the better he tasted. My hip brushed the hood of my Range Rover, and Max urged me closer. His hands were at my waist and then traveled around to squeeze my ass. My entire body was on high alert when I felt an eager portion of his body pulsing against my belly. I started thinking about that explosive night of passion at the party and I guess a whimper escaped my lips. Next thing I know, Max lifted me up onto my toes and his erection was grazing my clit. Oh God! I had no idea how badly my kitty was aching for attention. And I made the mistake of tightening my arms around him.

"That feel good to you?" he whispered against my mouth and all I could do was nod. "I know the feeling. All I've been able to think about was how good that pussy felt."

"Yes," I moaned. I felt like I was under a spell. His hands were all up under my skirt, touching my inner thigh. Oh his fingers were so close and my kitty purred with anticipation.

"CC, let me come over tonight and make love to you again," he murmured, his tone was low and husky.

Max was gyrating his hips and grazing my sensitive folds and I was so aroused that if he'd had a chance to ask me one more time I would have said to hell with that appointment and had him following me back home.

Click. Click.

Someone had remotely unlocked their car and was heading our way. Footsteps were close by. I dragged my mouth from his and drew a fast glance over my shoulder and saw two women watching us curiously. One of them was the woman who had been sitting with Max when I had arrived. I couldn't help but smile at the look of disappointment on her face.

"Damn, talk about bad timing," he murmured against my cheek. He then brought me back to my feet and slid his hands from up under my skirt.

I was breathing heavily as I pushed past him and walked around to climb into my Range Rover. Max stepped out the way and stood there with his hand pushed inside the front pocket of his jeans.

I pulled out the parking space, paused long enough to stare into his eyes that were hazy with desire, and when his lips curled into a confident smirk, I mumbled several obscenities, then put my foot on the gas and sped away.

Stupid! Somehow I had to find a way to get myself together because being around Maximilian James was starting to become as impossible to resist as a box of Hostess Twinkies. And I loved my Twinkies.

Blinking, I shook my head. I needed to find another man in my life—fast!

FIVE

By the time I had left the nightclub, a contract had been signed to cater the event. I stepped out the door and across the dark parking lot, then frowned. One thing for sure DJ Mecca was going to have to do something about the lighting. Guests weren't going to feel comfortable walking across a parking lot where they had to look over their shoulder. Worst case they would have to hire security.

A couple walked past me and the guy was tall and looked so much like Max, I had to do a double take. Unfortunately his woman caught me staring.

"Can I help you?" She had the nerve to stop walking and throw her hands in the air.

I was not for confrontation. "Sorry, I thought you were someone I knew." I figured if she thought I was looking at her instead of her man, she would quit tripping. Thank goodness it worked because she turned and they walked away.

"Damn you, Max." I knew he would be nothing but trouble. Why couldn't I get that man out of my mind? I shook my head and tried to concentrate on where I was headed. The club was the hottest in the area for happy hour and unfortunately I had to park all the way at the end of the lot. The sound of my heels echoed sharply against the concrete as I increased my steps.

I was reaching down inside my purse for my keys, when something hit me hard against the back of my head. "Awww!" I cried, then stumbled and fell hard against the hood of a parked car, landing on my face. It happened so fast it took me a few seconds to react. I was bleeding and I thought it was coming from my nose.

"What the—" I mumbled under my breath, but before I

could get up I was hit again and fell to the ground. Then my purse was being yanked from my arm. I was screaming and trying to catch my breath at the same time, but no sounds came out. Someone flipped me over and frantically I stared up at three thugs—one white and two blacks; my vision was blurred so I couldn't get a good look. Terrified, I scrambled away and tried to rise onto my feet but a boot sent a powerful blow to my stomach causing me to buckle over in pain.

"No!" I screamed and tasted bile and was certain I might throw up. The second hit knocked the wind out of me and I couldn't breathe… I couldn't get away. I was on the ground and held up a hand trying to get them to stop. Only they were standing over me, laughing.

I spotted my keys not too far away. I stretched out, fumbling to get a hold of the small pink mace can that dangled from the ring. I barely had it in my hand when one of the guys leaned forward and lifted me up off the ground by my neck. Gasping for air, I aimed the can at his face and sprayed frantically.

"Shit! You stupid bitch!' he screamed and clocked me hard in the face, and I fell back to the concrete.

"I can't believe you let that bitch mace you!"

That laughing hyena was a straight instigator and as a result the one standing over me, leaned down, and punched me hard in the mouth.

"No!" I screamed. My body was throbbing. I was scared and angry.

"Shut the hell up!"

And then something slammed across my head again so hard I was shocked I hadn't lost consciousness. I struggled on the ground and tried to get away but I was too weak to get very far.

"Don't hurt me," I asked in a panicked voice.

"Don't hurt me," one of them mimicked, making baby noises close to my face.

One of my arms was twisted beneath me. The other elbow was scraped and raw. My head hurt so bad.

"I think we need to show this bitch who's boss," a

different assailant said in an icy tone. As he flipped me onto my back and I caught a glimpse of a bloody knife tattooed on the inside of his wrist.

"No!"

I heard my skirt rip, my blouse was yanked open and I felt my legs being spread apart. I was completely powerless. I couldn't fight or kick. "Please… don't!" I pleaded. I was so weak I couldn't even scream, instead it was a strangled cry. My panties were being dragged down over my ankles and I silently sobbed because I knew what was about to go down.

Or at least I thought I did.

I could barely see out of my left eye while the right one was already swollen shut, but I swore I saw the one standing over me being tossed aside like a baby doll. I heard a scuffle and hard punches. There was a loud thump and I turned my head and saw a set of feet near the rear of the car. I struggled to a seated position with the mace can aimed and ready to use, but by then everything was silent. I spotted the white guy lying flat on the ground a few feet away and another even closer. Standing over them was a tall figure I couldn't make out in the poor lighting. I caught movement to my right and before I could scream the third assailant lunged at the man swinging a large pipe probably the same one I had been hit with twice. I kid you not, my rescuer twirled around and sent a hard kick to his middle section followed by a fist to his face, causing his body to flip before he landed hard on the ground, like in one of those martial arts movies. I was sobbing silently and trying to crawl away when the dark figure turned and looked over at me.

"Claudia, don't move."

I gasped and stared in disbelief as I watched him kneel down and as soon as he moved under the light my shoulders sagged.

Maximilian James.

Sobbing, I collapsed in his arms. Max was the last person I wanted to see me like this, but at the same time his strength and the comfort of his arms was exactly what I needed. I clung to his neck, sobbing hysterically.

"Shhh, I got you babe. No one is gonna hurt you. You're safe with me," he whispered against my cheek and I held on, too afraid to let go. Max lifted me effortlessly into his arms and I leaned in close, resting my head on his shoulder as he carried me away.

"My purse!" I cried.

"Relax, I got your purse and keys," Max assured me, and I was so grateful. I held on to him. Closing my eyes, I inhaled his masculine scent as he carried me away. I didn't care where he was taking me as long as it was far from here. Despite what had just happened, my heart was pounding like crazy. My protector.

"Thank you," I whispered.

He brought his lips to my cheek, kissed me then whispered, "Anything for you."

Once I was buckled in the front seat of his Tahoe, I sat there shaking. I think I was in shock trying to make some sense of what had just happened. Someone had attacked me and would have raped me if Maximilian hadn't arrived. A sob clogged my throat.

Max reached for his phone and started dialing as he turned the key in the ignition. Moments later, he barked into the receiver, "Dee, man. Claudia was attacked at The Hole. Yeah, yeah… she's pretty bad but I got there in time."

The rest of his conversation was a blur. I had tears running down my face and I was sobbing and wishing I could rewind the clock an hour or two and none of this would have happened.

"You're going to be okay," Max assured me as he backed out of the parking spot. I hadn't even realized he wasn't still on the phone.

I nodded and couldn't even bring myself to speak, instead I whimpered softly.

He gave me another long look, then put the car into gear and sped off down the street toward the interstate. I sat there with the incident running over and over in my mind. It couldn't have possibly happened to me. Why had I been that stupid to be on that side of town by myself at night? Max had warned me, but once again I thought I was untouchable.

Max rocketed onto the highway driving way past the speed limits. But he was a good driver and I trusted him. Hell, I don't know why but I did. I guess because Dereon was a cop and he wouldn't hang with someone who shouldn't be in his circle. The two were best friends so that had to count for something. Beside I didn't have anyone else I could turn to. I wouldn't dare tell my brother. He would call his boys and be ready to set it off in that parking lot. My parents would insist I move back home.

"You're gonna be okay," I heard Max say as he placed a comforting hand briefly on my knee and squeezed.

I snuck a peak at him. Max was concentrating on the highway. His hand was gripping the steering wheel so tight the dark skin on his knuckles had turned white. And there was a muscle at his jaw that was ticking a rapid unsteady beat. I swallowed. Max was not someone to be messed with. I shifted on the seat and winced at the sharp pain at my hip.

He took one hand off the steering wheel and took my hand in his. "Try not to move, boo, until I get the doctor to look at you."

"No! Please, no hospital."

He looked briefly away from the road. "I have to. You could have a concussion."

I rapidly shook my head. "There's no way in hell I'm going into a hospital looking like this. Just take me home. I'll be okay."

"Hell no! I'm not leaving you alone."

I shook my head wildly, wiping away tears. "I'll be fine. Now take me home." Why couldn't he just do what I said?'

"That bossy shit might work on some other brotha, but this man doesn't roll like that."

"Max, I—"

"Yo, let me finish, woman!"

Wow! I was too exhausted to argue.

"You got two choices, either I'm taking you to the hospital and having Christina call your parents or you're coming home with me. Which is it?"

Nothing turned me on more than a man who stood his grounds. I just wished it was someone other than Max, the man with the suspect baby mama. But I was in too much pain to argue. I took a deep breath and muttered, "No hospital." My father was the head of the department of internal medicine at Barnes Jewish Hospital. The last thing I needed was for him to find out.

I turned my head away from Max and closed my eyes. I felt helpless and needy. I don't do needy. But I needed someone and that person just happened to be Max.

Max's phone rang and he picked it up and started barking into the receiver. "Trey, get yo ass over to my place! And bring Brax with you. I'll explain later."

I groaned inwardly. Damn, everyone was going to know what had happened. As soon as he ended the call, I carefully shifted on the seat and glared at him with my one good eye. "Thanks a lot for telling everyone my business." I didn't mean to sound like a bitch but I had.

"I'm not about to give them all the specifics, but you were attacked. I'm sorry, but I don't take shit like that lightly. No man has a right putting his hands on a woman, especially not my girl."

"I'm not your girl!" I retorted.

"CC, this is not the time."

"Whatever," I mumbled with little conviction. I wanted to be angry and cuss him out for assuming I would even want to be with him, but I just didn't have the strength. Or maybe that was just what I was using as an excuse to deny the way he made me feel. Max was so alpha and Lord knows men like him were hard to find. But once again, I don't date men with baby mamas.

I closed my eyes again. By now my head was pounding. My body hurt and I just wanted to go to bed.

"CC, I know you don't want to talk about this, but you need to file a police report."

I buried my face in my hands. "No," I whined. "I just want to soak in the tub and sleep."

"Are you're saying you don't wanna press charges?"

"I'm saying please just leave me alone." Why couldn't he just let me feel sorry for myself?

"Then I'll handle things my way."

My eyelids snapped open. "What does that mean?"

"That means... don't worry about it. I'll handle it myself. Remember, I was there. I know what they look like."

Turning my head, I stared at Max again. "What are you planning to do?"

"Let's just worry about making sure you're okay."

He reached over for my hand and brought it up to his lips. I just stared at him and watched him kiss my knuckles. The tip of his tongue snaked out and slid across my skin. Max was gentle one minute and violent in the next. I had seen what he had done to those thugs all by himself. A shiver snaked up my spine. Maximilian James wasn't to be played with.

"Max, you're not going to do anything stupid are you?"

"Never that," he assured me.

I didn't like the way that sounded.

He released my hand and turned the steering wheel to the right, pulling off the highway toward South City, near the Fox Theatre.

"Where are we going?"

"I told you. To my house."

I closed my eyes and didn't even bother trying to argue because it wouldn't have mattered. Max does what Max wants to do. Besides I was in too much pain. My legs throbbed like crazy and my head was pounding.

You know you wanna go home with him.

I pushed the ridiculous thought from my head. No matter how badly my body yearned for Max, there would be no round two.

A few minutes later the vehicle came to a complete stop. I looked around. We were in an area that had been revitalized with big old houses that that slowly been restored over the last decade. I would have never pictured Max living in something so large and grand but then again, there were a lot of things about him that were a mystery.

Max climbed out, raced around and opened the door for me. I was struggling to my feet when he lifted me up into his arms and kicked the door shut. I closed my eyes, relaxed and just gave in to the feeling of being held in his big arms. Suddenly, I was very sleepy.

"Claudia, baby can you hear me?"

"Huh?" My eyelids fluttered open and Max was leaning over me.

"You might have a concussion so you can't be falling asleep," he said with the sexiest smirk I've ever seen.

I blinked and glanced around. I was in a bedroom lying across a massive bed.

"I ran you a bath and put some Epsom salt in it. It should help with the soreness."

He was so kind, I didn't know what to say except, "Thanks."

"Get undressed ... I'll be back in a few to check on you." He kissed my forehead and I watched him walk across the room and out the door without even bothering to shut it behind him. I glanced around the room but my head was pounding too hard to appreciate the large space. Slowly, I rose from the bed and limped over to the mirror and screamed when I saw my face.

Max rushed back into the room.

"My face! Look what they did to my face!" I was screaming and crying at the same time. There was no way this had happened to me. My lip was busted, cheek bruised and one eye was practically shut. My hair was all over my head. Realization swept over me. I had been attacked. Someone tried to violate me. I heard a loud pitched scream and it took a few minutes before I realized the person screaming was me.

"Claudia, baby, it's gonna be okay," he kept saying and Max dragged me into his arms.

"How could they do this to me?" I wailed and then I guess my legs collapsed because next thing I knew I was up in his arms and Max was carrying me over to a chair. He took a seat, settled me on his lap, and I buried my face against his chest.

"Baby, I'm so sorry this happened to you, but never again. I promise you that. No one is ever going to think about messing with my girl."

I know he was just saying that to make me feel safe. And I wanted so badly to believe him and yet I was shaking and so scared. My arms were wrapped around his middle and I was squeezing him tight. His arms were around me and I was glad. It had been such a long time since anyone had held me. Max felt amazing and I just didn't want the moment to end. As he rubbed a soothing hand up and down my back, the sobbing finally stopped and my body began to relax.

"I don't know what I would have done if you hadn't been there."

He rested his chin against the top of my head. "Don't talk like that. I was there and you are safe, that's all that matters."

I jerked back. "Wait a minute… why were you there?"

He stared at me. "I came to check on you."

I wanted so badly to scream, I didn't need his help. Only I had. A sob caught in my throat. "Thank you."

Smiling, Max kissed my forehead. "I would do it again. And hey," he said and then his hands were at my chin tilting my face toward his. I opened my eyes and gazed up at him again. "Babe, you are still beautiful to me."

"You're just saying that," I sobbed.

He kissed my forehead. "No, I'm serious. You're the most beautiful woman I've ever met."

Feeling like a big cry baby, I blinked away tears then sat up on his lap. "I don't believe you but thanks."

"You're welcome. Now I want you to take a bath and soak your body. You went through a lot tonight." Max gave me a slow lazy smile.

He got no argument there. Max helped me to my feet then took my hand and led me into the adjourning room. His bathroom was like nothing I had seen before. And my parents were rich and had a bad house but this bathroom was better than anything I had ever seen on HGTV.

The room was massive with granite his and her sinks, a Jacuzzi size tub and a large glass encased shower. Travertine tiles were on the floor and covered the entire wall. "Wow, this is nice."

"Thanks. It was my first renovation project when I moved into this house."

I often forgot he worked as a general contractor. I'd seen plenty of his projects to know he was good, but this was a bathroom to die for.

"Can I get one of these at my house?" I was joking of course.

"You can have anything you want, if you play your cards right."

I rolled my eyes and he howled with laughter. Just like a man to make it about him. He moved over and retrieved a stool from beneath a vanity and took a seat. "Get undressed and get in."

I guess he thought I was going to tell him to leave but I started unbuttoning my jacket and unzipped my skirt. As bad as I felt, I just didn't care. The outfit was ripped and ruined. I let it all drop to my feet then I removed my blouse, reached for my bra and unclasped it, then slipped out of my underwear as well. I wanted him to see that I really was beautiful. Our eyes met, then his gaze traveled slowly over my body. Last time I was naked the room was dark but this time there was no hiding. My breasts ached and there was a slow burn between my thighs. But the look on his face went from a smirk to a frown.

"What?"

He shook his head. "Nothing. Nothing at all. You are so beautiful."

I ignored his comment and before he could grab my arm I padded over to the mirror.

"Claudia, don't look!" He wasn't quick enough. I stared into the full length mirror and discovered why the frown had been on his face. My eyes widened with alarm. As high yellow as I was, there were bruises everywhere. No wonder my body hurt all over. Before I could start crying again, Max scooped me into his arms.

"Put me down!" I screamed.

"I will in a moment. Just chill."

Max carried me over to the tub then lowered me into the water. It was just right and felt so good. I slid low into the water.

"You okay?" he asked, concerned.

I nodded. His kindness was driving me crazy.

There was a loud chime and he turned and looked over his shoulder, then back at me. "That's probably Trey and Braxton."

I groaned and quickly put my hands over my breasts. "Please, I don't want to see them!"

"Babe, relax. I wouldn't dare bring them up here."

Of course he wouldn't. "I don't want to talk to them either. I don't want to talk to any of them. And please, please don't tell Christy."

He looked worried. "Dee already knows."

I had forgotten about that. Christina was probably already blowing up my phone anxious with worry, but I wasn't ready yet to talk about what had happened.

"Let me go down and holla at them. Try to relax while I'm gone." He winked and then left me alone.

I reached over and pushed the button and the jets started vibrating. The water beat against my already sore body. Tomorrow was going to be even worse. I was just thankful it was the weekend.

I slid further into the warm water and breathed a heavy sigh. I tried not to think about what had happened tonight and instead focused on Max and the way he made me feel, but I wasn't sure which was more dangerous to think about.

He had a way of making me feel safe and secure and there was nothing better than knowing a man had my back and he definitely was that person. Max cared enough about me he had come out to The Hole to make sure I was okay and that was something I just couldn't ignore. Coming to my rescue was heroic. I never thought of having my own personal hero but that was exactly what he had been tonight. Now, not only did I feel safe, but so freaking aroused.

Goodness. Why did he have to be so damn attractive?

And bravery only heightened the attraction, which pissed me off. Because no matter how much I wanted to ignore the man, my body refused to cooperate.

Why do you keep lying to yourself?

I tilted my head back, rested it on the edge of the tub and closed my eyes. I know I played a lot of games and tried to act like I didn't care about him, but it was a lie.

I was crazy about Max.

He was the closest I had ever come to finding everything I had ever wanted in a man since Isaiah. And deep down, I wanted more. I wanted the relationship, the commitment. To be able to call that gorgeous man mine. *All mine*. I couldn't remember the last time a man had managed to make me feel that way but there was something so special about Max that made me almost willing to risk it all, to take a chance at being with him. And then just when I felt my guard coming down, I remembered Parker and the baby.

SIX

"Don't fall asleep."

I opened one eye and then the other. "I wasn't sleep."

"Sure you weren't." With a smirk Max moved and took a seat at the edge of the massive tub. I could see he was trying hard not to stare at my breasts.

"Where's Trey and Braxton?"

"They went to pick up your SUV and bring it back here before someone steals it."

My stomach clenched at the mention of my attack. "That's probably a smart idea."

"I have a smart idea every now and then," he said with a sheepish grin. Goodness that man was sexy.

"How're you feeling?"

I nodded and dropped my gaze to the water. "Better. Thank you." Why was I suddenly nervous to be around him?

"Turn around so I can wash your back."

It wasn't a question. One thing about Max he rarely asked. It was always what he wanted. No second guessing. I guess that's what I liked about him.

I slid forward in the tub and handed him the washcloth. Max kneeled on the floor, lathered it and rubbed it across my back. Oh my, it was like a gentle caress. It took everything I had not to moan.

"Dee went to The Hole and checked out the parking lot, but by the time he arrived they were gone," he explained. "He said there was some trace evidence. Blood mostly."

Max dropped the washcloth and was using his palm instead. It was hard to think with his warm satin hand sliding across my skin. "It was probably mine since my lip's busted and I split my cheek."

"Or it could belong to that dude I clocked upside his head."

Despite the way I was feeling, I chuckled and looked over my shoulder. Max winked which made me grin.

"There you go. I've been waiting to see that smile again."

Max finished washing my back and then he rose from his knees and took a seat on the toilet. "Dee said you need to press charges."

"No." I shook my head then sprung up out of the water so fast I had to grab onto the tile rack for support.

Max shot up and grabbed my elbow steadying me. "Yo, take it easy," he warned and then I heard a slow inhale of breath. My eyes met his as they traveled slowly over my naked body. The intense look in his eyes caused my skin to heat in its quest. I guess seeing me naked and wet was too much for him. One can only hope.

"You good?" he asked like he was trying to fight for control. He looked far too serious and solemn.

I swallowed and nodded my head.

Max released his hold and grabbed a large bath towel and held it open. "Climb out slowly."

I stepped into his arms as he engulfed me in the soft material and drew me close. My chest was against his as he dried my back tenderly. I felt an erection pulsing beneath his jeans. Every muscle in my body was tingling with desire at the thought of lowering his zipper and begging he take me.

"You think you can finish drying off on your own?" As soon as I nodded, Max took a step back. "A man can only handle so much temptation," he added with a nervous laugh.

"I can handle it," I said and tried not to let my irritation carry over into my voice. He had no idea I wanted him just as badly as he wanted me.

"There's an extra toothbrush on the counter and I left an old t-shirt on the bed for you." With that, Max turned and made his escape.

As I dried off, I groaned. My nipples were erect. My body humming and the growing attraction was more painful than the blows to my side. He was my hero tonight and I was in a vulnerable state. I had to resist him or regret it later.

Avoiding the mirror, I reached for a bottle of lotion on the sink and rubbed it over my body then walked into the bedroom and slipped on the over-sized t-shirt that stopped about mid-thigh.

I was walking around the bed toward the door when Max reappeared. He was holding a tray in his hand with wings and fries.

"What are you doing? I was getting ready to come downstairs."

"Nope, I'm getting ready to serve you so hop in bed and get comfortable."

A meal in bed? This intimate scene was just getting way out of hand. "But you don't have to do that. I'm quite capable of walking down to the kitchen."

Max walked across the room and sat the tray on a small coffee table in the sitting room. "Tomorrow maybe, but tonight I want you to take it easy."

"But I'm okay." I wasn't really but I had to find some way to break through this euphoria of sexual tension that was stirring around the room.

"A few minutes ago you almost slipped in the tub."

"I just got up too quick," I protested.

"Regardless, you're on my watch and I'm not taking any chances. Now get in bed."

I was too hungry and tired to argue with him so I did as he said and climbed into bed and underneath the sheet.

"I sure hope there's something stronger than water in that glass."

He chuckled. "I got just what you need."

Yes you do. In more ways than one.

Max placed the tray on the bed beside me then reached over and fluffed my pillow. "I thought maybe you'd need something strong to calm your nerves."

"You thought right." He took a seat beside me and then placed the tray onto my lap. "Thanks. This looks great."

I took the glass and brought it to my lips and as soon as I felt the tequila sliding down my throat, I moaned . "Man I needed that."

Max winked and brought a hand up to caress the side of my cheek. "I told you I got you."

Yes he had. Everything about this moment was magical; me lying in his comfortable bed, his delicious scent surrounding me, Max staring at me with eyes dark and smoldering, and the gentle way he was taking care of me. It was so easy to get caught up in the moment and fall under his spell. It was a struggle, but I would have to strong.

"The food looks good," I said, desperate to break the mood.

"I bought the wings in bulk at Sam's Club. A few minutes in the oven and it's just as good as in the restaurant."

I brought one to my lips and took a bite." Ouch!" I cupped my mouth.

"What's wrong? Too spicy?"

"No, the sauce burns my lips."

"Damn, I didn't think about that," he hissed as he pushed to his feet then hurried into the bathroom and came out with a cold washcloth. "Here put this on your mouth for a few seconds. It should take the sting away."

"Thanks." I pressed it gingerly to my lips and it cooled. "I think I better stick to the fries."

"Probably a good idea."

I eventually went back to eating my food and caught Max studying me. "You're handling the situation pretty well." He was looking at me so hard, I was afraid he saw the truth.

"I've gotta be strong, otherwise they win." I stuffed a fry into my mouth that got stuck so I took a huge swallow of water to push it down. Tears were at the surface of my eyes. I wasn't as strong as I led people to believe. "Thanks for the food."

"Any time, CC. All you have to do is holla."

His kindness caused a tear or two to spill from my eyes and splatter onto my fries. If Max noticed he pretended not to and for that I was grateful.

While I ate we talked about the weather, sports and I caught myself laughing. The effects of the alcohol had begun and I started to relax a little bit. Then I don't know what happened next but I was crying. I guess it finally hit me. Max lifted me into his arms and was carrying me into the sitting room. He sat down in an oversized chair with me in his arms. I lowered my head and buried my face at his neck.

"It's okay, babe," he assured me.

"Not it's not," I said trying to pull it together. "I'm supposed to be stronger than this."

"We all have moments when we just need to let go. You went through something that you should have never had to endure."

"I still can't understand why they would do that to me."

"Ignorant… stupid. There's probably no reason. I just want you to remember I'm here. I got your back."

His voice was tender and his kindness only made matters worse. I started sobbing again and he drew me close, and whispered encouraging words in my ear and kissed my cheek.

Gradually the tears stopped and I drew a deep breath as I said, "I remember when I was still in college, studying culinary arts. I had landed a summer internship with Suarez."

"The restaurant chain?"

I nodded even though he couldn't see me. "Yes, Mr. Jacob Suarez handpicked students each year to work in one of his restaurants. I was ecstatic because that meant I had a chance of being offered a job upon graduation." I paused long enough to shift slightly on his lap before continuing. "I had been working two weeks when he asked me if I thought I was capable of catering a luncheon at his penthouse for a few guests. Of course I told him I could. When he invited me to drop by his house, I was flattered and didn't think anything of it. I thought I was just checking out his kitchen I had seen in *Bon Appĕtit* magazine. But once I got there I had a bad feeling just like I did tonight. However, because I'm Claudia Ciara and nothing is going to stop me, I let him give me a tour of his house. I was staring out the window when he caught me from behind and attacked me."

I felt Max's grip tighten around me.

"I tried to fight him off, but he was so strong and had me

pinned to the floor. I was screaming and kicking and he would have raped me if his maid hadn't showed up."

"Thank God," Max said, as he threaded his fingers gently through my hair.

"I guess he forgot it was her afternoon to clean because he looked just as shocked as I was relieved. I kicked him in the nuts and ran out of his place."

"Did you press charges on the son-of-a-bitch?"

"Yes, but he denied the allegations and his maid collaborated his story. I was humiliated and lost my internship."

"Is that why you won't file charges?"

I nodded. "It won't make a difference." Again it would be their word against mine.

"Not this time. I was there. I saw what happened."

He brushed the hair away from my face as I said, "Nothing's broken. I'm alive… they didn't rape me. I rather just forget."

"I understand your reluctance. And I support you however you decide."

"I appreciate that." I told him, then expelled a long breath and rested my head back against his chest.

"You never have to worry about that again. I'll never let anything happen to you."

"Why are you so nice to me? I always give you a hard time but you're still so nice. Why is that?"

He trailed his fingertips down my arms. "Because I want you in my life and the sooner you realize that the easier things are going to be for both of us."

My heart was pounding like crazy. What I was feeling… what I was thinking was just too overwhelming.

Let me just say being that close with his mouth only inches from mine was just way too intimate to say the least. I was feeling so vulnerable and yet the next thing I knew I was tilting my head and meeting his lips halfway.

Why did his kisses have to be so freaking delicious? It was really all his fault because if he wasn't so irresistible none of this would be happening. Instead, my hands came around to circle his neck, granting him better access. Max's large arms tightened and he cradled me close to his chest. I was sure he felt my nipples beading beneath the t-shirt. A moan slipped from my throat. The kiss was deep, hot and intimate. Max pushed his tongue inside my mouth. I swirled my tongue meeting his confident strokes. Oh, the man was good enough to teach Kissing 101. That was just how good he was. It wasn't until I felt his warm, calloused fingers caressing my kitty that I jerked back and ended the kiss.

Between labored breaths I said, "I don't think that's good idea."

Against my mouth, he whispered, "Why not? It's not the first time I've tasted you or even touched you. I know how it feels to be inside your body."

And I know how good you felt inside me. My pussy clenched at the memories.

I drew back and struggled to focus on his face. "Yes, and I'm feeling vulnerable, but I don't want to confuse what's happening for something else."

With his fingers still sliding across my folds, he said, "What do you think is happening?"

I panted, struggled to get control of myself. Oh hell no. He was taunting me again. "Nothing, which is why I think you probably should drive me home."

"Nope."

I met his gaze. "Then what's happening is you have kidnapped me."

Max chuckled heartedly. "No, it means you're going to spend the night with me. I need to keep an eye on you."

I glared and pushed his hand away so I could think straight. "I feel fine."

"Maybe," he declared. "But you could have a concussion and I'm not taking any chances."

"Max, I—"

He brought a finger to my lips, silencing me. "Woman would you just hush and let me do my job."

His words warmed my heart and made me smile. Goodness I loved when he was in control.

"Okay, I'll stay." I mean what choice did I have but to have agreed since he wasn't going to let me have it any other way.

"Thank you." A crooked smile claimed his mouth.

"What's going to happen is I'm going to bed. It's been a long evening."

"You're right. You've been through a lot tonight." He gave me a funny look. "Forgive me, I got caught up in those sweet lips of yours."

I did a playful eye roll as I slid off his lap. "Max, you're truly a piece of work."

"Yeah that's what I been told," he confirmed with a hearty chuckle.

Smiling, I walked over to the bed and pulled the comforter back. "Which side is yours?" I asked and could barely look him in the face, because if he even dared to give me that hungry stare of his I was liable to do something crazy, like throw myself into his arms.

His grin was cheeky and fun. "I sleep in the middle."

Goodness he was making this difficult. "Good then it won't matter what side you sleep on." I walked around to the right side of the bed and made sure I didn't brush against him.

"I have some extra pillows in the closet if you would like another," he asked.

There were already four on the bed. The entire conversation about bed and pillows was intimate enough as it was. "No, I'm fine. I'm sure I'll be sleep as soon as my head hits the pillow."

"Well in that case, I'm going to let you get your rest." My mouth went dry as he casually rounded the bed toward me, with each step his body moved with precision. There was just no avoiding looking up at him. I lifted my head and still wasn't prepared for the impact of his kiss. Although brief it was no less powerful. "Good night. I'll be checking on you."

I just bet you will.

Turning, he moved across the room and was just about to close the door behind him when I said, "Max."

He turned back, brow raised.

"Thank you. Thanks for everything."

Long after he was gone, I was lying under the covers with a pillow in front of me and another behind me. Not to mention there were two behind my head. Yeah, I guess he will need to get some extra pillows out of the closet.

The bed smelled enough like him to make me feel so amazingly aroused. I noticed he had one of those Sleep Number mattresses. It was comfortable as hell. I sank into the comfort and breathed a deep sigh. It would be so easy to get used to this. The pampering, the attention, there hadn't been a man yet to treat me the way Max had tonight. And then there was him coming to my rescue. Nothing would ever be able to top that. Nothing.

I turned onto my side and groaned at the sharp pain at my side. I hurt. I hurt bad and should have gone to the hospital at least long enough for them to check me over, but I was stubborn.

Which is why I was in this mess in the first place.

I finally started counting backwards from a hundred and eventually I dozed off to sleep until I heard someone calling my name.

"No!"

I cried out and woke up abruptly from the nightmare, and when I opened my eyes and saw Max, I burst into tears.

Max didn't seem to mind and pulled me into his arms. "Shhh, hey babe, it's okay. I'm here," he whispered. "It was just a dream."

He kept saying that over and over and yet it had felt so real. I held onto him, crying against his bare chest. I was sobbing hard and slobbering all over him and yet his hold tightened.

"Were you dreaming about the attack?"

I clutched him closer, practically digging my fingernails into his back. When I finally spoke, I barely recognized myself. "I... you weren't there... you weren't there." I was crying again and practically hysterical. Max reached over and turned on the lamp and I dropped my face.

"Hey," he put his hand beneath my chin and tried to tilt

my face but I resisted.

"No, I don't want you to see me like this."

"You are beautiful to me, even with snot running from your nose."

"Do I really?" I raised my hand up to cover my nose, but his hand whipped out and stopped me.

"Nah, I'm joking. I just wanted to see those big pretty eyes of yours."

I couldn't resist a sad smile. It was bad enough I had been beaten up. I'm sure the swelling had gotten even worse.

"I look terrible don't I?"

Reaching up, he stroked my hair. "I look at you and all I want to do is go back down to that parking lot and beat their asses all over again."

"Thank you," I whispered and realized I was trembling.

I didn't resist when he held me close and I closed my eyes and rested my head onto his chest. It was still dark outside. I had no idea what time it was, but I was certain we should still be sleeping. "I should have listened to you and not gone down to that hole in the wall."

"CC, for as long as I've known you, you've been stubborn. Nothing's gonna change that."

"Yeah and you see where it got me."

"There's no point in blaming yourself. You're here now, safe with me."

I breathed in the scent of his skin. As good as it felt pressed up against his chest I don't know if safe is the word I would have used. "Do you think the police could catch them?"

"Maybe, but they were gone by the time Dee got there, and the cameras in the parking lot are a piece of shit."

"I probably wouldn't recognize any of them if I saw them again." I couldn't help it. The tears started to flow.

He tightened his hold. "I'd recognize them, especially the tall one. I stared him right in the eyes before I punched him dead in his mouth."

I couldn't resist a smile. "Yeah, you were like Captain America out there."

He drew back and stared at me. "Captain America? I

thought I was more like Wolverine."

I searched his hands. "I don't see your claws."

"And I don't want you to either. Only when I'm angry and I don't think I can ever be really angry at you. Even though you have a way of pissing me off almost every week."

I gave a sad chuckle. Yeah, he was right. Every single time I was at Christina and Dereon's new house, Max was there, trying to ask me out.

Reaching up, I cupped his face with my hands and caressed the stubble across his cheeks. "I owe you one. Once my face heals I'm going to take you out… my treat."

"You got yourself a deal." He leaned in and gently kissed my lips.

I yawned and Max reached over for the lamp and turned it out. "Get some sleep. We'll talk in the morning." He kissed me gently on the forehead and then started to rise from the bed. "I'll—"

"No!" I cried and yanked him back down on the bed.

"What's wrong? Talk to me."

"I want you to sleep in here with me tonight."

"Claudia, I was in the spare room when I heard you screaming. I don't know if I can lie next to you all night and not want you."

I lifted my head and didn't care if he saw the water welling in my eyes. "Please Max. I can't be alone."

He looked like he was having a hard time deciding before he finally said, "Sure babe, whatever you need."

I breathed a sigh of relief. Wearing nothing but boxers, he stretched out on the bed beside me and tossed the sheets over us. It felt so good when he wrapped his arms around me and pulled me against his chest. I tried to ignore the erection I felt pulsing against the cheek of my ass, but I was keenly aware cotton underwear was the only thing separating us. He released a slow breath that made me smile. I'm sure it was going to be difficult just to hold me all night and not be able to do anything else, but I was grateful for him trying.

"Max, I—"

"Claudia, go to sleep." It sounded almost like a warning.

I closed my eyes and snuggled close, our heads side by side on the pillow.

"You'll always be safe with me," he said and brought his lips to my ear and kissed me.

SEVEN

It took me awhile to wake from a deep sleep. I rolled to my side and blinked several times as I waited for my eyes to focus, then gasped when I realized I wasn't at home. Memories of the attack came rushing back, including Max rescuing me.

After my nightmare, he held me in his arms with his large, hard body behind me. A couple of times he even patted my hand, waking me just enough to ensure I didn't have a concussion. I don't remember the last time a man had made me feel so secure.

I shifted on the bed, and continued to lay there. I wasn't ready yet to face him. Last night, I embarrassed myself, crying my heart out and showing vulnerability. That was something I preferred a man never to see. Showing weakness sets you up for heartbreak. I had a hard enough time fighting my attraction for Max as it was.

Yawning, I did a full body stretch then rolled over and froze.

Max was coming out the bathroom.

"Sorry, didn't mean to frighten you."

I couldn't help it. My eyes started traveling over his bare chest that was sprinkled lightly with brown hair and narrowed all the way down... I forced myself to breathe quietly, and pulled my eyes back to his face as I sat upright on the bed. "I thought you were in the kitchen."

"I was but decided to get a quick shower in and check on you. It's almost ten."

"Ten?" I whistled softly. "I slept that long?"

He leaned toward me. "You had a rough day. How are you feeling?"

I drew another deep breath. "I would feel a lot better if you'd put on some clothes."

Chuckling, Max moved over to a tall chest of drawers and pulled out a pair of red boxers, then dropped his towel. Goodness, the back view was just as enticing as the front!

"You hungry?"

Yes, and it wasn't for food. "Sure, let me freshen up first."

I got up from the bed and groaned as I felt a stabbing pain at my side.

"Are you in pain?" Max was at my side in the blink of an eye.

"I'm fine," I said and practically jumped back trying to put some distance between us. He was just looking too good bare- chested and in boxers.

"I'll have your food ready by the time you come down."

"Are you cooking?" The only time I ever had anyone make me breakfast was when I spend the weekend at my parents' house during the holidays.

Max shook his head. "No, while you were sleep I drove up to this little café not too far from here and picked us up something. You're gonna love it."

I would have loved it more if he would just get dressed and go downstairs. He bent his head and kissed me lightly on the lips, and yet it was still powerful enough to make my body sizzle.

"I'll see you downstairs." Dragging a t-shirt over his head, he left the room.

I rushed off into the bathroom and shut the door. Damn, what in the world was wrong with me? *Nothing*. I was a woman with needs I knew Max was quite capable of handling. I wasted no time splashing water onto my face.

Get it together. Get it together.

I washed my face, brushed my teeth and stared at my face. The swelling had gone down some, but one side of my face was dark and bruised like I had participated in a boxing match. There was no way in hell I was letting anyone see me like this. It was embarrassing enough that Max had.

With a heavy sigh, I walked out into the carpeted hallway.

I'm nosy, so I opened each and every door and peeked inside. One of the bedrooms he was using for a home office, another, a workout room, and then there were two guestrooms. I went down the staircase toward a grand foyer where a huge crystal chandelier hung overhead. The smell of coffee hit me at the bottom step. I padded barefoot across the gleaming hardwood floors into the kitchen. Max winked when I entered.

"Have a seat."

I lowered on one of the bar-height stools, surrounding a large center island.

"Your house is gorgeous." My eyes took an appreciative sweep of the massive kitchen with white and gray subway tiles, stainless-steel appliances, black marble countertops, and distressed pecan-colored wood flooring.

"Thanks, the house belonged to my grandfather," Max explained and there was no mistaking the pride in his voice as he pulled a second Styrofoam container out the microwave. "He left it to me when he died and I've been renovating it for the last four years."

"You're doing an amazing job."

"Thanks." He put the food on the counter, pushed one in front of me, and reached for two forks.

I waited for him to take a seat before I looked inside and gazed at eggs, bacon, grits and pancakes. I glanced up to find Max staring at me. "Are you going to sit and watch me eat?"

"Yeah, as a matter of fact I was planning on it," he joked and brought a slice of bacon to his lips. "Does it bother you?"

What bothered me was the way Max was staring at me like he wanted to sop me up in syrup and lick me up and down. "No, not at all."

He gave a hearty laugh. "I want to make sure you keep up your strength."

"Do I look like a woman who doesn't eat?" I said it as a joke but his face was so intense and serious I had to draw a deep breath.

"I think you look great, but I'm not about to take any chances. You're on my watch."

"I'm fine."

"You went through a lot last night. If I hadn't been there..." Max stopped and I saw the fire in his eyes. I felt sorry for any man who'd ever crossed him.

"Well the good thing is you were there and I will never be able to thank you enough."

His mouth curved in a slow grin. "I could come up with a few ways."

I tossed a grape at him and don't you know he caught it between his teeth. Were there any limits to this man?

"How's the omelet?" he asked.

"It's wonderful."

Max nodded knowingly. "I love their food."

"How'd you find this place?"

He stretched out his long legs as he explained. "I actually ran across it by accident. One morning I ended up getting a flat in front of the restaurant and by the time I had the tire fixed, the food was smelling so good, I went inside and got something to eat. I've been eating there ever since."

We ate and laughed and that comfortable feeling washed over me again. By the time I was done eating, I decided it was time to be on my way.

"Did Trey bring my Range Rover?"

He nodded. "Yep, he dropped it off last night."

"I'll have to remember to thank him." As a distraction I allowed my eyes to travel to the clock, hanging over the sink. "Do you mind getting my duffel bag out of the trunk? I should have a change of clothes in there."

"Sure. I'll grab it as soon as we're done."

"Thanks." Clearing my throat, I added, "I think it's time I head home."

"I don't want you to leave."

I met his heated gaze calmly. "I can't stay here forever."

"No, but you can at least stay the weekend and let me take care of you."

I looked at him, lips parted. My mind and body were at war. "I don't know what to say."

"It's easy, CC. You can stay or go, but I hope you'll stay."

I drew a deep breath. Deep down I wanted to stay, and as

bad as my face looked, I didn't want to run into my neighbors or friends. There would be a lot of questions, I wasn't up for explaining. Yep. That's my excuse and I was sticking to it.

"Okay, I'll stay."

He smiled and was clearly pleased with my decision. "Good decision. How about I barbecue?"

"Are you any good?" I asked with a chuckle and Max tried to act offended.

"Woman, I'm a beast on the grill," he said with a wink.

Rolling my eyes playfully, I replied, "This I gotta see."

I got up and helped him carry the dishes to the sink. He gave another mischievous wink, one minute I was laughing, and the next, Max was dragging me into his arms.

"This weekend, the only thing I'm tryna prove is how good we are together."

Max ran his mouth along my cheek and neck, making me hot, causing my flesh to hum with anticipation. "You want me too, don't you?"

I wasn't sure exactly when my hands came around to grip his biceps. "Yes, I want you."

His lips were then crushing mine giving me the kiss I'd tasted in my mind since we'd had lunch at Tommy's. Max took my mouth slow and deep and I dug my nails into his flesh. Screw my swollen, cracked lips. All I cared about was having his tongue dancing with mine. There was nothing gentle about him as he sucked the tip of my tongue, claiming my mouth, dominating the kiss, leaving me breathless and clinging to him. Max cupped my breast and squeezed, dragging a low gasp from my throat.

"Your nipples are sensitive. I like that."

I gave a nervous laugh as his thumb made contact with my nipple again. "It's my spot," I murmured, sounding as desperate as I felt.

His hand was inching up my knee, sliding under the t-shirt while his mouth dropped down to kiss my neck. I tried to hold back a moan, but there was no fighting how Max made me feel.

He cupped my breast, and brought his lips to mine again.

The stroke of his tongue matched the caress of his thumb across my nipple. He could have easily pulled down the t-shirt to expose my breasts but settled for finding my nipple through the fabric with his teeth, nipping, sucking and pulling, driving me crazy.

Desire roared through my body. I tried to keep up with his mouth but I was more focused on the direction of his hands.

One went under the t-shirt, gliding across my breasts, down my belly, and through the patch of hair between my thighs. I pressed and ground my mound against his fingers, eager for him to explore even further.

"Open your legs," he growled.

I parted my thighs and watched as Max lowered to his knees. Gasping, he parted my slippery folds with his fingertips, and with one thrust he pushed inside me.

Max," I moaned and arched off the counter. What I was feeling I couldn't even bring to words.

"Oh, that pussy is fat," he hissed. And when he pulled his long fingers out to the tip then pushed in again, I thought I would lose my mind. I was wet and aroused, cum trickling down my inner thigh.

He increased the rhythm and I started rocking my hips, meeting each delicious stroke. "Yes," I moaned. "*Yesss.*"

With his fingers still buried, Max leaned forward, and I sucked in a breath at the first touch of his mouth. He started licking hungrily and then sucked at my folds, flicking his tongue against my clit. My head lolled forward and I made the mistake of opening my eyes and I swallowed hard.

Max was staring at me, watching my responses as he pleasured me. His eyelids were hooded with lust. Knowing he was on his knees with my legs spread and his long fingers buried deep between my legs only heightened my arousal.

"You have no idea how sexy you look standing there," he said.

Soft whimpers slipped from my lips as his tongue swiped along my folds and then his lips nibbled away at my clit. He was gentle and demanding, encouraging and possessive, taking his time, knowing how to apply just the right amount of pressure before easing back. I was aroused and tilted my pelvis closer to his mouth, desperate for an orgasm that was close but never close enough.

My eyelids lowered as his tongue swept over my clit in a circular motion.

"Feel good to you?" he asked, his warm breath heating my tender flesh.

As if he really had to ask. "*Yessss,*" I whimpered,

I grabbed onto his shoulders as his tongue parted me. Max then slid two fingers inside, pushing even deeper this time, and began pumping in and out at an excruciating pace. I tried to muffle a cry as his fingers twisted, driving me crazy, but once his lips clamped down onto my clit, I screamed.

"Max!" Shuddering, I cried his name as an orgasm erupted. Nothing had ever felt so good. Max continued his pleasurable assault as I bucked and rocked against his mouth until he had drawn out every last moan.

As I struggled to find my breath, he rose from the floor, leaned in and kissed me.

"You good, babe?" he asked, his lips against mine.

"Are we fishing for compliments?" I teased.

"Not at all. I saw the look on your face. I felt the way your body responded when you came. I know you liked it." His hands were at his waistband and his eyes were on me as he lowered his boxers. My clit pulsed at the sight.

"Let me go get a condom," he said eyes locked on mine.

"I'm on the pill," I told him and reached out for his hand, drawing him closer so he was standing between my thighs. I didn't want to wait. I needed him now, pounding into me.

"Are you sure?" he asked. His dick jolted against my thigh.

It was hard to think with him being so close. "Positive, now quit stalling."

"You are something else, you know that?" he whispered. With his hands at my waist, he walked me backward into the family room.

My eyes never left his and there was no denying the dark

intensity of his gaze.

"I want you down on the floor, doggy style," he ordered.

I lowered onto the area rug and rose up on my knees with my ass in the air, then looked over my shoulder at him and could barely breathe. He was stroking his hand along his dick. Damn! It looked so delicious I wanted it inside my mouth. But for now I needed it desperately inside of me.

He moved to the floor and said, "Spread your legs for me, babe."

I did as he instructed.

"Damn, you're sexy," he hissed as he positioned himself between my thighs. "I could sit here all night and stare at you." He touched my ass, spreading my cheeks, then his long fingers traveled slowly down along my moistened folds again, parting and preparing them for a welcomed invasion.

"You need to quit teasing me," I whimpered and rocked my hips, urging his fingers to come and play.

"Tell me what you want?" Max asked and slid one finger and then another inside me. "I want to hear you say you want my dick inside of you." He pumped his fingers in and out until I was whimpering and rocking my hips wanting to feel him even deeper.

"Please Max. I want you. I want to feel your dick inside of me."

"That's it babe. That's what I wanna hear." In a matter of seconds, he was wedged between my thighs, gripped my hips, spreading me wide. He slowly eased inside, pushing all the way in. I cried out and then he was penetrating hard and deep, again and again.

"This is my pussy," he groaned.

I sucked my breath in on a hitch. "Yes, your pussy."

"Mine," he said between pumps.

Max could have said anything, and I would have agreed just as long as he didn't stop. The first time we had sex was good but this time, without a condom, it was so amazing, I was whimpering and moaning his name all at the same time.

"It's your pussy. Oh God! It's your pussy," I chanted.

"Shit, you feel good," Max groaned and steadied his

strokes.

Reaching around, his thumb massaged my clit again. "That's it baby, come for me," he whispered as he begun to move faster, driving even deeper inside her. Within seconds he was fucking me harder and burying himself so deep I wasn't sure how much longer I could hold on.

"Come for me," he coaxed, and I finally let go.

A powerful climax tore through my body. I cried out, screaming his name. Max continued to pound me from behind, and shortly after I heard a loud moan, his body tensed, then he and I collapsed onto the rug. "Oh shit! That was good," I managed between giggles.

"I think I put my name all over that pussy," Max teased.

"Whatever." I rolled over and popped him playfully across the head. Chuckling, he drew me close in his arms. We rolled around on the floor and then were kissing.

"All jokes aside, I am a very patient man, Claudia, and I intend to have you as my own."

I drew a shaky breath because I knew he meant every word.

EIGHT

Hours later I was rubbing my belly with satisfaction. "How in the world did you learn how to cook like that?" I asked in awe.

Max stared across the patio table, his mouth a saucy grin. "I spent a lot of time watching the cooking channel. I've never been domestic inside the house, but outside… I told you I was a beast."

I shook my head and stared down at the stack of baby back ribs on the table. When Max said he had skills with the grill, I had no idea he was that good. The meat had been so tender and the homemade sauce amazing, I was almost tempted to eat another. I just didn't have the room.

"That sauce, did your mother teach you how to do that?"

I noticed his brown eyes blazed with some unrecognizable emotion. "My mother never taught me a thing."

Damn. I inhaled suddenly then released my breath slowly. "I'm sorry I had no idea."

He shrugged a massive shoulder and tried to act like it was no big deal but I could tell by the pain in his eyes, someone had hurt him.

"I was in foster care practically my entire life."

I swallowed hard. "What happened? Where were your parents?" I couldn't believe I had blurted out what I was thinking, and yet, I was curious.

His voice sounded hollow as he spoke. "My mother was only sixteen when she had me and not interested in being a mother." Max paused and took a long swig from a bottle of water. "I stayed with her off and on until I was ten-years-old and then she just stopped coming around all together."

Goodness, his story was so sad I didn't know what to say.

My parents could be a little dysfunctional at times, but after thirty-seven years of marriage they were still together. My eyes searched his as I asked, "Did you know your father?"

"Sure, I knew. He was this old cat who managed the apartment building. My grandmother had my mother at sixteen followed by three other kids. That woman never worked a day in her life. A straight up project chick. When she couldn't pay the rent, she sent my mom down to see the landlord to work off the debt. Eventually she got pregnant with me." There was such a look of raw emotion in his eyes, I flinched.

I really didn't know what to say.

Max seemed angry, when he said, "Mom used to talk to me about it like it was a normal thing to discuss with a child. She always said you have to do what you have to do to survive in this world." He was staring out the window, across the yard, the muscle at his jaw ticking. Wow! His mama was definitely a trip.

There was a long silence and I reached for another grilled ear of corn, desperate to do something because for the life of me I had no idea how to break the mood. How could someone do that to a child? I just don't understand some women.

I licked my lips and tried to come up with something. "Max, I'm so sorry," I said apologetically. "I can't even begin to pretend I understand what your life was like because I couldn't imagine my mother not being in mine."

"You can't miss something you never really had," he said and forced a smile. "You know I ran into her at Target about a year ago?"

"What?" I put my corn down and gave him my undivided attention. "What happened?"

"She was pushing a shopping cart with a small boy inside. There was also this cute little girl running alongside her."

I was practically leaning over the table. "They were hers?"

He nodded. "And they looked good. Clean... hair combed... nice clothes on. Even my mother looked like a million dollars in slacks and a cashmere sweater."

I was holding my breath.

"So I walked toward her and if you'd seen her face you would have thought she had seen a ghost."

"Oh my goodness! My happened?"

"She acted like she didn't know who I was. I said 'hello Mom' and she tried to pretend I had her confused with someone else."

Oh snap!

"Some guy… I think he was her husband, walked over and asked if I was bothering her, and when she glared at me, I just walked away."

"You're stronger than me because I think I would have lost it." My mother, turning her back on me, I couldn't have beared it.

Max cleared his throat and shifted his gaze to his plate as if he needed a moment to collect himself. And I gave it to him. Men appreciated that.

He shrugged a massive shoulder. "I think it's because of where I came from that it made me stronger and the man I am today. I would never treat my children that way."

Now I'm starting to understand.

Reaching across the table he grabbed another rib and brought it to his lips. "Enough about my pathetic life, tell me something about you. Did your parents abandon you?" he joked and I gave him a sympathetic smile.

"No they're still together. Mom's a lawyer and dad's a doctor."

His gorgeous smile had returned. "Sound like the Huxtables."

I rolled my eyes even though I was so proud of them. "Pretty much. I have a sister who lives in Denver. She's a nurse, and a younger brother who just got accepted to medical school."

"Sounds like you probably had a great childhood."

I yawned and stretched. "Let's just say my father was one who always told us, 'I'm the one who's rich, not you.' We had to find our own way. Bad grades weren't acceptable and scholarships were a must. My parents were workaholics so my mom's mother lived with us until she passed away about eight years ago. She was my rock. Nana listened when my mother was busy preparing opening arguments for court the next day or dad had to spend long hours at the hospital." I shrugged. "I guess it's typical when you have two workaholic parents."

"How do your parents' feel about the career you chose since everyone else went into the medical field?" Max asked between chews.

I smiled across the table at him. "My mother thought I was going to be a lawyer like her, but I found law so boring. Cooking and designing cakes and pastries was something I loved to do."

Max leaned back in the chair and crossed his arms over his chest as he stared at me with curiosity. "How did you get into blowing sugar into art?"

I laughed. "It just happened by chance. There were two classes I loved; chemistry and wood shop."

"You were into wood shop?" I could tell he didn't believe me.

I nodded. "Hey, there's more to this pretty face than meets the eye." I winked. "I loved carving flowers out of wood, working with a blow torch, and blowing glass. Anyway, one day my mother asked me to clean out the pantry. I found sugar and all this food coloring and decided to have some fun. The next thing I knew I had made a bouquet of flowers out of sugar."

Max smiled and looked clearly impressed. "You are truly talented. I remember the cake you did for Dee and Christina's housewarming party."

That was some of my finest work. I had designed little pairs of stilettos all around a cake. It was a joke that Christina was going to be high maintenance.

"What about you? When you're not doing construction what else do you like to do?"

"I dabble in music," he managed while chewing a rib.

I nodded. "I noticed you had what looked like a recording studio in one of the rooms upstairs."

He nodded. "Yeah, I like to write songs."

"Really? That's a wonderful hobby. I like to write poetry

when I have free time, which I can't remember the last time that was. You like to rap?"

Max smiled. "I can spit some lyrics but I'm more into love ballads."

I laughed. "Oh snap! Like Usher and Neyo?"

He gave another grin. "Yeah, something like that." He pointed down at my hand. "You've got sauce on your fingers. It's a shame to waste it."

Max shocked the breath right out of me when he reached for my wrist. Dragging my hand close, he bent his head and his warm mouth slowly sucked each one of my fingers. A quivery sensation shot up my arm and lodged low in my body. When he finally released my hand, he gave a boyish grin that made my stomach do a backflip.

"All gone." His voice was low and intimate.

Max rose and started clearing the table. Eager to break the spell, I got up and helped him. I was amazed at how natural it felt working side by side in the kitchen.

"You still have enough food left to feed a football stadium!" I commented.

He shrugged as if he was used to it and chuckled. "All I gotta do is tell the fellas I cooked and they'll come over and smash all that food."

"You ain't lying!" I laughed along with him because he was telling the truth. I had seen the way the guys had eaten at a couple of cookouts.

By the time we got everything shined down and the kitchen spotless, I felt ready for a couple of ibuprofens and another nap.

"I think I'm going to go upstairs and lie down for a bit."

With a worried frown, Max took two strides toward me, then wrapped his long fingers around my upper arms, as he said, "Are you feeling okay?"

"No, I'm fine. Just feeling a little light-headed and..."

Before I could get out the entire sentence, I was in his arms. While he was carrying me up the flight of stairs to his bedroom, I rested my cheek on his chest and closed my eyes, focused on the fit and fill of his arms. Sex had been explosive and so unexpected, and being this close only had my body aching for more.

Max lowered me onto the bed then fluffed the pillow behind my head. He disappeared in the bathroom long enough to come out, holding a cup in one hand and two ibuprofen in the other. "Open up," he ordered and obediently I stuck out my tongue and swallowed the pills down with water.

"I wish you'd stop treating me like a baby," I scowled and pushed the glass away. Max placed it on the nightstand and looked at me.

"You're not used to a man treating you like a queen, are you?" he asked curiously.

"I-I…" His eyes never left mine. They were dark and intense and shadowed with heavy lashes. I was at a loss for words.

"I believe in catering to my woman."

"I'm not your woman, Max," I corrected despite the warm feeling coursing through my body.

"Yes, you are." Leaning forward, he brought his mouth down over mine and kissed me long enough to have my lips parting and inviting his tongue inside. By the time he drew away I was breathing heavily and feeling more light-headed than ever.

"Get some rest. I'll be right here." He winked and reached for the remote.

"You don't have to stay."

As he pointed the remote and clicked, he replied, "Yes I do. You said you're feeling light-headed, so I need to make sure you're fine."

I rose up on my elbows. "Are you always this overprotective?" I asked with humor in my voice.

"No babe. You just bring the caveman outta me." Max engulfed me in another sensual kiss. "Now get some rest."

It seemed almost criminal for me to want him but my heart was pounding as I watched him walk in the small sitting area to the right of the room and flop down onto an oversized chair.

"Have you watched the series *Power*?" he asked.

Instantly, I slid off the bed and padded over to where he was sitting. "Is that the one with 50 Cents?"

He nodded. "Yeah that's it."

"No, but I heard it's good."

As he clicked Starz On-Demand, he said, "Yeah, it's real addictive."

As soon as I was within arm's length, Max yanked me down onto his lap. He felt so solid and strong, and I felt secure. I pressed my cheek against him, breathing in his masculine scent. And as we watched, he caught me up with each of the characters. The series was really good, but I think by the time he started episode three, I had already fallen asleep.

"Babe?"

I opened my eyes and Max was standing over me. With a smile, I did a deep stretch. "What time is it?"

"After nine." He took a seat.

"What?" I jackknifed on the bed. I looked through the blinds and sure enough it was dark. "Why did you let me sleep so long?"

"Because you were tired and you needed the rest."

He was so considerate and caring. I felt it in the way he looked at me and the way his large hand moved gently along my cheek.

"I guess I was tired. Thank you. I can't remember the last time I slept so much."

"You're welcome." He brought his lips to mine, a soft, gentle kiss. "You hungry?"

"Maybe for something light, like a salad. But I can go down and make it."

In a voice low and hoarse with emotion he said, "Babe, I got this. That's if after we eat, you agree to go out back and check out my hot tub."

I laughed. "I don't have a swimsuit."

"You won't need it," he replied with a mischievous wink.

NINE

"I can't believe I'm doing something crazy like this." I was laughing.

"Enjoy life, babe. You only have one."

He strolled across the kitchen floor and then unlocked the door that led to his patio. "The lid's already off and the water's nice and hot."

That sounded nice on a cool day like today.

Opening the door, he stepped aside and I moved out onto the deck wrapped in a white towel. I tiptoed over to the hot tub in the corner and dropped the towel, shivering as the brisk air brushed against my naked body. Quickly, I stepped inside. Max wasn't lying. "Get in," I urged. "The water feels amazing."

Nodding, he looked down at me and replied, "I figured tonight would be perfect. I really don't get to use the hot tub as much as I used to."

"Oh, such a shame," I moaned. I was already submerged to my chin, grinning at him.

I watched as he dropped the towel. Oh God. His dick was hard and standing at attention. Max jumped over into the water, sending a wave flooding in my direction.

"My hair!" I screamed, although my hair was the last thing on my mind.

"Sorry babe." He backed me into a corner and pinned his arms on either side of me. I draped my hands over his shoulders, tilted my chin, and met his deep stares. I loved when he looked at me that way.

"This feels really nice," I said calmly.

"You feel even better," Max murmured.

Chuckling, I settled back against the wall. "Can you get sex off your mind for a moment?"

"Sex is always on my mind when you're around."

His words had me hot, willing, and wet.

He kissed my lips and cheeks, and then he nudged my thighs apart and stood between my legs. "I can't seem to get enough of you," he growled.

Neither could I. My fingers slid down across his pecs to his stomach and then traveled lower through a patch of silky fine hair to his cock, which I grabbed in my hand.

Max released a slow breath.

With a saucy grin, I began to stroke him under the water.

"Oh damn, you got skills," he hissed, as my hand moved up and down his length loving the way his erection jerked beneath my touch.

While my fingers worked their magic, his lips trailed light kisses up my shoulders and then his tongue slid between my breasts, sliding over my nipples again and again, winding my desire tighter. He teased my peaks as they strained for him to put them inside his mouth. My head was spinning. The desire to have him inside me again was so intense I could barely breathe.

It was his turn to touch me. Max stroked across my pubic hair, then lowered to my folds. On the upward stroke, his thumb grazed my clit, and I flinched, then arched my pelvis into his touch.

"Oh," I moaned and brought my hands up to run along his back and arms.

"I can't stop thinking about being inside of you."

Excitement perspired on my skin. "Why think if you don't have to?"

He gave a strangled laugh. "Like minds… think alike."

Taking my hand, he moved over to the bench and took a seat. "C'mere," he said and yanked me toward him. I straddled his hips, sliding my knees out on either side of him. "I want you to ride me," he said.

A raspy little moan escaped my throat. "Ride you? Are you a machine?"

"No, I'm a high-powered race car. And I need a tune-up."

"Is that so," I chuckled then began winding my hips and rubbing my nipples along his chest.

"Hell yeah," he growled against my lips.

I slipped a hand between us, reaching down for his erection, and then slowly lowered onto him, moaning with pleasure while the warm water lapped around us.

"That's it babe. Ride this dick."

I moved up and down, enjoying the feel of him inside of me. It was good, so very good. I gyrated my body, twisting my hips and savoring the overwhelming feeling. "Yes, oh yes!" I moaned. "It's good. You feel so good."

Without warning, Max thrust upward inside me so hard and deep I didn't realize I was holding my breath. I brought my hands to his shoulders to steady myself while I felt every inch of him pumping into me.

"I thought I was driving this car," I moaned my lips brushing his ear.

"I like being in the driver's seat," he said, setting a rhythm. "Now look at me."

I opened my eyes and met his dark intense gaze as he took over control, not that I cared. His hands were planted possessively at my waist, lifting me up and down as he pumped away.

"Yes," I moaned and wanted so desperately to close my eyes and rest my head on his shoulder, but I bit my bottom lips and held on. I watched his face as Max took over, pounding into me.

His jaw was clenched as he gripped my hips, guiding our strokes.

"Shit, that pussy's good!" he howled.

His cock was hard and buried so deep I felt each and every stroke, and I wanted all of him, filling me with pleasure until I couldn't prevent the cries from escaping.

"Max, fuck me.... oh God, fuck me, please!" I was begging and I didn't care just as long as Max kept doing what he was doing. He stroked me over and over.

"CC, I don't know how much longer I'll be able to hold on," he murmured between pumps.

"Me either," I whispered. An orgasm was fast and approaching. My stomach muscles tightened and my head lolled to the side.

Max upward thrust became more powerful and so intense, his hands at my waist tightened to keep me from falling. His thighs slapped against my ass, and my legs were starting to cramp. Desperate cries slipped from my lips as he pounded into me repeatedly until there was no holding back any longer. I came hard and screamed his name and then my pussy squeezed him until his breath came in little groans.

"Damn baby, that's it! Let it all out." Max's pumps did not slow up and I continued to ride him.

"Shit," he grunted and after two hard pulses, he came. He rode the last wave of pleasure, and I sighed in contentment then slumped against him, breathing heavily. His hold loosened and I shifted off my knees, and settled onto his lap.

"Woman, you are addictive."

"Am I now?" I liked the sound of that.

His attention drifted from my eyes to my mouth. "We could get used to this. If you'd just let me."

I was giving it more consideration than he'd ever know. What we had was so comfortable I was also growing attached.

"What's going through your mind?" His hands were sliding lazily down along my spine, and our gazes locked.

"I'm not sure" I said hugging him.

"Yes, you do," he replied boldly. "Do you want me in your life? Just be honest with yourself for once and answer the question."

I wondered if every woman dreamed of having a man this gorgeous crazy about her, wanting just her, looking at her the way Max was looking at me. There was no point in denying it any longer. "Yes, I want to be with you."

"Then stop fighting it, babe."

It took me just a few moments to decide, "Okay."

* * *

I couldn't believe I had fallen asleep again. But I had.

I woke up and Max was no longer lying beside me. A smile curled my lips as I thought about the last two days.

It was crazy, but my body couldn't seem to get enough of

him. Max was my new addiction.

After our rump in the hot-tub, we went back in the house and spent the rest of the evening, sipping wine, curled up in his chair and watching more marathon episodes of Power. He was right. The Starz Original series was addictive and I was so drawn into the story I almost forgot I was sitting on the lap of a man more gorgeous than the entire cast.

And I do mean almost because as soon as the first season was over, Max wasted no time reminding me what my body craved most. Shaking my head, I tried to understand where he got all that energy.

I rolled over on the bed, opened my eyes and stared up at the ceiling. The room was dark so it took a few seconds for my gaze to adjust. While blinking, I was sure I heard music playing. I rose and padded down the hallway and there was definitely music drifting from downstairs. I figured Max was listening to his iPod.

I descended the stairs slowly. A song I had never heard before was playing and it was beautiful. The voice sounded almost like Johnny Gill and John Legend rolled up in one so I wasn't sure who the recording star was, but I was determined to find out. I walked down the hall and moved toward the room on the other side of the kitchen and when I rounded the corner, my mouth dropped.

Max was sitting on a bench in front of a black baby grand piano tucked in the corner of the room. Why hadn't I noticed it before?

Probably because you were too busy getting down on all four.

The room was dark except the light filtering in from the sliding glass door. It was beaming down on him as if under a spotlight on stage. Max's playing was phenomenal, his long fingers gently pressing the ivory keys. I could tell he'd been playing piano for a long time. And his voice was so beautiful! His eyes were closed and he was so caught up in the song, he had no idea I was standing at the entrance. Totally mesmerized, I leaned my head against the wall and just listened. The tremble of his voice I heard all the way down to my toes. I kid you not. Max had talent and could practically run circles around half the singers currently playing on the radio.

"Tell me you feel my love."

Oh my! He was singing a love song and I hung onto his every word, and caught myself imagining he was singing to me.

"...how good you feel when I'm inside you."

My body tensed all over. I had always had a thing for a man who could sing, but a gorgeous man with a beautiful voice... Damn! I was so caught up in the images running through my mind that I didn't notice he had stopped singing.

"You're up," Max said, breaking the spell.

I gasped and shook off the effects of his beautiful eyes shining brightly at me. "Please...don't stop."

"I didn't mean to disturb you," he said apologetically.

Immediately, I shook my head and started toward him. "No, not at all. How come you didn't tell me you could sing like that?"

With a smile, Max slid over and patted a spot beside him on the bench and I took a seat. "I guess I never thought about it."

"And you were killing that piano!" I lightly punched him in the arm. "Shame on you! You said you dabbled in music. That sounded like more than dabbling. You were better than Tyrese's last album."

Max chuckled. "You better not let him hear you say that."

"I'm serious! You are so freaking talented." I was talking with my hands and getting all animated, he started chuckling and mimicking me.

I waved my hand at him. "Whatever, laugh if you want to."

"I'm not laughing at you, babe." He leaned in and kissed me hard on the mouth. "Glad you're starting to feel better."

I winced. "Ouch! I'm not feeling that good."

"Sorry. You want me to get you some ice?"

"No, I'll be fine." I swung around on the seat and put my hands on the keys and played a little bit of chopsticks, then blushed when Max started laughing. "Hey, that's all I know.

How long have you been playing?"

"I've had a gift for music all my life."

"Really?"

He nodded. "One of my foster mothers had a piano and she taught me how to play."

"Nice woman."

He gave a far-off smile. "She was. We would spend hours playing that old piano and singing gospel songs. I really thought Ms. Stringfellow was going to adopt me, but my mother wouldn't allow it."

While he spoke, visually I could see him as a little boy sitting on the bench, legs swinging in the air. My heart went out to him for having a mother who was so selfish, she stopped him from having something she could never give him.

"Play some more," I begged.

I sat there watching his fingers and listening to his mesmerizing voice as he sang. I was so caught up in the moment and could have listened to him play all night. By the end of the second song, I yawned. Max caught me and frowned.

"C'mon, CC. Time for bed."

"No, I wa—"

He had already put me over his shoulder and was carrying me back up to bed.

TEN

"You stupid bitch!" he snarled.

I jackknifed on the bed, arms whaling in the air. Shuddering, I looked around the room and then breathed a sigh of relief.

I was safe, naked, and in bed. Not only was I in bed, but Max was still lying beside me.

I looked over at him curled in the sheets. He was knocked out, but that was no surprise. Until the wee hours of the morning he had put in his work. We kissed, licked and touched, and I cried out in pleasure when he buried his tongue between my thighs and tasted me. When I didn't think I could stand a moment longer, he buried himself deep inside. I was caught up in the way he made me feel like the most important person in the world, and I loved every moment of it. During our in-between sex breaks, we talked about life and made plans for the following weekend.

I was crazy about Max. That was something I couldn't deny.

I slid from the bed and sighed. Every inch of my body was sore and completely satisfied. I could barely stand and I was almost tempted to get back in bed and curl beside him, but I had to pee and couldn't hold it a moment longer.

The sun was peeking through the blinds. I glanced out and noticed it had been raining. I grabbed one of his t-shirts from the chair and disappeared into the bathroom. While I relieved myself I found myself purring in satisfaction. Max was an amazing lover and I couldn't think of a single thing to complain about.

Girl, you got it bad.

I moved to the sink, washed my hands and gazed at my

reflection in the mirror. I still looked like shit. There was a black circle still around my eyes and my cheek was red but at least the cut was healing, and the swelling was gone from my face. I guess that counted for something. I shoved my fingers through my hair that was a wild unruly mess of curls. I couldn't believe I hadn't run a comb through it in two days.

Being around Max filled me with the weirdest sort of contentment like I could just be myself around him. I didn't have to worry about my hair, make-up, and putting on false pretenses. I had allowed him to see a part of me I rarely allowed anyone to see. He'd seen me crying, broken, and extremely vulnerable. It was so out of my norm it scared me, and I decided to resist the driving urge to climb back in bed. If I didn't take a moment to pull it together I was going to fall hard.

I pulled the t-shirt over my head and Max's scent enveloped me. It was warm and familiar. Damn, I really do have it bad.

Needing a little time alone, I decided to head downstairs. Thinking over a cup of coffee was always a good move. Over the years, I've made some of my best decisions while sipping a caramel macchiato at Starbuck's.

As I headed downstairs, I found myself thinking about just how much I really liked his house. I could see myself living here and that frightened really me. My heart was pounding like crazy. My mind was moving too fast and I needed to slow it down. But at the same time I didn't want to. The weekend had been a wonderful start to something, and I had a feeling I was in for one amazing ride.

I crossed the cool wood floor into the kitchen and winced at the wonderful soreness between my thighs as I headed straight for the coffeepot. I needed a pick-me-up right away. While I waited for the coffee to brew, I stared out the window at the beautiful backyard. The grass was thick and plush.

I don't know what it was but I felt so relaxed and alive with Max. I know a great deal of it was because he had come to my aid, but there was more to it than that. We connected. He made me laugh, and allowed me to cry on his shoulder. He provided compassion, and had brought me pleasure in ways I had only dreamed about. Maximilian James was the total package.

I had my back to the kitchen entrance, waiting for the coffee to brew when I heard heavy feet coming down the stairs.

"Hey beautiful," Max greeted as he padded across the wood floor.

"Good morning."

Max looked scrumptious in boxers and his chest bare. He pulled me into his arms. "I woke up and my bed was empty," he rasped just before he bent his head and kissed me long, and deep.

Goodness, even his morning kisses were delicious.

"You want some breakfast?" I asked against his lips.

"Yes, breakfast sounds wonderful. I think I worked up a bit of an appetite." He kissed me once more, then swatted me playfully across the ass. I jerked away laughing. Max winked, then grabbed another mug from the cabinet.

"You want to go see a movie or something today?" he asked as he reached for the carafe and filled it to the rim.

I smiled. I could definitely get used to him including me as part of his day.

"Uh-uh. No way. I saw how my face looks!" I had to force myself to frown.

"Babe, you look beautiful to me."

Doesn't he know it isn't about him, it's about me? And there was no way in hell I was letting anyone see me like this. "Besides, I'm really dying to go home and change clothes. We can crash at my house and play dominos or something."

That got his attention. "Dominos? What you know about playing bones?"

I gave him a confident grin. "My father taught me when I was young."

"Then it's on." Max spooned enough sugar in his mug to make me cringe. Talking about adding a little coffee to his sugar.

"What are you hungry for?" I asked with my head inside

the refrigerator and felt him come behind me. His hands were now palming my bare ass beneath the t-shirt.

"What I'm hungry for you can't find in that fridge."

Tingles of pleasure roared through me as I felt the head of his erection pressing against my ass. Max brought his lips to the back of my neck. I giggled and replied, "Yes and then we'll both die of starvation."

"At least I'll be happy." He kissed me once more, then reached over for his mug and took a sip. "I'm going to go up and take a shower."

After he left, I was both relieved and disappointed that Max hadn't insisted on satisfying his hunger. Memories resurfaced of yesterday morning being bent over the kitchen table, and heat rushed to my face.

"Goodness you got it bad, CC," I muttered under my breath.

Within minutes I had bacon frying on the stove and then started scrambling the eggs while I sipped my coffee. After two days together I was looking forward to sharing another with him as well.

I was draining the grease from the bacon when the doorbell rang. Max was still in the shower so at first I ignored it. But then when I heard someone leaning against the bell, I got annoyed and decided to go see who the hell it was. I swung it open and immediately stalled.

"What the…"

A short petite woman allowed her voice to trail off as she turned to the big Amazon chick standing beside her, who spat, "Who the hell is you?" Her head was twisting sending microbraids flying through the air.

My brow rose and I simply gave her the look and said with a fake smile, "Can I help you?"

"Nah, b—"

Before she could say something that might have landed her a punch in her thin lips, the petite chocolate chick cut her off and said, "Is Max home?"

I allowed my eyes to roam over her beautiful face, brown skin, high cheekbones and amazing eyes. She was a pretty woman and I couldn't help but wonder what her relationship was with Max. That was before I allowed my eyes to peruse the length of her and noticed her protruding stomach and suddenly remembered we had already met.

Parker… his suspect baby mama.

"He's in the shower," I replied and it took everything I had not to stare at her stomach. She looked adorable carrying a child. Why did I suddenly feel ridiculously jealous?

"Who are you?" she asked. Her expression was almost comical.

"Yeah… who the hell is you?" Her sidekick was nothing but an instigator. There was no way I was feeding into that shit.

"Why don't you ask Max who I am," I replied and I noticed Parker barely blinked an eye.

"You know I'm carrying his baby, right?" she said with a look that was so confident and cocky, I had the urge to slap her.

"I know there's a slight possibility." I had to reiterate that part because according to Max there was a strong chance it was not his child.

"*Possibility?*" she was waving her hands in my direction and it pissed me off. "There's no possibility. This baby is Max!" she replied rather arrogantly.

"I know that's right." Amazon gave her a high-five.

I held up my hands in surrender. "Listen, I'm not here to be the judge or the jury. That's between you and Max." I wanted to make sure she knew I could care less, even though deep down I was scared out of my skull.

Parker kept giving her friend odd looks then zeroed in on me. "Damn girl, what happened to your face?" She was trying to act like we were suddenly best friends.

My hands immediately came up to cover my cheeks. Damn, I forgot. "I was in an accident."

"Yeah, with someone's fist." Her sidekick was acting like she was whispering, but it was clear she wasn't really trying, then she started laughing all loud and embarrassing. Parker smirked and tried to act like she was trying not to laugh.

"Well, my girl here needs to talk to Max... not that it's really any of your business." That big chick had shameless attitude.

This right here was a ghetto hot mess and I wasn't about to stoop to their level.

"Let me go tell Max you're here." I started to shut the door but Amazon pushed past me and stepped into the house.

"We'll wait inside while you get him."

Parker followed her inside. She held her head high and strutted in like a peacock. At that point, I was invisible to them.

"Missy, this is the couch I was talking about. I told you I was with him when he bought it, right? It's Italian leather."

They were feeling the material like they were stroking a cat. You could tell they weren't used to quality. What the hell was Max doing with someone like this, I wondered. I wasn't starting to think that maybe I didn't really know him after all.

I left the two of them alone because obviously Parker already knew her way around the house. I went upstairs into the bedroom and Max was coming out of the bathroom. Damn. I was trying to stay mad, but it wasn't easy with him standing there with water running off his naked body.

"You have company."

He was digging through his dresser drawer when he asked, "Who is it?"

"Parker."

His head whipped around and his brow rose. I know he was trying to get a reaction out of me but I wasn't going there.

"I'm gonna go down and see what she wants," he said to me.

I felt like telling him he didn't have to ask me for permission. That was his problem, not mine. Instead, I slipped on my shorts, and headed back downstairs and toward the kitchen. The two were sitting in the living room playing his entertainment system.

"Oooh girl... that's my song!"

They screamed and started singing, Candy Rain, off-key.

Oh my God, they were embarrassing.

I scrambled eggs in a bowl and listened as Max came down the stairs and went into the room. Just as I suspected, he wasn't too happy about them messing with his music. There were a few choice words as I poured the eggs into the skillet and then I heard, "What the hell is *she* doing up in here?"

I was pissed and didn't even bother to listen to any more after that. In fact, I was so mad I ended up tossing the eggs down the garbage disposal.

I heard the door shut and then things were quiet. I figured Max moved outside so they could talk in private. That was my cue to go upstairs and get dressed.

The weekend was officially over.

I practically ripped off his t-shirt and slipped into the shower and within minutes I was drying off. I looked out the window and saw him standing at the car talking to Parker and I actually felt another twinge of jealousy. Damn, I haven't felt like that about a guy in ages. But sure enough, the longer I watched the worse that feeling became.

Parker moved in so close her belly rubbed against his arm. And she had put on this sad face that I'm sure worked on most guys. I wondered if Max was that naïve.

She's pregnant so that wasn't saying much about his character.

Yep, that was definitely not a life I wanted to be a part of. The thought of our weekend ending gave me a sick feeling at the pit of my stomach, but I ignored it. No man is worth all that drama.

Max finally stepped back, folding his arms to regain some of his personal space, but it was a little too late for that.

I slipped back into my workout shorts and sweatshirt and was sliding into my running shoes when I heard Max racing up the hall.

"Yo, babe! Where you at?"

He made it into the bedroom before I could respond.

"Sorry about that," he said and sounded sincere as he rubbed the back of his neck.

I shrugged. "No apologizes. That's your reality. Actually I'm glad she came."

His dark eyes glittered suspiciously. "Why is that?"

"Because it brought me back to *my* reality." I was struggling to lace up my shoes as I spoke.

With a groan, Max stretched out on the bed, his arms folded behind his head, one leg bent. "CC, don't go there. She dropped by to see if I was going to her appointment tomorrow."

"And she couldn't call?" I could just see the two of them sitting in the clinic together like a couple, waiting to hear their baby's heartbeat. Damn the vision was so vivid it ripped at my chest.

Max licked his top lip and was behaving all nonchalant. "She did try to call, but I turned my phone off."

So had I, before my meeting with DJ, and the minute I climbed into my car I was cutting it back on. There was no telling who had been looking for me.

I finally rose and stared down at him. Damn, he looked good lying on the bed. "Thank you for everything, but I gotta go."

"Can we talk about it?"

Sighing, I said, "No. I don't want to talk about Parker. She was the reason why I didn't want to get involved with you in the first place and you know that."

"Yes, but I was hoping you had a change of heart and would be willing to give this man a chance."

So did I. "For a moment there I almost thought I could but after seeing her, I just can't deal with that ghetto hot mess!" I tossed my hands in the air. "I'm trying to wrap my mind around how you could have possibly gotten involved with someone like her, and the only answer I can come up with is that I really don't know you at all."

He had the nerve to laugh. "Is that what you came up with?"

"Personally I don't see anything funny about this situation. In fact, it's kind of sad." Max was still laughing at the situation and was starting to piss me off.

"Claudia, why don't we go downstairs, sit, and talk like two adults?"

"Are you listening? I don't want any part of this," I

replied with a hand now propped at my hip.

Max growled and grumbled under his breath before saying, "So you're telling me what happened between us this weekend didn't mean anything to you?"

I swallowed because I would be lying if I had answered yes. "What I'm saying is regardless of how I feel about you, I'm not interested in being a part of any baby mama drama and you're going to have plenty with that one."

He took an arrogant stance. "Wow! I would think you would at least have respect for a man who owns up to his responsibilities."

Furiously, I folded my arms and growled, "I thought you said that wasn't your child?"

"So if you believe that... then why are you running away?" He straightened with a fluid grace that reminded me of a predator moving in for the kill. If he touched me then I was going to be back in his arms so I jumped out of his way.

"You don't know for sure and I can't sit around hoping you're right. Now excuse me, I need to get home." I grabbed my purse, rushed past him and was down the stairs and out the door before he could even stop me. I eyed my car keys on the table in the foyer and scooped them up along the way. I was climbing into my Range Rover when Max stepped out onto the porch. Quickly, I put the key in the ignition and backed out the driveway. Otherwise, I would have probably changed my mind and stayed.

As I peeled away, I searched around in my purse for my phone and turned it on. It was time to return to reality.

Thank goodness Trey had brought my vehicle to Max's house. I don't think I could have beared having Max drive me home. Trust me, I know I owed him a lot for what he had done for me, but there was no way in hell I was going to allow my gratitude to stand in the way of what I believed in. I said it once and I'll say it again... I don't do ghetto baby mamas and that one he had was straight out of the Wikipedia. In all honesty I actually felt sorry for Max because if that child was his—and the way my luck ran, it would be—he was going to have to be bothered with that woman for the next eighteen years. I sure hoped he was mentally prepared for the drama. Personally there was no way in hell I could stomach it. In fact, mine was already churning and I felt sad. Max and I could really have been good for each other. He was so nurturing and funny, and most of all he was all man. Goodness, I got goosebumps every time I thought about him coming to my rescue and scooping me into his arms. What impressed me even more was his ability to lie beside me and hold me and not try to get any. Speaking of sex… It just didn't get any better than him. By the time I hit the major intersection, I actually felt like crying.

Don't you dare cry!

I sniffed and took several necessary breaths then licked my dry lips.

CC, you're better than that. We don't cry over men.

It would have been easier if Max wasn't everything I ever wanted in a man and yet he was all wrong for me. Where was the irony in all of that?

ELEVEN

My phone rang and I pushed Talk on my Bluetooth. "Claudia, where are you?" Christina said the moment I answered.

I turned at the stoplight. "I'm on my way to my house."

"I'll meet you there."

What the hell? She hung up on me. I sighed. There was no doubt in my mind, Christina was pissed off and about to lecture me for leaving my phone off. She was going to have to get over it.

By the time I had made it to the driveway. Christina was already climbing out of her BMW.

"It took you long enough!" She hurried over in a pair of Manolo heels and wrapped her arms tightly around my neck. "Oh my God! I was so worried!" Christina pulled back and then her eyes widened. "Look at your face!"

Dammit! I couldn't even meet her gaze. "It's not as bad as it looks." Actually it was worse I had just done a fabulous job of covering up most of the bruises with makeup. Christina followed me into the house and to my kitchen.

"Why didn't you answer my calls?" she accused and then raised her voice. "You had me worried out of my mind!"

Her eyes were locked on my face. She looked so scared, I felt guilty. "I'm sorry. I really didn't mean to worry you but I wasn't ready to talk to anyone." I retrieved two bottles of diet iced tea and signaled for her to follow me into the sunroom. The floor-to-ceiling windows were one of the main reasons why I had bought the house.

Christina sucked her teeth. "Oh? So now I'm just anyone?"

I shook my head. Maybe I should have ignored her call a

while longer. "You know what I mean."

"No, what you're about to do is tell me what happened! Dereon tried to explain but he was so pissed I could hardly understand him."

I took a seat in one of the white wicker chairs and waited for her to sit on the love seat before I said, "I was leaving the meeting with DJ and these guys attacked me in the parking lot. I was trying to get away but…"

"Shit! I'm so glad Max showed up," she interrupted.

I was nodding as I popped the cap on the bottle. Every time I thought about Max and what he'd done, I felt like crying. "Christy, I don't know what I would have done if he hadn't showed up when he did." I tried to sound cheery, but tears were already swelling up in my eyes.

"Oh Claudia, I'm so sorry! I don't want to think about what would have happened if Max hadn't been there." Her eyes looked like they were tearing, which caused mine to tear some more. It's good to know my best friend really cared about me.

I blinked my eyes and forced a bright smile. "Christy, girl… Max came out of nowhere then started doing these Jackie Chan moves."

"*What?*"

"I'm serious. He knocked all three of them out." I laughed at the memories. "I can't begin to tell you how good that felt."

She shook her head. "Unbelievable! Dee said by the time he got there the guys were gone."

"Yeah, it pisses me off they're going to get away with attacking me, but at least Max spanked that ass."

"What did the police say?"

Oh boy, here we go again. "I didn't report it."

A worried look appeared on her face. "What? Why not?"

I waved a hand at her. "Because I don't want to go through all that. Max has already lectured me, but like I told him, it's not going to make a difference. They were already gone."

"But you still should have reported it. You never know what might happen," she scolded.

"Well it's over now." I guess she figured I really didn't want to talk about it because she let it drop.

Christina let out an exaggerated sigh. "I think we just need to leave that contract alone. A place like that would ruin our reputation." Christina never wanted to work with DJ Mecca in the first place. I was the one doing it as a referral for a customer who had brought us a lot of business when we were first getting started.

"I agree. We worked too hard to get where we are. I'll call DJ in the morning."

"So what's up with you and Max? After spending a few days with him I'm sure you finally have a different feeling about him." Christina was looking into my eyes.

I took a big thirsty swallow from the bottle before admitting, "Actually I was starting to think differently about him but that was before his crazy-ass baby mama and her bodyguard showed up to the house talking crazy."

"What?"

I frowned and stared through the glass out into my fenced backyard. "I'm serious. She was carrying on and acting like she owned the place."

Christina leaned in close like she was afraid she might miss something. "Where was Max?"

I turned my eyes to her. "In the shower, so I answered the door, and there that crazy chick was standing."

"What did she want?"

"I don't know. He went outside to talk to her. By the time she left I was ready to go home."

There was a brief moment of silence. "I really wish the two of you could get together." Christina leaned back on the couch and had the nerve to look disgusted.

"Not happening," I muttered sheepishly.

"What do you mean, not happening?"

"We're friends. And I thank Max for everything he did for me, but I'm just not interested in going there with him." I cut her off and changed the subject before she could object. "You want to go looking for a dress tomorrow?"

"My sister and I went yesterday... something's wrong

with her and Evan."

"What do you mean, something is wrong?"

She arched an inquisitive brow. "You know my sister is like my mother and will never admit anything is wrong in their home, but I could tell something isn't right. She kept trying to reach Evan but he wasn't answering her calls or texts."

"Do you think he's having an affair?"

"Who knows and Portia wouldn't believe it if he was." She shook her head again, and then it was her turn to change the subject. "Is there is anything I can do for you?" It took me a moment to realize she was back to my accident again.

The last thing I wanted was for her to start fussing over me. "No, I'm fine. I'm just glad to be home." I lied. I actually liked being at Max's house a little too much. "I probably won't be in the office for a few days. I have a cake to design on Friday for Margie Fox, so I'll definitely be in then."

"Right. A cake with a dozen white doves for her birthday." She nodded as she remembered the order. "If you need anything, please let me know. I'll be glad to bring it to you."

I waved my hand at her. "Thanks I really appreciate it, but I'm fine."

I knew she didn't believe me, and that's why I loved her so much because Christina knew me better than anyone.

"We really need to finish unpacking," she commented and had the nerve to turn up her nose."

"And you need to pack and get your condo on the market," I retorted.

"I know." She finally rose and reached down for her purse. "I will just as soon as I have a chance. Next weekend Mom and I are meeting with the wedding coordinator to make sure we have every detail covered. The last thing she wants is to be embarrassed in front of her friends."

I gave a rude snort. You would think she was the one getting married, not her daughter. But Jeanna was married to a millionaire of her own.

After Christina left, I went upstairs, stripped off my

clothes and decided to take a long soak in the tub. I caught another glimpse of my face in the mirror and I wanted to cry when I saw how pathetic I looked. I didn't want anyone to see me like this, all black and blue. I sunk low in the tub and thought about the attack.

"Thank you, Max," I whispered.

Despite how I felt about him, he would always be my hero and I would forever be in debt to him.

By the time I made it back into my bedroom, I was actually feeling a lot better about myself. I had never been a victim and I wasn't about to start acting like one now. I slipped into a pair of white cotton shorts and a pink top with spaghetti straps. Forget the bra, I was at home.

My phone was buzzing and I looked down to see it was my mother calling. I drew a deep breath. I'd rather ignore her call at least until tomorrow, but if I didn't answer she was likely to send my father or brother Clayton Jr. over to check on me. If either of them saw my face they would be packing up my suitcase and carrying me back to their house to live.

"Hey Mommy," I managed in a baby voice, but Aokia wasn't buying it.

"Don't Mommy me. I've been calling you for the last couple of days. Do you know how worried I've been?"

I hated lying to my parents, but sometimes it was necessary. "Sorry, I went down to the lake for a few days. You know the signal is terrible there."

"That's no excuse. You should have returned my calls."

"You're right, and I'm sorry. I just got home and was planning to call you in the morning."

There was silence, which meant she was pissed. My mother might be four-eleven and Japanese, but Aokia was not one to be messed with.

"We're planning a barbecue for your father's birthday. I hope you can find time in your busy schedule to come."

I was pretty certain my bruises would have faded by the first weekend in October. "I have a wedding that weekend, but if it's on Sunday I'll be there."

"Perfect. Your father will be happy to hear that." Some of

the ice had thawed from her voice, which meant I was back to being her favorite daughter again. "Guess who your father saw in the hospital cafeteria yesterday?"

I spread lotion onto my body as we talked. "Who?" I was certain it was another one of his boring colleagues he raved about all the time.

"Isaiah."

"What?" There was no way I had heard her correctly.

"Yes, he's interviewing for a position in the family medicine department." She went on and on about his conversation with my father, but by then my mind was traveling back. I had loved that man like no other. For seven years of my life, he was my entire world. We were supposed to have been married when he decided to join *Doctors Without Borders* and left me with a wedding dress I couldn't return.

That was five years ago.

Now he was back looking at joining Barnes Jewish Hospital, the same hospital that had offered him a position before he turned it down to follow his calling.

"He asked your father if you were married."

My heart gave a flutter, but I kept my tone steady. "And what did Daddy tell him?"

"That you were single."

I rolled my eyes. Isaiah probably thought I had spent the last five years mourning over him.

"I'm planning on inviting him to your father's birthday dinner." She paused, waiting for a response that I didn't give her. "I think he's ready to settle down and start a family."

"And you really think I still want to marry that dude?" I said incredulously.

"Claudia, as I told you before you can't stand in the way of a man and his faith. He felt compelled to dedicate to a cause. If anything, you should have more admiration for him than before." She always tried to make everything sound so simple.

"Why, because he decided he'd rather live in a third world country than be married to me?" I shook my head. Imagine what that decision had done to my ego. Oh no, not my mother. We'd had this argument so many times before.

She sighed the way she does when she is unhappy with my behavior. "At least give the man a chance to explain." There was more silence. "The two of you could have a great life together."

At one time that was all I had dreamed about... spending my life with Isaiah, but that was before *Cater to You* had begun to thrive... and before I met Max.

Part of me wanted what Isaiah and I once had. The other half wanted Max without the baby, the mama, and the drama. My emotions were so conflicted. I didn't know what to think or feel.

"I'll think about it, Mommy."

She breathed a sigh of relief. "That's all I ask. You know all your father and I want is for our children to be happy. And if Isaiah isn't the one then I understand, but sometimes your blessing is staring you right in the face."

When I lowered my eyelids the only face I saw was Max.

You are so screwed.

TWELVE

"He won't let us out the contract." Christina's long-lashed eyes grew wide with disbelief.

"What? Why the hell not?" she barked, while standing in the door to my office with her arms crossed.

"Because we already shook hands."

I was pissed. It was my first day back into the office and I had been on the phone for the last half hour, talking to DJ about nulling the contract at The Hole. And despite me getting my ass kicked in his parking lot, he refused to cancel our agreement. Arrogant bastard.

"He said nothing personal boo, but business is business."

"Are you kidding? That prick!" Christina pushed away from the doorframe and was sulking as she walked toward my desk.

"Right." I blew out a long breath. "I should have listened to Max in the beginning and stayed away from that place."

For the longest neither of us said anything.

"So now what?" Her facial expression was not a happy one. I couldn't blame her. I had gotten us into this mess, so it was my job to get us out.

"I guess I'll have our attorney review the contract and see what we can do. I haven't deposited the check yet so maybe that will count for something," I said faintly.

Christina was pacing around my office. "There has got to be a way out of this mess. I'm going to talk to Dereon and see what he has to say."

I nodded. "Whatever it takes at this point, because that is one party I don't want to do. Who's to say those guys won't be in attendance."

"Exactly! I was thinking the same thing." Her eyes were

wide with fear and I know she was worried not only about me but also about our reputation.

I was pissed and worried as well. "How could I have been so stupid?" I must have looked as dumbfounded as I felt because Christina shrugged her shoulders.

"How would you know? We aren't from the street. His money was green just like everyone else's. Besides George referred him and we've been working with George for years." He was also one of our oldest customers and a good friend of Nelly. It was because of George that we'd had the opportunity to cater an album release party for the rapper. The party was the buzz on Access Hollywood and TMZ. Ever since that night, *Cater to You* had been in high demand.

Christina took a seat, wearing a red pants suit that looked striking against her milk-chocolate skin. "Have you tried reaching George?"

I sighed dramatically. "Yeah, he's out of the country for an undisclosed amount of time."

She sank back in the chair and mumbled a string of obscenities that would have made even a rapper blush. "I think from now on we need to start screening our clients' locations before we decide to go into business with them."

"I agree. We are at a level now that we can afford to be a little picky."

We spent the next hour going over our catering schedule then Christina left for an appointment and I went into the kitchen to retrieve a soda from the fridge. I was wearing a long, black, knit skirt with high slits on the side and a simple long-sleeved shirt with a V-neck collar. As soon as I made a few phone calls, I planned to spend the rest of the afternoon in the kitchen designing a cake. Keeping busy occupied my mind. Since I had decided not to come into the office, I had spent the last few days unpacking boxes and was just about complete. I needed that, something to focus on, because I've had way too much confusion racing around inside my head.

First there was Max. I wasn't quite sure what I wanted to do with that situation. I'd been ignoring his phone calls all week. Luckily, I had parked my car in the garage and was able to pretend I wasn't at home when he had come pounding at my front door. I finally texted him to let him know I was alright, but preferred to be left alone.

And then there was Isaiah. Ever since I had talked to my mother, I had been thinking about him. I wasn't quite sure how I felt about seeing him again. I had even pulled out a few photographs of the two of us back when I was hopelessly in love and yet the memories were so faded I didn't quite know how to feel besides bitter that he had left me. Lastly, I was still having nightmares about my attack. Maybe I should have filed a police report.

I went back to my office and put the finishing touches on a contract I had been working on and by noon it was ready for Mia to send out. I then swiveled around in my chair and was reaching for the phone to update a client when I felt someone staring at me. I looked up and my breath stalled.

"Hey CC." Max smiled like I should be happy to see him. I hated to admit it but I was.

"Max… what are you doing here?"

His grin widened as he strolled into my office looking mighty tasty in blue jeans, a St. Louis Rams jersey, and powder-blue Timberlands.

"Since you've been avoiding my calls I thought I'd drop by and see if I could pull you away for lunch." As usual his stance was cocky and confident. The two things I loved in a man. And when it came to Max, it put him in a class of his own.

"I don't have time to go to lunch," I snarled. "I've got a million things to do and besides as long as I'm looking like *this*," I paused and pointed to my face. "The less I'm seen in public the better."

"You face looks good to me."

I gave a rude snort. "I wouldn't say all that." Most of the bruises had faded enough I could practically cover them with make-up with the exception of the dark bruise beneath my right eye. As soon as I had walked into the office, Mia had jumped out of her seat begging to know what had happened. The chick was so upset I had felt compelled to tell her.

"I figured you would say that, which is why I decided to bring lunch to you."

It was then I noticed the backpack he slipped off his back.

"What's that?"

He gave me this look that instantly made my nipples pucker. "A picnic."

I hated when he was so nice to me because it made it almost impossible to stay mad. How was it my mind refused to cooperate?

"A picnic?" I started laughing. Max and picnic were two things I would never had thought about putting together in the same sentence. "You're kidding?" I watched as he reached inside the bag and removed a blue blanket and spread it out onto my office floor.

"I got everything you like..., roast beef sandwiches, Cole slaw, chips, diet soda, and even homemade lemon pound cake from Mama Dee's Cafe."

My eyes widened as I rose from my chair and came around my desk to look inside the pack. "How in the world did you know that was my favorite?"

He gave that smile of his that melted my heart. "I got friends in all places."

"I just bet you do." I rolled my eyes and tried to behave as if I wasn't impressed. "Well, I hate that you went to all that trouble, but you're wasting your time."

I guess since I had allowed my guard down for even a second, Max took that as an opportunity to surge pass my defenses.

"C'mere." Max took hold of my arm, dragging me into the wall of his chest. I probably should have pushed him away, but that was hard to do with his juicy lips closing in on mine. And once again I was falling for his charm and bullshit. Dammit. Max was so sexy and enticing that rejecting him wasn't quite that easy even if I wanted to. And to be honest, I didn't. I would beat myself up over it later, but for now I wanted to savor the moment for all that it was worth.

I parted my lips and his tongue slipped into my mouth. Goodness, he was such an amazing kisser that desire shot through me so fast it made my knees buckle. I moaned and lifted my chin, seeking each stroke of his tongue. My arms came around to hold him while his hands moved to cup my ass. I was moaning and he was lifting me to my toes and crushing me against him.

I felt so comfortable in his arms I wanted to cry. Why was it this man had a way of making me feel good in ways that others could not? All I could think about was the pleasure blossoming in all of the right places. When he grazed his teeth over my bottom lip, I released a cry of distress. "Enough!" I jerked away from his embrace, then waved my hand letting him know I wasn't trying to hear anything he had to say. "Keep your lips to yourself!" I snapped then walked over and closed my office door and couldn't even look at him because I was afraid he would see what I was hiding.

Max chuckled. "Your mouth says one thing, but a few seconds ago your lips were moaning a different tune."

Oh no he didn't. "Where's Parker?" I folded my arms beneath my breasts and gave him a hard look. "I'm sure she's looking for you."

"I'm not worried about Parker. This is about you and me." He was so cocky.

"There's no you and I," I snapped.

"You're lying to yourself. We spent the weekend together. You want me just as badly as I want you." He was laying it on thick. Standing in my office, licking his lips, while staring with those amazing eyes, caused butterflies to churn my stomach. "We can work through it if you'd just give us a chance."

The way he was talking was such a turn-on, and yet I tried to convince myself I didn't want to hear anything else he had to say. Damn, why did he have to be so sexy?

"Babe, I'm sorry for the way things went down the other day. I promise you it won't ever happen again."

His voice was so low, sexy and enticing, and damn if I didn't feel myself on the verge to give in. The longer I spent time around him the more blurry the line between what I wanted and didn't want had become.

Max leaned back against the edge of my desk and my

eyes landed down at his crotch. Images of him holding his penis in his hand flooded my mind.

"Babe, I miss holding you in my arms," he confessed in this deep, enticing voice and I knew I really needed to have a long talk with my conscious later.

I was ready to try one last attempt at resisting when Max closed the distance between us and started tickling me until I was screaming and laughing. "Stop it!"

"Tell me you miss me, CC."

"Stop Max!" I was struggling trying to get free of his grasp.

"Not until you admit how much you like my kisses."

"Okay, okay!" I screamed. "I like your kisses!" He finally stopped but instead of releasing me he took my hand and got all serious.

"How are you feeling?" His eyes were moving all over my face. "Your face looks like it's healing. How are the other bruises?"

I dropped my eyes briefly in an attempt to regain some ground. Not that it helped. His voice was so alluring and his eyes… I could get lost in them forever. "I'm better really, thanks to you."

"So now you owe me," he winked.

"Owe you?" My eyes jerked to him. Just like a man. I should have known he was going to want something in return. "Owe you what?"

He smiled. "Lunch… now sit." He tapped my nose with the tip of his finger and dragged me down to the floor and onto his lap.

"Do I have to sit here?" I was already breaking out in a warm sweat. Like I said being that close was just too intimate and comfortable.

His grin widened as he kissed my cheek. "Babe, I love holding you in my arms, but I would never make you do anything you don't wanna do. You know that." His voice was so mesmerizing and sincere.

"I know." Damn he was making it hard with his pretty white teeth and perfectly barbered goatee. Did I tell you how much I loved a man with a goatee? Instead of sliding off his lap, I reached inside the bag and removed the perfectly wrapped foods and laid it on the blanket. "I'm starving," I said stubbornly and he chuckled. Max knew his charm was working on me.

I handed him one of the sandwiches, then I folded back the aluminum foil. A thick roast beef sandwich was inside. "This looks good."

"I got it from Wally's on Florissant Road. They make the best sandwiches in North County."

I turned up my nose. "What were you doing in North County?"

"I went to do an assessment on a possible flip," he managed to say between chews.

"Really?" I had seen firsthand some of the projects they had done. Reggie Hodges, a general contractor and owner of RDH Construction and his friends—Dereon, Maximilian, Trey, and Braxton bought and flipped homes that were fabulous. "Did the house seem like something you might want to invest in?"

He nodded. "Yep, I think it's one hell of a deal. I need to discuss with the crew first. Reggie is busy working on a project for the city so I'm going to take lead on the next renovation."

"Aren't you nice?" I teased.

He shrugged. "That's what friends are for. Me and Reggie grew up in the same hood."

"What hood is that?"

"Wellston."

"Wow!" Right in the hood.

"He was raised by his mother. His father was a deadbeat. His moms worked a lotta long hours, so I hung at his place," he explained as he chewed a chip. "Ms. Hodges was firm. She kept us busy around the house… off the streets and outta trouble." His eyes sparkled with what appeared to be fond memories.

"You ever thought about reaching out to your father?" I suddenly blurted out.

While Max took another bite, he frowned. *Stupid, CC! Why did you have to bring up his parents when you know it's a sore spot with him?* Luckily, he had a soft spot for me. "Nope, why should I?" Even though he tried to act like he didn't care, I could tell his father not being in his life hurt him. "I think I've done good without a father.""

"Yes you have." I felt compelled to lean over and kiss his cheek. "You have no idea how many times I wished I didn't have a father." I rolled my eyes but found myself laughing as I reached for a chip. "I'm serious. Growing up I used to say, "I wish you weren't my dad," so many times it practically rang in my ears. Daddy was strict. Even though we were well-off, he made us work for our allowances. And I had to have a job every summer to buy my own school clothes. I know that sounds spoiled and stupid after hearing about your life but to me it was a big deal." I smiled and filled my mouth with coleslaw before continuing, "Then my senior year my dad told me I had three choices after high school—college, the military, or get out."

"Wow that sounds like my last foster mom. Since I was in the foster care system I got all kinda grants." He popped the cap on a grape soda. "Yep, I did that all on my own."

"Really? You went to college?" I didn't mean to sound so surprised but I was.

Max chuckled and shook his head. Yes, he might have found the question silly, but I was being serious. "Yep, I got a degree in music from the UMSL."

My brow rose. "Really? Music?"

He nodded. "I told you I've always loved music."

"As beautifully as you play the piano I can understand why. Are you planning to someday teach?"

"Nah. I've always been interested in writing songs."

"So how did you get into home renovations?"

He laughed as he bit into his sandwich. "I used to stay with this disabled dude before his daughter stuck him in a nursing home. He had a workshop with all kinds of tools and he taught me how to use them. Before long I was fixing all kinds of stuff around his rundown house. Through high school and college construction work was how I kept money in my pocket. Now it's a means of making a living."

I loved staring at his lips while listening to Max talk about his life. He always found a way to make something so pitiful seem not so bad. "Good for you. Lord knows, Christina and I wouldn't be where we are today if it wasn't for my parents believing in us."

"What do you mean?"

"I mean we started our company in the basement of their house," I explained between chews. "I refused to accept any money from them, and Christina wasn't interested in taking from her father, who's a millionaire by the way. Together we scraped and struggled and launched our business with sweat and tears."

His appreciative eyes scanned the space I called my office. "And look how far the two of you had come."

I grinned because sometimes it was even hard for me to believe how far we had come and yet we had made it on our own. Christina was right. We were at a point in our career that it wasn't always about the money. We needed to start picking and choosing our clientele carefully.

"Why you frowning?" Max asked. Damn, that man doesn't miss a thing.

I blinked and then drew a long breath as I said, "I was thinking about the mess I put us in." I slipped off his lap, and sat Indian-style as I met his curious gaze. "I tried to break our contract with The Hole, but DJ Mecca refuses to let us go even after I told him what happened," I said by way of an explanation.

"*Are you fucking serious*?" Max was pissed. Trust me. The last thing I wanted was to upset him.

I nodded and said grimly, "I'm afraid so. He wants to hold me to my end of the contract."

Max muttered something under his breath. "You said Mecca is the one holding you to the contract?"

"Yes, do you know him?" I searched his eyes.

"Yeah." Max gave me a hard look, then shook his head. "I wish you had listened to me."

"I know I fucked up and if you've forgot I've already been punished for it!"

His expression softened. Leaning forward, Max kissed me hard on the mouth. "Babe, I'm sorry. I'm not mad at you."

I sighed and raised my eyes to the ceiling. "Good, because I'm already mad enough on my own. Now I'm just trying to find a way to get my company and Christina out of that mess," I pouted.

He stuffed several chips in his mouth and was quiet long enough to chew and wash it down with soda. "I won't make any promises, but let me see if I can rectify this situation."

"That would be so great! Christina and I would appreciate anything you can do."

"It would be my pleasure. DJ and I have bumped heads quite a few times over the years. Once more won't hurt. Then again… maybe it might."

I had a sudden flashback of the other night. "Oh hell no! I definitely don't want a repeat." I jumped up from the floor and glared down at Max like he had stolen something. Who's to say the next time he'd be able to just walk away. There was always the chance those guys would be somewhere watching and waiting for him to return.

"Worried about me?" he said as he rose and closed in the space between us.

"Yes, because I don't want your blood on my hands." I rolled my eyes.

He chuckled and stole a kiss. I tried to act serious, but it was useless. I started grinning, but then his face grew serious and his eyes darkened. My mind was screaming. I knew it was probably time to put an end to this little picnic and send him off to find Parker, and yet my heart was racing with anticipation.

When his lips brushed over mine there was no denying it. I wanted him bad. *Really bad.* My nipples were tight. And I felt my body leaning close to his rock-hard chest. His lips were delicious; mouthwatering, heart-stopping, panty-creaming delicious. The kiss deepened fast and my pulse was banging so hard I felt light-headed.

"I missed you," he murmured, his voice dark and deep.

Desire and longing swirled down into my belly. The smooth talker knew exactly what to say because I fell for it every time.

Max's breath was warm and his calloused fingers sliding over my shoulder was turning me to Jell-O. I shivered as his fingers slid across my skin and then my breath hitched as his hand shifted, sliding lower, toward my breast.

Dammit. I want him. Despite all the lectures I'd been giving myself the last few days about values and holding firm to your beliefs, for the life of me I couldn't remember any of it. I had never, and I mean never, wanted a man so damn bad in my life. And what was even better… he wanted me too.

The problem was I wanted more. A lot more. I wanted a life and a future with Max that I could never have. I wanted it all dammit.

I wanted him to keep me up all night, screaming with pleasure. I wanted him to send my mind and body to places I'd never dreamed. I wanted love, excitement and sex, and I wanted it right now in my office even if I knew it couldn't last. Just one more afternoon of crazy mind-boggling sex with the one man my body desired.

"This is crazy," I murmured against his lips.

"You make me crazy," he agreed as his tongue slid over my lips.

Bringing my arms up, I wrapped them around his neck, leaned into his touch and gave a low moan of delight.

I wanted his hands over every inch of my hard body, touching, feeling and even tasting me. I felt wicked, naughty, and alive.

As you would have thought he had read my mind because he descended until he was down on his knees, reaching under my skirt, and lowered my panties to my ankles.

"Someone might walk in," I protested.

Ignoring me, Max grabbed my ass, and shoved me toward him until his tongue and my moist lips collided. I let out a cry of shock before I could stop myself, followed by a sigh.

"Open up for me, babe." His breath was warm against my thighs. I kicked the panties aside and then spread my legs apart, allowing Max all the room he needed.

Within seconds, I was gripping the edge of the desk for support. Oh damn, it felt good. He was licking and sucking and invading between my folds with his tongue. And I found myself trying to fight what I was feeling.

Max pulled back a little and hissed, "Relax."

That was easy for him to say. He wasn't the one being held firmly in place for his personal assault. His tongue was delicious, confident and skillful, and before long I was arching off the desk and into his mouth. Raging heat tore through me. Max's tongue stroked me over and over, dipping inside before sliding up to my clit.

"Oh Max," I moaned and whimpered. It had been too long, a few days too long since I had enjoyed the comfort of his arms, the feel of his amazing fingers and his tongue, and my body was ready.

I was dying to come and scream his name.

With his fingers, he opened my folds, reached forward, and sucked my clit.

He wasn't making it easy to stay quiet. I was squirming on the desk, breathing heavy and ragged. An orgasm was creeping up on me. I could either hang on tight and enjoy the ride or make him stop before I embarrassed myself.

I decided to go with my first thought. Enjoy the moment.

Max increased the pressure, gripping me hard, his tongue was everywhere. "You taste so good," he murmured.

The hard edge of his voice was a turn-on and I shed my last bit of resistance. I brought my hands up and cupped the back of his head and drew his mouth as close as I could. "Oh Max, dammit, don't stop. It feels so good."

He was holding me in place. His lips were warm, wet and had me feeling desperate and out of control and then an orgasm ripped through me. Quickly, I bit down on my lip, stifling a scream. While gripping his head, I rocked my hips. Max continued to slide across my labia and I shuddered and moaned in ecstasy.

"Shit," I whispered as my body began to settle back down.

Max rose and unfastened his jeans. I barely had time to adjust when he was lifting my legs up off the floor and sinking deep inside of me.

"Damn, I missed being inside of you," he groaned, which made my body shudder. "Now lock your ankles around my waist."

As soon as I had my strappy heels resting against the small of his back, he pushed me down onto the desk. Parting my legs wider, he buried himself all the way as far as I could accommodate. Oh my, he felt huge! While I clawed desperately at his back, he began to stroke. Nothing slow or easy but long, deep, satisfying pumps that had my bottom lips trembling, screams from my throat were desperate to explode.

He was so addictive. I couldn't stay away from him for too long no matter how hard I tried. I had to have him, had to feel him deep inside of me. He lifted my ass off the desk, drawing me closer, spreading my legs wider, leaving me open, and allowing him plenty of room to pound inside of me. There was nothing gentle about his strokes and I was glad. They were deep, hard and arousing. I wanted it to last forever, but in reality I wasn't sure how much longer I could hold on without screaming in ecstasy at the top of my lungs and Mia hearing me.

"I wanna watch you come again," he growled and brought a hand down between us and grazed his thumb across my clit. Max was staring down at me, eyes, dark and hooded. I was thrashing around like a wild woman on the desk, knocking supplies onto the floor. And then he changed his rhythm to short quick strokes as his fingers continued to caress me. A loud cry escaped my lips and Max followed, the two of us moaning and crying out with pleasure. It sounded so good. I eventually collapsed while his shudders and groans went on and on until finally his body went limp on top of mine.

"You got me," he said in a lazy, satisfied voice.

I wasn't sure what he meant. Well, I had ideas but I

decided to ignore the comment, instead my fingers slid up and down his back. Max lifted slightly, easing some of his weight off of me, then kissed the sides of my face and neck.

"I hope you don't have thin walls."

I giggled, because I'm sure Mia had heard quite a bit, but she would never admit it if she had. "That's the beauty of owning your own business," I managed between breaths. "You can do what you want to do."

Max chuckled and rose. I unlocked my ankles and sat up on the desk. "Okay bossy lady." He winked. "You have somewhere I can—"

"There a bathroom behind that door." I said cutting him off and pointed to the far corner. One of the things we loved about the storefront suite was the half-bathrooms in each of the offices.

Once he was gone, I slid off the desk. This craziness that was going on inside of me didn't make any sense. One minute I was saying no then the next my body was tingling and begging for him to take me like a caveman.

I adjusted my skirt and reached down for the trash can and started cleaning up our little picnic. There was still lemon pound cake waiting to be eaten. I smiled thinking about how Max had taken the time to find out what my likes were. Oh, he knew exactly what he was doing and I was no fool. I wanted to be with him just as badly as he wanted to be with me. There was no denying it. I wanted that gorgeous man all to myself, except for that one thing standing in my way.

I cleared the containers and was folding up the blanket when I heard buzzing coming from his blue jeans that were still on the floor. I know I had no business being nosy but I couldn't help myself. I made sure the bathroom door was still closed, then I kicked his jeans to the side and his cell phone slid out of his pocket. With my foot, I turned the phone over and stared down at the screen. And I got angry all over again.

Parker was calling him. I knew it was her because the picture he had saved was staring me right smack in the face.

Stupid.

I felt like an idiot for giving in to his picnic seduction and even more ridiculous for spreading my legs. I was truly embarrassed. I struggled enough as it was trying to fight my feelings for Max and then all was forgotten by simply being in his presence. What the hell was wrong with me?

I picked up my panties and tossed them in my drawer. There was no way I could put those back on.

The door flung open and Max came out smiling. He is so cocky. I guess he had every reason to be since he had gotten exactly what he had come for.

"You got a brotha strutting around like a peacock," Max joked. I swallowed when I spotted his dick swinging between his legs.

"Parker called," I said and then turned my back.

Max had one leg in his boxers when he came over and wrapped his arms around my middle. "Don't start," he warned.

I wiggled free. "I'm not starting anything. Like I said, nothing has changed. Thank you for lunch and great sex, but I've a cake to design."

He raised a brow gave me a long intense stare as he slipped his legs inside of his jeans. "So it's like that now?"

"It's like what?" I shrugged. "What we have is fun, but that's all it is. That's all it can ever be," I replied hoping to wrap up the conversation and send him on his way.

Max shook his head like I was the one being ridiculous. "I'm not about to argue with you, Claudia. Not when I'm in such a good mood." Before I could stop him, he swooped in and caught my lips in a deep sensual kiss. I took a moment to enjoy it before I broke it off. Of course it was at that moment his phone started vibrating again. Max picked it up off the floor but not before I saw it was Parker calling him.

I started fuming. "I guess you better go see what she wants. I've got work to do." I rushed to the bathroom without another word and shut the door. By the time I had cleaned myself up and came out, Max was gone.

* * *

The rest of the day I was a mess. My body was still

humming, my nipples were aroused and my mind was flooded with images of Max down on his knees, staring up at me as he ate me out. Damn, I'm still shivering as I remembered how good his tongue had felt stroking along my kitty kat.

Thank goodness I kept an extra change of clothes in the closet because my skirt was wrinkled, panties were torn and soaked. While I was creating doves for the cake, cum was still sliding down my thighs. I made several trips to the ladies room, wiping away evidence that Max had put in his work again.

Why is it you always fall for the one you can't have or don't want? As I completed that thought I knew I wasn't being totally honest. I wanted Max with my last breath, and he wanted me. The problem was he was wrong for me. I wanted a simple man and there was nothing simple at all about Max. He was complex and his baby mama only complicated things even more. All I could do on the ride home from work was think about what if things were different? What if he didn't have a baby on the way? Would we be together? And the answer sung in my heart a high-pitched, hell yes! Life would be so much fun, exciting, I don't think I would ever have a dull moment with Max in my life. But the baby was something I just wasn't sure I could deal with.

I made it into the house, kicked off my shoes and padded down the hall to my bedroom. My panties were off before I had even hit the door and I tossed them in the washer machine at the end of the hall. Oh, they were definitely moist. Two pair in one day, I was going to have to invest in panty liners. Max stayed on my mind the rest of the evening. By the time I had finished eating a Lean Cuisine meal, I was staring at my phone and trying to convince myself not to pick it up and dial. By seven, I finally gave up and sent Max a text message.

THANKS FOR LUNCH.

There… I did it. I pushed the phone away and decided to get lost in a book. I reached for Sasha Campbell's latest release, *Consequences*. That was one author who sure knew how to write some drama. Any other time I would have been all caught up into finding out how the story unfolded, but instead I kept looking over at my phone for a text, which was crazy since my phone would chime like a bell upon receipt. After a while I started to get pissed. Why hadn't he texted me back? And then my mind started playing tricks on me and I started wondering if he and Parker were together. I don't know why I even cared, but yet and still I did. I reread the same page three times and was finally flipping the page when my phone vibrated. I practically jumped off the couch.

I SHOULD BE THE ONE THANKING YOU FOR LUNCH... IT WAS MIGHTY TASTY.

Why was my coochie tingling as I read into the meaning of his message? Max was so damn nasty and yet I liked it. I liked it a lot. My phone vibrated again.

TOU

I texted him back.

WHAT DOES THAT MEAN?

Max texted right back.

THINKING OF YOU.

I was just about to type TOU2 when I had to stop myself. What the hell was I doing starting something that I had no intentions of finishing?

I tossed my phone aside and reached for the remote. I had recorded the latest episode of Ballers and I was dying to see what happened next. Denzel Washington's son was definitely some kind of cute. He and The Rock were definitely the distraction I needed, because Max was under my skin and I had to find a way to get him out from under me.

I wasn't going to message him no matter how tempting it was, I would wait until Max reached out to me again.

THIRTEEN

Three days later, I still hadn't contacted Max. Unfortunately, neither had he. Not a single word from Max, and I had this sinking feeling he had finally gotten tired of the rejection and decided to move on. I should have been happy at the possibility, and instead, I was in a panic. It was crazy, but I loved it when he was trying to get my attention. Even though I behaved as if I wasn't interested, but in reality I really was interested in more ways than I truly cared to admit. And that's what scared me.

Somehow I endured a long weekend without hearing from him. Thank goodness I had a wedding cake to design and a blown art sculpture of a schoolhouse which took me practically all day Sunday to create, requiring my undivided attention. However once I was done with my creations, I was back at home thinking about Max.

Sunday evening I sent him the text message that had been sitting in my phone.

TOU2

But by time I had gotten back from lunch on Monday, I still hadn't heard from him. And I was fuming.

"Okay, I've been trying to go over this menu with you for the last half hour and you're not paying me the slightest bit of attention. What's going on with you?"

Christina's voice snapped me back to the present. I looked at her, blinking. She was right. I'd been so busy thinking about Max and hadn't heard a word she said. "I'm sorry. My mind is somewhere else."

"Missing Max already?" she teased while twirling the cocoa-colored beads dangling around her neck.

Despite the way my heart was pounding at the mention of his name, I faked a frown. "No, not at all. I wish he'd just leave me alone."

As always, she didn't appear at all happy with my

response. "I don't know why you don't give him a chance. He earns just as much money selling his songs as those doctors and lawyers you date."

I swiveled around on the chair. "What did you just say?" I needed clarification.

"Selling his songs." Her brow rose. "You didn't know he was a songwriter?"

"I knew he wrote songs but I didn't know he wrote *sellable* songs." Of course Christina looked pleased that she knew something I didn't. "Ummm, I'm gonna need for you to explain."

"Dee says Max has been writing songs for a long time. He has a song on Jodeci's new album. He's written for Iggy Azalea and even Usher."

My jaw felt like it had hit the floor. "I had no idea."

"Don't the two of you talk?" she questioned.

"Yes, we talk!" I barked and realized how defensive I must have sounded when her brow arched. "But I guess when he told me he dibble-dabbled in song writing I didn't realize how in-depth he really meant." Damn! Am I that shallow that I never asked Max about something I knew he was obviously passionate about? "I just thought he was a contractor who had a passion for music."

Christina shook her head. "Yes, just like I had no idea Dereon was a cop."

"Yeah I guess so." It had taken her months to find out Dereon was working undercover. Before, she had sworn he was a drug dealer.

"You do know he's in Atlanta meeting with Jermaine Dupre this week, right?"

"*What*? When did he leave for Atlanta?"

Her elbows were resting on her desk. "On Saturday. Dereon dropped him off at the airport."

"No wonder I haven't heard from him," I mumbled under my breath.

Christina leaned in and searched for any kind of reaction. Well, she wasn't getting one. "He should be back either Thursday or Friday."

I looked at her and rolled my eyes then reached for a pen. "C'mon, let's get back to work."

"Uh-Uh… You're pissed." She stared me down.

"Hell yeah, I'm pissed! He came to my office, ate my damn pussy and then didn't even bother to tell me he was leaving town."

"Is that what you two were doing in there?" Christina exploded with laughter. I didn't mean to divulge so much information but I was just too upset to be thinking straight.

"Not once did he mention he was going out of town!"

She grinned wickedly. "As angry as you are, the brotha must have skills."

Christina gave me this look and next thing I knew I was laughing. "Oh, trust me. The man is good!" She started laughing as well. It was either laugh or I was going to start screaming. "I still can't believe he didn't tell me."

"Why should he?" Christina said and sobered quickly. "Either you want the man or you don't."

"Wha…What are you talking about?" I squawked.

She sat there with her arms crossed against her pink cashmere sweater. "You heard me. You want his itinerary but then you don't want anything to do with him. Make up your mind, Claudia."

She was right but I wasn't ready to admit to anything. Not just yet.

"I'm serious," she snarled with attitude. "If you want that man then you better get him before someone else does."

I was pissed off and Christina knew it. I closed my eyes and rubbed my face with my hands. I just didn't want to think about Max being with anyone else even though I wasn't sure yet if I wanted him to myself.

"Did I tell you Isaiah was back?" I waited for my words to register and then it was her turn to be stunned.

"What? When?"

I knew my ex-boyfriend was just what I needed to change the subject. "Mommy said he just got back and interviewed at Barnes Jewish Hospital."

"Have you seen him yet?" Her eyes were dancing with

curiosity.

I shook my head. "No… not yet."

Christina leaned back on the chair. "Sooo, you going to see him?" she pressed and turned her brown eyes on me.

As I crossed my legs, I nodded. "He asked about me. Mom invited him over for Daddy's birthday party, but I think he and I need to meet in private first."

"Definitely. You don't need an audience," Christina said shaking her head and sending her expensive weave bouncing flawlessly. "Ooh I can't wait to see him!"

I shivered at the thought of seeing Isaiah. At one time he had been the love of my life. How would I feel when I did see him again? "No, I think I'm going to reach out to him before the weekend and ask him out to lunch or something."

"I would love to see him! I'm surprised he's still single."

I was also surprised. I would have thought after all these years he would have hooked one of the nurses or maybe even another doctor who had worked abroad.

"Nope, Mommy said he's still single and ready to finally settle down."

She tossed me a dirty look. "Damn girl. What if he wants to continue where you left off?"

That wasn't possible. I wasn't the same person anymore and I was sure he wasn't either. "I don't know." Because I really didn't. I thought that part of my life had been over. Years ago, I stopped dreaming of my ex coming back to St. Louis and the two of us having a do-over.

"Who knows… in the end you might have two men fighting over you." Christina held up two fingers to emphasize my position.

For a second there I had forgotten about Max, but all it took was the mention of him and my entire body started to vibrate. What I felt for Max, I had never come close to feeling with Isaiah even though I had loved him with all my heart. Maybe those feelings for Max were just lust.

One could only hope.

I had a site visit to do, so I left shortly after and headed downtown to a Women's Alliance Council Meeting. The president wanted to hold a retirement party for her mother at the center to celebrate forty years as a nurse. The entire time I was taking a tour of the banquet room and kitchen, she gave me details of the type of meal they wanted catered, I found myself comparing Max to Isaiah. They were definitely day and night but there was something about them both I had found attractive.

By the time I was heading home, I was scrolling through my contacts until I found the number my mother had given me earlier in the week and dialed.

"Hello?"

There was that familiar voice I had fallen in love with so many years ago, but instead of it being panty-drenching deep, it made me smile.

"Hey Isaiah, it's CC."

"Claudia…, what a nice surprise!" He actually sounded happy to hear from me. I couldn't resist a smile.

"The same here. Mom told me you were back in St. Louis, I couldn't believe it."

"Yes, I'm ready to settle down. Buy a house… and start a family."

I managed to keep the bitterness from my voice, even though at this point in our life we should have been thinking about starting a family. "I guess better late than never."

"I'm hoping it isn't too late," he said and then paused, catching me completely by surprise. The Isaiah I remembered had never been that straight forward. I was right. He had changed. I tried to contain my excitement.

"How about we get together for lunch?"

I could hear Isaiah's breathing getting heavier. "I would like that very much. I'm flying out in the morning to speak at a symposium in San Francisco, but I'll be back on Friday. May I call you when I get back?"

"Yes, absolutely."

I ended the call and was smiling the rest of the way home. See, maybe there's hope after all.

It wasn't until I got back in the house that my mind strayed back to Max. Okay, I'm lying. I hadn't been able to think of anything else but him, which was why I had called Isaiah in the first place. I still couldn't believe he had left town without telling me. In fact, by the time I got done taking a shower, I couldn't stop myself from texting him.

OUT OF TOWN? WOW! REALLY?

It wasn't until after I had hit Send that I regretted the message. Oh my God! I was acting like a raging lunatic and sounded like some jealous girlfriend.

Thank goodness, Isaiah was going to be back in town. I needed a distraction and I needed it now.

FOURTEEN

By Friday I was pissed. Max never responded to my text. Can you believe that? He had totally blown me off. Me…Claudia Ciara Winters. I was so mad I had to catch myself from snapping out on the chick at the lunch counter for giving me the wrong amount of change.

I decided to go by the renovation site and talk to Trey and find out when Max was expected to return. I know Christina had said Thursday or Friday and I guess I wanted to see if he was already back, even though that wasn't going to do anything but piss me off even more.

If my memory served me right, Max had said they were working on a two-family apartment building on Geyer Street near Soulard Farmers Market. I drove around the block a couple of times looking for the house that looked under construction and spotted Trey out front painting the trim.

I parked my Range Rover in front of the building, then walked up the sidewalk. Trey was smiling down at me from the nine-foot ladder.

"Whassup, Claudia? I didn't get a chance to catch up with you at the party."

He was handsome with the whitest teeth. Rich mahogany skin stretched over chiseled cheekbones. He was truly going to make someone a happy woman. "No problem. The party was packed. I didn't get a chance to mingle with everyone myself."

"What are you doing around here?"

I tried to shrug and act like it was no big deal. "I was over at the market and remembered you all were working in the area and decided to ride by and check it out. Very nice." Damn I was good. Trey looked like he believed me so that was really all that mattered. "How old is this house?"

"It was built in eighteen-eighty-five. It was a total gut job." I took a moment to take in the brick structure. There were white shutters on each of the windows. The front door was a bright yellow.

"There are two bedrooms in both units."

I nodded as I admired the space. It would make a great place for someone who wanted to be in walking distance of shopping, restaurants and bars.

"Hey, Claudia."

I looked up as another incredibly handsome, dark chocolate man with cornrows and a sexy goatee stepped out the door. "How have you been?" he said in a low masculine voice.

"Hi Reggie. How's Berlin doing?"

He had large sepia eyes and the deepest dimples when he smiled. "Cranky and moody."

Trey gave a rude snort. "She was like that long before she was pregnant."

"Ha-ha, I see you got jokes." Reggie scowled, then looked back at me. "Berlin's starting to adjust to the idea of being a mom."

"Please tell her I said hi. When you get a chance give me a call and I'll make her another batch of truffles."

"I definitely will." He turned and looked up at Trey. "Brax and I are about to hang those doors as soon as Dee get back."

He nodded. "I'll be up to help in a minute."

"When's Max getting back?" I blurted. I couldn't help it. I was dying to know.

Trey grinned, then he looked past me and tilted his head. "There he is now."

"What?" My head whipped around in a panic. The last thing I wanted was for him to see me here. Now he really was going to think I was stalking him.

A black Escalade pulled in front of the house and three drop-dead gorgeous men stepped out. Dereon, Braxton, and Max.

My stomach did a slow roll and I was sure my tongue was

hanging out of my mouth. Goodness. Max was wearing khakis that emphasized his powerful thighs and an orange Polo shirt that showed off how absolutely yummy his body was. I couldn't have run if I wanted to, instead my feet were firmly planted to the ground.

"Yo, look who we found waiting at the airport with his thumb out like a hobo!" Dereon joked as the three strolled across the lawn.

"Whatever man! Yo, Reggie, man. When I told Dee I brought back a few buckets of Garrett's Popcorn, he broke his neck to pick me up."

"Hell yeah. You know that's my shit," Dereon said and gave him a playful elbow to the ribs.

They were going back and forth and even Trey and Reggie chimed in, but I didn't hear a word they were saying. All my attention was on Max and when he met my eyes and moved toward me, my breath stalled.

He was smiling, showing off beautiful pearly white teeth. A diamond earring was in his left earlobe and a dimple dented his right cheek. "What's up, CC?" he said as he scooped me up into his arms and swooped in for a kiss.

For the life of me, I had no intention of kissing him back, really I didn't, but once I felt his hard chest against my body and those big powerful arms, drawing me toward him, I was a goner. Not to mention his lips were so lethal I had no choice just to part mine with a moan and allow his tongue to slip inside.

"Oh hell no! Y'all not about to do that shit here!"

Max drew back and gave Dereon a hard look. "You got a lot of nerve."

The gang roared with laughter and the sound shook me back to reality. I was supposed to be mad at Max, not making out with him.

"Put me down," I ordered.

He swung around and kissed me one last time before planting me back on my feet. "You couldn't wait to see me?"

I drew back. I couldn't believe how arrogant he sounded. So why did his cockiness turn me on so much? "I had no idea you were coming home today."

"Sure you didn't." Don't you know he had the nerve to laugh.

I pointed at my chest. "I was at the market and decided to swing by on my way home."

"Really? What did you buy?"

Oh damn. I wasn't expecting that. "What does it matter? I'm leaving now." I started walking away, but of course he scooped me up and carried me to my Range Rover.

"Put me down!"

"I will in a minute. Relax."

I was squirming in his arms trying to get him to release me. The crew shook their heads, chuckled and went back to work. I needed to get away from Max. Being against him just felt too damn good. He wouldn't let me go until we were at the curb leaning against my vehicle.

"Pop the locks."

"Why?" I asked even though I was pushing the button. As soon as there was a click he reached for the handle and opened the door.

"Get in," he ordered.

"I asked you why?" I said as I climbed inside.

"Because I need a ride home." Before I could protest, he closed the door, walked around and grabbed his things from the Escalade, then hopped in on my passenger's seat.

"I don't want to take you home." I was being a brat, but so what.

"Now it's my turn to ask why?"

"Why? Because I'm mad at you."

I put the car into Drive and headed down the street.

"Yo, CC. What are you mad about?"

I just stared out the windshield and kept driving.

"So now you're gonna ignore me?"

"Nope, I'm going to drive you home."

He chuckled.

"What's so funny?"

"You, boo." He slid low on the seat and I caught my eyes wandering over to stare at his crotch. What was wrong with me? I was supposed to be angry?

"I heard you're a songwriter."

"You heard right." he said just as easily as if I had asked him the time.

"Good for you." There was that sarcasm again.

I reached over and turned on satellite music. Thank goodness Nicki Minaj was rapping nice and loud. Max was apparently a fan because he was dancing on the seat, which looked extremely sex. The man had rhythm and had me feeling wet in all the right places, but I was determined to stay angry at him.

"I met Nicki once."

"Hmmm...."

"Yeah I was at an awards banquet for a single I had written for Kelly Rowland's last album, and she—"

"How come you didn't tell me you were a songwriter?" I finally blurted because there was no way I was going to ride in the car with him a moment longer without understanding why.

"I did tell you I dabbled with music."

"*Dabble*? Writing songs for celebrities, there is nothing small about that."

He shrugged. "It pays the bills."

"Obviously." There was that sarcasm again. "I guess I wasn't privy to this information."

"Nope, that's not it. I just didn't think you cared," he commented with a shrug.

I tore my eyes away from the traffic and glared at him. "What made you think that?"

"C'mon babe. You haven't made things easy for me. I try to get close to you and all you've been doing is throwing shade my way."

I decided not to answer because what he said was true. But I had my reasons.

We were silent the rest of the ride. I pulled in front of his house and left the motor running.

Max opened the door and stepped out. "Get out."

There he was, bossing me around again.

I shook my head. "No, I have things to do."

"CC…, get out the car." There was a lethal warning in his voice. I either get out on my own or he was coming to get me. That really wasn't a bad idea. Only I wanted to make the decision. I blew out a long breath, cut off the vehicle, then climbed out and shut the door. With my arms crossed, I leaned back against my SUV. Max stepped off the curb, came around to my side and I glared at him.

"Okay, I'm out. Now what?"

"Talk to me."

I said nothing.

"Tell me why I piss you off so much, because I really don't have a clue." His eyes twinkled with amusement.

I shrugged. "I don't know. You just do." My comment snatched the grin from his lips.

Max moved in until his knees brushed against my thighs. "Hey," he began and reached up and tilted my chin so I was looking at him. As I stared into his eyes I felt my body melting. "CC, what do you want from me?"

I swallowed and blurted from the heart. "I want nothing and everything."

"You got me babe." Max pinned me against the door and the feel of his body caused an ache to start between my thighs. "You have no idea." He captured my lips in a hard kiss that stole my breath away, his woody scent filling my nostrils.

With a mind of its own, my back arched, drawing me even closer. All resistance faded and it was all about how good Max tasted. I loved the way he kissed, fluid and confident, tongue dipping inside, stroking and coaxing, causing me to moan and my body to heat all over. The kiss deepened and I wrapped my arms around his neck and I tilted my head, giving him better access. His hands were at either side of my head, pressed against the glass, holding me still. I gave in to his touch and the savory taste of his mouth. How was it, this man controlled my mind and my heart? What Max wanted, Max got every time, and I was a willing participant.

When he finally drew back I grumbled and protested because I should have been the one ending the kiss, not him.

I looked up at Max, staring down at me. His eyes were dark and unreadable. I was breathing hard and feeling squeamish almost.

"Do you want me?" Even though his voice was soft and gentle, his question was direct and to the point.

How could he ask me a question like that after a kiss like that? My mind was scattered and my body heated, and aroused.

"And I'm not talking about just sex, Claudia. I want to know if we have a future."

"I don't know… I don't know," I murmured, because there was still the issue of Parker and the baby and like I'd said before, it was hard to think straight with him this close. "Can we just leave it about sex for now?"

He let out a loud playful growl then lifted me into his arms. "You are a hard ass, you know that?"

I rested my hands on his shoulders and purred, "I thought you liked my ass?"

"Hell yeah and I'm getting ready to tap that ass."

Laughing, I wrapped my legs around his waist as he carried me to the house and up to the front porch. I slid to my feet while he opened the door, then followed him inside. My eyes traveled appreciatively around the fabulous foyer while he disarmed his alarm.

"Where'd you find the artwork?"

He tossed his keys on a green table and followed my gaze. There were several unique urban paintings with vivid images of African-American children playing in the hood, hanging on the walls. "I was at an art show where I met this new artist and ended up buying all those pieces hanging there."

"You, at an art show?" My brow quirked. "She must have been cute." I tried to hide my jealousy, but I don't think I did a good job.

Smiling Max came over and wrapped his arms around me. "Lacey is tall, exotic looking, and very beautiful," he whispered and planted kisses at my neck. "She's also married to a recording artist that I've been working with under a recording label I'm launching."

I'd be lying if I didn't say I felt relieved. Call me selfish, but I didn't want to share Max with anyone.

He took my hand and led me up the stairs and once we reached his room, he dragged my shirt over my head.

"You don't waste any time, do you?" I teased.

"This is just about sex, right?" He winked.

I guess I put my foot in my mouth on that one. "Oh yes, definitely."

He unclasped the front hook on my bra and my breasts spilled free. "Good. I haven't seen you all week. Now I'm getting ready to tap that ass." He pushed the bra over my shoulders and down my arms.

"I was thinking maybe we could talk first. I wanna hear how your trip went."

His eyes were already focused on my breasts. "The trip was great."

"Well..., did you sell your song?" I hissed at the end when he reached out and captured a nipple between his finger and thumb.

"Yes, I sold my song."

"And then you just mentioned starting a recording label..." A moan, long and deep, escaped from between my lips. "Damn, I'm trying to show I care," I whispered while wetness moistened my inner thighs.

"Later, baby. Right now, I need to taste you." Max dipped his head and took a breast into his mouth.

"Oh God!" His lips felt so good suckling away at my nipple that I struggled to keep from falling onto the bed. Max was teasing and sucking with his luscious lips and I felt the powerful sensation right smack between my legs. The throbbing became intense, powerful with every swipe of his tongue and teeth.

"Since it's just about sex, I need to make sure you're pleased," he whispered. His breath was warm and wet against my flesh. My nipple was raw by the time he traveled over to the other breast. Desire raced through my veins all the way down to my kitty. Max latched on and suckled hungrily.

"Max," I gasped and then he was teasing and nibbling

while his hand came up to give my other breast equal attention. Oh my, his fingers were magical!

I was growing hotter and wetter by the second while his fingers rolled and plucked at my nipple and I couldn't even think straight. Max brought his lips to mine, which only increased the throbbing between my legs. I moved in closer, arching my body until my pelvis cradled the large erection straining beneath his zipper. His fingers came around to unfasten my pants and I was so desperate to have him, I did the same. My fingers quickly unfastened his belt and reached for the zipper of his khakis. He had my slacks down at my ankles, and then released me long enough for each of us to shed the rest of our clothes. My hands frantically pulled down my panties at the exact moment he removed his boxers for my viewing pleasure.

"Look a there," I purred and playfully licked my lips.

"You want this?" he said wrapping his hand around the entire girth and closed the space between us.

I bit my lips, trying to be coy and sexy. "Oh yes, I want it. The question is do you want this?" I asked and stroked my kitty.

"You forget…you already gave it to me." He pulled me into his arms and palmed my ass.

"I did?" I was good at playing dumb.

"Yep, my name is written all over that pussy." He urged me forward, pushing my legs open wide. The need to be one with him overwhelmed me and suddenly I just couldn't get enough of his touch, taste, whatever. I dragged his mouth down to mine and kissed him with all of the passion that had been simmering over the past few days. He pushed my lips apart and drew deeper inside my mouth. He kissed me, licked me, sucked at my tongue, and yet it still wasn't enough. I wanted more. A helluva lot more.

Max lifted me off my feet and I brought my legs up around his waist and his stomach rubbed against my sensitive folds.

"Awww!" I cried out at the sudden contact.

The friction of the fine hairs on his stomach against my

clit worked me to the point I wasn't sure if I could take anymore. I threw my head back as pleasure vibrated up my throat.

Max tossed me playfully onto the bed and I giggled and stared up at him still standing near the edge. "What are you waiting on?" I asked and then noticed his erection throbbing in my direction. "Hmm, I think I know of what you're waiting for." Smiling, I slid down until my legs were dangling over the side of his massive bed.

I reached out and brushed my thumb across the chocolate head. Max groaned as I swirled the precum all around the tip. Then I leaned forward and took a lick.

"Shit, that's good," he hissed and gripped the top of my head and started guiding me not that I needed any help. I slid my lips up and down his length, then swallowed him deep down my throat, sucking, nibbling, and teasing for a few heart-pounding moments. Our eyes met, locked and I didn't stop. I wanted him to see how much I enjoyed having his penis inside my mouth.

"You like that?" I coaxed.

"Hell yeah," he hissed. "You got skills."

"I'm just getting started," I announced with his dick still between my lips. Then I took him as deep as I could, teasing the head, nibbling then suckling some more.

"Babe, stop… stop! I don't wanna come inside your mouth," Max warned then pulled away.

I leaned back on the bed, grinning as I swiped the back of my hand across my lips. "You're ruining all the fun."

"The fun is just beginning." Max pushed me onto the mattress and spread my thighs apart. "Now wrap your legs around me."

I did as he said and then Max drove into me with enough force to make me arch off the bed.

"Oh baby," I moaned as I felt his full length.

I guess I was tight because Max groaned, then stilled for a moment. I felt the head of his penis pulsing inside me. "You feel so damned good; so tight and wet and hot."

See, I knew it.

"And you feel so huge." I brought my arms around his back and then started dropping kisses along his neck and shoulders.

Max adjusted his weight on top of my body, then brought his palms to my thighs and pressed down, spreading my legs even farther apart. I shifted slightly just as he plunged deep, and then withdrew, pulling out just shy of the head, then pushed forward again. He rotated his hips at a slow, teasing rhythm and waves of pleasure flowed through me.

"You like this dick?"

Like it? Shit, I loved it! I love it so much I hated to think about him doing to any other woman what he was doing to me. "Yes, I like it. Ooh baby, it's so good!"

Max was plunging deep again, sending a burst of fire racing through me.

"Tell me it's my pussy!" He pumped faster, driving me insane.

"It's yours," I cried. "It's your pussy." He pounded harder and I raked my nails down the length of his back. "Don't stop! Please don't stop," I whimpered. It was so good my eyes welled with tears. Lifting my hips, I drew him deeper and rocked my pelvis, meeting each pump with an upward pound of my own.

"Come for me babe. I need you to come." He sounded desperate like he was holding on to his own release waiting for me to get mine.

"Yes, yesss!" I cried out and felt his entire body tense as I came. "Yesss Max!"

"Oh shit!" he cried and I opened my eyes as he threw his head back and exploded in a loud groan that echoed in my ears. Every muscle in my body tightened and then I was shouting along with him, enjoying the final wave.

"C'mere." Max rolled onto his back and dragged me on top of him. My heart was pounding hard and so was his. I rested my cheek at the curve of his neck and savored the feel of his damp body. His thighs were on the outside of mine, and his cock still buried inside me. The head of his penis pulsed with each breath. As soon as my breathing slowed, I propped my head up with my hand and said in a soft voice, "Tell me about you and Parker. I want to know how the two of you met." What I really wanted to know was how she had ended up pregnant but I was sure he would get around to that.

Max stared up at the ceiling in deep thought. I got the impression what he was about to say was almost painful.

"We used to have the same foster mother."

That was not at all what I was expecting to hear. "Really? How did that work out?"

"Parker and I were in high school just trying to survive. We had both been bounced around so many times that neither of us wanted to do anything to get kicked out. Aunt Penny was actually pretty nice as long as you followed her rules." He grinned and I just waited because I was anxious for him to speed it up and get to the good part.

"I was already living with Aunt Penny when Parker came to live at the house and we got to be pretty close, like brother and sister."

I wanted to say brothers and sisters don't have sex, or at least they didn't in my house, but instead I continued to say nothing.

"Parker's mother was a stripper and her stepfather had been trying to climb into her bed ever since he and her mother got married. When she took a pair of pliers to his nuts, her mother put her out the house. Can you believe that shit?"

"It's sad but unfortunately it happens a lot." I was sure to see an episode this weekend on *Lifetime*.

"Anyway after I turned eighteen and left for college, she and I kept in touch. She was messing with a bunch of knuckleheads. By the time she had turned eighteen I tried to look out for her, even tried to get her to go to college with me so I could keep an eye on her so she wouldn't get caught up with some drug dealer because I knew that was where she was headed," he explained.

"And did she?" I asked because I was trying to hurry this story along.

"Yeah, but I stopped that shit cold. She lost her job waiting tables and I let her stay with me while she got herself together. We tried a relationship for a minute but it didn't work. Parker is needy and jealous and I couldn't take being accused every time I walked out the door of being with someone else."

Yeah, I could see that.

"Eventually she moved out on her own and was doing good until about seven months ago. She came over, upset about a break-up with a boyfriend. We got to drinking and one thing lead to another and the next thing I know we were in the bed having sex. The next day I had regrets and she did not. She had hoped we'd get back together. When I told her I no longer had feelings like that, Parker went off and I didn't hear from her again until the day she appeared on my doorstep to let me know she was carrying my seed." Max paused and dragged a hand down across his face. "This is really hard for me, because, as a man, I vowed if I ever had kids, I would always be there for them. Parker knows that better than anyone how I feel about taking care of my responsibilities. And that child is my responsibility until I find out otherwise." He then reiterated how he was certain the baby she was carrying wasn't his because he had used a condom.

I just hoped he was right.

The next question was hard to ask, but I felt like it had to be mentioned. "Have you ever thought about marrying her?" After all that was the right thing to do even if I couldn't stomach the idea.

Max hesitated long enough for me to know that he had.

"Oh boy!" I blew out a long breath and rolled onto my back.

"Hey." Max rolled toward me and stared into my eyes. "I honestly thought about doing the right thing and marrying Parker if for some slim chance that boy is mine. But then I told myself it wouldn't be fair to her or the child. And then you walked into my life and I terminated that idea."

I shook my head. "I don't want your decisions to be about me."

He gave a slight smirk. "It's too late for that. I'm crazy

about you."

"I..." My voice trailed off because Max had totally caught me off guard with that one.

"Why is it so hard for you to accept that I want you in my life? The days of juggling more than one woman and sleeping around are over. I want one special lady to come home to." Max was saying everything I wanted to hear and had my heart pounding like crazy.

"And I want just one man in my life," I whispered and couldn't have torn my eyes away from him even if I had tried.

Max brought a hand up to caress my cheek and I leaned into his touch and could feel my naked body starting to respond.

"Claudia, go out with me."

"What?" I searched his eyes and then started laughing but he was looking so serious.

"I want to take you out on a date."

I laughed. "A date? You act as if we've never done anything together before."

"I didn't say that. I said I want to take you out on our first real date."

He was staring down at me with those beautiful eyes that it took me a moment before I found the breath to say, "Sure, I would love to go out with you."

In fact there was no one else in the world I'd rather spend time with than him, and that scared the hell out of me.

FIFTEEN

I don't know why I was nervous. I mean, it wasn't as if Max and I hadn't been out together before, and yet I had tremors. My armpits were sweating and I couldn't get my mind right to save my life. I guess because things were officially different with us. There were no more games, no more avoiding the truth. Max and I were in a relationship.

Every time I thought about a man that gorgeous being all mine, I got goosebumps. Trust me, I've had relationships before but never anything quite that fine… and I do mean fine. Every time I thought about Max, which was practically all damn day, I had to pinch myself to make sure I wasn't dreaming. I truly was Maximilian's girl.

On Saturday, I spent most of the morning pampering myself, nails, hair, and bikini wax. I wanted to make sure when he saw me there was no doubt in his mind who he was dealing with—a one in a million kinda gal.

Christina and I headed to the West County mall and spent three hours scanning the racks until I found the perfect little black dress. Afterwards we were both starving and headed to the food court. Of course, Christina keeps antibacterial wipes in her purse and had to sanitize our table before she sat down. That girl was always good for laughs.

"Claudia, you're glowing?"

I arched an eyebrow. "Glowing?"

"Yes. Your face is shining and you look so happy." Christina was sipping her drink, being way too observant. I watched the way she was staring at me like she was trying to figure me out. "So is Max responsible for that glow?"

I took a bite of my grilled chicken sandwich and dropped my eyes so she couldn't read what I was feeling, or see the big smirk that was dying to curl my lips. "I'm looking forward to this evening," I replied and shrugged.

"Uh-uh, it's more to it than that." Christina was pointing all in my face as if she had just caught me with my skirt up. "You're falling in love and don't want to admit it."

I rolled my eyes because there was no way in hell I was allowing that thought to even infiltrate my mind. I had fallen in love too often with the wrong men for the wrong reasons and I refused to even let the word come into existence until I knew for sure where the relationship was going, and that the emotion was for real this time.

"I'm not like you," I retorted and quickly stuffed a fry into my mouth.

"Since when?" she said and had the nerve to have attitude. "We are more alike than you care to admit. And last I checked that was a good thing." She laughed and stabbed a fry with a fork. "You're crazy about Max." It wasn't a question; it was a statement. "Is that so wrong?"

"No." To be totally honest it felt amazing and that's what scared me. Now that Max and I talked and I had a chance to understand him better, I was finding it harder to ignore my feelings for him. "It's just been a long time since I've had a man—correction—my own man in my life."

"And he's fine and rich too! That's even better to have on your arm and call your own."

I giggled like I was back in high school. It felt good calling Max mine. And to think of all the years I had wasted dating men who weren't worthy, to have finally found someone who really wanted to be with me. Just thinking how lucky I was had my heart pounding like crazy beneath my breasts.

Christina startled me from my thoughts. "You didn't tell me where Max is taking you tonight?"

I shrugged and felt myself smiling all over again. "I don't know. He wouldn't tell me… he wants it to be a surprise."

Her eyes twinkled. "Look at Max trying to be mysterious!"

I started laughing with her. "Yeah, that man is full of surprises."

She gave a rude snort. "If he's anything like Dereon, you'll get all dressed up and he's taking you to White Castle."

We roared with laughter.

I shook my head. "No, he told me, dress to kill."

We finished our lunch and I went home, napped, and then it was time to get ready. I showered, sprayed on my favorite fragrance, *For Her,* then slid into my outfit. The simple Christian Dior black dress fit me perfectly, clinging to my curves like a second layer of skin. It showed off my small waist and round breasts while revealing quite a bit of cleavage. There was no way Max would be able to keep his eyes off of me.

At eight there was a soft knock at the door. I had just slipped into a pair of red and white candy striped heels. I took one last look in the mirror, then hurried down the stairs and flung it open.

"Ms. Winters?"

My jaw dropped when I spotted a round, bald white guy on my porch, and the black limousine parked out in front of my house. "Did Max send you?"

He nodded. "Yes, and your chariot awaits." He held out his arm and escorted me down the stairs. I waited for him to open the door and then I slipped inside expecting to find Max, only it was empty.

"Where is Max?"

"I'm taking you to Mr. James."

Mr. James? What in the world was going on?

The chauffeur shut the door and I watched him walk around and climb behind the driver's seat. As soon as he started the limo, soft jazz filled the air.

Grinning, I leaned back against the leather-cushioned seat, feeling like Cinderella on her way to the ball. I couldn't believe Max had had a limousine pick me up from the house. I quickly removed my cell phone from a small clutch purse and texted Christina. She was going to freak out when she found out. Limos and Max were two things I never expected to say in the same sentence. I was starting to think more and more I had the dude pegged so wrong.

During the entire ride, I sat there thinking about Max and how much I liked him. I mean I really, really liked him. He was full of surprises, had an amazing personality, and treated me like a queen, but most importantly he had my back. The parking lot attack had proven that. I would be a fool to not want to be with a man like him.

So then what's the problem?

The problem was Parker. I know, I know. That whole baby mama mess, I just needed to push that aside, wait, and worry about it once the baby was born. Only that was easier said than done. But for now—at least until the baby was born—I was going to enjoy Max and see where our relationship led. Maybe, just maybe in the end, Parker and the baby would no longer matter to me. Or better yet, the baby would turn out not to be his. One could only hope.

The driver pulled off in one of downtown St. Louis's trendiest nightlife areas with restaurants and nightclubs that were regularly crowded until the wee hours of the morning. Back in the day I was right there making sure I was a part of the scene, but I guess I'd gotten tired of that life and now preferred a quiet and more intimate setting. However, when the chauffeur pulled in front of *Mystery*, a restaurant slash nightclub, I felt myself getting excited. I'd heard about the new, happening spot and had been meaning to check it out but never had the chance. Now it seemed I was going to be able to peek inside.

He parked, then came around, opened the door and helped me out the limousine. Pointing toward the door, he said, "Please go inside, Mr. James is waiting."

"Thank you." I gave him a three finger wave then turned and stared at the big sign flashing over the door. *Mystery.* Yep that would sum up my evening so far because Maximilian James was blowing my mind.

I smoothed out the front of my dress and moved toward the building where a man, wearing a dark suit was standing outside.

"Welcome," he greeted and then held the door open for me.

I stepped inside and was immediately caught up in the vibe. A knot of excitement coiled in my chest. There was an acoustic singer on stage sounding every bit like Corinne Bailey Rae, and the sound had me rocking my hips. My eyes swept the place. It was crowded. All of the tables were full, and the seats around the two bars were gone. The cornerstone restaurant was clean with modern designs and slanted windows, overlooking the brightly lit city streets. I was impressed.

"Welcome, do you have reservations?"

I gave the hostess a weird look because I wasn't sure and I noticed all the others sitting in the lobby waiting for a table. "I'm meeting someone here," I explained. Hopefully, Max had already arrived.

"Name please."

"Maximilian James."

As soon as I said his name her hazel eyes lit up with recognition. "Yes, of course. Claudia, right?"

"Yes," I replied. Max had left my name with the hostess and she made it her business to remember. *Talk about class.* If the food was as good as the service, I would definitely be back.

"Follow me," she instructed with a wave of a heavily jeweled hand.

As I brushed past a group, waiting to be seated, some skinny chick rolled her eyes at me. She obviously didn't like that I was being seat, while she had to wait.

Not my problem.

The hostess led me across the floor to an elevated section of the restaurant at the right of the stage. It had to be VIP. There were only about eight linen covered tables on that level. I climbed the four carpeted steps and followed her to an empty round table in front. "Please have a seat. Your waiter should be with you shortly." She smiled at me once more before she left.

I took a seat and was feeling so special. Limo service, VIP seating, and wonderful music, it couldn't possibly get any better than this. Max had definitely earned himself an extra serving of CC tonight.

The waiter came and poured wine into my glass and then I ordered mushrooms stuffed with crab for an appetizer while I waited. I was sipping from the flute and enjoying the performance when I looked up and spotted Maximilian coming my way. Oh damn! I had never seen him look so good. The crisp gray suit was well-fitted and showed off his broad shoulders and tapered waist. I let my eyes travel up and down his frame. *Goodness, remodeling houses does a body good.* Max was gorgeous, his nutty-brown features masculine, and beautiful but his appeal went beyond his fabulous body. It was his charisma and confidence that had drawn me to him, and his dick that had me hypnotized. Max was definitely one of a kind. And I was out on a date with him.

I swallowed. My heart was beating rapidly beneath my breasts and my throat was so dry I had to take another sip of wine.

"You made it," he said in greeting as he climbed onto the platform. My hands were sweating by the time he came over and dropped a kiss to my lips. And when Max finally lowered onto the chair across from me, my body was on fire.

"You are full of surprises, you know that?"

Max winked and looked so cocky, but like I said that was one thing I liked most about him. "I like to keep things interesting."

"Well, you're definitely doing that." I had to practically drag my eyes from his gorgeous face and forced myself to look around. "This place is nice. I've heard a lot about it but hadn't had a chance to check it out."

He poured himself a glass of wine as he spoke. "I'm glad you're here. Tonight is our amateur night when we allow new talent to showcase their skills."

"Hold up! Did I just hear you say *ours*? You work here?" I looked at him cockeyed.

He raised the flute to his lips, took a sip and then gave me a perfect-ass smile as he replied, "No… I'm a silent partner."

I practically choked on my wine. "Wait a minute! Back it up." I held up my hand silencing him. "You're a contractor, a songwriter, and a restaurant slash club owner. Is there anything else you have forgotten to tell me?"

"No, I think that about sums it up." He winked at me over the rim of his glass and my heart rate kicked into overdrive. I always said I wanted a challenging relationship with a man who constantly kept me guessing, but this was starting to be a lot to digest all at once.

"How long have you owned this place?" I asked, returning his stare.

"We're getting ready to celebrate two years," he replied while staring down at my breasts. I knew he wouldn't be able to keep his eyes off of the cleavage in this dress. "You hungry?" Max asked.

"Very."

"Then I suggest the ribeye, garlic red potatoes and the succotash, and then there's peach cobbler for dessert."

My stomach growled. "Mmmm that sounds heavenly."

The waiter returned with my appetizer and took our order. I wasted no time fixing a plate and started eating. Max and I were talking about the club and the performers he had lined up for the week when there was a round of applause and the female singer left the stage.

I leaned in close so he could hear me. "She's really good."

"Yes, I signed her for my label last week. Will you excuse me?"

Signed her? What the hell was going on? I didn't even have a chance to ask before Max was rising from the chair. He reached inside his pocket for something that looked like a microphone and clipped it to the lapel of his jacket. While I chewed I stared up at him with curiosity.

"Can I have everyone's attention?"

Yes, that was a mic. His voice boomed across the floor. What in the world....?

"I want to thank all of you for coming out for amateur night. For me, this evening is exceptionally special because I'm in the presence of a very special lady."

I sat there frozen, unable to speak. No, he wasn't doing what I thought he was doing.

Max turned and looked down into my eyes. "Claudia, my

life has not been the same since you've walked into it, and I never want to know what it feels like to see you walk away."

I heard shocked whispers and gasps. I couldn't get a word around the lump of emotion in my throat. All I could do was nod and then he gave me this smile that made me feel like the luckiest woman in the entire state of Missouri. I wonder if he knew what was going through my mind at the moment. There were a few haters, throwing shade my way, but the rest of the guests in the restaurant started to clap and then Max leaned down and kissed me soundly on the lips. I was just too shocked to respond. The next thing I knew he was walking over to the small stage and taking a seat at another baby grand piano that I hadn't even noticed sitting off to the side.

As soon as Max's fingers hit the keyboard, the room quieted while he sang.

"Beautiful lady… you make my heart smile…"

Music drifted from the stage and I was shaking all over. His voice was beautiful and the song was so personal it sounded as if he had written it just for me. My throat tightened, tears stung my eyes. This felt like a dream and again I had to pinch myself and realize it was real. A gorgeous man was serenading me in front of hundreds of people.

When Max finally finished and rose from the bench, the crowd whistled and applauded, and then stood to their feet. I was crying and feeling so proud of him that by the time Max winked at me, I was racing onto the stage.

Max circled me with his arms and I wrapped mine around his neck and kissed him. I didn't care that everyone was looking. Leaning back, I said in a choked whisper, "I knew all along you were going to be trouble."

Tossing his head back, Max roared with laughter.

SIXTEEN

Max and I had been a couple for nearly two weeks. I spent most of the time designing pastries, while Max and the crew finished the renovations on their flip. However, every single night we spent either at my house or his, and it was like living in a sensual haze.

There were the intimate candlelit dinners, the weekends with breakfast in bed, and of course there was the amazing sex. Max really knew how to get under my skin and it scared me. Each and every time he showed me how much he cared, it terrified me. I wasn't used to someone wanting to hold my hand whenever we were out together, holding me tenderly while we curled up on the couch, and he cradled me close to his body as we slept. It's crazy, but I felt alive and more attuned with the world surrounding me in some weird way.

I rose on Saturday and headed quietly down to the kitchen to make breakfast, wearing Max's t-shirt. I loved wearing his clothes. Max was still sleeping and after the work he had put in last night, he had earned his rest.

I had left my purse on the couch in the living room. I started the coffee maker, then padded into the family room and reached inside my purse for my phone. I had a blown sugar display to create tomorrow for a promotion party on Monday and was waiting for my client to call me back with the color choices for her balloons. For some crazy reason, she couldn't make up her mind. I looked down at my phone and frowned when I didn't see any messages from her. However, I noticed another missed call from Isaiah. He was definitely persistent. With a sigh I pressed the key and listened to his message.

"Hey CC, I've been trying to reach you. Would love to get

together and have that meal we discussed."

As I deleted his message, I drew another long sigh. I needed to call Isaiah back and let him know having lunch and catching up would be great. However, I needed to be honest with him and let him know I had moved on and was now seeing someone else. Only I couldn't seem to find the guts to just call or text him. For some reason it was hard for me to close that chapter of my life, even though I knew I was with the man I wanted to be with. I dumped the phone back in my purse, reached for a small sketch pad I had brought with me, then carried it into the kitchen. I poured myself a cup of coffee, then opened the pad and started sketching a design that had been racing around in my head all morning. I had finished my second cup and was standing at the counter, brewing my third, when a pair of arms came around my waist. I jumped.

"Oh shit! You scared me."

"My bad." Max pressed his warm lips to my shoulder and kissed it. "What are you doing up so early?"

"I had a design in my head and I thought I would draw it while it was still fresh."

"Can I see it?"

There was nothing better than a man who was interested in my work. "Sure." I walked over to the table, reached for my sketch and handed it to him.

"What do you think?"

"This is like the children in my painting, big eyes, full lips. Yo, are you planning to do this with sugar?" I nodded. "How you do this?"

I reached up in the cabinet for another cup as I explained. "It took years of practice, but when blowing sugar the most important thing to remember is keeping the sugar warm and delaying it from crystalizing."

"I'm going to have to come down and watch you in action because you're definitely good at it."

"Thank you, babe." I reached for the carafe. "You want some coffee?"

He nodded and while I filled the mug I felt his hands slide underneath the t-shirt until my entire ass was in the palm of his hands.

"Coffee can wait. I rather have you instead."

I released a sigh but didn't even bother to answer.

Max spread my legs, parting my cheeks and lifted me up until my coochie was wide open. Before I could draw my next breath, he was buried deep inside of me.

"Oh baby," I moaned and fixing coffee was the last thing on my mind.

I braced my hands against the counter and then pushed out my ass ready for Max when he pulled back then buried himself again. Oh my, would I ever get tired of him being inside of me? His cock spread me wide and then Max pulled out to the head then plunged deep again.

"Damn, I love this pussy," he grounded from between his lips as he continued to pump inside of me.

"And I love this dick," I whimpered and then my breath caught as Max created a rhythm that I couldn't even begin to explain. Two pumps, then three. Powerful, then he eased back, allowing me to breath before he was plunging deep and hard again.

"Whose dick is it?" he coaxed.

"It's mine. All mine," I moaned.

Max stilled and I closed my eyes. He wasn't the only one trying to hold on. All I had been thinking and dreaming about is Max and I, fucking until I couldn't even think straight.

"Hold up babe, otherwise this is going to end way too soon."

I giggled but slowed my hips. Max reached around and palmed my breast with his hand and I moaned.

"I love when you play with my nipples," I cooed.

"Oh yeah? Like this?" he said and rolled my nipple between his thumb and forefinger. "I love these titties."

I sucked in a breath. "Yes, Max. Just like that baby. Oooh, just like that."

I loved the way my man did everything he could to make me feel good. He paid attention. Knew my likes, and my dislikes. And one thing he knew I loved was him playing with my nipples. He had my body so aroused I started gyrating my hips again.

"CC, I said give me a minute. Do you have any idea how good you feel?"

"Probably as good as you feel. Max please," I said in my baby voice.

He gripped my hips, holding me against him. "You ready for a ride?"

I shivered. "Just fuck me now!"

Max chuckled but gave me exactly what I asked for. Gripping my ass, he pumped into me with hard, determined thrusts. To hell with taking it slow, it was all about reaching the finished line.

I held on tight, and rocked my hips back meeting each pound for pound. The sound of his thighs slapping against my ass was such a turn-on. I was moaning and whimpering, then crying out his name, the soft sounds of my voice echoing through the otherwise quiet house. Over and over he plunged inside my greedy pussy. He then reached around and his thumb stroked my clit and sent me bucking wildly against the counter.

"Please! Oh baby. I'm getting ready to come," I warned and gritted my teeth. My legs felt like they were gonna give up on me soon. An orgasm was close and felt like fire building in my lower belly. It took every ounce of willpower to hold on. My thighs were burning. My breasts were swinging and my nipples brushing the slick, cool granite only intensified the situation.

"I'm about to come," Max groaned and I cried out with my release as he continued to pound against me.

"Yesss!" I cried and then I felt him jerk and release a long growl before his hips finally slowed.

By the time Max pulled away my entire body was trembling. He took my hand. "C'mon, let's go back to bed."

* * *

I was starving by the time I finally got to eat and Max and I decided to spend the rest of the day together and had been hanging out ever since. First we went to breakfast at the diner he'd raved about and pigged out on stuff I knew I had no business eating. Next we headed to the mall and did some shopping. I swear that man loved to shop just as much as I did. I had been looking for an outfit for my upcoming visit to Atlanta, and when I found the perfect plum-colored dress, I tried it on and Max insisted on buying it for me. I'd never been one for accepting gifts from men but when Max had his mind set to something there's no changing it.

As we left the store walking hand in hand I had this feeling that someone was watching me. I had an identical feeling again after we left Footlocker. Maybe I was just being paranoid, although usually I loved a lot of attention. And when you're walking with Max it is definitely guaranteed. Women couldn't keep their eyes off of him but who could blame them. Max is not only tall, but gorgeous, so there is no way you can ignore him. Any other woman would probably be trying to plant a tracking device on his fine ass, but not me, I was confident in who I was and what I brought to the table. He was everything I needed in a man and it was my job to continue to show him his search for a soul mate was finally over.

I finally blew off the paranoia and figured I was just caught up in the moment, which was probably true, and went back to enjoying my afternoon with Max.

We had just gotten some ice cream and were heading toward the parking garage when he started squeezing my hand.

"What's wrong?"

"Just keep walking." He was practically dragging me to the car.

"Max, what's going on?" I started looking around trying to see what had made him so tense. And here I thought I was the one being paranoid.

"CC, would you just listen and keep walking." I didn't like being bossed around and was planning on giving him a piece of my mind. We walked across the parking lot and over to his SUV. Max opened the door for me and waited until I was seated before he said, "Lock the door and don't get out."

"Where the hell is he going?" I muttered when I noticed he didn't walk around to the driver's side. I turned around on my seat and followed him as he walked across the parking lot. He was shouting something and waving his hands in the air like some lunatic. "That dude has lost it," I mumbled under my breath. Before long I couldn't even see Max anymore. Quickly, I turned on the seat and got the door open.

"Get back in the car!" Max called out and I froze.

Where the hell did he come from?

Max climbed in and slammed the door behind him. "Didn't I tell you to lock the door?"

His angry tone put me on the defensive. "I'm not a kid!" I snapped and immediately regretted it. I tried to snuggle up against Max but his mind was somewhere else. "What was that all about?"

The moment he turned and looked at me I knew I wasn't going to like what he was about to say.

"Two of the guys who attacked you were at the mall," he said cutting to the chase.

I jerked upright on the seat. "What?"

He nodded and searched my eyes for my reaction as he spoke, "I spotted one of them before we had gone into Macy's and by the time we were leaving there was the other."

Oh my goodness! I had been walking around the mall all that time and had no idea my attackers had been there. They could have been standing a few feet away and I would have never known. I was shaking so hard, I was ready to puke.

"I think I'm going to be sick."

Max reached out and put a hand on my arm. "Babe, it's going to be okay. As soon as they realized I saw them, those cowards ran away, but I got a license plate number."

I searched his dark hooded eyes. "What are you going to do with that?" My voice was trembling and my knees knocking.

"I'm going to give it to Dee after you go down to the police station and file a report."

I felt like this conversation was a song stuck on repeat. "Max I—"

"Woman... I don't want to hear it! If I hadn't been there they could have followed you back to the parking garage and there is no telling what might have happened this time."

For a moment we both fell silent.

For me, I think I'd been dealing with the attack pretty well. But now, knowing they had been in the mall, I had reached my breaking point. He was right. They could have knocked my naïve ass in the back of the head and I still wouldn't have had any idea what any of them looked like. For me, that was very scary.

Max leaned over and kissed me, and I tried to relax.

"Alright," I said sadly. "I'll go."

SEVENTEEN

The rest of the weekend was crazy. I went down to the station and filed a report. You should have seen the way the female officer was turning up her nose at me for not filing sooner. It was almost as if that bony wench thought I was lying. However, trust and believe when Detective Dereon Sanders stepped into the room, she was like a puppy on a leash. All that eye rolling and sucking her buckteeth ceased. Dereon said he would make sure that someone competent was assigned to the case and as soon as he had information about the car, he'd let us know. However, on Sunday Dereon called to say the vehicle those dudes had been driving was stolen. So we were back to the drawing board.

That was why I didn't want to file the report in the first place. What was the likelihood we would run into those guys again? Probably next to none.

On Monday, I had too much going on to worry myself about my attackers. I figured as long as I stayed on my side of town I wouldn't have to worry about seeing them again. Even though I had no idea what any of them looked like.

I spent most of the morning creating a two-tier cake with sugar-blown soccer balls all over it for a team luncheon while Christina made two sausage lasagnas big enough to feed an army. Daphne, a culinary arts student, who was currently working as an intern was there to assist. She's the first student I had successfully been able to teach how to do sugar displays. Together, she and I loaded up the company van with *Cater to You* airbrushed in pink on the side and delivered the food. Afterwards I dropped her off at her mama's house. Hey, she didn't have a car and usually traveled by bus, but I didn't mind helping out a kid who was trying to better herself.

I had a two o'clock appointment with a new client that Mia scheduled just yesterday. It was for a last minute party that needed to be planned sometime in the next two weeks. I hated rushing and so did Christina, but if they were willing to pay the extra fee for quality service then who were we to turn down their business.

I parked my Range Rover and was climbing out when I heard a familiar voice calling my name. I turned my head around and as soon as I saw the man stepping out of a white Jaguar then cross the street, I almost fainted.

No fucking way!

It was Isaiah or at least he looked like he could be Isaiah but goodness this man had so much swag, I couldn't stop staring. He stood about six-two with an almost perfect nutmeg complexion. He had always had a headful of dark curls but now he wore it short and neatly cut. Knowing Isaiah the way I did, he'd just left the barbershop because even his goatee was trimmed and razor sharp.

And then there were his eyes. How in the world could I have forgotten how wide and golden they were? And when he smiled, dimples appeared at both of his cheeks. He was handsome. Not as fine as Max, but definitely eye-candy.

Isaiah winked as he came closer, undressing me with his gaze while taking in all of my curves. "What's happening CC?" He greeted me with that larger than life voice of his. And when Isaiah came over, sliding his arms around me, memories of our past came rushing back. "How you been?" he asked when he finally released me.

I was grinning and blushing like some crazy fool. "I've been good. I can see time has really been good to you."

He shrugged one of those strong shoulders of his. "Just trying to stay in shape." He had never been one for compliments. That was one thing I had always loved about Isaiah was how humble he could be.

"Well, whatever you're doing is definitely working." He released me and I took a step back.

"I could say the same about you. You're still as beautiful as you were in high school, but then I expected no less from you."

I started batting my eyes and struck a pose, making sure he saw my good side. I was glad I had taken a little extra time in my appearance this morning. My hair was up in a ponytail, my makeup flawless even though I was sure my lipstick was long gone. Nevertheless, I had decided to wear a cream blouse that emphasized my C-cups and a brown pencil skirt that hugged my curves in ways that made me proud to know I had gotten some of my most important features from my father's side of the family.

We were standing in the street beside my vehicle, grinning at each other like two damn fools. Isaiah always had perfect teeth and sexy thick lips. We used to have such a great relationship together, laughing, making love, planning our future. This man was supposed to have been my husband.

"What are you doing here?" I was so nervous I could barely get the words out.

"I got tired of you ignoring my calls and decided to come down here and see you." He reached out and took my hand in his. My heart sped up in a good way. Isaiah had always been a touchy feely kind of guy. Being affectionate had always been one of his strong points.

"I wasn't ignoring your calls. Just been super busy," I began and glanced down at my watch. "In fact, I'm late for a meeting." Although at the moment that client was the last thing on my mind. I could have stood there, staring up into his gorgeous face all day. I don't know if I was attracted to Isaiah or simple just missed having him in my life.

"Well I don't want to keep you, but I do want to take you out to lunch tomorrow, if you can squeeze a brotha in."

"Lunch?" It was probably a good time as any to tell Isaiah I was seeing someone, but like I had said before I just couldn't bring myself to do that. Strange. I had always said if he had ever come back into town he wouldn't have a chance in hell of getting me back. However, I wasn't going to lie to myself. I was curious. Curious to find out if there was still something there. One thing for sure I was definitely feeling him. He was dressed in a pair of jeans, a Sean John t-shirt and Chuck

Taylor's. I smiled. He always did love his chucks. "I think my schedule is free for lunch tomorrow," I replied.

"Good. I'll be by to pick you up at noon."

He didn't even wait for me to agree before he was kissing me lightly on the lips, and then turned and walked back across the street.

"Make it twelve-thirty!" I called after him. No way was I going to let him think he was running things.

"I'll see you then, CC." He was chuckling but never broke his stride toward his car.

I didn't even wait for him to pull away. Oh no. I wanted him to see me strut toward the building in a pair of mustard-yellow pumps. As soon as my back was turned a wide goofy smile curled my lips as I headed toward the glass-front building with *Cater to You* over the door. I was gushing like a teenager who had been asked out on her first date. Goodness, wait until I tell Christina!

Of course, it was going to be an innocent lunch, strictly two friends catching up over casual conversation. Now I just needed to drop by the mall and find the perfect outfit that screamed to Isaiah what a fool he had been to let a good women like me go.

I was giggling as I walked through the door. Oh my, the games woman play.

"Claudia," Mia greeted. "Your appointment is already in the conference room with Christina."

"Thank you." I offered her a slight smile then hurried into my office, left my purse, and reached for a spiral notebook and pen. As soon as I took a look in the full-length mirror on the back of the door, and liked what I saw, I sashayed down the hall to the small conference room and stepped inside. My heart nearly stopped.

Christina was all smiles. "Claudia, there you are. This is our new client —"

"We already know each other." I tossed the woman a nasty look.

Parker turned on the seat and gazed up at me with this tickled look on her face.

Unfortunately, Christina was clueless. "Oh, I had no idea the two of you had met."

"We have a mutual friend." I walked across the room. "Christina thanks for stepping in but I think I can handle this client all by myself."

She gave me a weird look and I nodded my head, letting her know I got this and would explain later.

I waited until Christina left and I heard the door click before I glared over at Parker. "What do you want?"

She had the nerve to be sitting in my conference room, smiling like she had not a care in the world. Braids were swept up in a ponytail and her face was scrubbed free of make-up. She looked young, innocent and pretty. "I asked you a question. What do you want?" I barked.

Parker shook her head, chuckling, sending her braids flying around her damn head. "I want what all of your customers want. I want you to plan me a party."

"A party?"

"A baby shower." She made a show of rubbing her stomach. "But I need you to put something together quick because this little boy is due in two weeks."

It was taking everything I had not to put my foot up in her ass. "I don't know what kind of games you're trying to play."

"Who's playing games? I need a shower. I heard you were the best and I figured you wouldn't mind since Max is paying for it."

"Max?"

"Of course, there isn't anything he won't do for his little boy. You should have seen his face when he got to see the sonogram. I can already see we're going to have him wrapped around our finger."

I moved over to the table and glared down at her. "What do you want?"

She turned her evil eyes on me. "What I want is for you to understand that for the next eighteen years I'm gonna be in Max's life. And we both know this little boy is always gonna come first." She was talking with her hands.

It was my turn to laugh. "I would never stand in the way of Max and his child."

"Well good. I'm glad you know your place," she tossed in.

"Bitch listen, don't get it twisted. The only reason why I haven't thrown your ass out is because you might be carrying my man's child." I pointed at my chest.

"There's no maybe about it. This is his baby," she hissed, then rolled her eyes at me.

"And how can you be so sure? Max said he used condoms."

"Condoms aren't a hundred percent." She had this look on her face like it was a private joke or something. I felt sorry for Max for getting involved with her in the first place.

"Either way it doesn't matter."

"Oh it's gonna matter, trust me." There was sarcasm all in her voice. I just stood back and watched as she pushed out of my chair. "You might not think it does now but it will. I guarantee."

A hand flew to my hip. "What's that supposed to mean?"

"You'll see." She then winked and waddled to the door but before she opened it Parker turned her head and said, "Oh, by the way, can you do me a favor… remind Max we have an appointment on Friday." With that she stepped out the door.

I stood there for the longest time fuming over what had just happened. There was no way that chick had come to my job like that. But she had and as much as I wanted to reach out and touch her, I couldn't because she was pregnant. And she knew it. Damn, why did Max have to be tangled up with someone like Parker? Why couldn't I for once have what I wanted? Get what I felt I deserved? Was that asking too much?

"Who was that?" Christina asked, snapping me away from my thoughts.

I took a seat before saying, "That was Max's Parker."

It took a moment for it to register and then her eyes got large and round. *"Max's baby mama."*

"*Suspect* baby mama," I reminded her. "Although, the

way that chick was talking I'm starting to think there may be a chance that's Max's baby."

"Really?" Christina rounded the table and took a seat and raised an incredulous eyebrow at me. "Oh my God! I can't believe she had the balls to come in here thinking we were going to plan her a baby shower."

"And she was planning to send Max the bill."

She was dumfounded. "What? Ain't that some shit."

I shrugged. "Parker probably figured since I'm dating Max I would have given her a discount."

Christina started laughing and despite how miserable I felt I found myself giggling as well. "I don't know whether to laugh or cry over this ridiculous situation. I'm serious. This is something you'd see on one of those ghetto reality series."

"I know, right." She stopped laughing and looked over at me, her expression had gotten serious. "Now that you know the type of woman she is, what's your thoughts about this whole situation? I mean have you ever thought about what things would be like if you and Max decided to make things permanent?"

I shook my head. "I think about spending my life with him all the damn time. And just when things are good between us, I get slapped in the face with his baby mama issues. I just don't know if I can deal with that."

Christina hesitated, then answered truthfully, "You might have to. Especially if that baby ends up being Max's."

I worried my bottom lip with my teeth while I took a moment to think about her question. "You know, sometimes I wonder if I'm as crazy about Max as I think I am."

Her eyes widened with surprise. "Claudia… Why you say that?"

My gaze shifted to the table. "Because whenever I'm confronted with his drama, I find myself thinking about Isaiah and what could have been."

"What? Are you serious?"

I nodded my head. As much as it saddened me to say it, I was starting to reconsider the relationship again. I just didn't want to do baby mama drama and that chick pretty much guaranteed she would be a permanent fixture in my man's life, and I wasn't sure if I was the woman for the job.

"Matter of fact, as I was coming into the building, Isaiah caught me in the parking lot and asked me out to lunch tomorrow."

Christina's jaw dropped. "What? How does he look?"

I had to take a deep breath just to contain myself. "Christy…he's so freaking sexy it's unreal!"

Her brow rose and I could tell she was skeptical. "Are you serious? He's always been cute, but sexy?"

I winked. "I'm serious. The years have done him some good. You can tell he had been in the gym and everything."

"Really? This I gotta see." I must have had a silly grin on my face because she leaned in close. "Uh-uh, hold up! I thought this was just about lunch but the way you're talking and looking, it sounds like it could possibly be more going on."

After that baby mama crap I was definitely considering the possibility. "I'm not going to lie, the moment I spotted him I started thinking about what could have been."

She gave a rude snort. "Yes, but remember he left you to run off to Africa to provide medical treatment to the underprivileged."

I should have known she was going to go there. "Yeah, yeah, but it doesn't seem so wrong anymore."

"What? Did you forget all the days you spent crying your eyes out and I had to come over and make you get your funky ass in the shower?'

I gave her a dismissive wave. "I wasn't that bad."

"No, it was worse," she retorted. "That man shattered your heart. Now mind you, I understand he felt it was his mission, but I know what you went through and for him to come back and think he can just start where you left off truly blows me away."

I shrugged and leaned back on the chair. "Who said anything about starting over? I just want to see if the chemistry is still there and weigh my options."

"Options?"

"Yes, options. There is no telling how Max is going to act once this baby is born. My worst fear is he decides he wants to be a family with Parker."

"I met the chick, that ain't happening," she replied with a rude snort.

I had to chuckle at that. "Okay, maybe not, but if I decided to share my life with him then I'll have to deal with her ass. I'm just not sure if I can deal with a constant reminder every single day."

There was a long pause. "So are you going to plan her a party?"

I rolled my eyes. "Hell no! She better go visit the Party Store and hand Max the bill." Christina was bent over with laughter. "You're laughing, but I'm serious."

"I know you are and that's why I'm laughing," she said and then sighed. "Max is such a good guy. Knowing him he'll head right on over to the baby store and pick up everything that baby needs."

I shook my head because I knew it was true.

She met my eyes. "I guess that's what makes him a great guy."

I drew a long breath. "Yeah and that's the problem." He was a gentleman and I already knew he was going to be an awesome father. The other issue was Parker had known him long enough to know that as long as she had Max's baby, he would be at her beck and call.

And that's what bothered me so much.

"I think the two of you need to sit down and talk about this so you can move forward," Christina suggested and she was right. I needed to talk to Max and let him know how I felt, but I had a feeling it would just lead to another heated argument.

"I'll talk to him about it tonight," I replied.

Christina cleared her throat. "Or maybe we won't have to wait that long."

I followed the direction of her eyes and saw Dereon and Max stepping into the conference room. Damn, those two were something to look at. Dereon with all that dark chocolate swagger and Max looked too scrumptious today to put to words.

"Hey, babe!" Christina was practically shouting as she jerked up from the chair and came around the table to greet her fiancé with a big fat kiss. It was embarrassing watching them so I looked up at Max just as he drew close, leaned forward and covered my lips with his.

"What are you two doing here?" I asked, and pulled back to look into his eyes.

"We came to give you this." He reached inside his pocket and removed a bunch of ripped sheets of paper and dropped them onto the table.

"What's that?" Christina asked.

"Your contract with DJ." Dereon was strutting proudly around the conference room.

My eyes shifted from one to the other. "Oh shit! You got him to cancel our contract?"

Max gave Dereon a weird smirk and responded, "Let's just say we were able to convince him it would be to his best interest." He held up his fist and gave dap with his best friend.

"Yes!" I jumped out the chair and threw my arms around his neck. "Thank you so much."

Max gave me a long look, then winked. "Anything for you babe. I told you, I got this."

"Yes, I guess you do." Smiling, Max gave me a long sensual kiss until I heard Christina clear her throat.

"The two of you need to go and get a room," she muttered as she took her fiancé's hand and led him out the door. "I'll see you later. Max thanks so much for your help."

Dereon paused in the doorway. "Whoa, baby, what about me?"

"Don't worry, I plan on rewarding you in just a few minutes," Christina replied with a saucy grin. I already knew how my girl got down. She winked at me and headed out.

I turned to Max and smiled up at him as I said, "I don't know how to thank you for getting us out of that contract."

"I can think of a few things."

I laughed and leaned in for another savory kiss then

remembered less than an hour ago, I had been kissing Isaiah with those same lips. So why didn't I feel like a slut?

Max leaned me back against the table, his body close to mine. I loved the way he felt, hard and manly in all of the right places.

He lifted a curious brow and smiled. "How's your day been?" I appreciated the way he always took the time to make sure things were right in my life.

I inclined my head coolly. "It's was great until your baby mama showed up."

The color drained from his face. "What? Parker was here?"

I pushed away from him. "How many baby mamas do you have?"

"Just the one suspect. What the hell did she want?"

I gave a rude snort. "She wanted us to plan her a baby shower and send you the bill."

"What the..." he started cussing under his breath as he paced across the room. Max spun around. "What did you tell her?"

"What do you *think* I told her... hell no!"

Closing the gap between us, Max reached up and cradled my face with his hands. "Babe, I'm sorry."

A thought came to mind and I searched his eyes as I said, "How did she even know where I worked?"

Max hesitated before answering evenly, "I had one of your business cards in my car and she saw it."

I held up a hand. "Whoa! Wait a minute. What was she doing in your car?"

"I took her to an appointment," he replied gently.

"Oh really? So is this going to be a weekly thing?"

He blew out a long breath. "Babe, she has an appointment every week until the baby is born. I can't just turn my back on my child."

I arched a cynical brow. "But you said it wasn't your child."

"I said I doubt it very seriously. I used a condom."

"But they aren't a hundred percent." There I was using

Parker's words.

Max dragged a hand across his head I could tell he was getting frustrated. "CC, look… I know this is hard for you."

"Damn right it's hard! You keep telling me there isn't going to be any drama and yet I have already had two encounters with Parker. That bitch came to my job!" I was yelling and I didn't mean to, but it was just something about her that bothered me and the way she was gloating about having my man wrapped around her finger once the baby was born bothered me even more.

He inched closer and slid his fingers up my arm. "CC, there's no reason to get all worked up."

I removed his hand. "Are you defending her?"

"No, not at all. She had no business coming here, and I'm definitely gonna talk to her about it, but we gotta all find a way to get along," his voice was husky with emotion.

"Then tell her that," I hissed. "I'm not showing up at her job. By the way, does she even have a job?"

"She's an LPN."

I figured she was sitting at home collecting a check from the state and another from Max. "Well good for you. You got yourself a nurse." I attempted to step around him, only he grabbed my wrist and drew me close to him.

"Babe, don't be like that. We can work through this. I'll talk to her this evening."

My heart clutched. "This evening? So you're going by to see her."

He pulled in a deep breath. "I'm gonna work on the crib and help her get the nursery together."

I was too through with this conversation. "She doesn't have friends to help her?"

"It isn't their responsibility. It's mine. Why's that so hard for you to understand? Would you rather I was a deadbeat father?"

"I rather you not be a father at all! At least not to her children."

I practically choked on a sob that was lodged in my throat. Okay, I was jealous. There was no other way to put it. I was jealous he was going to have a baby with another woman and that woman was going to make sure to throw that in my face every chance she got, and I just couldn't stomach the thought.

"Listen Claudia, I'm crazy about you, but I'm not gonna argue with you about this. I'm sorry she came to your job and I will definitely check her ass for it, but you gotta understand this is something I have to do."

I was too stubborn to answer him and allowed the awkward silence between us to drift and expand.

We were both upset and right now was probably not a good time for us to be talking about Parker. Max was the first to break the spell. "Look, I gotta go. I'll call you tonight."

He didn't wait for an answer before he was tipping my head back and kissing me. His lips were so delicious, it was almost enough to make me forget about my problems, but not really.

I watched him leave and stood there with my arms crossed, fuming and feeling like an idiot. I guess the situation bothered me more than I cared to admit and yet I liked Max so much I couldn't have walked away from our relationship even if I had wanted to. And that's what pissed me off.

I had fallen in love.

The realization caused my knees to buckle and I quickly moved over to one of the chairs and took a seat. How was it even possible, I asked myself that I had fallen in love with a man who was about to have a baby by some crazy chick? Parker represented everything that I tried to stay clear of my entire life.

I heard laughter coming from Christina's office, then there were heavy footsteps going down the hallway and the bell rang overhead. I was so glad they were gone because I seriously needed that time to regroup.

"Are you okay in here?"

I looked up to see Christina standing over me. "I heard you talking loud."

I cringed. I tried to always keep it professional, especially in the workplace which was why I rarely ever mixed business with pleasure. However, when it came to Max, I had a hard time keeping my head on straight.

"No, I'm not okay but I'm going to figure it out."

She stepped around and leaned against the table beside me. "Girl, I can't even begin to imagine what you're going through. As selfish as I am, I would have said 'deuces' and moved on, but you've always been stronger than me."

That may have been the true in the past, but when you're dealing with a man you loved it's a total different ball game.

"Christina, I really don't think I can deal with this, and yet I can't imagine my life without Max being in it," I said sadly.

She placed a gentle hand to my shoulder. "Just pray about it."

Maybe that was the answer. But at the moment I was starting to think of the alternative. Isaiah. Maybe the Lord was trying to tell me something.

EIGHTEEN

I ignored Max's call that evening because the last thing I wanted to talk about was the baby crib he had set up at Parker's place.

The next morning I got up and took extra care in making sure I looked exceptional. I decided on a form-fitting sweater dress that encased my body and showcased everything I had to offer. I was just finishing up an appointment with a client when Isaiah called to let me know he was parked outside the office.

I grabbed my purse, exited the building and did a double-take when I saw the car parked out front. A white Bugatti. The French car was the epitome of luxury and style, and very expensive.

"First a Jaguar, now this. You balling like that?"

He laughed. "No, I actually bought this car for cash. All those years working overseas I didn't spend a dime of my trust fund, so I thought I would treat myself with something nice with the interest I'd earned."

I had always known he was well off, but maybe I had never truly paid attention to how much.

I got comfortable on the seat. Soft jazz was playing.

"It's really good to see you, CC. How have you really been?"

Did he think I was about to bare my soul and tell him about all the moments I spent crying over him? No way in hell. Even if I had been lonely and miserable, he would never know. I planted on the perfect smile. "I've been great. Business is booming. We are thinking about expanding."

"That's good. What about your personal life. How has that been?"

Men were so sneaky. That was his way of trying to find out if I was seeing someone. I probably should have told him right then and there, but I just couldn't bring myself to do it. I guess part of me wanted to see just how far Isaiah was willing to go with this. "If you're asking if I've been dating. Of course I have."

The way his Adam's apple bobbed I could tell he didn't like my answer.

"As beautiful as you are? I would be a fool not to know that men have been practically breaking their necks to get close to you."

"How'd you know?" I teased and he started laughing, which was a good thing. The situation was uncomfortable enough as it was.

"How about you? I'm surprised some woman hasn't snatched you off the market?" I licked my bottom lip and noticed how his eyes lit up when I did.

"No, I went to Africa on a mission and once that calling was fulfilled I decided it was time to get back home and focus on another important mission." He laced his fingers with mine and I felt all giddy inside. I knew he was talking about me and him. Like I said, I wanted to see how far he was willing to take this.

"How are your parents?" I asked even though Mom saw them at church every Sunday and kept me up-to-date.

"Dad finally decided to retire from the bank."

"Really?" His father had been CFO of Liberty Trust, one of the largest financial services in the Midwest.

"Yeah, he wants to buy an RV and he and Mom travel around and see the world. Mom is ecstatic."

I smiled. "That's a wonderful idea. Mommy can barely get my father to take a yearly vacation. I know he's really excited to have you joining the team at Barnes."

"I'm excited too. I truly feel like God is blessing me with everything I've dreamed." He brought my hand to his mouth and pressed his lips to it.

I felt a shiver of excitement because everything he was dreaming had been my dream for so long. Was God finally listening? The problem was I wasn't sure if this was what I wanted. Nevertheless, that baby mama drama had me rethinking my choices and looking at possible other options.

Isaiah pulled up into valet at one of my favorite Italian restaurants. One of the attendants held the door open for me and I climbed out just as Isaiah came around. He handed over his keys and put the orange slip in his pocket, then draped an arm around my shoulders possessively, and led me inside.

We were immediately escorted to a table at the center of the crowded restaurant. I eyed the lasagna on one plate and seafood pasta on another and my stomach growled. I was so looking forward to a meal.

Isaiah helped me into my seat, then sat in the chair beside me and looked around the room. "I see Luciano's hasn't changed much."

"No, not at all. I think it has grown even more popular since they opened a second restaurant downtown."

A server came and poured us both a glass of water and white wine then delivered a basket of bread. I wasted no time dipping it in olive oil.

"You're going to be full before the food arrives," he warned.

"Trust me, no I won't."

Isaiah shook his head and grinned. "You always could put away some food. I just don't know where it goes."

"I can point to a few places." My thumb was directed at my thighs.

"You don't hear me complaining."

I laughed at his compliment. I looked across the room and my jaw dropped.

"What?"

I tilted my head. "That man coming into the restaurant. That's Portia's husband."

He looked over his shoulder. "Little Portia? I did hear from Mom she got married."

"Yeah he's a pediatrician and Christina thinks he's having an affair." I watched him walk across the restaurant and out onto the patio where a beautiful woman was seated. As soon as she spotted him, she rose from her chair and I watched in horror. It wasn't the kiss it was the way he looked at her as he kissed her.

"Ain't that some shit," I mumbled under my breath.

The waitress came to take our order and I grabbed the menu and quickly decided on the lasagna. As soon as she left, I was staring out onto the patio again. He and the female were now holding hands across the table.

Wait till I tell Christina this.

"Hey, earth to Claudia." Isaiah snapped his fingers and I blinked.

"Sorry, I just hate seeing men think they can get away with shit."

"I would never do you like that."

He reached over and put his hand over mine. I looked down at it then back up at him and rolled my eyes. "You broke my heart."

"And there hasn't been a day that has gone by that I haven't regretted what I did." I could see the remorse, but that didn't mean I was going to make this easy for him.

"I wanted to be your wife."

He released a long, shaky breath. "I know you were, but there was no way I could let you marry me when I had no idea which direction my faith was going to take me. That just would have been unfair to expect you to put your life on hold for me for five years."

"That should have been my decision, not yours." I don't know why he wanted to even talk about this because every time I thought about the way he left, all it did was make me angry. I had spent all those years waiting and hoping he would come back to me.

"I want to apologize for what I did. I was wrong and I was stupid. But I'm here now and I want nothing more than to be your man and make things work." He brought my hand to his lips and kissed it. "It was good then so I know it could be even better now."

I wanted so badly to have what we once had, and if Max wasn't in my head I would have been straddling Isaiah's chair right about now, but I wasn't the same woman.

"I can't make any promises, but let's see how things go?" There I said it, or at least that was all I was going to admit. I just wasn't ready to say anything about Max. The fact I was mad at him didn't help matters at all.

I looked over at Dr. Evan Smith. He and the woman were staring into each other's eyes. I knew that look anywhere. The brotha was in love with someone who wasn't his wife.

"Will you excuse me? I want to take a picture of the pond out back."

I rose and before Isaiah could stop me, I stepped out onto the patio and over to the railing. There were geese swimming in the water and the view was breathtaking but I was more interested in what was going on over at the table to the far right. I walked all the way around so there was no way Evan could miss me, and the second he spotted me his eyes grew wide.

"Hey Evan, how are you doing? I saw you sitting here and thought I would stop by and say hello to you and your wife—" I faked a gasp. "Oops, I thought you were Portia. My bad." I scurried away and waited until my back was turned before I broke out in a smile. I reached inside my purse for my phone and took a few pictures of the lake before I swung around and snapped a couple of Evan and his side chick. By the third, he caught me and jumped out of his seat. As he made his way over to me, I pretended to be scrolling through my phone.

"Claudia, I need a big favor?" he said in this low voice. I'll have to admit Evan smelled quite delicious.

"What kind of favor?"

His gold-green eyes locked with mine. "I need you to not tell Christina you saw me," he added casually.

"What did I see? You, having lunch with a colleague?" I said, shrugging since he obviously thought I was an idiot.

A cocky smirk curled his lips. "Yes, that's exactly what this is."

"Or is there more since I saw the two of you kissing and holding hands?"

That instantly wiped the smirk from his face.

"Listen, Portia is delicate. She wouldn't understand if she knew I was having lunch with a female colleague."

I folded my arms. "Why is that I wonder?"

He smiled. "Because she gets a little jealous and I don't know if you noticed, but she can be a bit insecure."

"So what?" I said protectively. "That gives you the right to mess around behind my friend's back?"

He didn't even look the slightest bit fazed by my comment, so I rolled my eyes and stared off into the pond.

"Look, I would appreciate it if you didn't say anything."

"I'm not making any promises to you. The only thing that would stop me is I don't want to see Portia get hurt. Now if you'd excuse me I have a date for lunch. I'm single and single people can do that." I pushed past him and strutted back into the restaurant.

"Everything okay?" Isaiah asked curiously.

I nodded. "Yeah, I'm good. Let's eat."

I was reaching for my fork when Isaiah placed his hand over mine. "Every man isn't like that asshole. I loved you… hell, I never stopped loving you. I want to show you that there are some good—sometimes stupid—men out there. But regardless I want to cherish you and treat you like the queen that you are. I just ask you give me a chance."

I stared at him and I knew Isaiah was being serious. And I was at a loss for words.

* * *

After lunch I went back to work. Christina had already left for the day and that was probably a good thing. I wasn't sure if I ready to tell her about Evan or discuss my lunch with Isaiah. I needed a moment to think. She was busy planning a wedding and the last thing I wanted to do was upset her. This was her moment, but at the same time, I would want to know if it were my sister.

By the end of the day I was still thinking about my lunch with Isaiah.

I just ask you give me a chance.

I leaned back in my chair and thought about how much I had once loved Isaiah. Could I ever feel that way about him again, now that I'd met Max?

Damn that man.

If he hadn't walked into my life it would be a no brainer. But now that I knew what it was like to be with him, to have him buried deep inside me, I just wasn't sure if anyone, including Isaiah could ever measure up in comparison.

Mia was packing up for the evening and I locked up the building and we left together.

While we walked, I could tell the girl was distracted.

"Mia, you okay?"

She took a moment before she looked up at me, chocolate eyes wide and inquisitive. "I wanted to apologize again for Shalisa being drunk at Christina's engagement party."

I gave her a dismissive wave. The girl had already apologized to me three times before. "That's old news."

"I'm glad you said that," she began, then paused and hesitated. "Shalisa is really sorry and if you can ever find it in your heart she would like another chance to make things right."

"I—"

"She promises it will never happen again," she blurted out.

I sighed and continued walking. "You really go out of your way to help your little sister."

She shrugged. "All we got is each other."

When we reached her Ford Focus, I stopped and turned to her. "I promise I'll give it some thought."

My answer caused her to smile. "Thank you."

I said goodbye and walked over to my SUV. Shalisa better be glad I had a soft spot for her big sister. *All we got is each other.*

I was still thinking about Mia, and wondering what she meant when Max called my phone.

"Hey babe. You still mad at me?" His deep voice poured into my ear like warm honey.

"I was never mad." I lied. "Did you tell Parker not to

come back to my job?"

"Yeah, we talked. It's all good."

I seriously doubted that. I tossed my briefcase in the backseat and climbed in the car. "I forgot to tell you, Parker asked me to remind you, she has another doctor's appointment on Friday."

"Babe..., don't be like that." I could tell he was getting frustrated but I didn't care. He was supposed to be mine.

"Can I come over tonight?" he asked, breaking the silence.

My nipples hardened at the mere thought of being with him, but I just couldn't allow myself to be controlled by my body. I knew what I was doing was right. Max needed to be with Parker and the baby, and I needed to do what I should have done five years ago, and that was marry Isaiah.

As I pulled out the parking lot, I replied, "No, I've gotta lot of work to do this evening. Can I have a raincheck?"

"Sure babe. Is there anything I can do for you?" His tone was sincere and seductive.

I fought back tears. "No, I'm fine but thanks for asking."

NINETEEN

It had been almost a week and with each day I had been avoiding him more and more. It was a struggle, but I had pretty much convinced myself Max was not what I needed in my life. Instead I'd been hanging out with Isaiah. Dinner, movies, we even bowled on Friday. And on Sunday, we decided to ride together to my father's birthday party. It wasn't until we pulled up in front of my parents' house that I remembered my mother had also invited Christina and Dereon. By the time we had arrived, his black Infiniti QX56 was parked in front of the house.

"Damn," I mumbled.

"What's wrong?" Isaiah turned off his car and swung around on the seat. His eyes locked with mine.

He was cute, especially when his attention was focused on me. I had to say that for the last few days he had done everything in his power to make me feel important. Even this evening, I had opened the door to find him standing there with an edible fruit arrangement in his hand. The new Isaiah was sexy, thoughtful, confident, and irresistible.

"I forgot Christina and her fiancé were coming for dinner."

He was studying me. "What's wrong? You don't want them to see us together."

How did he know? "No, not at all." I just wasn't ready to hear the lecture. "I just forgot. That's all."

He smiled, causing his dimples to wink at me then reached over and stroked the side of my neck, heating my skin in its path. "That's cool. It will give me a chance to congratulate the happy couple." He cupped my chin and drew me close and captured my mouth in a familiar kiss. With each touch of his lips he brought back memories. I just hoped it would be enough.

We climbed out and I stared up at the place I once called home. Over five-thousand-square feet of living space that Mommy insisted on having cleaned almost every day even though they only used half the house. It was a two-story stone-front house, with four-bedrooms and breathtaking views to the garden and lake out back. As soon as I knocked on the door, Daddy swung it open, and gave a knowing look. "Come on in, come on in," he said merrily before ushering us inside the house. His smile stretched across his dark, mahogany face as he opened his arms wide for my embrace.

"Happy birthday, Daddy." I kissed him on the cheek.

"Thank you sweetheart."

I waited as he gave Isaiah a bear hug and noticed my father was starting to gray at the temples. I actually like the distinguished look. Clayton Winters was about six-feet with an athletic build. A personal trainer and healthy living was his testimony. He had a wide nose, champagne-colored eyes, and a friendly smile.

The two of them were whispering and I drew a breath. My father made it no secret what direction he wanted his daughter to take.

"Christy is in back with your mother."

Nodding, we stepped across the cherry-wood floor and down the hall. The custom-built home had nine foot ceilings, and crown-molding in every room. I rounded the sterile white kitchen and made it out onto the sunroom. It was glass—encased just like mine only bigger and much more elegant.

As usual, Mommy was filling glasses with her fresh-squeezed lemonade. As soon as Isaiah stepped out into the room, I waited for everyone's reaction.

"You made it." Mommy was smiling, her eyes crinkling in the corner.

I looked over at Christina as she and Dereon were exchanging a look that said, "I'll explain later."

I blew them off and walked around the table and gave my mother a kiss and embraced her small petite frame. "Hi

Mommy."

"About time you got here," she scolded although the look in her slanted brown eyes told me she was happy to see me and Isaiah together. I wish I could say the same about Dereon. He mean-mugged him through most of the meal and even when he and my dad took a seat out on the deck and were smoking cigars I could hear Dereon giving Isaiah the third degree. But that man took it in stride. Isaiah was so laid back he surprised me.

My brother Clay arrived with his chick of the week. I hadn't seen him in almost a month so I was the first one to throw my arms around him. "Where have you been hiding? I said and ruffled his curls.

"Buried deep in those books," He replied and grinned.

My brother was handsome. His Asian features were more prominent than mine; slanted eyes, spiky dark hair, small lips. Clay was about five-eleven and whenever he wasn't study he was either hanging with a girl or pumping weights. As a result, he had an impressive physique that drove the girls crazy.

My aunt and uncle arrived, and Mommy went into the kitchen and checked on dinner. I don't know why she was making such a fuss. Her cook, Amelia, had prepared the meal, and even set the table in the formal dining room before she left for the evening. I would make sure the dishes were loaded in the dishwasher before I left.

Christina was sitting beside me when she leaned over and whispered loud enough for me to hear, "Girl, you ain't lying. Isaiah is fine!"

I smirked. "I told ya." My eyes strayed back out on the deck to catch his amazing profile. He looked sexy as hell taking a long drag from one of my father's cigars.

"You know Dee is going to tell Max you were with another man," she warned.

"So what?" I said and shrugged. I was trying to act like I didn't care, but in reality I was worried. The last thing I wanted was to piss Max off. "Max and I aren't married. He's got enough to worry about with the baby coming and all." I was being sarcastic and Christina knew it.

Dinner was served and all of us made our way to the dining room. There was laughing and joking and I noticed how Isaiah fit in perfectly with my family. He even chimed in on a few stories. Amelia had made her sweet potato pie and with a scoop of vanilla ice cream it was to die for. We pigged out, laughed and then the family moved to the grand room where we played a few rounds of Taboo, girls against the guys. Naturally the women won. The guys then went out to the garage to look at an old car my father was trying to restore while the women cleaned up.

Christina and I were stacking plates in the dishwasher when she said, "Portia just texted. I guess I need to call and see what's going on." Christina released a heavy sigh. "Sometimes I wonder if marriage is the right thing. Maybe it isn't what it's cracked up to be."

My eyes met her with alarm. "How can you say that? Dee adores you."

She shrugged a shoulder beneath a mocha wrap dress. "Look at all the husbands my mother has had. And when it comes to Portia, Evan adores my sister, buys her anything in the world she wants and yet I can tell she isn't happy."

I figured at this point I had no other choice but to tell her what I had seen. "Christina, I have something to tell you."

I saw the look on her face and I hated to be the one to say it. "I saw Evan with another woman."

"What?" she cried. "Where?"

I told her about Isaiah and I having lunch and spotting Evan and the other woman. "She looked like a doctor."

Her eyes were blazing with fury. "I knew he was messing around! As soon as I my sister told me how he was acting, I knew it had to be another woman."

"You should have seen his face when he spotted me. I thought he was going to pee on himself."

"Did he say anything to you?" Christina asked curiously.

I reached for another glass and loaded it in the top rack and I replied, "Don't you know he had the nerve to ask me not to say anything?"

"Asshole. Portia's been dying to start a family and he told her no, not yet."

"Really?"

Christina nodded. "He's a control freak. Portia likes those kinds just like my mother."

"Your mother doesn't have a problem holding her own," I reminded. Jeanna was a force to be reckoned.

She didn't look convinced. "Maybe... and maybe not."

I rinsed off the eating utensils and asked, "Are you going to tell her?"

Christina shrugged. "I don't know. She said she's coming by my house later but I just don't know if I want to tell her. To be honest I really don't think my sister could handle the news. She acts so damn fragile at time."

I had to agree with her. Portia had given up a career to be a wife. I wasn't sure how she would even earn a living without Evan.

"Well, if you need proof, I took photos."

"What?" she blurted. "No freaking way!"

I held up a finger. "Hold up." I left the kitchen and hurried to retrieve my phone.

"I can't believe you took photos!" Christina barked when I returned.

"I figured Portia might be in denial if she didn't see it for herself." I unlocked my phone. They were the last ones I had taken. I opened the first photo then held out the phone.

Christina practically snatched it from my hand and I wasn't surprised that her mouth was hanging open. "I can't believe he has his tongue down her throat!"

"That bastard had the nerve to be cocky too." I snapped my fingers as something registered in my head. "I bet you that was him I had heard in the closet, talking at your party."

"What?" Her mouth was still hanging open.

"I heard this guy on the phone, talking to this female. I knew he sounded familiar but I just realized that was Evan I had heard."

Briefly Christina closed her eyes and shook her head. "He left the party early. Said he had an emergency at the hospital. I can't believe that bastard is messing around on my sister like that!" She drew in a deep breath. "I guess I need to find the right time to talk to her."

Nodding, I stacked the last of the forks in the dishwasher and closed the door. "Men ain't shit."

Christina winced. "How can you say that?"

I lifted my head and trapped her with my gaze. "It's true. You give them your heart and look what they do to you and then they think they can say sorry and everything is supposed to be okay."

She gave me a weird look. "Are we talking about my sister, or Isaiah?"

"What make you say that? He and I are good."

She stopped wiping down the counter and gave me her full attention. "Good in what way? Dating? Having sex... in love again?"

"Why you all in my business?" I didn't mean to snap but I did.

"Because you need someone to keep you on task. Answer this question for me... Why are you here with Isaiah?" Christina had her arms crossed and was leaning back against the counter as if she was waiting for the shoe to drop.

"We've been dating and we decided to come together."

"No I mean why are you dating him when that's not what you really want to do?"

I dropped my head so she couldn't look me in the eyes because if she did she would know. "Of course it's what I want. I wouldn't be going out with him if I didn't. We've talked and put the past behind us. Now we are working on trying to have a future."

"But you're not in love with him anymore," she reported.

I rolled my eyes. "I've always loved Isaiah."

Christina shook her head. "But you're not in love. Not the way you are with Max."

"How do you know how I feel about him?" I asked suspiciously. Did my best friend have x-ray vision or something?

"I saw the way you looked at Max. Anyone who saw the

two of you together would know you were in love."

My eyes shifted to the travertine-tiled floor. "I'm not in love."

"Are you going to stand there and tell me I'm lying?" she accused.

I glared over at her. "I'm going to tell you to mind your business. I know what I'm doing."

Christina gave a dry laugh. "I don't think you do and you keep it up you're going to lose the best thing that has ever happened to you."

I thought about what she said the rest of the evening and again while Isaiah drove me home and yet I wasn't ready to believe that Isaiah and I were never going to be. It wasn't fair! He was single, rich, educated and with no kids or baby mamas. Why couldn't I love him again?

"I had a great time as always," he said as he walked me to the door.

Dad had stopped me on the way out to let me know just how proud he was of me. What more could a girl want but the approval of her father? I'm not saying they wouldn't like Max, but I already knew my parents loved Isaiah and life with him could be wonderful.

"Would you like to come in?"

There was a cocky smirk on his face as if he had known all along I was going to ask. He had no idea the turmoil that was going on in my head. Parker and the baby weren't going away. Imagine my relief when he shook his head and declined.

"No, I better not." He looked down at me with a soft smile on his lips. "It's been a lovely evening, but if I stay I'm going to want to do a lot more than just talking. I don't want to rush things with you. I'm trying to court you the old-fashion way." He lowered his head until his lips covered mine. The kiss was soft, gentle and nice, nothing like the ones I shared with Max, but I kept telling myself it didn't really matter.

Liar!

"Dang girl. Those lips are too soft and tempting," he

teased then kissed me once more and pulled away. "Open the door and get inside before I change my mind." He was staring at me with this hungry look in his eyes and I knew he meant it. Once I was back in the house, I slipped into a pair of sweats and a t-shirt, grabbed a carton of butter pecan ice cream and curled on the couch in front of the television. I still had a library of shows I had saved on my DVR to watch.

My phone rang and my heart started pounding all crazy when I saw it was Max. I made myself take a deep breath, let it ring a bit before I finally answered it.

"Hello?"

"I can't believe you answered."

Yep, neither could I. "What do you want Max?" I said and didn't bother hiding my irritation.

"What do you mean what do I want? I want you."

Yeah, and I want you too. But being with him meant bringing drama to my life.

"You're quiet. I'm a big boy. Tell me you don't want me?" he insisted in that husky persuasive voice of his.

"I didn't say I don't want you."

Now he was getting all defensive. "You sure in the hell act like you don't. I haven't seen you in days and every time I call you're either blowing me off or not picking up the damn phone." He blew out a long breath. "I thought we were better than that?"

I sat there with ice cream running down my arm. He was right. I had been behaving like a spoiled brat who wanted things her way but was it so wrong to want a man all to myself?

I blew out a long shaky breath. "You're right. I should just be honest with you."

"Is there something you need to tell me?" he insisted. "If so, just tell me. No, you know what? Hold that thought. I'm on my way over." *Click.*

I couldn't believe he had hung up on me. I sprung out of the chair and put the ice cream back in the refrigerator then hurried up to shower and change into something attractive. The last thing I wanted was for him to take one look at me and question why he was even crazy about my frumpy looking behind in the first place. I slipped into a pair of jeans and a pink sweater. I decided to just mousse my hair and let it dry naturally.

I was back downstairs watching television by the time the doorbell rang. Once again my heart was pounding like crazy. I slowed it down, but then my coochie started purring.

Uh-uh, there will be no sex. He's just here to talk.

All that pep talking went out the door in the wind the moment I swung it open and spotted Max standing there. Even in black sweatpants and a matching hoodie, he managed to still look irresistibly handsome.

"Hey," was all I could get out my mouth as I stepped aside so he could enter. Max put his car keys in his front pocket of his pants then pulled me into his arms. His lips covered mine and I felt myself melting again. I forgot all about breathing as we fed on each other's mouth. I let the kiss go on for a while, but as soon as I felt my kitty starting to purr again, I gently eased back and gasped for air.

"I thought you came over so we could talk?"

He chuckled and brushed a hand across his head. "I seem to forget my last name when I'm around you," he admitted.

I know the feeling.

I signaled for him to follow me into the living room. I took a seat at one end of the couch while he took the other.

"So babe, what's going on?" His dark gaze was absolutely mesmerizing.

I got right to the point. "Did you and Parker work things out?"

"There's nothing to work out. I told you, I plan to be there for her until we find out if that's my seed or not."

So in other words, nothing had changed.

I shook my head. "See the problem is I don't know how I feel about all this."

Leaning forward, he rested his elbows on his knees and murmured, "It's not like I've lied to you."

See now he was pissing me off. "I didn't say you did, I'm just—"

"Hold up," His phone rang and he held up a finger telling me to wait until he finished his call. "Hey, what's going on?" Max rose and started walking around the room and the moment I saw him stall, I knew what was up before he had ended the call.

"Parker's in labor."

I didn't know whether to laugh or cry. The moment of truth was finally here. "Then you better get going."

He towered over me and said, "Babe, come with me to the hospital."

"What?" I sprung from the couch.

"Please, you're my girl and I need you there with me." His voice was stressed.

I looked at him, and saw the fear and excitement in his eyes. "I guess since you put it that way, okay, I'll go." Besides I was anxious to get my eyes on the little boy.

TWENTY

I slipped on my running shoes and a jacket and followed him out to his vehicle. He was trying to act like his normal joking self, but I could tell he was nervous because he kept saying the same thing over and over. And every time we were at a stop sign he tapped his fingers impatiently on the steering wheel and looked down at his watch.

"Max, relax. We've got plenty of time." I knew enough about babies to know they usually took hours to arrive. "How's she getting to the hospital?" I asked, hoping that we weren't stopping to pick her up along the way.

Damn, I'm selfish.

"One of her home girls is bringing her. She attended all of her Lamaze classes with her."

I tilted my head and studied his handsome profile. "I'm surprised she didn't ask you."

He swallowed. "She did but I decided I needed to draw the line somewhere."

I felt like cheering.

When we arrived at the hospital it was after ten so the parking lot was relatively empty. Max parked and we walked through the emergency room doors and to the front desk. While he talked with the nurse I looked around. The television was playing the news and there were quite a few people sitting in the waiting room. Two females in particular, were pointing and looking at me. *And so the drama begins.*

"They said she's been admitted and was just wheeled up to a labor and delivery room on the floor."

I nodded and kept looking at the women. "Do you know them?" I asked.

Max followed the direction of my eyes, then groaned. "Yeah, that's Parker's crew."

I guess that should have been obvious the way they were mean-mugging me. I decided to ignore them especially after Max took my hand and led me over to a chair.

"What's up Max?" one of the girls said. She had enough weave in her head to cover an entire horse.

He gave a head nod. "Hey Nora... Shay. How's she doing?"

"Acting a damn fool," the skinny one said causing the other to cackle like a hyena. "You should have heard her going off in the car. I was ready to pull over and push her ass out."

They chuckled and Max joined in. I barely broke a smile and focused on watching the news.

Max draped an arm over my chair and I rested my head on him. It was cold in the building but he was there to keep me warm.

"Maximilian James!"

We both sat up and looked over at the nurse standing near the desk calling his name. He rose and pulled me up beside him. "I need you babe."

Nodding, I followed him over to the nurse.

"Are you Maximilian James?" she said and gave him a disapproving look when she noticed me holding his hand.

"Yes I am. How's Parker?" he asked eyes attentive and worried.

"Contractions are about three minutes apart. She's asking for you. Follow me and I'll take you up. *Just you,*" she added, then turned and walked away.

Max stalled. I released his hand and urged him to follow her. "Go. Fathers aren't supposed to sit in waiting rooms. Go see your son be born."

He hesitated a moment longer and then the nurse had the nerve to suck her teeth impatiently and say, "Are you coming or not?"

"Go," I urged.

"Thanks babe... you're the best." Lowering his head, Max pulled my lips in for a kiss, then eased back, turned, and hurried to follow the nurse.

I was all alone.

The last thing I wanted to do was sit over there with Parker's friends staring me down. I moved over near the automatic door, texted Christina to let her know Parker was in labor then passed the time playing word games on my phone. Eventually I started having the munchies and hit up the vending machine for some cookies and a diet soda then I wandered back over to watch television. Parker's friends were no longer in the waiting room. I wasn't sure if they had gone up to see her, or if they had left, either way I decided to watch a little television while I waited. *Cheers* was on and I watched one episode and then another and after drinking all that soda I needed to pee. I went in search of the ladies room and when I stepped out the stall one of Parker's friends, the skinny one, was standing at the sink.

"Hey," she said.

I nodded and moved over to wash my hands.

"Are you and Max a couple?" Her big round eyes were checking me out from head to toe.

"Why?" I asked with straight attitude because if I went with anything else she would have thought I was a punk. Maybe now she would think twice.

She held up her hands. "Hey, I was just curious, that's all. He looked happy with you."

While I washed my hands, I eyed her suspiciously through the mirror. "Yeah we're a couple."

"I figured as much." She crossed her arms. "And how do you feel about him having a baby by Parker?"

Did she really think I would answer that? I shrugged. "That's between the two of them."

She just stood there as if she was contemplating something. I balled up my left fist just in case she decided to strike me in the head. Being attacked once was more than enough.

"If I tell you something, do you promise to leave my name out of it?"

I eyed her inquisitively. "I don't even know your name."

She rolled her eyes. "It's Shay but I'll deny it either way."

"Okay, so what is it?" I said like it was no big deal.

"Well... Parker has been trying to have a baby and trap a man for years."

I figured as much but I kept that observation to myself.

"She has this thing," she paused and stared at the door like she was expecting someone to come barging in at any moment.

"What kinda thing?" I coaxed before she clammed up and changed her mind.

She leaned in close and I smelled liquor on her breath. "I know Max is hoping that baby isn't his, but he might as well get ready to deal with that crazy bitch until his son is old enough to leave home."

I swung around and faced her. "How can you be so sure and what kinda thing does she have?"

"You know what... I probably shouldn't be saying this but I am." She looked me dead in the eyes. "Parker pokes holes in the condoms she uses with a pen."

"What?" I'm sure what little color I had drained from my face.

Shay nodded. "She even showed me. She'll take a brand new box and poke holes through the condom wrapping with a safety pin. Then when a guy comes over, she pulls one out of the box like it's no big deal."

"What the hell? How many men has she done this to?"

She suddenly dropped her eyes and looked as if she had confessed more than she had wanted. "Too many."

I couldn't believe it. If what she said was true, then there was a good chance the baby she was carrying might be Max's after all.

"Why are you telling me this?" I asked frowning.

Shay huffed in frustration. "Parker pissed me off a few months ago when I found out she fucked my man so I consider this payback. However, like I said, if you tell anyone I will deny it." With that, she left the ladies room. I just stood there shaking and thinking there was no way in hell this was really happening.

My cell phone started ringing and I looked down at my caller ID. It was Christina. I walked out the room, across the waiting area and stepped outside the sliding door so I could talk to her in private. A cool October breeze was kicking up its heels.

"Hey."

"How's it going?" she asked.

"It's going. He's upstairs probably helping her deliver the baby."

Christina blew out a long breath. That's my girl. Sharing in my frustration. "Now at least you'll finally know."

"I guess but I have a bad feeling about all this." I looked over my shoulder and made sure no one was around, then went on to tell her what Shay had told me in the ladies room.

"Are you kidding? Who does that shit?" Apparently Parker did. "Are you going to tell Max?"

I walked around the circular driveway as I spoke. "I don't know. Shay will deny it and I don't want him to think I'm being a hater."

"Are you planning on going up to see the baby after he's delivered?"

"I don't know. I'm here because Max asked me to come. But to be honest, if I had driven my own car, I would have already left." I released a long frustrated breath.

"I think it's all going to work out. Just hang in there. I think Max is worth it."

That was the only thing keeping me there.

"The reason I was calling was to tell you Dereon said they found the stolen car."

"What? Where?"

"Off of St. Louis Avenue, not far from the Greyhound station."

My heartrate increased. "Did they find out who was driving it?"

"Not yet. Hopefully the police will know something soon."

A man was walking in my direction and I put some distance between us. I'd already been attacked once in a parking lot. I definitely didn't need that happening again.

We chatted a little longer then I hung up and went back

inside to the waiting area. Shay and that other chick were back and laughing at King of Queens. I caught Shay looking at me out the corner of her eye.

Ignoring them, I was watching television as well when the door blew open and Parker's big Amazon friend came plowing into the room.

"Yo, it's official. She had a boy!"

"Aw-ight now."

"Missy, how's she doing?"

Missy spotted me, gave me a long stare, then started grinning. I focused on the television and pretended I wasn't even listening.

"She's doing good. She pushed that little boy out like a pro. You should have seen Max's face when he saw the head coming out. I thought that dude was gonna faint."

"Hell nah!"

"But that little boy looks just like his daddy," Missy added, probably for my own benefit. My stomach clenched painfully.

There were all talking loud at the same time and I tried to keep a straight face and not jump to conclusions.

"C'mon y'all, let's go up to see her real quick before we head home."

Missy waved for them to follow, but before she passed me, she stopped and towered over my chair. I lifted my head slowly and glared up at the hairs on her chin.

"If I was you I would find myself another man."

"If I was you, I would get the hell outta my face!" I sprung from the seat and I couldn't believe it when she jumped back. Good. I was sick of their shit.

"Missy, you gonna let her get away with that." I should have known the one impersonating a horse would be an instigator.

She sucked her teeth and gave me another hard stare, then had the nerve to start laughing and the other two joined her.

"What the hell is so funny?" I spat. My hands were at my waist and my chest was heaving.

"You, boo. A female with any respect wouldn't be sitting

down in the waiting room while her so-called man is up on the floor bringing his son in the world with another woman." She was laughing again. "Y'all c'mon."

They headed toward the elevators. I noticed the nurse behind the desk trying to pretend like she wasn't listening but there was no hiding the smirk on her face. I sat back down onto the chair, feeling like a damn fool. She was right, what in the world was I doing here? If I had my own vehicle, I would have already been half-way home.

"Babe!"

I swung around and spotted Max walking across the emergency room with a smile like I had never seen before. His entire face was lit up.

"Did she have the baby?" I asked as if I didn't already know.

He lowered his head and kissed me, then smiled against my lips before pulling back. "Yes, nine pounds and fifteen ounces."

"That's a big baby."

"Yeah he's a little man." The joy on his face was something I would never forget.

"I'm happy for you. Really."

"C'mon, I want to take you up and introduce you to my son." Max laced my fingers with his and led me toward the elevator.

"So he really is yours?" I held my breath as I waited for an answer.

He shrugged. "I don't know yet. We'll have to take a test once Parker is feeling better." He searched my eyes. "Hey, how are you?" he said and leaned forward and kissed me soundly on the mouth. "Thank you so much for coming with me." Max draped an arm around me and we stepped into the elevator. Once the doors shut his lips covered mine and I sank into the kiss. I wished this moment could last forever, just me and him, no one else.

I heard someone clearing their throat and opened my eyes to see the elevator had arrived on the floor and the doors had slid open.

Missy gave me the eye, then looked at Max. "Parker's looking for you," she snapped.

"I'll check on her in a minute." Max took my hand and led me off the elevator. I smirked as I walked past. I know it pissed them off he had brought me up onto the floor and I wasn't going to let them know how I really felt.

Max led me down to the end of the corridor to a glass-encased room. "I think he's down here." There were dozens of small bassinets lined in front of the window for everyone to see. My eyes traveled over all of the tiny little boys and girls. They were so precious and innocent. None of them asked to be in this world.

"There he is!" Max shouted loud enough for one of the nurses to turn around and smile.

Slowly I walked over to the glass, holding my breath. I was both anxious and afraid to see him at the same time. My eyes settled onto the little boy lying there with his eyes wide open as if he knew he was being looked at.

I gasped. He was so beautiful I wanted to cry. He had a head full of dark curly hair and a strong nose. It was similar to Max's, but it was too soon to tell. He was pecan brown but his ears were dark so I was sure he was going to change over the next few days. But it was the eyes that were dark and intense. It was too soon to be sure but they definitely looked familiar. My entire body was shaking. This was a Derwin and Melanie moment for the television series, *The Game*.

"What are you going to name him?" I asked.

Max came up behind me and wrapped his arms around my middle, then rested his chin on my shoulder. "Maximilian Jr."

I was stunned. The test hadn't even been done and yet he was already claiming the little boy as his. Hell, I couldn't blame him. He was so adorable who wouldn't want him in their life, but at the same time it meant that this was the moment I had been dreading. I stood there, staring, with tears running down my face. This was so unreal.

"He's beautiful." Really, what else was there for me to say? Max had already pretty much decided he was going to be a father to this child, regardless.

"Yeah, he is quite handsome," he said and chuckled.

We continued to stare until a nurse pointed at her watch and then the blinds slowly slid down over the windows.

"I guess I better take you home."

I nodded. That sounded like a wonderful idea since I needed to be in the office in a few hours.

Max held my hand out to his Tahoe and never let it go the entire ride home. Once there he climbed out, came around and scooped me into his arms. I think that was the first laugh I'd had all evening.

We went inside and Max reached up and brushed a lock of hair away from my face and our eyes locked before I became fixated on his mouth. His luscious mouth. Instantly his lips were all over me. Soon we both forgot about everything but each other. I wanted to talk about us and what was going to happen now that the baby was here, but when Max reached down and cupped my breasts with his hands and it was all she wrote. My body came alive and when his fingers caught my nipple I was pudding in his hands. Damn him! Max knew my spot quite well and there was just nothing I could do about it. I tugged him into the living room, ready to remind him of what he had right here with me.

He broke the kiss and his lips traveled down to my neck. I was already reaching down for the drawstring inside his sweatpants. Max stopped kissing me long enough to raise my sweater over my head, then he was unclasping my bra and lowering his mouth to my breasts. I cried out and arched my body, drawing my nipple even further between his lips. I don't have any idea how our clothes came off. His thick, long, chocolate dick sprung erect in front of me, and I was leaning over doggy-style against the couch. Max buried himself balls deep inside of me. Within seconds he was pounding so hard I had to hold on and steady myself so my knees wouldn't buckle. Not that I was complaining. The sex was rough and intense. Max brought his hands around and gripped my hips, guiding and controlling the rhythm.

"Oh, this pussy is good!" he groaned.

"No, the dick is good. It's so good!" I was screaming, panting and breathing heavily. My man was definitely a force to be reckoned with. It was one for the record books because the next thing I knew I was coming and Max was only moments behind. You would have thought he was howling at the moon.

I collapsed on the couch laughing with him rolling beside me. Our bodies were completely covered in sweat and I was satisfied. His gaze met mine and I couldn't help but smile. He held me in his arms planting kisses along my neck and shoulder and I took it as a sign that everything was the way it should be and nothing had changed. We were going to be alright. I could feel it.

By the time my heart slowed, I kissed him once more, then rose from the couch, eager to slide into my bed. "C'mon let's go upstairs." I could already visualize another long night with my legs wrapped around his waist. But as I stepped out into the foyer, I heard the ruffling of clothes and realized Max wasn't following me. He was getting dressed.

I swung around. "Aren't you coming upstairs?"

"No, I'm going to spend the night at the hospital. After they get done with all of his tests and assessment, my son's gonna spend the night in the room. He'll be a little too much for Parker to handle tonight, don't you think?"

Dumfounded, I just stood there not sure what to say. "Yeah sure." I watched as he disappeared in the bathroom and then came out a few minutes later.

"How about I come by your job tomorrow and take you to breakfast?" Max walked toward me. I was standing there naked and feeling ridiculous.

Somehow I managed to lift my head and smile. "Sure, just call me." My body was humming with humiliation. I barely remember returning his kiss or walking him to the door. It wasn't until I heard his vehicle pulling out my driveway that I finally snapped out of my funk.

"I don't know if I can do this," I muttered as I walked up to my room trying to figure out if he was really worth it.

TWENTY-ONE

When my phone rang, I had been at it for three hours straight; ordering food, arranging for wait staff, and preparing a new contract for Mia to fax over to a client for signature. Being busy was definitely a welcomed pleasure, especially since I had yet to hear back from Max.

Yesterday he was supposed to have taken me out to breakfast, but called at the last moment to say the baby was jaundiced and he wanted to stay near. Today his son was being circumcised and he didn't want to miss it. I suggested meeting for dinner, but Parker was being discharged later and he wanted to be there to take them home.

Feeling jealous was an understatement. I also missed him like crazy. Just two weeks ago, we were spending every night together and I had been feeling on top of the world, now I was back to thinking about him, yearning for his touch, and his strong arms.

Thank goodness I had too much to do, otherwise, I don't know what I would have done. I had a blown sugar design I had to prepare for a company Halloween party and needed to stay focused.

The sugar mixture began to boil and I reached for a pastry brush and brushed the crystallized sugar off the sides of the pot. The mixture needed to reach three hundred degrees before I turned it off to cool.

"So this is where the confectionista is hiding."

I glanced over my shoulder as Isaiah walked into the room and grinned. "Hey, what are you doing here?" I asked.

"You were on my mind so I thought I'd drop by and see you." He moved up behind me. Without taking my eyes off the sugar I tilted my face, offering him my cheek.

"What are you making?" he asked.

"I'm preparing the sugar for some Halloween art, ghosts and pumpkins," I explained as I dipped the candy thermometer into the pot. Instantly the sugar began to crystallize on the gadget. I turned off the fire then removed the pot from the heat. "I'm going to be making a dozen of them. They will be table centerpieces."

"What are you going to do next?"

"Once the sugar cools to two hundred-fifty degrees, I'll add the orange food coloring, and flavoring, then pour it into a glass measuring cup I have warming in the oven.

"Why warm?"

He was asking a lot of questions, but I liked it. "Because it could crack and make a huge mess."

"Hmmm, amazing."

"Yeah, I think so," I wiped my hands on a towel. Isaiah stepped back, allowing me to turn away from the stove. "I'll make two more pots. One white, and one black." Smiling, I slipped off my apron and took in his appearance.

"You look nice," I purred appreciatively. He looked breathtaking in navy slacks and a white button-down shirt. Expensive loafers were on his feet.

"Is it safe to kiss you?"

I nodded playfully. "Yes, it is."

He drew me close and brought his lips down over mine. The kiss was sweet and mannerable. For once I wish he'd be hard and reckless. I sighed then drew back from his hold, ending the kiss.

"Guess what?" Isaiah's eyes were twinkling with excitement.

"What?"

"I was officially offered the job."

"Oh wow! Congratulations!" I cried because I really was happy for him.

"Thank you. It feels really good to finally be back where I belong. Now I just need to put a few things in place and everything will be as it should be." I noticed the way he was staring at me as he spoke.

"How about dinner tonight to celebrate?" he suggested.

How could I say no when he looked so happy? "Sure, but only if I get to treat."

"Okay," he replied even though we both knew he would never allow me to pay. He was just too much of a gentleman for that. "What time shall I pick you up?"

"I should be done by eight."

"Eight it is."

I tilted my head and was ready for the next kiss. Just as we pulled away, Christina came waltzing into the kitchen. "Hi Isaiah." She sauntered over and he engulfed her in his arms.

"Christy, Isaiah got the job."

She drew back, eyes wide. "Congratulations, not that I'm surprised." She gave a dismissive wave and playfully rolled her eyes. "There was no doubt in my mind they were going to hire you."

"I appreciate the vote of confidence," he said and winked. "Well, I better get out of here. CC, I will see you at seven."

As soon as he was gone Christina swirled around on the heels of her orange pumps. "Where are you going tonight?"

I shrugged and reached for the thermometer. "We're going out to celebrate."

"The two of you have been spending a lot of time together."

I added the orange food coloring as I replied, "Might as well. Max is just too busy for me right now."

"Aren't you being a little selfish?"

I whipped around and looked at her. "You gotta lot of nerve. You're the queen of selfish."

She laughed and leaned against the counter. "Yes, but everyone knows I'm selfish. You, on the other hand, are not."

I stirred until the color was uniform, then reached for the maple flavoring. "I guess I feel left out. The baby is something he and Parker are enjoying together. I'm just trying to figure out where I fit in."

"Has he said anything else about the blood test?"

I shook my head. "Nope and I'm not bringing it up anymore."

The whole thing with Max and his baby mama, and Isaiah

coming back was really starting to drive me crazy. It probably should have been an easy decision but I couldn't even figure out which direction to turn.

I could tell she was trying to think of something to make me feel better. "I could only imagine what Max is going through right now. Being a father. Dee would be a nervous wreck, waiting on me hand and foot."

"He waits on you hand and foot now."

"Yeah, I guess he does," she said with a smirk. "But I imagine it would be so much more intense. You gotta give the man some time."

"I am. And in the meantime I will hang out with Isaiah." I was being stubborn.

Christina scowled. "All you're doing is giving that man hope."

"Maybe there is hope," I said and shrugged.

"And maybe you're a fool," She retorted.

I ignored her comment and reached inside the oven and with a mitt, removed the glass cup from the oven then slowly poured the orange sugar mixture inside.

"You and Isaiah are too much like brother and sister. You need to leave that idea alone before you mess around and end up losing Max."

I glanced at her and away. "How can I lose something I never had? Parker and the baby were in his life before I came and they will be there for the next eighteen years. She has already made it clear that she isn't letting anyone close to him. How can I compete with a child?"

"You know what they say… if you can't beat 'em, join 'em. I'm sure Max wouldn't have a problem letting his son be a part of your life."

"I bet you Parker will." It wasn't a dare. It was a fact.

Christina gave a rude snort. "Now that I can't argue."

"I don't want any drama," I said with growing frustration.

Christina waved a negligent hand, as her eyes darkened with wisdom. "No, but you love Max, so you need to ask yourself if he's worth fighting for."

I was still thinking about our conversation much later while I was pulling the sugar, creating pumpkins and ghosts. Somehow I managed to think and work at the same time which is something I rarely do. Once the centerpiece was done, Christina and I cleaned and prepped the kitchen to prepare for the catered meal we had to prepare in the morning.

I went home exhausted. I think it was more mental than physical and if Isaiah hadn't texted, I would have forgotten about our date. Instantly I hopped in the shower then climbed out and searched for something to wear. I didn't dare sit down because if I did I was sure to have fallen asleep.

He drove us to an authentic Indian restaurant, decorated with old-world charm. Sitting across from Isaiah was like déjà vu. Indian restaurants used to be our spot. Even now looking at him, I remember how much I loved just being in his company.

"What's your spice level tonight?" His lips twitched.

It has always been a contest, whose food was spicier than the other. "My stomach isn't like it used to be. I prefer to enjoy my food."

When our waitress arrived we ordered garlic nann, which was a garlic herb bread. I wanted coconut curry shrimp medium hot while Isaiah decided he wanted his lamb Indian hot.

"You still like watching the DIY channel," he asked between chews.

I nodded and smiled because he had remembered. "Oh yeah but a lot has changed since you've been home. I watch HGTV. House decorating, flips, rehabs you name it. It is so addictive."

"Remember how we used to dream about the house we wanted?"

I nodded. "Of course I do. We used to spend hours just riding around, picking out our dream home." My smile widened at the memory. "Oh yeah. There we were, two dreamers."

"But look how far we have come," he said and placed his

hand over mine.

I stared at his face, taking in how handsome he was. In fact Isaiah seemed to get sexier each and every time I saw him.

As we ate dinner I found myself watching his mouth, the way he ate, his chew, and compared him to Max.

"What's on your mind?" Isaiah was staring at me, brow was quirked as if he had asked me a question I had missed.

"Did you say something?" I said and wiggled my shoulders trying to clear my head.

"I asked if you ever thought about what if things had been different between us?"

"I used to all the time." And I was pissed at him for even bringing it up.

"And now?"

I rolled my eyes and stabbed a shrimp with my fork. "Now, it's too late to live in the past." Even though that was exactly what I had been doing.

"But there is always the future. I had a lot of time to think," he managed between chews. "And I realized back then I was scared of commitment."

"Scared?"

He nodded gloomily. "Seriously. I'm not going to lie, I was terrified so I panicked and ran."

I watched him bite into his lamb and waited until he swallowed to ask, "How come you couldn't have just told me you weren't ready for anything permanent?"

"I really don't know why. It sounds so simple now."

Ya think.

Isaiah frowned. "I guess I didn't want to disappoint my parents, your parents and especially you. Everyone wanted us to be together and I started questioning if we were together because everyone expected us to be or because that was what we really wanted."

I rested my elbows on the table and took a moment to think about what he had just said. "I think it was probably a combination. I had planned on marrying you for as long as I could remember. I think it just became something that was expected to someday happen, but when you left and went to

Africa, I realized what I felt for you ran deeper than that. I truly loved you."

"Me too. I've spent many nights lying in my bed feeling like I had made the wrong decision."

I gazed at him for several seconds. "And do you still feel like you made the wrong choice?"

He hesitated. "Working overseas was something I had to do for me. I felt compelled to give my time, but I should have told you I loved you and asked you to wait. Hell, I should have married you the way we always planned and found a way to make it all work. Instead I gave up something I wanted so badly for something I needed to do. That's something I'll always regret."

Our eyes locked. His gaze was deep and passionate. "I can't believe we are finally able to talk like this."

A smile twitched my lips. "That's what was missing from our relationship. Communication. This time I plan on doing everything to show you how much I want you in my life, permanently."

His voice was raw with emotion. *Permanently* sounded like a lifelong commitment. Once upon a time, yes, but now it was something I just wasn't sure I wanted anymore.

Much later we were sitting on the couch in my living room. I raised my glass. "Let's toast to you…much success as the newest addition to the family practice team at Barnes Jewish Hospital."

He clicked his glass against mine and we both took a sip at the same time. It was getting late, and I had a busy day tomorrow, but instead of sending Isaiah on his way I decided to invite him in for a drink to celebrate. "This is a start of a new life for you. Are you sure you're ready for the commitment?" I teased.

He laughed so hard he ended up spilling white wine on his shirt and my couch. I jumped up and went into the kitchen for a towel.

"Sorry," he said when I returned. "I can be such a klutz."

I paused, towel in hand and gave him a sweet smile. "I hope you don't say that around the patients. I could just see you with a scalpel in your hand."

Laughing I started soaking up the spill on the couch. "Why don't you take your shirt off so I can clean that stain for you?"

I looked down at the couch and didn't bother to look up again until the spill was absorbed and when I rose and spotted Isaiah standing there with his shirt off, my jaw dropped.

"Here you go."

I took the shirt but my eyes never left his chest. Oh my, he had a beautiful chest.

And no taco meat.

I really don't know who made the first move. Maybe it was him but it could have been me. All I know was his arms were at my waist, drawing me closer.

"I missed you," he growled playfully against my lips.

"Really?" I purred and I placed a hand to his chest prepared to push him away but I felt one of his pectoral muscles flex and instead I caught myself sliding my fingers along his chest.

Isaiah lowered his head until his lips were against mine and within seconds our tongues were dancing. He was a great kisser. Over the years he had gotten more experienced and a great deal more confident.

For a fleeting moment I started to think that maybe I needed to stop while I still could, but then Isaiah reached up and cupped my breasts. The motion was torturously slow and arousing. I don't know what was worse; sex, hard and fast, or foreplay that was sensual enough to drive you insane. And then he found my nipple and I felt my body relax and a sigh escaped my lips.

"I haven't forgotten your spot," he murmured.

I couldn't believe how assertive he had become. My body was getting hot, the temperature rising and my knees ready to give out. After all these years, Isaiah remembered what I liked. That meant so much I gave in to what I was feeling—aroused, sexy, and horny.

I brought my arms around his neck and arched my body into his touch. His hand made its way underneath my blouse and his fingers slipped under my bra.

"I want you," he said and I no longer felt the need to object. All the anger and resentment I had felt for him over the last five years was gone. I wanted to let the past go and see what the future could bring.

Isaiah released my breasts long enough to help me unbutton my blouse. The entire time I was working those tiny buttons through the holes, he stood there, looking at me, eyes blazing gold with lust. I shrugged out of the blouse, followed by my bra and then he gently pushed me back on the sofa. Isaiah wasted no time bringing his lips to my nipples and suckled like a newborn. His mouth was a little rough and the whole time I found myself wondering if Parker was breastfeeding. It's crazy and definitely a mood killer but I couldn't help it. Max was probably right there, all three of them one big happy couple. I don't know why I cared so much except the fact that I loved the idiot. The one thing I swore never to do again after Isaiah. But apparently tonight was about do-overs and getting things right. And Isaiah was offering me a second chance at what could be an amazing life together.

I shook off thoughts of Max and allowed my hands to run up and down Isaiah's back. The dude was in such amazing shape. Muscles were rippling beneath my fingertips and the feeling made him all the more attractive to me. His lips had traveled down to my belly button and then back up to my nipples. I was squirming beneath him because I was beyond the foreplay. I brought my hand around and started working at his pants while he bunched my skirt up at my waist and slid my panties down my legs. Isaiah rose long enough to slide his slacks down and then his boxers and when I saw his cock it took everything to hold it together. It wasn't anything close to what Max was packing and for the first time I noticed it was crooked and curved to the left.

He removed a condom from his wallet, quickly slipped it on, then lowered back on top of me, bringing his lips to mine. We kissed and his tongue worked its magic to the point my body was starting to get heated, but I realized it was because I was thinking about Max and his magic stick. Isaiah didn't try to put it in right away. My mind was so consumed with Max that I had no idea how long Isaiah had been winding his hips and dry humping me. I peeked a look at Isaiah, teeth gritted, perspiration beading across his nose, and I suddenly wondered what in the hell was I doing. I can't do this. "Isaiah, I—"

"I'm sorry. I'm really sorry," he blurted as he rolled off me with frustration and took a seat at the end of my couch. What was he apologizing for?

"What are you talking about?"

He gave a nervous laugh. "I guess I was so excited about being with you, I ejaculated prematurely."

I sat up on the couch. "Prematurely, as in when?"

I could tell he was embarrassed. "The moment I laid on top of you."

Seriously? I looked down at the condom and sure enough he had dropped a load. I breathed a sigh of relief. Isaiah had that problem back in college . And this was one time I was grateful.

I looked at him sitting there with his eyes closed, jaw tight with humiliation. Back then I had been willing to work with Isaiah because I loved him, but not now, not when I knew there was something else waiting for me.

You can't keep playing with people's emotions.

Reaching over, Isaiah placed a gentle hand to my knee. "I'm sorry. I promise next time will be better."

I had a strong feeling there wouldn't be a next time.

TREY

"I think her office is somewhere over there," Reggie said over the heavy beat of the music blasting in my Avalanche.

I let my eyes travel up and down the street looking for the building. I didn't come to Clayton that often so I wasn't familiar with the area but for some homemade truffles, I was willing to go door-to-door if I had to.

Reggie pointed to the strip of storefronts across the street. "Hey, Trey, there it is over there."

I looked over and there in fancy script letters was *Cater to You*. "Pink, I shoulda known," I said and chuckled as I pulled the car into the parking lot across the street.

"Yeah those ladies are definitely something else, but Berlin loves those truffles so I'm gonna give her exactly what she wants."

"How's she feeling, man?"

Reggie scowled. "Morning sickness still kicking her ass. Now she's complaining of feeling fat."

"And you think giving her truffles is going to make her feel less fat?"

My man tossed his head back with laughter. "Hey, I'm willing to do whatever it takes. You'll find out when you decide to have a baby."

"Oh hell no! I gotta get married first and I ain't ready yet to give up that playas card."

"Never say never, bruh."

I'd been hearing that same thing for years. There were just too many women out there. Why chose just one when I could have a different female in my bed any night of the week?

"Park there," Reggie suggested.

I squeezed between two pickup trucks. Reggie and I climbed out and were laughing at some dude walking by in a tight-ass suit when I spotted two guys attempting to break into a vehicle.

"Hey Reg.... isn't that Claudia's Range Rover?"

His head whipped in the direction I was looking. "Hell yeah." He muttered then stormed in their direction. "Hey, what the hell y'all doing?"

There was no way I was letting Reggie confront those two alone, so I followed. At the sound of his voice, they looked up, saw us coming and took off across the busy streets. Cars were honking and one of them, a blond guy barely missed being clipped by a car before he jumped out the way. I dashed out in front of a black SUV and followed Reggie who was in hot pursuit of a tall, lanky black man. I noticed the other making a detour between two buildings and I raced down the sidewalk heading his way. There was no way I was letting him get away.

The white guy looked over his shoulder and when he realized I was still following him he picked up speed and hurried down to the end of the block. He tried to jump over a car and ended up flipping and falling in the middle of the street.

"Where you think you're going?" I yelled as I yanked his stocky ass up off the concrete and twisted one arm behind his back.

"Mothafucka let me go!" he snarled and tried to jerk free but I held onto him.

"Not until the police get here." I walked him down the street back toward the office. "I don't know if you know this but that SUV you were messing with... it belongs to a very good friend of mine."

"I wasn't messing with no vehicle!" he said and continued to struggle but he was no match. Pedestrians were looking. I even saw someone drag out their cell phone and snap a few photographs. Yes, I'm sure it probably looked strange, but unfortunately I wasn't letting him go until the police arrived.

"Keep moving," I demanded when his steps slowed,

trying to be reluctant. "I hate to have to clock you upside your head."

At the warning, his steps increased and I instructed him to make a right at the corner. Holding firmly to his arm, I led him up the street and over to the suite.

"Go through that door," I ordered and pointed to the glass door. He opened it with his one arm, and I braced the weight with my hip then followed him inside.

I hauled him into the lobby and noticed a beautiful woman sitting behind the desk. As soon as she spotted me, she jumped from her chair and hugged the wall.

"Can I help you?" she asked and I could see the surprise in her beautiful brown eyes.

I nodded and forced the man down to his knees. "Can you get Christina and then call the police?"

I hated to see the fear on her beautiful cinnamon-colored face. Maybe bringing him inside wasn't such a good idea.

As she slid past me and down the hall, I watched the sway of her luscious hips. She was short and thick, just the way I liked them. The skirt she wore complimented her curves, while leaving plenty of room for me to slide my hand underneath if I needed to.

There was a loud thump. I swung around as Reggie came through the door, pushing the assailant to the floor with a hard shove.

"I was wondering where you were," he managed between deep breaths.

"Man, I was wondering the same about you."

"Everything alright?" he asked and held out his fist and gave me dap.

I nodded. "It's all good. I just sent some fine honey to grab Christina and call the police." The black dude tried to rise to his feet, but I brought my foot to his back and shoved him back onto the ground. "Stay down. And you… you get down too." I released my hold on blondie and waited until he was lying on the floor as well. "Next time rob someone's car at night when you have a better chance of getting away with it."

"Let me call Dee." Reggie whipped out his phone and

dialed Dereon. He answered just as I heard running feet. I looked up to see Claudia and Christina both wearing aprons, rushing into the lobby.

"What in the world is going on?" Christina asked. She would probably have a fit if she knew she had flour on her nose. I didn't have the heart to tell her.

I pointed down at the two. "We caught these two breaking into Claudia's car."

"What?" Claudia jerked back and looked from me to Reggie with her eyes wide and then down at the two. "What were they doing at my car?"

I shrugged. "I have no idea but Reggie's on the line with Dee now."

I gave her a hard stare. "Claudia, do either of these guys look familiar to you?"

She cautiously drew closer and looked at both of them from above. They were lying face down. "I can't see their faces," she said and I heard the way her voice shook.

"Wait... what's that on his wrist?"

I reached down and turned the black dude's arms so she could take a closer look.

"That's it! That's the tattoo I had saw on one of the guys who attacked me! I remember that bloody knife. Oh my God!" she screamed and backed away. Christina ran over and comforted her. Shit! Max was going to have my ass for this.

The guy attempted to get up from the floor, but I kneeled down with my knee at his back. "Where do you think you're going?"

He mumbled under his breath.

"Say one more thing and I swear I'm gonna put you to sleep!"

There were sirens coming from a distance, which was a good thing. I wasn't sure how much longer I would be able to restrain from punching one of them especially now that I knew these were the guys who had attacked Claudia behind The Hole.

What were they after?

By the time the two were being hauled away in handcuffs,

Dereon rushed into the office.

"You girls okay?"

"Baby, Reggie and Trey caught them trying to break into Claudia's car," Christina exclaimed and she and Claudia rushed over. Dereon put an arm around each of them and they all started talking at the same time.

I noticed the beauty had returned to her desk and I couldn't keep my eyes off of her. She was cinnamon brown with dark, wide set eyes and a small nose that was so cute, I had the urge to walk over and touch it. And then there were the high cheekbones and lips that were full and pouty. Her features resembled Naomi Campbell so much I wondered if maybe she too was from Jamaica. She wore her hair pulled back in a bun which left her long neck exposed and there were silver hoops dangling from her earlobes. The way she had my loins heating, there was no way I was leaving before I had a chance to find out if she was single.

"I can't believe they thought they could break into her car in the middle of the day. I wonder what they were looking for?" Reggie spat.

Claudia shook her head. "I have no idea."

"Well, the police are out in the lot right now taking fingerprints. Once they get done I'll let you check and see if anything is missing." Dereon kissed her cheek then turned to me and Reggie. "Good job, bruh."

I gave him a head nod. "No problem."

Claudia walked over and wrapped her arms around my neck. "Thanks Trey." When she drew back I saw the fear still in her eyes. Those dudes were going to have hell to pay.

"Any time, baby girl."

Dereon was walking to the door when he turned and said, "Hey, y'all knuckleheads stick around. The police will want to talk to you before you leave."

"No problem." I was in no rush. I leaned in and whispered near Claudia's ear, "Who is that?"

"That's my assistant, Mia." A soft smile curled her lips. "Want me to introduce you?"

I squeezed her shoulder then shook my head. "No need. I

can handle that on my own." My eyes locked in on her profile as I strolled over to her desk, rubbing my palms together. I don't know how long I was standing there before she glanced up briefly at me.

"Can I help you?"

I licked my lips. The ladies love it when I do that. "I sure hope so. I'm Trey. I thought I would come over and introduce myself."

"Why?"

"What?" Her question knocked me off my game.

"Why did you come over and introduce yourself?" she asked impatiently.

I was taken aback by her response. That was not at all what I wanted to hear. "I figure since everyone else knows each other I would come over and make your acquaintance. I'm Trey by the way." I held out my hand. She looked at it and hesitated before finally taking it, but she barely shook it before releasing it.

"Nice to meet you. Are you the one picking up truffles?"

"So you do know who I am?" I said with my signature smirk. "Yep, that would be me. It's my mother's birthday."

Nodding, Mia rose from her seat and without saying a word left, and then came back shortly carrying two small pink boxes tied with a white bow. "There's one for you and the other is for Reggie."

"Thank you," I replied and tried to make eye contact only she refused to look at me.

"They're delicious. I hope your mother enjoys them."

Watching her mouth as she spoke I discovered something else was equally delicious.

"Thank you and you have a good day." Mia spun her chair around, picked up the phone and made a call.

Breathing in deeply, I tried to keep my composure, but it wasn't easy considering I wasn't used to anyone blowing me off like that. I'm serious. Women were usually throwing themselves at me. But it seemed Mia wasn't like all the others, instead, she was the type of women who could easily get under my skin.

Somehow, some way I was going to find a way to get her attention because it appeared it was going to require a great deal more than impressing her with heroism.

One thing about me, I loved a challenge.

MIA

I dialed the phone and was practically holding my breath as I waited for Trey to move away from my desk. I couldn't believe he was talking to me.

I had spotted him at Christina's engagement party. The entire night I watched him, hoping he would have at least made eye contact. Only he never looked my way. He was too busy flirting with every woman who came within ten feet of him and there had been plenty. It seemed they all wanted to get close to Dereon and his crew. Not that I could blame them. The men were definitely something worth looking at. Trey in particular. That man stirred up feelings and desires I hadn't experienced in a long time.

I finally stopped playing with the phone and returned it to the cradle then swiveled around on my chair. Trey was standing outside the building, talking to a police officer, who had a notepad, probably asking questions. There was nothing more attractive than a man who wasn't afraid to jump in and aid a woman.

Claudia and Christina walked back into the suite. I rushed around my desk and joined them.

"Are you okay?" I reached out and ran a comforting hand along her back.

Claudia was nodding and trying to hold it together, but I could tell she was scared. I had only gotten tidbits of what had happened to her last month. All I knew was someone had attacked her in a parking lot while she was out doing a site visit. I had seen the bruises she'd tried to conceal. Believe you me, I knew blows to the face when I saw them.

She nodded her head rapidly and said in a shaky voice, "Yes, I'm okay, just shocked they were trying to get into my vehicle. I feel so violated."

I nodded knowingly. I knew the feeling. I remember when my car had been stolen. That's what I get for dating a crackhead.

"Have you called Max?" Christina asked and took her hand in hers.

Claudia shook her head.

I wasn't sure what was going on between the two of them. She had been hanging with that other guy, Isaiah, a lot lately. He, too, was gorgeous to look at, but I pictured her being with Max. He was so sexy.

With a sigh, she released Christina's hand. "I guess I better go to my office and try calling him."

Christina nodded and once Claudia left she turned her focus on me. "Mia, can you get that contract over to Eileen Barter? I'm supposed to call her at four so we can go over it on the phone."

I nodded then returned to my desk. While I printed the document, my gaze strayed over to Trey again. He was talking with his hands and licking his lips. That gesture was a turn on. And that wasn't the only attractive thing about him. He was around six-feet-two, with mahogany skin, large eyes, and the most amazing lips. Someone like him could definitely make me forget my problems at home.

I frowned then sighed deeply as I reached for the contract off the printer and headed to the fax machine. While I waited for the call to connect, I allowed my eyes to wander over to Trey again.

If things were different, I would have given him a run for his money.

TWENTY-TWO

"Are you doing okay?"

By the time the police and the guys had cleared away I was in my office shaking. I couldn't believe the police now had the guys who had attacked me. Maybe not all of them, but at least two which Dereon was certain would eventually lead them to the other.

I looked up at Mia's concerned face. The last thing I wanted to do was worry the girl, because she seemed to have enough problems of her own, dealing with her sister.

I nodded. "Yes, I think I'm going to be okay. I-I just can't believe they tried to break into my vehicle."

She took the seat across from me. "I don't mean to pry, but do you know why they have targeted you? This isn't random, you know."

I shook my head. "I have no idea. I really don't have any idea." *Why was this happening to me?*

"You're shaking!" she cried and then rushed around my desk and wrapped her arms around me. "Hey, it's going to be okay." I hugged Mia. "Thank you. I really appreciate your concern."

She drew back slightly and gave me a hard look. "Of course I'm concerned! You and Christina are like family to me."

I released a long breath of air and forced a smile. "I'm just glad they finally caught them. Now I can stop looking over my shoulder."

She gave me a big hug and released me.

"I overheard Dereon saying there was one more?" Mia walked back around my desk as she spoke.

A feeling of dread slid down my spine. I was worried that

as soon as he found out his friends had been arrested, he was liable to come after me . "Now that they have the two, I'm hoping they will find him quickly."

"CC, where you at?"

I heard shouting coming from the front office. Mia and I both turned to the door at the same time heavy footsteps could be heard coming our way.

"CC!"

I rose from my chair just as Max came round the corner and barged into my office. As soon as I saw him, I rushed past Mia and into his arms.

He held me tight then eased back. "Look at me," he said searching my face. "Are you okay?"

I nodded and tears rolled down my cheeks.

"I'm going to leave you two alone," Mia muttered then walked quietly out of the room.

"Baby, why didn't you call me?"

I dropped my gaze, hating for him to see me like this again. "I tried, but your phone went straight to voicemail."

His hand was caressing my cheek and emotions I couldn't even begin to describe were dancing across his face. "I plan on getting to the bottom of this."

I searched his eyes. "Who do you think is doing this?"

Max shook his head. "I don't know but I think DJ is pissed you broke your contract and this may be some kinda retaliation."

My knees felt ready to give out. "What? You think he had the men jump me in the parking lot?"

"No, but I think he knows who did it." He drew me closer to his body and I pressed my cheek against his chest. "I made you a promise and I intend to honor that."

"What are you planning to do?" I mumbled against his shirt.

"Handle it."

The tone in his voice caused my head to whip back and I searched his eyes. Max leaned forward and kissed me. The pressure of his luscious mouth relaxed my body and eased my mind. There was no need to think, only feel as my entire body tingled. I moaned and Max's tongue eased inside. I met his smooth strokes while my fingers caressed his thick, dark hair. With one kiss, he had me once again feeling reckless and out of control. No one kissed like Max There was his confidence and determination to make sure the kiss was thorough and satisfying.

He finally ended the kiss and wrapped me tightly in the circle of his arms. "Since I know what they look like, I need to go down to the station and identify the two men."

I sighed and was anxious for all of this to be over. "I remembered the tattoo on one of the guy's arms."

Max released his hold then drew back and gazed down at me. "You're coming with me. Get your purse."

"But I have an appointment this afternoon," I protested.

"Cancel it. You've been through a lot and I'm taking you home." I was feeling both annoyed and aroused at the way he always took control.

As I reached for my purse, I noticed his eyes strayed over to the bouquet of white roses that had been delivered earlier. "Do I need to be jealous?"

I stared at him. "That's the same question I was getting ready to ask you." The flowers had arrived this morning from Isaiah. There was no way I was even going there. I decided the best way was to handle it was to flip the script.

He pinned me with his dark penetrating eyes. "The only woman I want is the one I'm trying to protect. Now quit stalling and grab your things."

After the afternoon fiasco I refused to leave my car in the parking lot. Max followed me down to the police station. My phone rang and I noticed it was Isaiah. I decided to ignore it. He would have heard the fear in my voice and the last thing I wanted to do was tell him what had happened. There is no way he would have been able to resist telling my parents. They still didn't know about my attack and this would only make things worse.

I shook my head as I thought about what Max had said. Would DJ Mecca do something like this to me? I just couldn't understand why? Even when I sent over the contract cancellation for him to sign, and called him on the phone, he didn't give off any indication he had some kind of beef with me.

My mind was racing, searching for other possibilities. This was one time I was willing to let Max do whatever it took to find answers because I couldn't spend the rest of my life looking over my shoulder and wondering who was going to come after me next.

MAXIMILIAN

I walked into the club and headed straight to the back. I'd been at The Hole enough times I knew where I was going.

It was unusually crowded for a happy hour, but I noticed all the men wearing the same funny hats and realized there must be a private party going on.

My eyes traveled left and right scanning the place. Security was tight as usual. They were standing there, looking bored, however, in a few minutes they were going to be throwing someone out the club.

Behind a large elevated stage, I headed down the hall with long determined steps. My chest was heaving and my fists were already balled and ready to punch something or in this case someone.

A large guy stepped out in my path. "Can I help you?"

"No you can't," I mumbled and then pushed him out of my way. I expected him to strike again, but he didn't, probably because Braxton and Dereon were right behind me.

When I reached the large corner office, I stopped and looked over my shoulder. "Y'all stay here. I got this."

They nodded and stood in position outside the door. I pushed it open, unannounced, and stepped inside. DJ Mecca was sitting behind his desk, eating what looked like fried rice.

"Whassup, Max? I hear you're a new daddy. What do I owe the pleasure?" he said with a big shit-eating grin.

"Claudia Winters." I stormed over to his desk, grabbed him by his collar and yanked him up out the chair.

His eyes snapped up to meet mine. "What the—" That was all he could get out. Probably because I had my hand pressed against his windpipe. I threw him back hard against the wall and he cried out. "Max... man, whadda I do?"

"DJ, you're fucking with me! Don't you know I could cut your life off right now and no one would care?" I snarled. He tried to move away, but I closed in on him. "I asked you before what happened to my girl in the parking lot and you said you didn't know, so I'm going to ask you again. Only this time not so nicely." Primitive male rage rushed through my veins and I felt capable of destroying whoever had dared to lay a hand on my girl, in fact I had no problem taking them apart.

There was some commotion outside the office door, but I had no doubt my boys could handle that. DJ had all my attention.

"I told you I don't know." He had the nerve to shrug his shoulder. "I guess next time she needs to remember to come inside before dark."

I punched him hard in the chest before he could get the next word out and he gave a loud grunt as he buckled over.

"I'm not playing with you anymore, DJ. There were three guys, two are in custody but there's one more missing. And I know you know who that person is."

He looked up and shook his head. "I told you, I don't know."

"Wrong answer." I punched him again and then just kept on punching him. I think I was just pissed. Pissed about the whole situation with Parker and the baby; the not knowing, and the games she was playing were driving me insane. I was pissed because I loved a woman with all my heart who wasn't sure if she wanted to be with a man with a child. Hell, I couldn't blame her. It took a strong woman to deal with Parker's daily bullshit. However, as soon as the pediatricians gave my son a good report of health, it was going to be time to get my lawyer involved and I was ready to play dirty if I had to. I loved Claudia and I wasn't letting her get away. I also wasn't allowing anyone to think for even a second they could get away with putting their hands on her. That shit was coming to an end today.

I sent another blow to his face.

"Yo, yo, Max, man, chill out!"

Dereon raced into the office and had to practically drag me up off of DJ. He was lying on the floor, groaning, and holding his nose.

"Shit!" he shouted as he slowly rose to a sitting position.

My knuckles were bloody and yet I had no regrets. I should have done this to him years ago.

Dereon tried to wedge himself between us. "DJ, I advise you to tell Max what he wants to hear, otherwise I'm not going to be able to hold him back."

He staggered to his feet and leaned against the large desk for support. As soon as his eyes reached mine he started laughing; that hard obnoxious laugh that would always register in my head. "Damn Max! If I had known you had a mean right hook I would have hired you for my security team." He kept on laughing and I lunged at him but Dereon stopped me. Braxton stepped inside the doorway. I turned and he gave me a small head nod.

Hearty laughter escaped his lips. "Looks like the Calvary is all here. Oh no, wait… there are two of you missing."

"Cut the bullshit DJ!" Dereon ordered. "Otherwise I'm going to find a reason to have this place shut the fuck down. We all know there is a lot of illegal business going on in here."

That got his attention.

"Fine. I'll tell you what you want to know." He rested his hip against the edge of the desk and folded his arms against his round frame.

I brushed past Braxton and looked him dead in his beady eyes. "What's the name of the dude?"

He waved his hand like I was bothering him. "Tommy Vane. He used to work security for me until I found out his punk-ass was stealing."

"And where can we find him?"

He smirked. "Now that part is on you, but he's usually here on the weekend running a tab."

Braxton grabbed my arm. "C'mon Max. You got what you wanted. Now let's go."

I looked at DJ a moment longer, with blood trickling

down into his mouth, smirked, and turned away.

"Hold up! It doesn't stop there," he called after me.

All three of us turned around. "What are you talking about?" I spat.

Despite one of his eyes being swollen shut, they twinkled with mystery. "Who do you think hired them to shake up your girlfriend?"

"I'm not in the mood for your games. What are you talking about?" I barked.

He laughed dryly. "C'mon now you're taking away all my fun. And you know I was more than willing to get a little payback," he added with that same smug look he had given me several years ago.

"It's not that hard to figure out. But let me give you a hint. It's the same sweet little honey I've been banging off and on for the last few years... the same one that's calling you, Daddy. Hell, that might be my kid for all we know."

This time Braxton wasn't swift enough. By the time he reacted, I already had DJ pinned flat on the desk. The small of his back landed with sharp impact against the wood.

Dereon tried to pull me off him, but I refused to let go. "Max, it ain't worth it," he warned, but my eyes didn't once stray from DJ's face.

"Are you telling me Parker hired them?" I screamed.

DJ gave a loud, chilling laugh. "Hell yeah. She's the one who had me call my boy to schedule the party." He was bleeding and laughing hysterically. "I guess it's true. Good pussy will make a nigga lose his mind."

It took Trey and Dereon both to pry my hands from around DJ's neck. With a loud growl, I yanked free of their grasp and stormed out the club.

TWENTY-THREE

I was on the phone talking to Isaiah when I heard a car pull up. "You have a great time. Tell Nathan I said hello." Isaiah was flying to Chicago to attend his cousin's bachelor party. I heard the doorbell and slid my feet in my slippers and left the room.

"I will. And sweetheart we're going to talk when I get back."

Yes we are. "Okay," I said as I padded quickly down the hallway. "I'll talk to you later." I ended the call, leaving the phone on a small table, then hurried down the stairs. The bell rang again just as I swung it open.

Max stepped into the house and gathered me into his arms.

"Hey babe," he said on a breathless gasp as he plastered his lips to mine. I wrapped my arms around his neck. The kiss was wild and punishing.

"Max, I…" I tried to speak and to get him to slow down. But it was no use.

He kicked the door shut and stopped kissing me long enough to carry me up the stairs. I put my legs around his waist. His palms were planted at my ass.

"What's wrong?" I asked because he looked so serious and intent.

"I just need to be inside you," he hissed. And who was I to complain?

Max stepped across my bedroom and lowered me to my feet. We wasted no time stripping off each other's clothes. I slid onto the bed and he immediately followed me, climbed over me, crushing my breasts, then caught my hands, pinning them above my head. His mouth was touching mine again, nipping me hard and possessive at my lips, cheek and throat.

Something was definitely bothering him or maybe it was just the chain of events from afternoon morning, or his cell phone that had been vibrating in his pocket since he had arrived. Whatever it was had him fired up.

"I'm sorry babe... I can't wait," Max moaned and wedged my thighs apart with his knee. Immediately, he thrust into me, his cock warm and hard, and I gasped and arched off the bed. There was nothing slow about the way he was moving with long, confident, and steady strokes.

"Shit!" he hissed.

His lips were wild, my body ached, thighs trembling, but he kept on pounding hard and fast, never slowing down. And in a matter of minutes, I felt an orgasm starting to build.

"Yes baby..., yesss," I cried.

I raised my legs, sending him deep to my g-spot. Max drove faster and harder and when he stiffened his hips and jerked, I came with him.

We lay there both breathing heavily. Max was still on top of me, his damp flesh warm against mine. I trailed my fingers down along his back.

I loved him. There was just no denying the way I felt about him. Max was in my heart and in my soul. And I wanted him to stay there forever. The last thing in the world I wanted to have to do was share my man with someone else, but with Max I was starting to think, I may be willing to do whatever it took to make things work between us.

His breathing had slowed and I had a feeling he was on the verge of falling asleep. My body tingled at the mere thought of having him in my bed all night again.

"Are you ready to talk?" I asked breaking the silence.

His phone was ringing again that same annoying ringtone that identified Parker was calling.

"Don't you need to get that?" I said getting a little irritated.

He rolled off of me and onto his back. "Nope, but you and I, we need to talk about something."

He was serious and I rolled over onto my side so I could look down at him. "Okay, so go ahead and talk." I'm sure by the tone of my voice he knew I was already expecting the worse.

Max turned his head to the side and had this confused look and I don't know why, but I couldn't keep a straight face. I started laughing and he chuckled and drew me into his arms.

"You are truly something else," he muttered as I leaned in for a kiss.

"Yeah, I know," I said.

"Yo, seriously we need to talk," he whispered against my lips.

I had never seen him look that serious before and to be honest I was afraid of what he might say. His phone started ringing again, but this time it was a different ringtone, which meant it wasn't Parker.

Max sat up on the bed, then rose, and retrieved his phone from his pants.

I lay there waiting to see the expression on his face. When I noticed him reaching for his boxers, I knew it couldn't be anything good.

"That was Parker's home girl, Missy. Max Jr. has a fever of a hundred and three."

"What?" I jerked upright on the bed. "That's high." I've never had kids, but I knew what was considered dangerous.

"Parker is taking him to the hospital. I told Missy I would meet them there." He stopped and dragged a hand across his hair as he sighed. "Listen, Claudia I would invite you, but there is so—"

I waved my hand silencing him. "No, don't worry about it. Go, be with your son. We can talk later."

I could see there was something else he wanted to say, but instead I slid my naked butt off the bed and over to him and turned his shirt right side out for him while he disappeared into the bathroom long enough to clean himself up. By the time he came out he was fastening his belt.

"Babe, there is some—"

I placed my fingers against his lips, cutting him off. "We'll have plenty of time to talk later. Right now you need to get to the hospital with Parker and Lil' Max." I was really trying to show him I wasn't all that selfish. If we had any chance of making this things work, I had to learn to accept that Max was a package deal.

"You're the best, you know that?" he teased.

"And don't you forget it," I told him and handed him his shirt.

Max yanked it down over his head, pushed his arms through and gave me a quick kiss then sat down and started putting on his sneakers.

Claudia, you might as well get used to him being a daddy to his son.

By the time he had his shoes laced, I had slipped into a nightshirt and slippers.

"Babe, I better get outta here."

I forced a grin. "Come on, let me walk you to the door." I laced my fingers with his and led Max down the stairs. I didn't know what to say and it seemed he didn't either. The moment felt weird and slightly off and now there was a lump in my throat.

"I'll call you later," he said.

I tilted my head and stared up into his eyes. "Please do. I want to know how he's doing."

Max took my other hand and pulled me closer, then dipped low and covered my lips with his. I savored the taste and feel like a starving woman, and almost cried out when he ended the kiss. "I'll call you."

I nodded and watched him walk out the door and down my steps, and didn't leave the front porch until his SUV had reached the corner.

My mind was a mess. I was in love and so damn confused I didn't know what to do anymore. Being with Isaiah would have been so simple and easy, but I've learned nothing worth having ever comes easy. My relationship with Max was definitely proof of that.

TWENTY-FOUR

The next morning I sauntered into the office and stopped dead in my tracks. "What the hell is going on in here?"

Mia laughed. "You tell me. All these bouquets are for you."

"What?" I glanced around at the assortment of roses. There had to be at least a dozen vases with a dozen roses each. "Who in the world sent these?"

"Isa—oops." She stopped and brought a hand up to cover her mouth. "Sorry, the flowers are so beautiful, I couldn't resist."

While I shrugged out of a long, beige trench coat, I laughed. "Don't worry about it. I would have done the same thing if I was you." Isaiah was really laying it on thick. He was out of town but still trying to let his presence be known. He wasn't making ending the relationship easy.

"Where would you like me to put them?" she asked inquisitively.

I already had a bouquet in my office. "How about we decorate the entire suite with them? We might as well all enjoy them."

"Okay, good idea. I think I'm going to keep this one right here on my desk."

Mia was smiling enviously at the yellow ones in a white vase perched on the corner of her desk. At the back of my mind I wondered if a man had ever bought her flowers.

"What did you think of Trey?" I said suddenly out of the blue.

Her brow quirked. "The one who had the dude in a headlock?"

"Oh so you had noticed him?" I said with a laugh.

She tried to hide a blush. "Who could miss him?"

I draped the coat over my arm and slung my purse higher on my shoulder as I asked, "Did you think he was cute? He asked about you."

Mia shrugged and said, "He's okay. I prefer light-skinned men."

My brow rose with disbelief. "Are you kidding?" I shook my head and giggled. "Girl you've got a lot to learn." I reached over and retrieved my mail from the bin and shuffled through it. Junk. Good. "Are the students here yet?"

"Yep. Christina stepped out for a moment but she already has the crew in the kitchen preparing the luncheon."

I had no doubt. Christina was very meticulous and organized. "Please tell Christina to come and see me when she arrives."

Mia looked up from her computer and nodded. "Will do. Oh, and your mother called."

I nodded. Knowing her, she wanted to talk about Isaiah and me. Not happening today.

I started toward my office then swung around. "Is your sister available to help with the Hargrove wedding this weekend?"

Her eyes lit up with surprise. "Yes, I'm sure she is! I'll call her right now."

"And tell Shalisa no drinking this time. Otherwise, I'm done with her." If Christina had any idea she had been drunk at her engagement party, she would never have used her again. But I believed in second chances.

Mia nodded. "I'll tell her. Thank you so much. With that deadbeat man of hers she really needs the money."

Nodding, I turned and headed to my office. I put my purse away, made a cup of coffee, then sauntered toward the kitchen. From the hall, I smelled smothered onions and garlic. I stuck my head in and my eyes swept the six culinary arts students, who were hard at work. I didn't bother them, because that always seemed to make them nervous, instead I returned to my office. There was a text from Max. He was swinging by to scoop me up for lunch. I got excited and forced myself to get to work. He had called last night to let me know the fever was down and under control. As I swiveled my chair around in front of my computer, I grinned. I had a feeling that everything was going to work itself out.

I was reviewing invoices when I heard Christina coming up the hall.

"I wasn't expecting you in the office today," she said and was standing in my doorway wearing the hell out of a gorgeous blue pants suit. The jacket tied at her small waist. I gave her a weird look because I really don't know how she managed to cook dressed like that. "Why wouldn't I be in today?"

It was her turn to look at me strange. "Because of everything that happened yesterday."

I rolled my eyes at the comment. "I can't stop living. Besides, they caught them breaking into my car."

"Yes, but there's one more missing, and there is no telling what that crazy bitch told him to do to you." She looked mad enough to hit someone. I was sure I looked confused.

"Whoa, time out!" I held up my hand. "What are you talking about?"

"I'm talking about Max's baby mama—whatever her name is—hiring those creeps to attack you."

I was sure my jaw dropped onto my desk. There was no way in hell I had heard her correctly. "What did you say?"

"I said...." The rest of Christina's sentence trailed off and then she gasped. "Oh no! You didn't know?"

My entire body pulsed with shock.

"I'm sorry. I thought Max had told you." Christina looked so worried for spilling the beans. I would have felt sorry for her, if I wasn't already feeling sorry for myself.

"Parker hired those dudes?" Even saying it out loud it still seemed unreal.

"That's what Dee told me." Christina shook her head. "Now I wish he hadn't. I wonder why Max didn't tell you?"

"I don't know." Probably because he was too busy last night trying to get between my legs. I felt like a complete idiot.

I was in love with a man who ... I was so pissed I didn't even bother to complete the thought. "I can't believe this." Max was off playing family man, while wifey was busy plotting to get me out of the way so she could have him to herself.

My entire body was humming with betrayal.

Silly me, had truly believed Max cared about me and wanted me to be a part of his life. Instead he was only out for what he had wanted, and who knows what that was. Maybe since I had rejected him for so long I was a challenge to him.

"I can't believe this is happening to me!" That man had come to my house, made love to me like tomorrow wasn't promised to us, and then left when he had known all along what his baby mama had plotted to do to me.

Christina leaned across the desk and put her hand over mine. "I'm so sorry. Really I am. Is there something I can do?"

I closed my eyes and shook my head. "No, I just need a moment alone."

I was hurt and pissed at the same time. I couldn't even focus on my work. Instead I grabbed my purse, told Mia to hold all my calls and then walked out the building to my Range Rover before Christina could stop me. I didn't even bother to look around to see if anyone was following me because I was just that pissed to even care.

I decided to head to the flip-house first. I figured Max either had to be there working or off somewhere with Parker's ass, holding hands and singing, "We are family...."

Numbly, I drove. The more miles I traveled the more time I had to think about Max and the angrier I became until I had my foot on the gas going ninety. By the time I reached Soulard, a riot of emotions were tumbling through my mind and settling right smack at my gut.

The first vehicle I saw on the street was Max's. My heart thumped and was logged so far up my throat I thought I would choke. I parked my car behind Trey's truck and got out, slamming the door behind me.

Braxton was coming out of the house as I was walking up. "CC, what's—"

You know that expression, 'talk to the hand', well that's

what he was doing, because I cut the conversation off before he even had a chance to get it started. As soon as he jumped out the way I marched up the stairs and into the house.

"Max… Max where are you?" I was shouting as I paraded through the completely renovated house. Trey poked his head out the bathroom, but the look on my face told him to get out of my way.

"Babe! I'm upstairs!" I heard Max say, using the term of endearment that I had learned to love so much. And it all had been a game. I couldn't get up those stairs fast enough. Max stuck his head outside the door of one of the bedrooms and had the nerve to be grinning at me.

"Hey babe, c'mon in here." He signaled for me to follow, and trust me, I didn't waste any time. Of course the moment I stepped into the room, he tried to get a kiss but I pushed him away.

"When were you going to tell me?"

He had the nerve to try and look confused. "Tell you what?"

I couldn't believe he was standing there pretending he didn't know what I was talking about. "That Parker hired those men."

I looked in his eyes hoping to see he had no idea what I was talking about and that Christina was wrong, but instead I saw the guilt. "Claudia I was planning on telling you."

I felt sick. And all the pain of being beaten and betrayed hit me hard in the gut. "When? When were you planning to do that, after I was attacked again?"

"I just found out yesterday. I was going to tell you once I verified the information and had proof."

"Proof? You need proof?" I was so hurt my knees buckled and I grabbed the wall just in time to keep from falling. Coming here had been a mistake and all I knew was I had to get away. I raced down the stairs.

"Whoa! Babe wait!" Max barked as he reached for my arm and stopped me. "Let me explain."

I yanked my arm free from his grasp and turned around and glared at him. I hated for him to see me with tears sliding down my face. "We have nothing else to talk about! I got attacked because of you and your baby mama drama, the one thing I wanted no part of. Stupid me gave in, because I was crazy about you and what did it get me? A psycho chick, hiring hitmen to jack my life up!"

"CC, calm down and let's talk. You just said you're crazy about me, so I know we can work this out."

The promise in his voice almost stole my resolve. Not now. Not after everything I had gone through. "There's nothing to work out. There's no trust left and I don't want to see you ever again."

I ran out the door blind, needing to put some space between us while crying like a damn baby. I heard Braxton calling my name but I didn't stop running until I was inside my vehicle. I gripped the steering wheel, trying to make some sense of it all. Hands shaking, somehow I managed to get the key in the ignition, but before I could pull off, Max jumped in next to me.

"Get out!" I screamed. "Get out of my car."

Somehow he maintained his composure. "Claudia, please, calm down and listen."

I glared at him and was angry I still wanted him. "I don't want to listen. You said you needed proof, which tells me you don't believe Parker's involved."

"No, it means I'm trying to build a case against her, so I can get my son!" He stopped and dragged a hand down his face.

"But you don't even know if he's yours!"

He looked like I slapped him in the face. For a moment I was prepared to take back what I said because it was both selfish and mean, but then I remembered why we were arguing and changed my mind. "Get out of my car!"

"Claudia, babe chill."

I heard light tapping on my window and whipped my head around to find Reggie "Angrily, I rolled it down. "Will you tell him to get out my car?"

Reggie met his gaze and only the two of them knew what that look meant.

Max shook his head. "I'm not going anywhere until we talk." He had the nerve to slide low on the seat like I had all the time in the world to waste with him.

"I told you I don't want to talk!" I know I was sounding like some crazed lunatic.

"Yo, Max, man, get out the car," Reggie said in this soothing voice that irritated the hell out of me.

"Yeah, you need to listen to your boy and get out," I cosigned, but he blew both of us off.

Max turned on the seat. "CC, look at me." He reached a hand out and cupped my cheek, stroking it lightly with his thumb. "We're better than this. You are so right. I shoulda told you, but give me a chance to explain."

I saw Trey coming across the lawn and I pointed at him, then at Max, indicating I wanted him to get his friend before I hurt him because I wasn't hearing anything he had to say.

"CC, are you gonna let me explain?"

"No, go be with that crazy bitch, because I plan on pressing charges against her!"

"How are you going to do that if we don't have proof?"

Yeah, I guess he did have a point. I pressed my lips tightly together.

"That's what I'm trying to tell you, babe. Those dudes in custody refuse to talk. And before I confront Parker, I want to have proof so I can nail her ass to the wall. Reacting in rage won't get us anywhere. Instead she'll run and take my son away."

I folded my arms in front of me and turned away from him. I was a little calmer now but still angry. Trey and Reggie were standing on both sides of the car, waiting and watching. The whole thing was so humiliating—some Jerry Springer shit. This was not the life I had planned for Claudia Ciara Winters.

"The only reason why Parker is doing this is because I made the mistake of getting involved with you. I'm not about that life. I don't want no part of it and if that means I can't be with you either, then I guess this is goodbye," I said softly.

Max waved his hand in the air and glared out the

window. "Yo, Reg, y'all give us a minute!" he snapped.

I noticed Reggie backed away from the car and reached into the pocket of his jeans, giving us a moment of privacy. Even Trey took a few steps back, allowing us some time.

"No, I'm not saying goodbye." He cupped my face and stared at me. The muscle at his temple was pulsing. His hands were clinched. He was clearly angry. Good, so was I. "I love you, CC, and I know you love me, too, only you're too freaking stubborn to admit it," he said in a voice that was a rough whisper. "I'm going to give you a few days to think about it. In the meantime, let me handle my business."

I watched as he yanked open the door and shut it behind him as if he desperately needed to put some distance between us. I, too, needed to clear my head.

Reggie moved toward my vehicle and said, "Max, man, y'all just need to give each other some time to calm down."

It was Trey's turn to chime in. "Listen to him, Claudia because he would know. Just wait until Berlin finds out about this huge foreclosure he just bought. She's going to flip."

Reggie's heavy voice drew me from my daze. "Claudia, before I go knock him upside his head, is there anything I can do for you?"

I met his dark eyes and shook my head. "No, nothing, but thanks."

"Trust me when I tell you, my man didn't mean to betray you. Max is all about getting to the source and working with facts. Give him some slack… he really does love you."

His kindness had me blinking away tears again. "Thanks Reggie."

I put the car in gear before the damn broke and drove away feeling worse than when I had arrived. Why did relationships have to be so difficult?

I was just about to pull onto the highway when I brought the vehicle to a screeching halt.

Did I hear Max say he loved me?

TWENTY-FIVE

"Have you heard from Max?"

I carried over a dozen dresses and lay them across Christina's bed. She was finally moving out of her condo. I briefly glanced in her direction and said, "Oh yeah, he calls or texts me every day."

"That's a good thing," she said and flopped down on a long leather chaise.

I gave a rude grunt and tossed more clothes onto the pile. I didn't want to talk about Max.

"Where are you planning on putting all this stuff?" By stuff I meant piles of clothes and mountains of shoes.

"Dereon's converting one of the bedrooms into a large walk-in closet for me."

"Why am I not surprised?" I rolled my eyes and couldn't resist a laugh. It was definitely break time. We'd been going at it all morning. I walked over and took a seat beside her. "I've been dealing with my own drama I haven't had a chance to ask you, how does it feel to be getting married?"

While smiling, Christina drew a long shaky breath, and said, "It feels amazing. I had no idea how wonderful it could feel to be with a man you truly loved."

I knew what it felt like because I felt it every time I was with Max. I just hated that the moment didn't last.

"I can't wait to get married!" she exclaimed excitedly.

I smiled. "Have you decided on a date?"

"Yes, April."

"A spring wedding? That will be so nice!"

Christina blinked and looked at me. "I know. It's going to be beautiful. You know Jeanna has already taken over."

"What else is new? You just make sure your mother

coordinates a day that is not about her, but all about you," I ordered.

She nodded. "Exactly! Nobody is going to steal my shine." Christina turned on the seat. "Now getting back to you… I want you to have the same!" she whined.

I shrugged. "There's always Isaiah."

She scrunched up her nose. "I was talking about you and Max. Claudia, you have to find it in your heart to forgive him."

"Why?"

"You forgave Dee for telling me.

She was right. He had been apologizing to me ever since he found out Christina had blabbed her mouth. Didn't he know by now she couldn't keep water? I remembered Max saying neither could Dereon. "That's different."

"Either way, you gotta have trust. Dereon said –"

"Uh-uh," I began cutting her off. "I don't want to hear it."

"But Claudia…, Max is trying to track your attacker down. I overheard Trey saying he's even been back down at the club looking for him."

"What? He could get hurt."

She nodded. "Yes, he could but he cares about you and that's what people do."

"I think he told me he loved me," I said suddenly out of the blue.

"What?" Christina squealed. "Oh my God! And you didn't tell me."

"Because I don't quite remember him telling me. I was so pissed I was half listening."

She smirked. "What man would go out combing parking lots dressed up like Rambo if he didn't love you?"

I fell back on the chaise laughing. "You're stupid! I know he isn't dressed like that."

She shrugged. "Who knows? All that matters is that man loves you and is out there trying to right a wrong."

"But he betrayed me. That's hard for me to let go of. And Parker is still walking around the street because no one has reported her. Where's the justice in that?"

"You gotta have faith in your man."

My phone rang and I reached inside my purse and looked down at the screen. It was Isaiah. Talk about timing. He had been back for a few days, wanting to get together, but I had been blowing him off. I just needed time to think. And it was hard to do that with him constantly showing me what life would be like if we were together. Comparing the two of them wasn't fair, so I decided to just stay clear of them both. I hadn't seen Max in three days and I missed him so much but refused to subject myself to that life any longer.

The door downstairs opened and shut and then there were footsteps. "Christy, where are you?"

"We're up here!"

At the sound of Portia's voice, I nudged Christina in the arm and whispered. "Did you ever tell her?"

Quickly, she shook her head. "Nope, but you can."

I was all set to object when Portia appeared in the doorway.

"Hey, looks like you've been having fun without me," she said and smiled.

She was dressed impeccably in gray slacks and a pale pink blouse with ruffles at the sleeves. Black leather ballerina slippers were on her feet.

"No we're just getting started. Come join the party." Smiling, I signaled her in. We all hugged and gave each other air kisses.

"You can help put all the shoe boxes in that big box. The clothes are going in those hanging boxes just as soon as I get them assembled," Christina explained.

The pizzas arrived and the three of us dived in and packed away most of the room. As much stuff as she had, it was going to take several days. The movers and professional packers were due later in the week, but Christina didn't want a stranger rummaging through her clothes.

"Evan and I have been talking about starting a family," Portia announced, while carrying blue shoes over to the box labeled Blue.

Christina and I shared a look and I tilted my head urging

her to say something.

"Sis, come over here and have a seat."

Christina moved over to the bed and patted the space beside her.

"Sure, what's going on?" Her bone-straight, dark weave brushed the center of Portia's back as she looked from me to her. She took a seat and placed both hands in her lap. I could tell she was preparing herself for what was about to be said.

I was standing near the closet, watching as Christina said, "Portia, Evan is having an affair."

She drew in a breath until she was practically sucking in her cheeks. "No he isn't." I couldn't blame her for not wanting to believe it.

"Portia, your sister is telling the truth. I saw Evan in the restaurant kissing some chick. Here, I'll show you." I walked over and grabbed my phone then handed it to her once I pulled up the photos. She refused to take it like my phone was either diseased or she just didn't want the truth in the palm of her hand.

Leaning over, she stared at the photographs. I slowly scrolled through them until Portia squeezed her eyes closed and mumbled, "Enough."

"I'm so sorry." Christina leaned over and hugged her. I guess she was in shock because she didn't bother to raise her arms to hug her sister back.

"Yeah, I'm sorry, too, Portia but I had to let you know what I saw," I said softly.

Her eyelids flipped open. "Why? Why couldn't you just mind your business?"

I was flabbergasted. "Excuse me?"

Christina jerked back. "*Mind your business*? Girl, are you crazy! Claudia was trying to look out for you."

"Why? I didn't ask her to. What's it going to change by her telling me?"

I rolled my eyes. I didn't at all appreciate her attitude. "I would hope you would get in his ass and let him know you know."

She narrowed hazel eyes in my direction. "Why? I'm not

going to leave him."

This chick was stuck on stupid.

I shook my head. "Do you know a man has no respect for a woman who allows him to disrespect her?"

Portia's eyes sparkled like she had a big secret she was about to share. "How will he know I know unless I tell him?" She shifted on the bed and smoothed a hand across her hair as she spoke. "I have a wonderful life as a doctor's wife, a beautiful home and a hefty allowance to keep me dripping in diamonds and pearls. Why in the world would I give that all up for some other woman to take everything I have?"

I stood there in disbelief while I listened to Portia and Christina toss comments back and forth.

Portia shrugged a slender shoulder. "So what if Evan dips out every now and again. That just means that's one less day of the week I have to spread my legs, because someone else is doing it for me."

Portia had this smirk on her lips like she was so smart and we were the idiots.

"Thank you for looking out for me, but I'm happy with my life and my man." Smiling, she rose from the bed and got back to work.

Christina frowned while I was too busy picking my jaw up off the floor.

As I stood there listening, I had begun to wonder if that was the way I had been behaving with Isaiah. Wanting what I had always dreamed of, even though deep down I knew we would never be able to get back what we once had.

It was time for me to do some real soul-searching.

TWENTY-SIX

On Sunday I was lounging on the couch, reading a book when I heard my doorbell. I hurried to answer it and flung the door open to find Isaiah's smiling face. "Hey, what are you doing here?"

"Come with me. I want to show you something." He took my hand and pulled me out the house.

I grabbed onto the door frame and stopped him. "Now? Can I at least change my clothes?" I had on an old comfortable sweat suit.

He shook his head stubbornly and said, "No, you look fine just the way you are. You still keep a spare under a rock near the house?"

How in the world did he remember that? "Yes."

"Good." He turned the lock and shut the door, then led me down the stairs and into his Jaguar. I started laughing as he pulled the seatbelt across me. "Where are you taking me?"

"You just kick back, relax and let me handle this."

He shut the door and walked around to the driver's seat. I was curious, but knew he wasn't going to tell me, no matter how much I begged.

Isaiah started the car and warm heat flowed from the vents. It was still hard to believe it was November already.

"How was the wedding?" he asked as he pulled down the driveway.

"It was nice. Everyone loved the food and raved about the cake." Christina and I had catered a wedding last night, held at a roller rink. It was unique to say the least. I had even hired Shalisa again to help us host the event and she managed to stay sober and professional the entire night. I made sure to put a little something extra in her envelope.

"I'm so glad. Sorry I wasn't able to come and watch you in action."

I gave a dismissive wave. "No, I understand you have a lot going on with the new job."

He heaved an exaggerated sigh of regret. "Yes, but that's no excuse. I need to start making you more of a priority in my life."

He knew how to say the right things. Unfortunately, it was just five years too late

"Would you like to go have dinner later? I heard there is a new steakhouse not too far from here."

I turned my head and smiled. "Maybe if I have time to change clothes first."

He took my hand in his and it felt tingly and nice. Not the intense feeling I got with Max but it was nice just the same. "Guess who I ran into a few days ago?"

I turned on the seat, eyes wide with curiosity. "Who?"

"Jay Cobbins."

He laughed and we talked about his former roommate who ran naked across campus his sophomore year before the police came and locked him up. I was stunned to find out he was now a principal at a high school in Kansas City. During the drive, we joked and reminisced on school and mutual friends. I forgot all about he was taking me somewhere until he pulled off in the direction of one of my favorite neighborhoods in the Webster Grove.

I snapped my finger. "This is the neighborhood we used to ride through when we were dreaming about getting married and starting our own family."

Isaiah smiled and nodded. "There was this one street you always made me drive down real slow." His brow bunched. "I think it's around here somewhere."

I pointed ahead of him. "It's right up there. Just make a right at the next corner." It was strange how this neighborhood always gave me this warm feeling like I was finally home.

Isaiah turned down the tree-lined street. All the houses were custom built, two-story and very expensive. "Wow, it still looks the same over here," I said as my eyes traveled up one side of the street and then down the other until my eyes landed on my favorite house.

"Isaiah, stop!"

He pulled over to the curb and I immediately climbed out. I had forgotten I had on sweats and flip-flops. Not the look I was going for in a neighborhood like this but it didn't stop me from getting out and walking up the sidewalk.

The house was for sale.

"Look at that!" I had spent so many years staring at this house, imagining what life was like on the inside.

Isaiah moved beside me and stared ahead appreciatively. "This was the house, right?"

"Yes, it's my house!" I exclaimed and rushed over to the window and stared inside. "There's a double staircase just like I thought."

"Sweetheart, we really shouldn't be peeking inside," he scolded.

I kept on looking and didn't bother to turn his way as I said, "Why not? How else do they expect someone to see inside?"

"How about using a key?"

It wasn't until I heard a set of keys jingling that I turned and looked at Isaiah.

"You have the keys?"

Grinning, he nodded and walked over to the door, sticking the key in the lock.

"How in the world did you get the keys?"

"Don't you want to go inside?" he said and winked. Isaiah stepped inside while I stood there frozen on the porch. Whoa! I felt my heart pounding like crazy. How many years had I dreamed of this moment?

By the time I stepped into the foyer, which was bathed with lighting that gleamed off the marble floors, Isaiah was coming down one of the wrought iron railed staircases.

Like a kid in Willy Wonka's Chocolate Factory, I raced from one room to the next. Open floor plan. Twelve-foot ceilings. Crown molding. A kitchen to die for, and even a solarium, that looked off a beautiful backyard with a garden and a gazebo. The house was everything I had always knew it would be.

"What do you think?" Isaiah said. He strolled over and wrapped an arm around my middle.

"It's beautiful. Thank you so much for bringing me to see it." I was touched that he had gone out of his way to make this happen. "You sure know how to make a girl's day."

"I got something that I hope will really make your day. Look inside the refrigerator." He gave me a gentle push toward the big stainless steel appliance in front of me.

"What's in it?"

Isaiah was grinning. "Go and take a look."

I walked over and was almost afraid to look inside. Goodness, I don't know what I was afraid of. When I reached for the double doors and swung them open I gasped. There was a bottle of my favorite red wine, with a note tied around the neck.

WELCOME HOME.

My head whipped around. "Isaiah, wha—"

The rest of my words fell off. He was down on his knee.

"Five years ago I made a mistake of letting you go. Even though I was doing what I felt I was destined to do, I've regretted leaving you. Now I want to give you everything you have ever dreamed about. This house, babies… a life together. If you give me a chance, I promise to never let anything ever come before you again. He reached inside his pocket and pulled out the signature blue box and opened it." Claudia Ciara Winters will you marry me?"

I stared down at the beautiful solitaire diamond and then back up to his humble face.

"I-I don't know what to say."

Isaiah rose. "I know it's probably too soon, but at least tell me you'll think about it. I know we need time to rebuild what we once had, but I want you to know that I'm here to stay… I'm not going anywhere." He placed the ring on the counter. The gem danced off the light beaming from the skylights overhead.

"I dreamed about this," I whispered because I was at a loss for words.

"I want our life together to be like a dream." He put his arms around me and kissed me long and deep.

"I—I"

"Claudia, take your time and think about what I said and when you're ready you let me know," Isaiah whispered against my lips.

After we left the house, not once did he mention the proposal and I was grateful. I declined dinner but we stopped for ice cream before he dropped me off at home.

I spent the rest of the evening thinking about how wonderful a life could be with him as a doctor's wife. That was what I had dreamed of in high school, and college, and again when Isaiah left for medical school. But after listening to Portia talk about Evan and their marriage, I knew that dream was long gone.

A sob rose to my throat as realization sunk in.

It didn't matter the house, the prestige, or the childhood dream. I'd rather have Max and a ready-made family than a life without Max. The truth sucker punched me right in the gut.

I really was in love.

TWENTY-SEVEN

I was annoyed with myself for even thinking about Max for the umpteenth time today. It had been over a week since the big blowup. I'd been avoiding his calls, texts and visits and yet I still couldn't stop thinking about him.

Desperate for a distraction I decided to spend Saturday with my mother shopping. Something I rarely did because Mommy was only interested as long as she was looking for something, but once she found it, she was ready to go.

We were back at my house with our bags, sitting out in my sunroom, sipping iced tea when I heard the doorbell ring.

I hurried to answer it and pulled open the door, thinking it was my father coming for my mother. He had dropped her off on his way to the hospital to check on a few of his patients. Only that wasn't a sixty-two-year-old man standing on the other side of the door.

Instead he was gorgeous, tall and looked extremely sexy standing there in a Redskins jersey and jeans.

"Hey," Max said, giving me a smile.

I tried to act like I wasn't happy to see him. "Hi, what are you doing here?"

"I thought I'd see if you wanted to go for a ride."

I felt a slow, hot tingle of anticipation. "Really?"

"Actually I was missing you. My bed is lonely without you in it." There was another smile. "I was hoping I could convince you to pack an overnight back and head home with me."

My body was starting to get warm. The thought of spending the night with him was so tempting.

"Hmmm, I don't know if that's a good idea." I turned away and walked into the living room. I only half expected him to jump back into his car and leave. But instead he did like all alpha men, closed the door and followed me into the house.

Thank goodness he couldn't see the smile on my face.

"Coming home with me is a perfect idea."

I turned on my heels, eyes rolling. "It's always about sex with you, isn't it?"

The grin fell from his face. "Sex? Not that I don't love making love to you, but tonight, I wanna talk." He started toward me with this hungry look in his eyes that caused me to gasp and back away from his reach.

"I'm here because I love you, Claudia."

It wasn't fair of him to use the L-word. It was what made our relationship so complicated. I loved him. I loved him so much I wanted nothing else but to spend my life with him; I wanted it more than my next breath. But it was the selfish part of me that was keeping us apart.

The last few weeks had been difficult enough as it was, and now, seeing him had me feeling all kinds of things I didn't want to feel. Why the hell did love have to be so damn complicated?

"I want to be with you and I'm not going to stop until you admit you want to be with me, too." He moved toward me, eyes soft, expression serious. I knew if he touched me I was going to cave. "Tell me you don't love me and I'll walk away."

"That's not fair," I protested.

"Life isn't fair, but it doesn't change the way we feel about each other." He took my hand and drew me close enough for him to gather me in his arms, and I breathed in his light cologne that I loved so much. "I'll apologize every single day for the rest of our lives if I have to."

I gasped when I felt his lips on my cheek that traveled down to graze my neck. His arms came around my waist drawing me closer. "I missed you."

"I missed you too," I finally confessed.

"That's what your big daddy likes to hear," Max whispered against my skin and then he was kissing me.

Damn, I'd missed this man!

His lips were warm and wet and when Max slid his tongue along the seam of my mouth, I groaned and let him inside. I wrapped my arms around his neck, and tilted my chin giving him better access. Max took full advantage and dipped inside, and I sighed with pleasure. He gathered me into his arms, holding me tight, and I never wanted to let go.

"I love you," he whispered brushing his lips along my jaw.

I opened my mouth to respond when a cheerful voice called out, "CC, do you have— Oh, I'm sorry. I didn't know you had company."

I had completely forgotten my mother was in the house. I tried to move away, but Max held on tight.

"Hello I'm Maximilian James," he said before I could make the introductions. He reached out and took her small hand in his, looking like a giant standing in front of her.

"Maximilian, how nice to meet you. I'm Aokia, her mother." She smiled at him and then shot me a curious look.

He nodded. "It's a pleasure and call me Max. All my friends do."

My mother's slanted eyes gleamed with female appreciation. "So Max, how did you and my daughter meet?"

"Mommy, Max is friends with Dereon. They renovate houses together." I was trying my hardest to explain, but my body was still humming out of control.

"Oh okay. Well, it is definitely a pleasure to meet you."

"Now I see where CC gets all her beauty," he drawled, his mouth curved into a wickedly sexy smile.

Within seconds he had laid on the charisma and had my mother laughing and blushing like crazy. We took a seat in my family room and when I mentioned Max was a songwriter, my mother started asking about copyrights and if he had a good attorney.

It was wonderful watching the way the two of them interacted together like they had known each other forever and a day. Max had that kind of charm about him and I couldn't let him go no matter how much I tried to fight the way I felt about him. I knew deep in my heart there was no way I would ever marry Isaiah but it was nice to be able to dream for at least a little bit. I think when it came to Isaiah my biggest worry was hurting him and disappointing my parents.

"You're in love."

Mother's intuition. I should have known she would figure it out.

Mommy and I were in the kitchen clearing away the homemade salsa and chips I had brought out for us to enjoy. Max had excused himself to go out to his car to make a call. He said it was business. I figured it was Parker.

"Have you told him?" Mommy was never going to let up until I responded.

I shook my head.

She brought a hand to her slender hip and scowled. "Why not?"

One thing I had always had a hard time doing was lying to my parents. "I haven't got around to it," I mumbled and flopped down onto a barstool.

Mommy shook her head. "Why the hesitation?"

I didn't know where to begin or what I could tell her. "I don't think we're right for each other." I couldn't bring myself to tell her about Parker and the baby.

She pulled out the stool beside me and climbed onto the seat. My eyes met her intense stare. "I think you're lying to yourself about him. I also think you are fooling yourself if you think you and Isaiah have a chance because you don't. That ship has sailed."

I swallowed and stared into her brown eyes. "You think so?"

"I know so. Isaiah will always be a part of the family and like a son to me, but what the two of you had died a long time ago. I saw it when you were together at my house. I confirmed it this afternoon while watching you and Maximilian together."

My shoulders sagged with relief and I fought back the tears rising to the surface. "But Daddy will be so disappointed."

Mommy waved a manicured hand in the air. "Your dad

needs to mind his own business."

I had to snicker at that.

She leaned toward me and took my hand in hers. "All I have ever wanted was for you to be happy and you can't do that if you're trying to fool yourself. I know what I saw and what I saw were two people who are very much in love."

"Thanks Mommy," I said as a single tear rolled down my cheek.

TWENTY-EIGHT

"What were you and your mother whispering about when I walked in?"

We were driving to his house. I was sitting on the passenger side trembling with the realization that I loved this man enough to endure Parker, and accept his ready-made family.

"We were talking about you."

He grinned as he if he'd had no idea. "Me?"

I nodded. "I think she likes you."

"Well good. Maybe I'll have a better chance of her daughter liking me."

I punched him playfully in the thigh. "I do like you."

He roared with laughter. "Maybe so. Now I just need to get you to tell me you love me and then I can lasso your sexy ass in."

I loved the way he and I could laugh and joke with each other. It was natural and never once felt forced. My mom was right. Why had I wasted so much time fighting something when I knew all along what I really wanted?

"I need to make a quick stop before I head to my house," he told me and I nodded.

Max and I had stuck around until my father arrived to pick up my mother. As usual, he honked his horn and I walked her out to the car. I figured introducing him to Max wasn't a smart idea at the moment. Mommy reminded me to not worry about my father and focus on my own wants and desires. She and I agreed she'd prepare Daddy for the news long before Max showed up for Thanksgiving dinner.

Max pulled in front of a house that had seen its better days and left the motor running, and the heat blasting as he rushed inside. A few brief minutes later, I saw him coming out the door carrying a car seat, and my brow rose.

Max was picking up his son.

I sat upright on the seat and felt like I needed to fix my hair and makeup so I could make a good impression, which was ridiculous. Looking toward the house, I expected to see Parker, but no one came out. Quickly, I climbed out the car preparing myself for the introduction.

"Who do we have here?" I cooed.

Max was strutting and smiling from ear-to-ear. "Let me get him in the car and I can pull the blanket away so you can see him."

I nodded and watched as he opened the door and set him down on the backseat, then he moved away the blanket so I could get a closer look. I stared down and released a long slow breath. "Awww, he is so handsome." And I wasn't just saying that. He really was. Max Jr. was bigger than the last time I had seen him and sleeping peacefully, which was a shame because I really wanted to see his eyes again. But one thing I could tell was he had the same nutty brown complexion and thick curly waves of hair on his head.

"Parker is working late and asked me to pick him up. I hope you don't mind."

I shook my head. "Of course not."

I climbed back in while Max strapped him in the car seat. Once he was settled, Max climbed back in and laced his fingers with mine. "Hey," he began and waited for me to meet his intense gaze. "I know things have been crazy the last few weeks, but I want you to know everything is going to work out."

I loved watching his lips move as he spoke.

I heaved a heavily sigh. "I really want things to work too, but there's still the issue of Parker."

Max gave me this weird comical look. "Why are you whispering?"

I shifted my eyes toward the back seat. "I don't want him to know I'm talking about his mama."

Max started laughing and I joined in. Yeah, I guess I was

being ridiculous.

"Babe, if I don't find Tommy by the end of the week, I will personally drag Parker's ass down to the police station and make her confess." He brought my hand to his lips and I felt his warm mouth tickling my knuckles. "This has gone on long enough. Everything I love is right here in this car—you and my lil' man. And we aren't gonna be able to move forward with our lives until we get this issue resolved."

There weren't enough words to begin to explain what I was feeling, but love was definitely at the top of my list.

We made it to the house and Max Jr. didn't start crying until the vehicle stopped moving. I grabbed his diaper bag while Max carried him inside. That little boy definitely had a set of lungs on him.

"Hey.... What's the matter lil' man? You hungry?" Max had him in his arms cradling him close. I took a seat on the couch and watched him reach for one of the bottles and put it in his mouth and immediately he was sucking away. "There you go. Did Daddy make it all better?"

My heart nearly stopped. I sat there frozen. Here he was a big man who was so gentle and caring, pacing the room speaking in a soft soothing baby voice. This was the same man who had beat up three men in a dark parking lot. Max was hard, yet soft at the same time. Watching him now, I don't think I had ever loved him more.

He finished feeding his son, then walked around some more, while gently patting him on the back. Our eyes met and I blew him a kiss. Max made some funny faces and I chuckled softly. Then his eyes darkened and got real serious and intense. I couldn't look away. The chemistry flowing between us was more powerful than ever before. By the time the baby was sleep, Max had signaled for me to go upstairs. Quietly, I went up to his room and I was naked before I heard his heavy footsteps coming down the hallway.

As soon as he saw me, his eyes widened with pleasure. Max managed to remove his t-shirt before he dragged me close into his arms. The kiss was hot and I felt like I was drowning and he was my life preserver. I slid my arms around his neck and arched into him, determined to get as close as I could. He kissed me, urged my lips apart, and danced with my tongue. He was mine. I was his. The thought echoed in my ears while the kiss went on and on. Max's hands trailed around to grip my ass and drew me forward. He pushed my legs apart and lifted one along his waist until my pussy was flush against the erection straining beneath his zipper. Delicious tremors rocked my body.

He was mine and that down there throbbing behind his jeans was mine as well. The realization sent a burst of longing through me. My tongue danced with his and I sucked, drawing him deeper. My hands went to work, unfastening his belt and lowering the zipper. The friction of his jeans against my clit, I couldn't take much more.

"A little anxious," he breathed and it wasn't a question.

"More like desperate," I whispered against his lips.

Max growled then lifted me off the floor and tossed me playfully onto the bed. I watched as he shoved his jeans and boxers down in one smooth motion. His cock sprang free, large and in charge. I licked my lips and slid up on the bed and spread my legs. Max climbed slowly onto the bed, like a lion on the prowl, and settled himself between my thighs. He brought his lips down over mine as he drove into me with one hard thrust.

"Damn," he groaned.

I put my arms around his middle and he pushed deeper. Max made an agonizing show of pulling out almost to the head of his cock before pushing back inside. My breathing was increasing and he thrust deep, again and again, sending heat bursting through my body.

"This pussy is so good."

Then his strokes became faster and more intense, driving me insane. I raked my nails down the length of his back and lifted my pelvis to meet each deep pump. It wasn't long before I felt like my body was soaring through the air.

"Yes, baby, I'm about to come!" I cried.

Max pounded harder and faster, drawing my legs high along his waist. He was penetrating me so deep an orgasm hit me fast and I was flying. "Yess, yesss!" I screamed.

"That's it babe, cum all over my dick," Max hissed.

My body sang with pleasure while Max continued the wild ride towards his own orgasm. My heart was pounding like crazy. And I was still whimpering his name when I felt him stiffen. I opened my eyes to watch as Max threw his head back as he exploded.

Max's body went limp and he rolled onto his back, pulling me with him and I rested my head on his damp chest.

"I love you."

Max lifted up and stared at me. "What did you just say?"

I grinned. "I said I love you."

"Well it's about damn time you admitted it!"

I gave a rude snort. "Whatever dude. It's not like you make it easy for a woman to love you."

He sighed. "No, I probably don't, but I'm glad you do. I love you, too, babe."

"We'll see how much you still love me after you meet my father. Mommy wants you to join us for Thanksgiving."

"I can't wait." He shifted his body until I felt my back against the mattress and he was on his side. We just lay there staring into each other's eyes. "Where have you been my whole life?"

"Right here, waiting for you," I whispered.

Leaning forward he pressed his lips against mine and I savored the taste and the moment. I wasn't sure what the future would hold but right now everything in my life was perfect. Max dozed off and I lay there thinking about the kind of life we could have together. I heard whimpering, and decided to let Max sleep while I checked on the baby. I eased out from beneath him, slipped into his jersey, and tiptoed out the room and down the hall. The sound was coming from the second bedroom. I pushed the door open and sighed when I saw Max had transformed the room into a nursery. Everything was blue and white and the furnishings, high-end, dark rich woods. Max Jr. was fussing so I reached over inside the crib and lifted him into my arms.

"Hey, what's wrong?" I cooed.

He stopped and gazed up at me and I felt something in my chest tighten. He was beautiful with dark eyes and the perfect nose. He was staring at me like he knew who I was. "Hi Little Max. I'm CC. It's a pleasure to meet you." He was moving his lips like he was trying to tell me something and I felt tears at the corner of my eyes threatening to spill. Who couldn't love this little boy? He was the innocent one in all this mess. Max Jr. brought a fist to his mouth and started sucking. "You are so cute, you know that?" I whispered. "Just like your daddy." There was just no denying it. The little kid looked so much like Max. "Your daddy really loves you and I can see why." I continued talking to him in a baby voice and he just stared up at me as if he understood everything I was saying.

I heard movement behind me and then big strong arms were cradling us both. "I didn't hear him."

Smiling, I glanced over my shoulder. Max pressed his lips to my cheek. "It's okay. I need to get used to being around him. If I'm going to be a part of your life, then that means him, too."

"Did I tell you I was a package deal?" he joked.

I laughed. "I think I remember something like that."

I don't know how long we just stood there together staring down at him before Max Jr. dozed back off to sleep. I slowly lowered him into his crib, then Max took my hand and led me back to the room.

We took a shower together, then I slipped into shorts and a t-shirt I had left a few weeks ago, and followed him down into the kitchen. "Name your poison," he said with his head in the refrigerator.

"I'll take a wine cooler if you still have one."

"Coming right up." He removed a bottle then headed over to the drawer for a bottle opener and popped off the cap.

I took it from his proffered hand. "Thank you, baby."

"You're welcome." He kissed my lips as I heard the doorbell chime.

"Who is that?" I whispered against his lips.

His eyes widened. "Shit, I forgot Parker was coming to get him." Max hurried into the living room. I sat there waiting for him to open the door and then I heard throaty laughter. At first I started to just sit there in the kitchen counting the subway tiles until she left, but then I decided, why the hell do I need to hide? Max and I were together and she needed to get used to it.

I brought the bottle to my lips and took a swig as I padded into the living room. Her back was to me.

"Hello Parker."

Her head snapped toward me, and if looks could kill, I would be six feet under.

"What is she doing here?" she hissed.

Max shrugged. "That's my girl. Not that it's any of your business."

Her eyes rolled up and down my body. "Well, I don't want that bitch around my son!"

Normally, I would have just brushed it off, but I was sick of her shit. "You talking to me?" I pointed at my chest.

"Aren't you the only bitch up in here?" she barked.

I'd had enough of her. I leaped and Max brought me to a halt, but not before I saw Parker flinch and back up, eyes wide with disbelief. "Whoa! Respect the home. There is no need for all that name calling."

"You better check your baby mama!" I shouted.

I guess she figured she was safe as long as Max was there. Parker rolled her eyes at me. "She shouldn't be here."

"Parker..., you don't tell me who I can or cannot have in my house. But when you are here, you need to show me and my girl respect."

"I don't have to do a damn thang. Go get my son so I can get the hell outta here!" She was talking with her hands.

I could see Max was trying to keep his composure. I patted his arm. "Baby go on upstairs, and give us a minute alone," I said then my lips curled into a smirk. "I promise I won't hit her." For the life of me I couldn't understand why Parker was messing with me.

As soon as Max hit the top stairs I moved in closer and clenched my fists. "I know all about you hiring those guys to attack me."

That bitch barely flinched. "Attack you? I don't have any idea what you're talking about."

I stepped forward and was ready to jump for joy when she took a step back. "I think you do. Two of them are already in custody."

"Then I guess it will be their word against mine unless of course you have some proof," she tossed in.

I just glared at her.

Her lips curled in a satisfying smile. "That's what I thought."

Max came down the stairs holding his little bundle of joy. You should have seen the way her face actually softened at the sight of him.

"How's Mama's baby?" she cooed while Max put him in her arms. Parker carried him over to the car seat on the floor, near the couch, and gently strapped him in. "Daddy is hardhead. He's got other people around, breathing all over you." That crazy chick was talking baby talk about me. "Never again."

Max and I turned and exchanged looks.

"Yo, Parker, as long as I'm taking care of my son you don't have any control over what I do, or who I have at my house."

Her head and neck started twisting as she spoke. "Maybe not, but I control who comes around my son, including you. You want to keep seeing her… fine. You don't have to worry about seeing your son again." She picked up the baby seat with one hand and carried it toward the door.

"You can't keep him from me."

With a sinister smirk, Parker replied, "Watch me."

With that she walked out the door.

TWENTY-NINE

"I'm getting married at the Silver Oaks Chateau!" Christina squealed. "I still can't believe it."

The chateau resided on a twenty-eight-acre luxurious private estate in Wildwood. There was always a two-year waiting list, but someone cancelled for April, and Jeanna was able to pull a few strings.

"Wow! Talk about lucky. Now you'll owe Jeanna, and she's really going to take over," I mentioned as I finished decorating the last batch of truffles.

"I'm not having it. This is my wedding and I'm going to have things my way," Christina announced and slammed her hand on the table.

"Oh damn! If you turn into a bridezilla I'm kicking you down the stairs." My comment sent us both into a fit of laughter.

She shifted on the chair and said, "Hey, I tried to call you. Max came by yesterday and brought pictures of his son. Oh Claudia, he is so handsome."

"Yes, he is. I had a chance to spend the evening with him and I can see why Max is already in love with him. He really is a beautiful baby."

"So are you finally thinking about giving Max a fair shot?"

"After I deal with Isaiah. He proposed to me." I didn't mean to blurt it out, but I did.

"What? When?"

"The day after I helped you pack." I went on to tell her about him picking me up and taking me to my dream home. "You know the one I love on Mason Avenue."

"Oh my God! Are you serious?"

I was grinning and nodding at the same time. "He's such a good man, sexy, rich and he wants me." I blew out a long breath.

"Are you trying to convince me or you? Because if you really wanted to marry Isaiah, you would have already said yes." She snatched another truffle and waited for me to continue.

"Christy I—"

She gave a dismissive wave. "When Dee proposed I didn't need a second to think before I yelled, hell yes! You want to know why? Because I knew he was the man I wanted to spend the rest of my life with."

"I agree."

"If you agree then what's the problem?" she said although the look on her face said she already knew the answer.

"Max," I said following by a sigh. "I finally admitted to myself I love him."

"Oh my God! Did you just say, you love him?"

"Yes, aren't you listening?" I shook my head. "I love him with my every breath."

"Well, then you need to tell Isaiah and quit stringing that dude along."

I nodded. "You're right. I need to quit being selfish and find a way to tell him."

Before I could stop her, Christina reached out and quickly popped another truffle into her mouth.

"Stop it! I have to deliver these in the morning and I don't want to make another batch. I still can't understand a bunch of grown men sitting around eating truffles during a board meeting."

"Hey, who are we to judge as long as it keeps the lights on," Christina teased.

"True," I said and then my smiled faded. "Have you spoken to Portia?"

She did that eye roll thing again. "Yes, she and Evan are going to the Cayman Islands for a few days to spend some quality time."

I shook my head. "The things women are willing to put

up with."

"Speaking of putting up with… I hope you're ready to commit to a relationship. Don't play with Max's emotions."

"Yes ma'am," I said and winked. "I'm more than ready."

I glanced up from the icing and spotted Mia walking into the kitchen.

"You're late, Chica." I made a show of looking down at my watch.

I expected a string of apologies and then a long drawn out explanation, but instead, she barely looked at me as she walked into the room holding her phone out in front of her as if it were a murder weapon.

"Hey what's going on with you?" I asked her.

"Mia, honey, why are you late?" Christina asked and looked concerned and she had every right to be.

When Mia reached the table, she raised her head and the moment I saw her eyes I knew something was seriously wrong.

"Mia, you're scaring me."

She shook her head and squeezed her eyes closed as she spoke. "I don't know where to begin."

"How about at the beginning?" Christina suggested and I had to agree.

I wiped my hands, pushed the icing aside and removed my apron. "Okay, tell us what happened."

Her eyes shifted from me to Christina and back to me before she dropped her head. "Please let me start by saying Shalisa and I had no idea."

She looked like she was about to faint so I walked over, grabbed a chair and dragged it onto the floor in front of her. "Sit. Now talk."

Don't you know she turned her head, avoiding my gaze?

"Here, let me get this child some water. Maybe her lips are sticking together," Christina teased while trying to lighten the mood. While she rushed off to grab a bottle from a small personal refrigerator, I leaned back with my arms crossed beneath my breasts. Mia could barely look at me so I knew whatever it was, it was serious.

"Mia, something is wrong. The only time you look this upset is when you got bad news or that boyfriend of ours…" My eyes widened. "He didn't put his hands on you, did he?"

She gave me a look of alarm. "No, nothing like that."

"Then quit stalling and tell me what's going on? We've worked together for a long time. I want to know who or what is responsible for making you look like you just lost your best friend."

Christina returned, heels clicking as she sauntered over to us. "Here you go. Drink up."

Mia immediately took the bottle and took a long thirsty swallow. I looked at Christina with a brow raised.

"Okay, so what's up?" I demanded.

"Are you sure you wanna know?" she asked. After that song and dance, of course I wanted to know.

"Of course we do," Christina answered and managed to remain calm. I was personally starting to lose my patience.

Mia drew a long dramatic breath. "Okay, but you're not going to like what I'm about to say." Her eyes dropped to the phone in her lap and I swear you would have thought that girl had seen a ghost. "I was with my sister yesterday," she began and I was already rolling my eyes inwardly. I should have known this had something to do with her sister.

"She asked me to meet her at this diner near her apartment, said she needed to show me something." Then instead of continuing with the story Mia got this weird glazed look in her eyes like she had suddenly got lost in a time warp.

"And then what happened," Christina asked, and slid a chair beside her.

"Well I met her at the diner and immediately I could tell she was scared." Mia's hands were trembling so hard, I reached out and took the bottle from her.

"I asked her what was wrong and she showed…" she choked. "She showed me this."

Her watery eyes met mine and I looked from her to Christina then back to her. "What's with the phone?"

She took a long breath and I waited for what seemed like forever for her to continue. "It's not the phone… it's what's on it."

Mia reached down for the phone and tapped a few buttons and I was suddenly afraid of where this was headed.

She held the phone out and I expected to see a photo, instead we watched a video. I couldn't tear my eyes away from the scene playing before my eyes that sent the blood rushing from my face, and once it was over I stood there with my mouth hanging wide open. Did I really just see what I thought I saw?

"Where did she get that?" Christina asked. I was grateful because my mouth was so dry, I swung around grabbed the bottle on the table and took a long swallow.

Mia was sitting there tears running down her face. "Shalisa thought Meechie was messing around with this chick so while he was sleep she unlocked his phone and that's when she found this video." She wiped her eyes. "She said Meechie was always doing drug deals in his car so that's why he installed one of those dashboard cameras that people thought was a police scanner. But she never expected to find this..." Her voice cracked. "As soon as she heard your name, Claudia, she put two and two together."

I was shocked into silence. Somehow I managed to make it over to a chair and started hyperventilating. Oh my God! There was no way this shit was happening to me.

"Claudia, you okay?" Christina rushed over to my side.

"Hell no, I'm not okay. I just watched Parker pay someone to hurt me!" My stomach lurched up into my throat. This was just so freaking unreal. "How did her sister know about..." I stopped talking and had to restrain myself from crying.

Mia was looking up at the ceiling. "I told her. I'm sorry. I was so upset when I found out you were attacked at The Hole I had to tell someone."

Christina brought a comforting hand to my forearm and squeezed. "Well it's a good thing she had, otherwise we would never have seen that video."

I wish I hadn't seen it because I would never be able to get it out of my head. Ever. That cold-blooded bitch had really paid someone to get me out the way so she could have Max to herself.

While Mia gave us all the details about Meechie's real name being Tommy Vane, I felt like I was having an outer body experience. No matter how much I tried I just couldn't seem to wrap my mind around the fact I had been the victim of a plot for hire. Like I'd said, this was some shit out of the movies.

"Claudia, I am so so sorry for all of this. If I had known Meechie and Tommy was the same person I would have told you before," she explained. "Shalisa wanted to come and show you herself, but I told her I didn't think that would be a good idea."

She was right. It wouldn't have been.

"Tell me what you want me to do?" Mia was scared and practically pleading. "I will do whatever it takes."

Christina shook her head in disbelief. "Mia, it's not your fault, so don't start blaming yourself."

"I feel responsible for my sister and every stupid thing she does, including the men she deals with."

I was still digesting the news when my head whipped around. "Is that Meechie's phone?"

Mia shook her head. "No, Shalisa's. She transferred the video to her phone."

I was still trying to wrap my mind around what I had seen and yet I nodded then said, "Send the video to me."

Christina studied my face. "Are you gonna take it to the police?"

Our eyes locked as I replied, "Not yet. There's something I have to do first."

THIRTY

I was sitting in an exam room when Parker stepped in. As soon as she saw me, she jerked back, then glared. "How did you get in here?" she hissed while standing in the doorway.

"Easily," I began, then paused to cross my legs. "I don't know if you know, but my father is the head of internal medicine here at this hospital. Does Dr. Clayton Winters ring a bell? Anyway, all I had to do was toss out his name at the front desk, and say I was relaying an important message, and I was escorted to a room so we could talk."

The look on her face said she'd heard of my father.

"Well, what do you want?"

"I figured it was time we talked. Woman to… woman." There were several other things I would rather call her, but I guess now was not the time.

"Personally, we don't have anything to talk about."

"I think we do and if I was you, I would shut the door and take a seat."

She stared at me, then finally pushed the door with a click, yet she opted to lean against the sink instead.

"How's Max doing?" she asked with a coy smile.

"My man is doing quite well, but thanks for asking. He would be even better if you would let him see his son." It had been almost a week since that evening at his house, and she had been good on her threat.

"He should have thought about that before he decided to bring you around him!" she shouted angrily.

"I'm going to be in his life. Get over it."

"What you need to do is find your own man. That one belongs to me and our son."

I chuckled. "We don't even know for sure that he's his, but I hope he is for Max's sake."

"Oh, he's definitely his."

I glared over at her. "I guess you would know since you have a habit of sticking pins through condoms."

The look on her face was just what I needed to boost my confidence.

"Oh yeah. I heard all about your little scam. Just like I heard all about you paying someone to get me out of the way."

"Nobody is going to believe that story."

"Oh, I think they will. In fact before I go to the police with the evidence, I thought I would let you have a front row seat."

With that I held up my phone and her brow rose with curiosity. She was practically holding her breath while trying to act all cool like she had her shit together, but when the video started with her as the leading lady, Parker was suddenly looking like a scared little girl. I almost felt sorry for her.

The video ended and the only sounds in the room were Parker breathing heavily and me popping strawberry bubble gum.

"What's wrong Parker?" She was speechless. The look on her face… priceless.

"How did you get that?"

I shrugged. "It doesn't matter how I got it. I got it, and so does Max, and a few other people. The police will be coming for you soon. Looks like you're going to be facing assault and attempted rape charges—"

Parker quickly interrupted. "Rape? I never told anyone to rape you!"

I shrugged. "Tell it to the judge."

"Is that why you came here… to gloat?" she asked and glared at me.

"No, I came to ask you to allow Max to have shared custody of his son, and to stop interfering in his life. If you agree, maybe I'll get my mother's law firm to take on your case. I might even ask the judge not to be so hard on you."

She looked perplexed by my offer. "Why would you do that for me?"

"I don't spend my life walking around hating other people. I love my life and I'm surrounded by people who love me. And with a man like Max, what in the world do I need to be unhappy about?"

There was a knock at the door and you should have seen how big her eyes got.

"I guess you better hurry up and decide. Tick-tock," I said with my leg swinging.

I guess that was enough to convince her. "Okay, whatever you want."

I smirked, nodded, and rose. "Good luck, Parker. Maybe the next time we see each other you'll be ready to respect the fact Max and I are in love and nothing or no one is ever going to stand in the way of that."

With that I reached for the door and opened it.

* * *

I sauntered down the hall of the medical clinic until I found the office door with Isaiah Cunningham in gold letters. I took a deep breath, then tapped lightly on the door.

"Come in."

I cracked the door open just enough to peek inside. Isaiah was sitting behind his desk, tapping away at his laptop. He stopped and smiled when he spotted me. "Hey you." He signaled me inside.

Swallowing, I stepped into his office and shut the door. "Wow!" It looks like you've gotten all settled in." I allowed my eyes to travel around the room. Numerous awards and photographs of his time in Africa adorned the walls and bookshelves. In all the weeks, this was my first time visiting his office. I definitely sucked at being his girlfriend.

Isaiah came from around his large desk. "To what do I owe the honor of your presence, busy lady?" He lifted me off my feet and onto his desk. When I smiled, he slanted his lips over mine in an urgent kiss.

I drew back and brought my hand up to cup his face. His

dark eyes glittered with intensity. "You're such a good man."

"Thank you and you are a good woman."

I searched his eyes. "That's why I can't accept this." I reached inside my purse and removed the velvet box and placed it in his hand.

Isaiah stared down at his palm and then back at me. "It was too late, wasn't it?" he asked quietly.

I stared at a point beyond his shoulder and nodded my head slowly. "I'm in love with someone else." I hadn't planned on being so honest but our circle of friends was small. It would only be a matter of time before he would find out, or even saw us together.

"I hope he knows he's a lucky man."

Hot tears clouded my eyes as I whispered, "I'm the one who's lucky."

THIRTY-ONE

As soon as I stepped into his house, I locked my arms around Max's neck and dragged him down to kiss me.

Panting, Max said against my mouth, "Somebody missed me."

"Desperately," I whispered and pressed my mouth to his.

Max picked me up off the floor and kissed me long and hard. The pressure of his lips was soft and sensuous, and just what I needed.

It had been a long day. Parker and Tommy Vane had been arrested and along with the other two were now facing conspiracy, second-degree assault and attempted rape charges.

Max Jr. was where he belonged, upstairs, sleeping peacefully.

I wrapped my legs tightly around his waist. While Max carried me up to his room, his hand slid underneath my dress.

He jerked back, his eyes wide. "You're not wearing panties."

I grinned wickedly. "They would only be in the way."

"My thoughts exactly," he murmured against my lips.

The feel of his palms rough and calloused stroking across my ass, had ever nerve in my body on high alert. My kitty throbbed. My nipples ached. My body tingled to life.

He laid me gently on the bed and then removed his clothes and lay beside me.

"You're so beautiful," he crooned as he lifted my dress over my head. "All of you."

Max ran his fingers down my thighs. I snagged my bottom lip with my front teeth as he eased my legs apart, then leaned forward and kissed my mouth while his fingers explored between my thighs.

"I love you, CC."

"And I love you," I replied. "I'm no longer afraid to admit it."

"Tell me again," he asked gently.

I drew a long, deep breath as tears burned the corners of my eyes. "I love you, Maximilian James, with my every breath. I don't know how I could be so lucky to have you in my life."

He hugged me close. "No, I'm the lucky one." Max kissed me. "I hope you're ready, because I plan on making love to you all night long."

I raked my fingers across his hair then brought my hands down to cup his face, nearly drowning in the depths of his dark eyes.

"I was hoping you'd say until the wee hours of the morning," I teased as I felt his thumb slide across my slick folds and then I flinched.

"How about for eternity?"

I faked a frown. "Eternity isn't long enough."

"How about infinity and beyond!" We both broke into a fit of laughter at his attempt at imitating Bud Lightyear from the Toy Story franchise.

He finished taking off his clothes, and I released the clasp to my bra. Max rolled on top of me and wasted no time sliding deep inside. I moaned when he spread my legs wider, allowing him deeper access. I arched my back and dug my fingers into his flesh.

Within seconds we were lost in a euphoria of pleasure. And by the end of an hour, I was up on all four while he brought us both to another earth-shattering orgasm.

When I collapsed, spent, against his chest, with his fingers running up and down my arm, I knew in my heart that everything was going to be alright.

"I'm hungry."

"I'm not quite ready for you to get up just yet," he said.

I rolled onto my side. "We have to eat."

Max smiled softly. "I'm full on love."

I laughed. "You're full of crap."

He drew me close and released a long groan from deep in the back of his throat. "Babe, where have you been all my life?"

I cupped his face, stroking his cheeks with my thumbs as I stared into Max's eyes, and replied, "I've been right here, waiting for you."

EPILOGUE

Three Months Later

Shortly after ten o'clock, I pulled in front of Max's house and breathed a sigh of relief. It had been a long day.

Claudia and I hosted a wedding at the luxurious Frontenac Hotel that had been an elegant and sophisticated affair, one I was sure the bride and groom would never forget. Now I was eager for dinner, a long hot shower, and then spend the rest of the evening, lying in the strong arms of my amazing man. Since Christmas, Max and I had been practically living together.

Snowflakes were falling again, which came as no surprise. It had been a harsh winter and already Channel 8 News forecasted six more inches of snow before sunrise. I raised the collar of my wool coat up around my ears, then climbed out, and managed to make my way up to the door without sliding in my designer boots. I put my key in the lock and opened the door.

"Honey, I'm home!" I called softly.

"Babe, I'm back in the kitchen."

Smiling, I dropped my purse and keys on the table in the foyer, then slipped out of my coat, and hung it in the closet. I took a seat on the stairs long enough to slip the chocolate boots off my feet, then padded across the floor.

There was soft lullaby music playing in the living room. I dipped my head inside to find Max Jr. in his baby swing, sound asleep. Instantly, I reached down and lifted him gently into my arms. I know I was spoiling him by holding him so much, but I couldn't help it. Every day I yearned to touch him, and be close to that wonderful baby scent. I never knew I could love an individual so much, but I did, with all my heart.

Holding him snuggly against my breasts, I carried him to the rear of the house, into the kitchen. Max was sitting at the table, sipping a beer.

"Hey babe," he said and rose from the chair just enough to lean in for a kiss then I took the seat at the table beside him. "I just put him down," Max scolded, brow raised.

I gave a sheepish grin. "Sorry babe. I promise not to wake him, but after a long day, you know I need to hold this little man."

His smile became almost sad as he gave a head nod toward the center of the table. I followed the direction of his eyes and spotted a white envelope.

"What is it?"

"The DNA test results," Max said quietly.

I grew very still, understanding the importance of his announcement. "What did it say?"

He shook his head and took another long swig, finishing the bottle before he lowered it to the table, and replied, "I was waiting for you to get here before I opened it."

I held the baby protectively against me. Max's gaze met mine and we stared at each other for what felt like forever and my heart rate kicked up a notch. All kinds of things were running through my head.

The last few months had been rough. Parker had pleaded guilty for a lesser sentencing, in exchange for her testimony against the other three. Their trials had yet to be scheduled, while she had already started serving a one-year sentence. Since then Max and I had been juggling our schedules to share in the care for Max Jr.. I had even brought him into the office a few times for Mia and Christina to fuss over. Mommy pitched in and already she and Daddy were treating Max Jr. like he was one of their own. Surprisingly, Max and Daddy hit it off instantly. Thank the Lord for football season.

"You sure you want to open it?" I asked.

Max shifted on the seat and released a long breath. "I need to know."

I nodded and swallowed a large gulp of air as I watched

him reach down for the envelope. Max ripped it open then drew a deep breath before looking down at the paper in front of him. I noticed he flinched and then his eyes glazed unfocused. I held my breath, waiting for him to say something, and was too afraid to ask. He finally slid the paper across the table, and I immediately snatched it up with shaky hands and stared down at the results. My stomach clenched.

Max had been right all along. Max Jr. was not his son.

I swallowed a sob and struggled for the words to speak. Max Jr. stirred in my arms and I pressed my cheek against his, and started cooing in his ear.

"Let me have him." Max whispered and held out his arms. I handed him over. I knew he needed him close to him. "In the beginning, I knew he wasn't mine, but after he was born I wanted so badly to believe." Max drew a long, deep breath then stared up at the ceiling, his eyes cloudy. "I wanted to be his father."

The sight of him holding Max Jr. close literally broke my heart and it took everything I had to hold it together for Max's sake. "Being a father is more than just having the same DNA running through your veins. As far as I'm concerned that's your son and you are his father. Nobody has to ever know otherwise until you're ready to tell them." I sent a compassionate gaze in his direction. His eyes were filled with raw emotion.

Finally, after a long nail-biting moment, Max cleared his throat and said, "You're right. This is *my* son. That's *my* name on his birth certificate, and *nothing* will change that."

Pushing back tears, I walked over and wrapped my arms around him. "You are such a good man. Max Jr. is lucky to have you as a father."

He tilted his head and looked up at me. "No, he and I are the lucky ones for having you in our lives." I kissed his lips then stared down at Max Jr. while a tear slid down my cheek. At one point I would have been jumping for joy at the test results, but now, I couldn't bear the thought of Max Jr. not being a part of my life.

Max was staring at me again. "Babe, have I told you I love

you lately?" There was an amused note in his voice.

I laughed. "Not in the last hour, but who's counting?" I brushed the tears away.

It was over. It was done. It was time to move on because nothing had changed, and I was grateful for that.

I kissed him once more then moved around the table with a smile tugging at my lips. "How about I get dinner started and then afterwards you can give me that foot massage you've been promising."

Max laughed. "Actually, I have a better idea. How about I put my son to bed, and you join me in our room?"

Our room, I loved the sound of it. "I think I like that plan much better."

Max tossed his head back and laughed.

I smiled because in my heart and mind, I knew, everything was going to be alright.

ENJOY AN EXCERPT FROM

Say My Name

(Christina and Dereon)

Now available

ONE

"Would you like some company?"

Would I? Goodness! For a second there I thought tall, dark and chocolate would never ask.

"Yes, if you'd like," I said, trying to sound like it was no big deal, when in reality spending the evening together could possibly become the most important moment of my entire life.

Logan smiled and kissed my lips, sending goose bumps down my arms as I watched him climb out of his fully loaded Range Rover. I sat back against the butter soft seat and ran my tongue along my painted lips while my stomach bubbled with excitement. The evening was going better than I had imagined. We'd had dinner at my favorite Italian Bistro, followed by a horse-drawn carriage ride through the cobblestone streets of downtown St. Louis. For a first date, what more could a sistah have asked for?

I tried to remain calm, but I was already planning the next six months of our relationship, all the way up to the very moment Logan would drop down on one knee and confess his undying love for me while holding a beautiful five-carat platinum diamond ring in his hand.

Giggling, I waited for him to come around to the passenger side and open the door for me, the way a gentleman should. Yes, indeed. Logan was definitely everything a woman wanted in a man—money, looks, and charm. Did I mention he had money?

Last month, in Forbes Magazine, his father's software corporation was reported to be worth more than eighty million dollars. Carson Cambridge's health hadn't been the best, which meant Logan, who served as CEO, was next in line. Naturally, behind every successful man was a beautiful wife, and that's where I would come in. Before I let Logan leave, I planned to show him everything I had to offer.

I don't know how long I sat there daydreaming before I was startled by a knock on the glass. I jumped, then looked through the window to see Logan standing outside my door.

"Why aren't you getting out?" he asked.

Is he for real? Biting my tongue, it took everything I had not to comment as I reached for the door handle and opened it. So much for being a gentleman. I climbed out and convinced myself it wasn't important, then swayed my hips provocatively up the sidewalk towards my deluxe condo, my shoes clicking with every step.

There was nothing like looking fabulous, and I knew it, with a five-hundred-dollar weave that hung loosely around my shoulders. I was showcasing all my sweet curves in a black silhouetting dress that stopped mid-thigh and dipped daringly between my large breasts. On my feet were strappy high-heeled come-fuck-me shoes.

I sashayed to the door, stuck my key in the lock, then stepped aside so Logan could enter first. The look in his eyes told me he was impressed with everything he saw, mainly me.

"You've got a nice place," he replied after a quick sweep of the spacious room. Gleaming wood floors, a large spacious room and expensive contemporary furnishings.

"Thank you. I can—" Before I could answer, Logan snaked an arm around my waist and pulled me to him. I let myself go slack, unresisting, and moaned when he brought his lips down over mine. *Oh, my.* He would have been a fabulous kisser if it hadn't been for his tongue that was…licking me like he was part man, part puppy dog. And then there were his teeth.

If he bites my tongue with those sharp fangs, I swear I'll bite his ass. "You got me so hard I can't wait to be inside of you." Moaning, he cupped my ass and pulled me against his arousal. "I'm planning to give all of this to you."

Lucky me. What I wanted to asked was, *all of what?* Because it didn't feel like he had more than four inches to work with. Logan started rubbing and touching and I reminded myself of his wealth and the fabulous life we'd have together. Within minutes I felt my body heat up and I was turned on. Money does that to me. Or maybe it was because I hadn't had sex in almost three months. I'd been waiting, saving myself for the perfect man.

Ever since we'd met at a fundraiser a week ago, I'd had a feeling Logan was that perfect somebody. I couldn't wait to show him off at my sister's wedding next weekend. Jeanna was going to be so proud of me.

His hands reached for the buttons on the front of my dress, and I didn't object as he released one right after the other. My eyes were glued to his, staring deep into their chocolate depths. The fabric dropped onto my carpet and I quickly kicked the dress away, not caring where it ended up, then stepped back and propped a hand to my slim waist so he could see everything I had to offer.

The hunger in his eyes was unmistakable. "Christina ...you're beautiful."

I grinned. Not that he was telling me something I didn't already know. What woman wouldn't be gorgeous standing in a red satin bra and matching low-ride panties with a pair of red Manolos on her feet?

I sauntered toward him and he pulled me into his arms and swept his tongue across my lips, leaving them sopping wet. "So beautiful," he murmured. He slid a hand up to my breast and cupped it a little too eagerly. "Play your cards right and you won't ever want for anything ever again."

That was the plan.

He brushed a thumb across one hardened nipple and smiled triumphantly when I gasped. "That's it, baby. Give yourself to me." He massaged my breast slowly. "You want me?"

I pulled back slightly and stared up into his face. "Yes, Logan. I want you." *And everything you have to offer.*

Grinning eagerly, Logan reached for his belt buckle. Stepping back, I licked my lips thinking about the night I had in store for him. Trust and believe, before the night ended Logan was going to be mine. I had never been so aggressive with a man before, not that I was about to enlighten him of that tiny fact.

"You ready?" He exhaled a harsh, aroused breath.

"Absolutely," I answered in a low sultry voice. With a crook of my finger, I signaled for him to follow me up the stairs to my bedroom. My foot had barely touched the bottom step when I heard a knock at the door. Logan's brow rose and he looked clearly disappointed at the interruption. Well, he wasn't the only one. I was preparing to answer it when I heard loud pounding.

"What the hell?" I muttered under my breath. I padded to the door, looked through the peephole and spotted a woman standing there, balancing a small child on her hip.

"Who is it?" Logan hissed impatiently.

I looked over my shoulder and shrugged, "Some curly-headed chick holding a little girl." It was then I noticed his eyes grow round as saucers.

"What?" I asked, and suddenly I didn't want to know.

Before he could answer, the woman pounded her fist against the door again, but this time she screamed, "Logan…I know you're in there!"

Swinging around, I saw the fear on his face. "Who is that?" I whispered.

Logan was quiet for several seconds before he finally answered, "My wife."

"Your *what?*" I screamed. I don't remember him mentioning once in any of our conversations that he was married. How come that information wasn't available on the Internet?

"I want my daddy!" wailed the little girl at the top of her lungs while his wife continued to pound at my door.

In record speed, Logan zipped his pants and slipped his shoes back on. I was so shocked I didn't know what to say. I just stood there as he moved toward the door. "I'm sorry. I'll call you tomorrow," he said. Reaching up, he caressed the side of my face and then winked at me, like I was really that stupid and desperate. Logan had no idea. Unlike my mother, I wasn't interested in being someone's mistress. It was all or nothing with me. Being second was not an option.

Suddenly I found my voice and spat, "Do me a favor and lose my number."

I reached for the knob, swung open the door and stared at the woman with tear-stained cheeks holding the crying child in her arms. Logan looked from her to me, and when I refused to make eye contact he finally stepped out onto the porch and scooped the little girl into his arms. Mrs. Cambridge gave me a triumphant smile. I watched as she laced her fingers with her husband's, and the three of them moved out to the curb, climbed into their vehicles and pulled away, leaving me standing there with another disappointment and shattered dreams.

Other Books By Angie Daniels

Feinin' *Big Spankable Asses Anthology*
Tease
Seduced into Submission
Talk A Good Game
When It Rains
Love Uncovered
When I First Saw You
In the Company of My Sistahs
Trouble Loves Company
Careful of the Company You Keep
Intimate Intentions
Hart & Soul
Time is of the Essence
A Will to Love
Endless Enchantment
Destiny In Disguise
The Second Time Around
The Playboy's Proposition
The Player's Proposal
For You I Do
Before I Let You Go
In Her Neighbor's Bed
Show Me
Any Man Will Do
Coming for My Baby
Strutting in Red Stilettos
Running to Love in Pink Stilettos
Say My Name
Every Second Counts
A Beau for Christmas
Do Me Baby
Naughty Before Christmas
Time for Pleasure
For Her Pleasure
Beg For It

ABOUT THE AUTHOR

Angie Daniels is a free spirit who isn't afraid to say what's on her mind or even better, write about it. Since strutting onto the literary scene in five-inch heels, she's been capturing her audience's attention with her wild imagination and love for alpha men. The *USA Today* Bestselling Author has written over twenty-five novels for imprints such as BET Arabesque, Harlequin/Kimani Romance and Kensington/ Dafina and Kensington/Aphrodisia Books. For more information about upcoming releases, and to connect with Angie on Facebook, please visit her website at www.angiedaniels.com.

Made in the USA
Monee, IL
17 August 2020

38516444R00177